Kim Wilkins was born in London and grew up in Brisbane. She has degrees in English Literature and Creative Writing and was the 1997 winner of the Aurealis Awards for Best Horror Novel and Best Fantasy Novel and the 2000 winner for Best Horror Novel. Her books are also published in the UK and Europe. You can write to her at:

mail@kimwilkins.com

or find more information at

www.kimwilkins.com

Other books by Kim Wilkins in Gollancz:

The Infernal
Grimoire
The Resurrectionists

Fallen Angel

Kim Wilkins

The right of Kim Wilkins to be identified as the
author of this work has been asserted by her in accordance
with the Copyright, Designs and Patents Act 1988.

First published in Great Britain in 2002 by
Gollancz
An imprint of the Orion Publishing Group
Orion House, 5 Upper St Martin's Lane, London WC2H 9EA

A CIP catalogue record for this book is available
from the British Library

ISBN 1 85798 333 5

Printed in Great Britain by
Clays Ltd, St Ives plc

for Selwa
who understands everything about
the magic of words

... what in me is dark
Illumine, what is low raise and support;
That to the highth of this great argument
I may assert Eternal Providence,
And justify the ways of God to men.

John Milton, Paradise Lost

The reason Milton wrote in fetters when he wrote of Angels & God, and at liberty when of Devils & Hell, is because he was a true Poet and of the Devils party without knowing it.

William Blake, *The Marriage of Heaven and Hell*

An Introduction

I came to London to write and found myself practising magic instead. I suppose they're not so very dissimilar if you think about it — there are words in magic, just as there is magic in words. So be warned. There are a lot of words in this book.

I'm a journalist. I don't make things up, I write things down. You may have seen my by-line, Sophie Black, on any number of mindless articles in glossy, perfumed magazines. Writing one of those articles initiated my involvement with the Lodge of the Seven Stars. I liked to stock up on seasonal pieces; articles which I could sell to a few different publications at specific times of the year — Valentine's Day, spring, the anniversary of Diana's death — and I'd decided to do a Hallowe'en piece on the occult in London.

Hallowe'en was still five months away at the time, but my financial situation was dire and I was desperate to make an early sale. I was desperate to make any sale, really. My rent was crippling me, I'd already given up cigarettes and, if things didn't look up, coffee would be the next vice to go.

So I wandered in and out of every new age shop in London, fighting my way through hanging crystals and bangle-jangling customers, to ask the staff if they knew of a ritual magic group. I was answered by a lot of shaking heads, a few offers to take my phone number, and one recommendation to visit a bookshop called Seventh Star just off Camden High Street. "Ask for Neal," I was told. That is how, on a fine May morning, I met Neal Gardiner.

Seventh Star smelled good: the combined scent of citrus candles and crisp new books. I browsed for five minutes, astonished at the range of volumes. Jung bumped spines with Crowley, ufology lined up with urology, Hegel gazed across the aisle at the Koran. From behind a bookstand, I assessed the man at the counter. Early thirties; dark hair; a little goatee beard; pale eyes — maybe green or grey; a studied casualness, probably developed over the years to cover an innate awkwardness. I would have found him attractive under other circumstances, but my heart had just been freshly broken. No member of the male species had the power to interest me. I found a book on the Golden Dawn tradition and approached the counter.

"Hello," I said. "Is this a good introduction to ritual magic?"

He considered the book. "It's not particularly comprehensive. What information are you looking for?"

"I'd like to learn a little about the history, with a view to maybe finding a ritual magic group to practise in."

"The best way to learn is within a Lodge," he said. "What's your name?"

"Sophie," I said, "Sophie Cabrel." My *real* surname. I try not to let on to too many people that I'm a journalist. Letting on that I'm a journalist is simply the most effective way to shut them up.

"I'm Neal Gardiner. My wife and I are founding members of the Lodge of the Seven Stars."

"Do you recruit new members?"

"Not usually. I mean, no, we don't. But we've always had seven members and one of them just relocated to Edinburgh . . ."

"So you're one short?" I asked.

"Yes. Exactly."

"I'd be very interested to attend a meeting."

"It's not that simple."

"I didn't think it would be."

"I don't know you. I know nothing about you."

2

"What do you need to know?"

He looked around. Only a few customers browsed at the shelves. "If you'll wait here a moment, I'll see what I can do," he said.

I waited at the counter, hoping he wouldn't make me buy the book. I had barely enough money to pay my phone bill. I watched him go to the back of the store, disappear through a staff door, then re-emerge a few minutes later with a younger man.

Neal met me once again at the counter. "Joe can watch the shop for an hour or so. We could get a coffee."

The magic words. "I'd like that," I said.

We left the store and walked two blocks in silence. Neal was a fraction shorter than me, and he wore a blue zip-up anorak even though it was warm. His affected casualness seemed even more pronounced now that he was walking beside me, striding mock-confidently, hands thrust mock-nonchalantly in his pockets.

"I quite like that place," he said, indicating a cafeteria on our left.

"Fine."

We crossed the road and found a table inside. Two women, wearing spades of make-up, smoked in a corner. The grey haze curled around their heads. I rubbed my tongue on the roof of my mouth, imagined the cylindrical smoothness, the easy breathe-in, the warm tingly taste. I added up the days: it had been six weeks since I quit smoking, which meant it had been ten weeks since Martin had said that he was sorry, so sorry, but he needed to be by himself. The thought of Martin reminded me why I felt a permanent dull ache inside, like someone's thumb had jabbed me in the heart and left a bruise.

I slid into a vinyl seat. Neal asked me what I wanted.

"Large black coffee," I said, hoping he would offer to pay. I made a show of reaching for my purse.

"No, no," he said, "I'll get it."

3

"Thank you."

He walked stiff-elbowed to the counter and ordered our coffees. I envied the composure with which he pulled out his wallet, and offered the waitress a five pound note. If I hadn't chosen to live two streets from Euston station I might possess the same ease with my money, but even my sad, stuffy bedsit came at an immoderate price in that location.

Neal returned with our coffees. I let mine cool a moment.

"So, perhaps you should tell me a little about yourself," he said.

"What would you like to know?"

"Let's start with that accent. I can't place it."

I nodded. "It's a bit of a mixture."

"Go on."

"I was born here but my mother was Scottish, my father French. I spent my childhood in Paris until my father decided he preferred his secretary to his wife, and then I moved with my mother to Glasgow." I sipped my coffee to allow him to interject if he wished. It was too hot and I burned my tongue. Neal nodded to indicate I should continue. "I went to boarding school in Manchester, and did four months of a degree in journalism at university there, before I fell in love with one of my tutors and ran away with him to Los Angeles."

"Ah, I thought I heard California in there," he said, smiling as though I might be a movie star.

"Just faint, I'm sure. Anyway, Martin and I spent the last seven years there while he did a doctorate in economics. About nine months ago he got a position at the University of Sussex, so we came back to the UK to live in our dream cottage in East Grinstead."

"And?"

"And now I'm in London because he needed 'more space'."

"Oh. I'm sorry."

4

I shrugged lightly, as though it didn't matter.

"You really have lived all over the place," Neal said, spooning the foam off the top of his cappuccino.

"And left a piece of myself in every location," I said. "So I'm nowhere near whole."

"But very exotic."

"Thank you," I said. He liked me, I could tell. I can read people like road signs. "What else do you need to know?"

"Um . . . what do you do for a living?"

"I'm between jobs at the moment. I'm usually a waitress. I also study part-time."

"I see. And how old are you?"

"Twenty-eight."

"Why are you interested in magic?"

A crucial question: Neal wouldn't let me anywhere near his Lodge if I sounded too rehearsed or insincere — even though my reply was both rehearsed and insincere. "Purification of the self. Something's been lacking from my life for a long time, some aspect of the spiritual which I have been unable to find through any of the traditional channels."

"So you're looking for enlightenment?"

"We all are, aren't we?"

"I don't think so. I think many, many people have no interest in enlightenment."

This was the arrogance of the new-age disciple; as if football hooligans and hairdressers never wonder why they're here. "Perhaps you're right," I said.

"Let me speak to the others," he said. "I'm a good judge of character. I have a distinct feeling about you, and it seems fateful that you should show up and ask just a fortnight after Andy left. I'll okay it with the rest of the group, then I'll phone you and you can come along to a meeting."

"I'd like that." I suspected his "distinct feeling" about me was at least partially erotic interest: his gaze held mine too keenly, his body leaned forward too eagerly. As always, I was surprised. I saw myself only as a generic adult woman. Nothing about me stood out: medium blonde hair of a medium length, a medium complexion, medium hazel eyes, and a medium-sized body. Whatever it was that attracted the stolen glances on the Tube, or the sloppy leers in the Bishop's Gate on a Friday night, I could not see it.

I scribbled down my phone number for him and we chatted while we finished our coffees. He and his wife — she was reluctantly offered into evidence — owned the shop I had visited, and another one in Greenwich. Both stores did very well and they had just moved to a flat on Baker Street. His wife's name was Chloe and she didn't work because she was often ill. Unfortunately, he said, they were yet to have children because of Chloe's health. I liked him. I like people who are always willing to talk. I sincerely hoped he would call and that I could come along to the Lodge of the Seven Stars very soon. We said goodbye and I walked home.

Mrs Henderson greeted me as the security door slammed shut behind me.

"Have you got the rent?" she asked. Mrs Henderson was always direct.

I picked up my mail, leafed through it quickly. Found the envelope with the *Foxy* logo on the front. Relief. "Yes," I said, holding up the envelope. "The rent is right here."

"You're two days late."

"I'll bring a cheque down in a minute."

"May as well make it tomorrow. I already banked this morning."

"Sure."

"And I'd prefer cash."

"Sure. No problem." I was retreating from the lobby, up the creaky stairs. Hartley Manors sounded like a far more prestigious address than it actually was. It was damp and stuffy, the bathrooms were never quite clean, the heating was hit-and-miss. It had once been a bed and breakfast hotel, but Mrs Henderson now rented out the rooms on a

6

monthly basis as bedsits. Mine was on the first floor, overlooking the street. Even with the double glazing the traffic noise was unbearable, and now summer was approaching I would have to start leaving the window open for fresh air.

I threw my bag on the bed and pulled up a chair at my tiny desk, knocking my left knee as I did every time I tried to work in the cramped space; the skin was permanently blue with bruising. I began the business of opening my mail. A lorry roared past outside, making the window rattle.

I suppose I should admit why I chose to live in a crap bedsit with a good address rather than find something cheaper and less central. I could tell you that it was crucial for my research that I be so close to the British Library: St Pancras was barely a ten minute walk away. I could tell you that it was important to have a central London address in order to impress the publishing companies buying my work: freelancing is competitive, and if you look like you're doing well the magazines have more confidence in you. I could even tell you that there is a sports centre two doors down from me, and that I'm obsessed with squash (I am). But none of these reasons are the *real* reasons.

No. I just wanted to make sure Martin knew I was doing fine without him. When I first moved in I wrote him a brief note, enclosing my business card with the new address if he needed to get in touch about anything. Nonchalant. Independent. It was the most important thing in the world to me that Martin not find out how badly shaken I was by our break-up. He hated desperate and he hated weak, and if I behaved desperately or weakly he would never ask me to come back. I occasionally phoned our mutual friends, lying extravagantly about how well I was getting on, knowing that all the stories would find their way back to him.

And eventually, if I waited, he would call and ask me to

return. I knew this for a certainty because I always win. Nothing ever beats me and that may sound immodest, but I assure you it's true.

The mail that day proved bountiful. I had two cheques, including the large one from *Foxy* for a piece I'd written called "Spring-Clean Your Life". I had three invitations to submit articles I'd queried about, and a commission for a seven-hundred word piece about airline food, preferably funny. I figured that, in a month or two, when payments started to roll in and the commissions became more frequent, my money troubles would be over.

I didn't know then that, in a month or two, money would be the least of my concerns.

It poured with rain the night I attended my first meeting of the Lodge. I came up from Baker Street Station and my cheap umbrella instantly blew inside-out. Although it was the first day of June, summer looked to be the last thing on the sky's mind. I had to walk several blocks in the foul weather until I found the right address.

An attractive, plump woman met me at the bottom of the stairs.

"You must be Sophie," she said, as I hung up my umbrella and slipped out of my raincoat.

"And you must be Chloe." I liked Chloe immediately. She was pretty in the way only plump women can be, cherubic and clear-skinned, with a pleasant smile. She slipped her soft hand into mine to shake it, then led me up the stairs.

"We're very happy to have you here," she said, unlocking the front door to her flat.

"I'm happy to be here."

We walked directly into a warm candle-lit lounge room. Shelves swollen with books lined all four walls. There was no other furniture. Five people dressed in black robes stood talking with each other. They looked round as I came in.

"Sophie. Good to see you." This was Neal, advancing

across the room and giving me a firm handshake. "Come and meet the others."

Chloe intercepted us and handed me a towel, and I dried off my hair as Neal introduced me to the Lodge members. I committed their names and one or two notable character-istics about each of them to memory: Art, John Lennon specs; Deirdre, pale, blinking redhead; Marcus, heavy-jawed grin; Mandy, anorexic, pink-faced blonde. Then there were Neal and Chloe. All of them were somewhere between thirty and forty. Chloe was shrugging into a black robe over her powder-blue house dress. Nobody was naked under their robes. Unfortunate. It would have been a good angle.

"We might just have you sit among us as we do our ritual," Neal said, indicating that I should sit on the floor.

"Can I take my shoes off?" I asked.

"Certainly. Make yourself comfortable."

I eased out of my squelching boots and lowered myself to sit on the floor with my legs crossed.

"Close your eyes if you like, relax, and just listen," Chloe told me. "Maybe you'll see colours, or have visions. Many strange, wonderful things can happen during a ritual."

I didn't believe a word of it. I was a sceptic, absolute and entire. My micro-cassette recorder was taping the proceed-ings from the depths of my handbag. I kept my eyes wide open.

A few moments of silence ensued, and then Neal said, in a very clear voice, "Brothers and sisters of the Seven Stars, take your stations so that we may open the Lodge. Sentinel, secure the inner and outer doors."

Marcus went through a self-conscious series of motions — walking up and down, leaving the room, knocking, coming back in — then said, "Magister, the doors are secure."

"Warder," Neal said, "please ask for the current password."

Mandy went from person to person, leaned close as the password was whispered to her. I couldn't quite make it out, but thought they may have been saying "stardust". It all put

9

me in mind of Enid Blyton's Secret Seven, and I was careful not to smile.

"The current password is known to all but one," Mandy said.

"Sister," Neal said, addressing me, "you are witnessing a great and secret tradition. Do you agree not to share what you see and hear tonight?"

"Yes," I said, with all due circumstance. I was lying, of course. I thought I may never see these people again, so it hardly mattered what kind of promises I made.

Neal looked around at the others, waited a few moments. "Brothers and sisters, let us invoke the Higher."

Much muttering and mumbling followed, accompanied by a thorough censing of the room in sandalwood, and a bit of water from a silver goblet being splashed about. They walked right and then left in a circular pattern, held hands, drew pentagrams in the air, called out spells, invoked deities long-since discredited, and paraded about like self-important extras in a B-grade fifties Biblical epic. I admit, I wholly admit, that I took none of it in the least seriously. I watched and I listened, and I drew my conclusions. Despite their ridiculous behaviour, and despite the studied seriousness they all cultivated, it was abundantly clear that they were having the time of their lives. This was a cubbyhouse gang for grown-ups.

As the ritual wore on, I started to consider my options. There was nothing sinister enough here to provide an angle for a Hallowe'en article; but this was an interesting group of people indulging in an unusual practice. Was it worth more than a two-thousand word piece in *Foxy* mag? An Irish anthropologist had once made a killing writing a book about the time she spent practising as a witch with a coven in Chicago. Was there a book in this? Could I investigate these people, learn what motivated them, write an interesting account that would sell well in hardback?

Two questions plagued me: was it ethical, and what

kind of advance would it be worth?

"You have a lot to think about," Neal said to me later, unwittingly hitting on the very reason I had become distant and quiet.

"Yes, I have," I said.

"We're very happy to have you as an initiate in our Lodge," Chloe said, "but it's loads of work."

"You'd have to learn the godforms," Deirdre said, blinking rapidly, "and the Sephiroth, and the Hebrew alphabet."

I nodded. "It's what I really want to do."

"Neal is a great teacher," Chloe said, sliding a proud arm around her husband.

"I'm eager to learn."

"It's decided then," said Neal. "I'll give you some reading material, and you can work towards your initiation. Welcome, Sophie. You're one of us."

I began to learn. This involved daily thought exercises and meditations. It meant beginning to understand the complex chains of correspondences which revolved around Hebrew letters and the ten stations on the Tree of Life. My contact with the "unseen" world up until this point was limited. My Catholic father and Protestant mother had dealt with the problem of religion by introducing me to neither faith and hoping I would one day choose a side for myself. I wasn't even sure what star sign I was, given that some horoscope columns said that I was Capricorn, and some said I was Aquarius. I had a lot of information to fit into my brain, and it took up a lot of my time. Luckily, I have a good memory, so when Neal insisted on meeting me for lunch in Soho midway through the week, I could recite back to him some information about the Sephiroth and which pillars they were on.

"Good, good," he said. "Your enthusiasm is paying off already."

I curled some fettuccine onto my fork. We were sitting in

a grubby trattoria on Old Compton Street. "How long have you been involved in the Lodge?" I asked.

"Let me see . . . four years with the Seven Stars, but before that I was with another group in Islington. I've been practising for ten years altogether."

"You must have seen some amazing things."

"Yes, of course. Spirits, magical workings, messages from angels. One working we did, in the early days of the Seven Stars, cured Chloe's mother of cancer."

"Really?"

"Without a doubt."

"I'd like to hear more about that."

"We all have miraculous stories to tell." He then proceeded to recount a few of them. I sat quietly and he happily filled the silence.

"Have you asked for a child?" I said when he had finished.

"A child?"

"For you and Chloe."

He cast his eyes down, and I was afraid I'd made him sad. "Oh. Yes, we have done workings. But the Universe has other ideas, I suppose."

"Chloe's lovely," I said.

"Yes, she's a lovely woman," he replied. I wanted to ask why he hadn't invited her to lunch with us, but I suspected I already knew.

After lunch — he paid — Neal went back to the shop and I fought my way home through the crowds of tourists. I sat at the desk and wrote down everything I'd heard, spent a few hours working out possible chapter divisions, then plugged in my groaning old laptop and typed up another article I'd been working on about investments for single women. Not that I had any investments myself; I'd never expected to find myself single.

Neal and Chloe had me over for dinner the night of the next Lodge meeting. Chloe had a way with lamb and rosemary. I was debating whether to ease the top button of my jeans open and make more room when Deirdre arrived, bursting with a story to tell.

"We need to send out a warning," she said.

"A warning?" Chloe asked, as she scraped leftovers into a plastic container.

Deirdre set her bag down in the corner and pulled up a chair at the table. "Yes, over the psychic network. There's a Wanderer in town."

I sat very still and listened. What was a Wanderer?

"No, really?" Chloe said, sliding into her chair.

Neal leaned forward on his elbows. "How do you know?"

"I know because I saw her with my own eyes and spoke to her with my own mouth."

I dropped my head so they couldn't see me smile.

"What happened?" Chloe asked.

Deirdre glanced quickly at me, unwittingly letting on that trusting me was still an issue for her.

"Go on," Neal said.

"I was late for work, so I took the short cut through the cemetery. But when I hit Bunhill Row, I sensed a very strong psychic cry for help."

"Deirdre is a Sensitive," Neal said to me.

"I see."

"I followed the cry down the first side street. It was coming from an old building marked for demolition. When I went up the stairs, I found an old woman sitting in a corner in darkness. I asked her what she wanted, and she said she had a story to tell."

"What did you do?"

"I was wary, of course. I asked her what kind of a story it was. She said it was a story that needed telling, and then alarm bells started ringing in my brain. When I asked if the story came with a warning, she said yes, and I hotfooted it out of there."

"Well done, Deirdre," Neal said.

I was confused. "I'm sorry, I don't understand," I said.

"Have you ever heard about the Wandering Jew?" Neal asked.

I shook my head.

"The chap who was cursed to wander the earth forever telling his tale again and again until Judgement Day?" Chloe said. "You've never heard of him?"

Some vague impression of somewhere having read about the myth struck me. "Oh, yes, I know what you mean."

"It's a not uncommon psychic occurrence. There are those who find themselves under a burden to tell a story."

"Why?" I asked.

Neal shook his head. "You never ask why. The story they tell reveals why."

"But why can't we hear it?"

"Because," Deirdre said patiently, blinking with her left eye, "once they've told you, the burden passes to you."

This sounded so far beyond the limits of rationality that I almost laughed out loud. Founded on a fear of an implausible superstition, Deirdre had abandoned a needy old woman who probably had some fascinating tale to tell (most elderly people do). "And what happens if the burden passes to you?"

"You're under a spell. A curse. Until you can find somebody else willing to hear the tale, you have to wander the earth alone."

I considered all this information while they discussed the Wanderer.

"I'll put a message on Lodge-list as soon as I get to work tomorrow."

"Not everybody is on the Internet, you know. We'll have to ring around all the shops, ask people to put up flyers."

"We should do a cleansing ritual for you, just in case. The compulsion may still be clinging to you."

"I knew I was safe bringing it into the Lodge. We'll banish it."

The conversation continued around me, things I didn't understand. One question was bothering me. "How come this woman can't find anybody to hear her story, when the world is full of cynics who have never heard of the Wandering Jew?"

"Only those who are Sensitive will hear her call," Deirdre said, puffing up her chest proudly. "Only those who are already highly developed on the psychic plane can find her, and they understand the warning she gives."

"Oh. I see."

So, finding her meant years of psychic development. It was a good thing Deirdre had all but given me the address.

I never had a shortage of squash partners. I had already garnered something of a reputation at the Euston Sports Centre. What I love about squash is the speed, the precision, the gratifying *thwack* as I pound the ball with my racquet. I am very, very good at it. Every time I walked into the sports centre, one or two of the regulars would be upon me in seconds, demanding a rematch. I'd beaten them all: ex-champions, men twice my size, expensive women with expensive equipment. They simply didn't stand a chance. The sweaty, rubbery smell of the sports centre was, to me, the smell of victory. I was addicted to it.

The only person who had ever beaten me at squash was Martin, which went a long way to explaining my adoration of him.

On Thursday afternoon, I had just finished wiping the floor with a wiry Asian man who swore he had once played for Singapore, when I spotted Neal waiting near the weights room. I was sweaty, badly dressed, had my hair scraped back in a ponytail, and probably smelled bad. How fortunate. Nothing like a dose of bodily reality to cure a man of romantic notions, especially a man with a pretty, clean wife waiting for him at home.

"Hi, what are you doing here?" I asked, loosening my hair and towelling it.

"I went to your place looking for you. The landlady said you might be here."

"She was right. How did you get my address?"

"I thought you might like to go for a coffee."

"I'm filthy."

"Then perhaps we could just go to your place. I could wait while you have a shower."

"How did you get my address? I'm not in the phone book yet."

"My brother works for British Telecom."

"Oh." I tried to remember what kind of state I'd left my room in, and was fairly certain I'd filed away any evidence of my occupation. "I suppose we can go to my place, if you like."

"I just wanted to go over some of the lesser rituals with you."

I nodded. "Come on then."

When we arrived at Hartley Manors I let him into my bedsit, sat him at my desk with my magic workbook for him to check, and disappeared into the communal bathroom for a quick shower. Hoping the whole time that he wouldn't get curious and snoop in my files. I suppose most people aren't file-snoopers. I certainly am.

"Well done, Sophie," he said when I re-entered the room, freshly dressed in a white shirt and blue jeans. He held up my workbook in his left hand. "You've obviously been working really hard."

"Yes, I try to do a little each day."

"Is this your laptop?" he said, indicating my five-year-old Toshiba.

I nodded. "I think it's on its last legs, but it does the job."

"I have a laptop at the shop that I no longer use. You can have it if you like."

"No, I'm sure mine will go the distance."

"Really, I insist. Since we put the new computer system in, I haven't even opened it."

I shrugged. "Well, if you insist." I had never had a problem with accepting gifts, even the ones that came with complex, unvoiced expectations. I figured I could sell my old laptop to some desperate student and use the money for my next phone bill. I switched on the electric kettle and made two cups of coffee. Neal rambled on for a few minutes about the new computer system and how it had improved the efficiency of their stocktaking. He needed very little encouragement to talk. I handed him a coffee mug.

"Mmm, lovely," he said, after the first sip.

"I had a few questions about Deirdre," I said.

"Deirdre?"

"Well, more specifically about the Wanderer she met."

"What would you like to know?"

I sat in the windowsill, facing him. "Do you believe it?"

He nodded immediately. "Yes. Oh, yes."

"You see, to me it sounds a little . . . incredible."

He smiled. "You will see and hear many more incredible things in the months to come."

"I don't doubt it. What did she mean about a warning?"

"A Wanderer must warn you. That's their curse, to need to tell you a story but to be unable to find a willing listener."

"And why did we have to do a cleansing ritual for Deirdre?"

"Because the compulsion to tell the story can be so strong, it can be almost contagious. Deirdre may have found herself a few days later thinking obsessively about the story, wanting to return and hear it. She may have even passed it on to others she came into contact with."

"Like us?"

"Yes, like us. But, as she said, it's safe to bring it to the Lodge because we're all believers. We all did the cleansing ritual, and we're all aware of the dangers."

"I see."

"You're curious?" He looked at me closely, and I could tell he was wondering if *I'd* been thinking obsessively about the story, if Deirdre had somehow infected me with the old woman's malaise.

"Yes." I smiled.. "Not too curious, though. If you're worried."

"No, not worried. I think, though, that I should show you the LBRP."

"Aha," I said, scanning through my memory. "The Lesser Banishing Ritual of the Pentagram."

"Yes, it will help if you find yourself in any psychic danger. Sometimes entering the world of magic and ritual makes you vulnerable. You should probably be doing it every day." He put his coffee cup down on the desk. "Come on, stand up. I'll show it to you."

I did as he asked.

"Now, face east."

"Which way is east?"

"Where the sun rises."

I shook my head. "I'm not up at that hour."

"That way," he said, pointing towards the door. I turned around.

"Centre yourself."

I took a breath, closed my eyes.

"You stand at the very heart of the universe," he said. "There is a brilliant white sphere above you, a sphere of light. Reach up with your right hand, pull the light towards you, towards your forehead. And say *Atah*."

They had taught me a peculiar way of saying these magical words, very far back in my throat like a slow, vibrating whisper. It always made me want to cough. I did as he told me.

"Draw the light down through your body with your hand. Say *Malkuth*."

I did so.

"Now, draw the light across to your right shoulder."

I wasn't concentrating properly, and touched my left shoulder by accident. I felt Neal grab my hand. I hadn't realised how close he was standing. "No," he said, "your right shoulder." He moved my hand across firmly. For the next few passes, he kept his hopeful grip on my fingers, talking me through the ritual and standing uncomfortably close. He didn't seem to realise what a dangerous game he was playing. What if I had been interested in his advances? What then of dear, childless Chloe in her pastel dresses? Not that I credited him with the nerve to go through with an affair. The thought made me irritated. I shook him off and took a step back.

"I'm sorry, Neal, I'm not feeling particularly centred. I'll practise it by myself and show you at the next meeting. Okay?"

He backed off quickly, filled the gap between us with nervous chatter. "Yes, yes, practise it a while. It takes some time to get it right. Don't rush, don't rush." And on he went, making excuses for not finishing his coffee, picking up his jacket, opening the door. He was gone in a flurry of embarrassment within twenty seconds. I hoped he wouldn't forget about the laptop.

All the talk about the Wanderer must have got to me, because that night I dreamed of an old woman. She was holding out a key to me, and when my hand closed over it a flood of words and letters rushed into my head. They had scratchy edges which grazed the soft tissue of my brain. I cried out in pain and she said, "And you were so sure words couldn't hurt anyone." I woke up feeling unsettled — scared even — though I couldn't exactly put my finger on why. I had never been troubled by nightmares, but I was still getting used to sleeping alone. I missed Martin so much in those moments waking from the dream — missed him with a pain which was physical — that I cried until dawn broke.

I have always liked to work in noisy places. Silence is too heavy with expectation for a writer. First thing the following Wednesday morning, I collected my notebooks and walked down to Soho, intending to claim a corner in a coffee shop before it started to fill with the day's tourists. I found a dimly lit cafe playing Ella Fitzgerald, ordered a coffee and settled at a scarred table in a back corner. I assessed the other patrons. A few business types lingered over breakfast meetings, a group of Australian backpackers gulped down cappuccinos, and an earnest young couple shared their opinions on football teams. Everybody was smoking. *Everybody*. I wanted a cigarette so bad that my eyes watered.

I spread out my books and papers. First to hand were all the photocopies Neal had provided, with lists of correspondences which had to be committed to memory. I put them to one side and picked up the notebook in which I had scribbled the stories I had heard so far about miraculous healings, finding lost objects, communion with spirits. I was more sceptical than I can adequately express. My own experience of the Lodge meetings offered me no insight more astonishing than the fact that grown people could act so foolishly without embarrassment. The previous Friday's meeting had not even enabled me to talk once again of the Wanderer and her story. Whenever I brought the subject up, Deirdre would stonewall me and Neal would tell me to make sure I did my LBRPs and forget about it. Forgetting about it, though, was almost impossible. It was the most interesting lead that this magic ritual business had provided me with so far. I took out a fresh sheet of paper and played around with chapter titles and organising my ideas. As I pondered I doodled in the corner of the page, surprised when I looked down to see that I had drawn an old woman's face. I scribbled it out and reached for a new sheet of paper. I wrote a few paragraphs, experimented with styles and voices. I drank one coffee, then another, and another, stopping after three for financial reasons. I looked at my notes, at my writings. What I had was obviously far too little information for a book, and far too much for a standard-length article. How much longer would I have to keep attending those bloody meetings? They were already becoming tedious, and with Neal turning into an octopus the whole situation had lost its charm. The only thing of any interest at all was the old woman with the story which I was simply supposed to forget about.

I rummaged in my bag for my mini London A-Z. Deirdre had mentioned a cemetery on Bunhill Row, and I found it quite easily. Bunhill Fields Burial Ground. It wasn't far from Old Street tube. It wouldn't hurt to see if I could find the old woman's place, just as an intellectual exercise. Or just to see if she looked like the woman I had dreamed of. That would be worth writing about; not that I'd believe it was something supernatural even if I saw it with my own eyes, I supposed. Still, I packed up my things and left.

Outside, hot midday had taken hold of the streets. I shrugged out of my jacket and tied it around my waist. I walked to Leicester Square and made my way by the Underground to Old Street.

Bunhill Fields was a very pretty, very green graveyard; a little sanctuary of quiet from the screaming traffic on City Road. But even this sacred place was not free from the scourge of tourists, a group of whom asked me if I would take their photograph congregated around William Blake's headstone. It all seemed in poor taste to me, but I complied anyway. They offered to take my photograph and post it to me, but I declined. I walked through to Bunhill Row, unsure whether to head right or left. On a hunch I went left, and took the first side street. Deirdre had mentioned an old building marked for demolition. The whole area was peppered with construction sites, so I stood for a moment at the top of the street, surveying its length. One building about halfway down the block had a scaffolding and yellow tape decorating it. I walked up to it and stood out front, wondering if it was the right place. Something up high in a window caught my eye. I glanced up, thought I saw a brief flash of an old face moving away from the glass. I didn't know why, but I felt frightened, and for a few moments I was rooted to the spot. I even considered turning around and going home and forgetting about the old woman. But I don't like to be beaten by fear, so I pushed it aside and checked in my bag for my tape recorder, then went to the front door. It wasn't locked. Inside was very dark. I crept up the stairs, testing each one with my weight first. I saw many rooms without doors, where all the fittings inside had been torn out. At the top of the stairs I called out, "Hello?"

"In here," she answered.

I pushed open the door and found myself in an empty room. Empty except for a single bookshelf with a half dozen books on it, and a chair where an elderly woman sat, close to a grimy window. It was very stuffy and quite dark.

"Hello," I said. "I'm Sophie."

"It's a pleasure to meet you, Sophie," she said. She was thin, dressed in black, and her face was very pale with very soft features. Not too much like the woman in the dream, really, unless you were energetically looking for similarities.

"Look, this may sound a little strange," I said, "but an acquaintance of mine told me about you. She said you had an interesting story to tell."

"I do."

"I'm a journalist. I collect interesting stories."

"I'm happy to tell you my story, but it may be dangerous for you to hear it."

"Yes, yes, so I've heard. I'm afraid I don't hold much with such superstitions."

"Even so, I have cautioned you."

"What's your name?"

"I'd rather not say."

I pulled my tape recorder out of my bag, inserted a fresh tape. "Do you mind if I tape you?"

"Not at all. What you do with the story once I've told it does not concern me."

Copyright presented no problem, then. I nodded. "So, what's it all about?"

"Can you see the blue book over there on the shelf?"

I moved to the bookshelf, reached for the book.

"No, no," she said, "don't touch it."

I peered at the spine. "*Paradise Lost*," I read, "by John Milton."

"Have you read it?" she asked.

"No," I said, wondering where this was going. "I'm not particularly well-read in the classics."

"Never read it?" She seemed appalled. "But it's the greatest poem in the English language."

I'd always been rather fond of the lyrics to "Across the Universe", but I didn't tell her that. "It's very famous," I said.

"It's a first edition," she told me, nodding towards the book. "I've had it rebound, though. The old cover fell apart a long time ago." She frowned as if remembering something unpleasant.

"A first edition?" My gaze turned once more to the book, my fingers itching to pick it up. "You'd get a small fortune if you wanted to sell it."

"I doubt it's worth much, really," she said, glancing towards the window.

"It's stuffy in here," I said. "Can I open the window for you?"

"No, I'll never be able to get it closed again," she said. "I'm too weak."

"I can close it before I go."

"You might forget."

I shrugged. "What do you want to tell me about *Paradise Lost*?" I was starting to think she might just be crazy, not interesting, and it was growing very warm in the room. My breath felt compressed in my lungs.

"I want to tell you a story about three sisters," she said. "Do you have sisters?"

"I'm an only child," I said.

"Then it may be hard for you to understand the bonds of loyalty and love, and how they may be broken."

I was just about to ask if she was one of the sisters, when she said, "This is an old story. It starts in the 1660s. The eldest sisters are young women, the youngest on the threshold of adulthood."

I hesitated, then decided to stay and listen. In fact, I had a feeling I was *meant* to listen. I couldn't explain it then, and I can't explain it now. All I knew was that it seemed the most natural thing in the world to lower myself to the floor, sit cross-legged, stand my tape recorder on the bare floorboards in front of me, and say, "Go on. I'm listening."

And this is what she told me that first day. I've edited it for clarity, of course, but it's almost word for word.

1

Daughters Grow About
the Mother Tree

The most disruptive events sometimes occur on the most peaceful of days, and Anne Milton knew this. She had known it since she was a child.

Yet, so far, it was a peaceful day. She lay on her back in the ocean of long grass. Up above her, the sky was blue and infinite. The grass waved in the spring breeze, and the sun was pale on her face. She closed her eyes and entered the familiar world of her imagination. Heaven smiled on her, cherubs beckoned. She breathed great lungfuls of spring, felt herself drifting off on a tide . . .

"Anne! Anne!" Her youngest sister Deborah was calling her from far away.

Anne blinked her eyes open and was dazzled by the sky.

"Anne! Come to the house." The voice drifted awry on the breeze. "There's news of Father."

She sat up. Deborah stood on the edge of the field, scanning for her.

"Here," Anne called.

Deborah, dressed in her usual sober grey, beckoned grandly. "Come. Liza's here."

Liza was Father's maidservant. Anne hadn't seen her since they left London three years ago. When the King had been restored to his throne, Father had been imprisoned briefly, and Anne and her sisters had been sent to live with their maternal grandmother here in Forest Hill. The distance had suited Anne well. He was a terrifyingly brilliant man with an unforgiving tongue, and he reserved his cruellest barbs for Anne. *Dullard. Cripple. Simpleton.*

She pulled herself up and made her way towards the house, her left leg dragging slightly as it always did, refusing to heed her will. Deborah waited patiently at the edge of the field for her.

"What d-do you think has happened?" Anne said. Her words, even more than her legs, would not behave as she willed them. "Is he d-dead?" Although the thought brought a sense of relief, the guilt bit ten times more acutely.

"Don't say such a thing! I'm sure he is fine, but Liza won't tell until we're all together. Grandmamma's trying to find Mary."

Anne pushed open the door to the little wooden house. Inside was crammed with people and cats and a jumble of old and new furniture. The smell of boiling meat arose from the fireplace where Ruthie was cooking dinner. Liza, Father's skinny maidservant, waited by the window, keeping well out of the way of Uncle William and cousin Hugh. They were chasing Madam Cat around and around the room, trying to step on her tail. Great-uncle George dozed and dribbled on himself by the fire. The two sisters sat obediently on the long wooden seat adjacent to the hearth, and Anne folded her hands in her lap, trying to be as composed as Deborah. She had imagined she may never hear from Father again, never have to confront those old memories of London.

With a rustle of crimson silk Mary flounced in, her little dog Max held tight in her arms. Uncle William ate Mary with his gaze as he always did, his lascivious interest carelessly displayed. Mary rolled her eyes at him, then plonked herself on the seat and leaned in eagerly, her dark curls bouncing. "Do you think the old bore has finally given up the ghost?"

"Mary!" Deborah admonished. "You sound as though

26

you relish the thought. 'Tis abominable."

Max whimpered and wriggled in Mary's arms. She feigned innocence. "'Twasn't me that said it, sister. 'Twas Mad Mary." This was one of the middle sister's favourite jokes. When she said or did something outrageous she liked to pretend that she had been seized by a sudden, brief fit of insanity.

"Where's G-G—" Anne started.

"Grandmamma? She's coming." Mary turned her attention to Liza. "Well, what's going on?"

"I have to wait until Mrs Powell is here."

Mary muttered grimly under her breath, something about "stupid servants" but Anne couldn't entirely make it out.

"Grandmamma!" Mary called, her voice sharp in Anne's ear. "We're waiting for you."

"Yes, yes, here I am." Grandmamma thundered in on her enormous legs. She was a fat old gossip, and Anne mistrusted her, though Mary adored her. The old woman shooed Hugh and Will away and approached Liza at the window, her eyes gleaming. She, too, suspected that Father had passed on. Maybe she even imagined there would be an inheritance. "What's this news, then, Liza?"

Liza straightened her back and announced, "Ma'ams, your father is lately married."

"Married, Liza!" Mary exclaimed. "Why, that is not news. If he were dead, that would be news."

Grandmamma laughed loudly. "Never mind, Mary," she joked. "He will die in his own good time."

Liza drew her eyebrows down in disapproval, then continued. "Mr Milton has asked that you return immediately to London, to live with him and his new wife."

Anne felt as though she had been struck. Return to London? *No, no, no.* Every nerve shook loose at the idea. She opened her mouth to speak, felt her lips moving, but no words would come. Just the stupid stuttering beginnings of consonants.

Deborah turned to her and waited patiently. "What is it, Annie?"

"N-not —"

"Not what, Anne?" Mary asked.

She could see their pretty faces turned towards her — fair Deborah and dark Mary — expectant eyes upon her. She struggled to make the words leave her mouth. "N-not the house in . . . P-Petty France. Say we're n-not returning to the house in Petty France." The image came unbidden as it always did: a tiny boy, lying as though asleep. But not sleeping. Cold and pallid, his chill limbs flung limp across the bed.

"Why no, Miss Milton," Liza said. "For we have lately moved to a new house on the Artillery Walk to Bunhill Fields."

The warm thread of Anne's relief was almost lost among the icy guilt that memories of Petty France had awoken. Though she may never return to that room again, she feared she would never stop seeing it in her imagination.

"When are we to leave?" Deborah asked. She sounded bright and excited. Father's youngest daughter was his favourite.

"He has given orders that I return with you in not more than three days," Liza said.

Grandmamma threw her hands in the air. "Three days! Why, that's barely enough time to pack."

"London!" Mary said. "How thrilling! I shall see all the fine ladies and the cavaliers, and I shall take my new scarlet dress, Grandmamma." She laughed. "Father's too blind to see how low it is at the front."

Deborah leaped to her feet. "And I shall take my Hebrew grammar, and Father will be so proud to hear how much I've learned."

Mary sniffed. "Father won't even notice, Deborah."

"He shall, of course he shall."

"Come, I'll race you to the top of the stairs," Mary said. They dashed off together, leaving Anne rooted to the couch.

One of the cats yowled with pain as Hugh got a foot on its tail, and Great-uncle George woke with a snort. Grandmamma made plans with Liza, and Ruthie admonished Uncle William for tasting the soup. But Anne was aware of nothing but the churning of her stomach, and the guilty horror of remembering her baby brother's death.

"Mistress Mary, say you won't go."

Mary sat up, brushed the hay from her hair. "Sir Adworth, we have discussed this."

"But some other worthy will catch your eye in London. Some young, handsome man."

She carefully began lacing her bodice, plucking hay from her clothes. The stable had been cleaned that morning, and smelled of fresh hay and horses. "You know I'm not interested in young men."

He reached out and pulled her down beside him, forcing his hand inside her bodice to squeeze her breast. She assessed him coolly: his age-spotted skin, his grey hair, the sagging flesh on his chest. Yes, he was ugly and tiresome, but he was the wealthiest man in eight miles and he adored her. Grandmamma had always said, find a wealthy man who adores you and you'll never want for trinkets. It had proved sound advice. Sir Adworth had already provided silk for four dresses and dozens of strings of beads for her hair.

She smiled and shook her head coyly. "Come, Sir Adworth, you know you won't manage again so soon."

"Mary, what am I to do without you?"

"You'll find somebody else. Or haply your wife may open her legs to you again."

"I'm sure she has cobwebs growing between them."

Mary laughed, pushed him away firmly and straightened her clothes. "I must go. My sisters will be waiting." She stood, then helped him up. His knee joints cracked loudly, making her wince. He was the oldest lover she had ever had, at sixty years of age, and it alarmed her how quickly he could lose his breath or become pained in the joints.

"I have a parting gift for you," he said, recovering his balance and reaching into the purse under his cloak. He pulled out a delicate bracelet, silver and amber stones.

"Oh, 'tis lovely," she said, snatching it from his fingers.

"When you come back," he said, "you'll come to see me again?"

She looked him over, doubting he'd live another summer. "Of course. But Father may want us to stay in London."

Sir Adworth frowned at mention of her father. "I suppose you must do as he says."

"I must go," she said. "The carriage will be here already."

"Take care," he said, touching her cheek. "You shall always be the prettiest girl in the world."

She kissed him quickly on the mouth, then pulled the stable door open and ran out into the sunshine. She lifted her skirts so she wouldn't trip and dashed across the open fields. She saw Grandmamma's house in the distance, and caught sight of the large silhouette of Grandmamma walking towards her.

"Gran!" she called.

"Hurry, Mary, the coach is about to leave."

She kicked off her shoes and scooped them into her right hand, kept running towards the lone, dark-clad figure in the sunny field. Grandmamma caught her with a laugh. "You've been with Adworth?"

"Look what he gave me!" Mary exclaimed breathlessly, holding out her wrist.

Grandmamma inspected the bracelet eagerly. "Oh, good girl, Mary. But you should hurry. The coach is waiting."

Grandmamma enclosed her in a claustrophobic hug. She smelled of old wool and boiled ham. She whispered close to Mary's hair. "You're the only one I shall miss."

"I shall miss you, too."

"I shan't miss the puritan and the moron."

Mary giggled. "Gran, that's not very nice."

"Go," she said. "Find a wealthy man in London and make him marry you. And make sure you write me letters."

"Every day, if you do the same." Grandmamma had never been taught properly to read and write, so her letters would be full of entertaining spelling mistakes.

Mary took off once again towards the house, rounded the corner to see the coach, laden with their trunks, waiting out the front. Mary was keenly looking forward to London; even looking forward to meeting her new stepmother. Her last stepmother had been a beautiful, mild-tempered woman whom they had all adored. And London was so exciting, so full of people and promise.

Anne, Deborah and Liza were already in the coach.

"Come on, snail's pace," Deborah called out the window.

Mary poked her tongue out as the coachman opened the door for her, and she climbed in. Liza held a disconsolate Max on her lap. Mary had barely sat down when the coach surged forward, and they were on their way.

"Here, he doesn't like me," Liza said, thrusting Max into her arms.

"Dear little man, handsome little fellow," Mary cooed as Max licked her and settled into her lap.

Deborah leaned across and plucked a strand of hay out of her hair. "Have you been saying goodbye to Sir Adworth?"

"He gave me a bracelet." She thrust her arm out, but Deborah sniffed dismissively.

"Jewellery does not interest me."

"'Tis mighty p-pretty, Mary," Anne said.

"Your father wouldn't be happy knowing where you got it," Liza said.

"Shut up," said Mary. "'Tis none of your business, you're just a servant. And if you tell Father, I will beat you." She considered the bracelet vainly. "I'd wager it cost a pretty penny."

"You're such a fool for these old men, Mary," Deborah said.

"And you are jealous."

"Jealous? Hardly."

"'Tis n-n—" Anne's eyelids began to flutter, and her top lip jerked up and down. Her stammer always put Mary at the end of her patience, but she forced herself to wait — Anne was her sister, and despite what Grandmamma said, despite what Father said, despite what everybody said, Anne was not really a fool. For all that she sounded like one.

"'Tis not wrong to accept g-gifts from someone you love," Anne said finally.

"But she doesn't love him, Anne," Deborah said. Anne looked uncomprehending, and Mary reached out to touch her hair fondly. Her older sister's most endearing folly was that she always assumed Mary loved the men she dallied with; credited her with a fickle heart and nothing more dissolute. Anne didn't suspect that she lay with them, though Deborah had probably deduced it. Her little sister was far too watchful and clever for Mary's liking sometimes.

Mary fingered the amber stones and thought about Adworth. Neither of her sisters would ever understand the feel of victory she derived from her conquests: when they were inside her, all their power and dignity disappeared. The mighty became the vulnerable, the wealthy became supplicants, the most scholarly were as mindless babes; all they had care for was her.

"Sir Adworth is older than Father," Deborah was saying. "'Tis revolting."

"He's richer than Father, too," Mary countered.

"You are a fool, Mary. If he adores you so, why does he only ever meet with you in the stables? Why does he only buy you amber and silver, instead of rubies and gold?"

Mary opened her mouth to reply, but found too much truth in the remark to rebut it. Sometimes she hated Deborah for being able to say precisely what would hurt her most.

"P-please don't fight," Anne said. "Mary may love whomever her heart leads her to love."

"Love! Oh, I shall be sick!" Deborah exclaimed.

Mary, seething at Deborah's earlier comment, chose a barb that would be equally hurtful in response. "Sir Adworth said that Father was strook blind by God for siding with Cromwell."

Liza gasped and even Deborah could not speak for a few moments. Finally Deborah said, "That's not true. God would not punish a man who sacrifices himself for what he believes. Sir Adworth has never made a sacrifice in his life."

"You are such a tedious puritan, Deborah."

"I'm not."

"Then why do you dress like one and act like one?"

"I simply prefer plain clothes," Deborah said. "Like Father. And I believe in Christian liberty — each man should be able to worship as his conscience dictates, for we cannot know for certain what God is or what God wants of us."

"That's one of Father's ideas, too, is it not?" Mary teased.

"Father is a wise man."

Mary contemplated Deborah for a few moments. She was the only one of the three of them who resembled their father: his soft, fair complexion, his pale red-gold hair, his wide hazel eyes. Anne and she were dark like their mother, though Mary flattered herself that Anne was less robust, more pinched in the face, her hair lanker and straighter. Deborah, the youngest by four years, already towered over them both. She often wore her long hair loose, and despite her taste for sober colours, her stature and the golden sweep of her hair drew gazes wherever she went.

"I know not why you worship Father so," Mary said finally, and she meant it. It wasn't just another dart thrown into the argument. "He's unkind to all of us, you included."

"He is angry because he is blind. We must do our best for him."

Mary leaned back in her seat. The coach bumped as it hit a stone on the road. "I only hope that his new wife is kinder to us than he is."

"I'm sure she will be," Deborah said. "What say you, Liza, for you have met her?"

Liza shook her head. "'Tis not for me to judge, ma'am."

"Is she nice? Is she kind?" Mary asked.

But Liza would not answer, and her silence spoke volumes.

Evening had descended on London by the time their coach rattled up towards Father's house. A butcher's wagon blocked the Artillery Walk, so they pulled down their trunks and set off on foot up the hill. The Walk was a dark, narrow alley, the upper jetties of buildings blocking out the sky. A light drizzle dripped mournfully, making the ground muddy. Deborah kept her eyes on her feet so she wouldn't slip.

"It is the one on the left where you can see the light in the window," Liza called behind her.

Deborah blinked rain out of her eyes. Why had Father chosen the darkest, narrowest street on the block? Then she admonished herself, for she suspected she knew. Since the return of the King, Father's fortunes had foundered. Perhaps the Walk was all he could afford. After the wide open fields and fresh air at Grandmamma's place, dank, noisy, cramped London would be hard to get used to.

Moving ahead of them, Liza pushed open a door. The girls hurried inside and stood dripping in the doorway.

Liza indicated the door on her right. "He'll be in there."

"Liza?" Father's voice. "Is that you?"

"Yes, Mr Milton, sir," Liza said, ushering them through ahead of her. "Your girls are home."

Father sat, straight-backed, in his austere chair by the fire, his head cocked slightly to one side as though he considered a conundrum. He was surrounded by low bookshelves, a harpsichord, and a carved writing desk which he could not use now he was blind. In one corner of the room, two battered trunks of books were stacked, more books haphazardly perched on top. He was dressed sombrely, his jacket closely buttoned and his white collar crisp, if slightly stained, above it.

But he was not the puritan Mary denounced him for: Father would never allow himself to be part of a flock. Deborah felt a surge of love and admiration for him. His shoulder-length hair glinted gold by the firelight. Only a few strands of grey were visible and his pale face was still remarkably youthful. As always, Deborah was amazed by his eyes. Even though he had been blind for many, many years, his gaze appeared to be alert. He had trained his eyes to follow sounds almost precisely. Nobody who met him for the first time would be able to guess his blindness until he miscalculated and glanced slightly too far to the left or right, or until he let his guard down and his eyelids drooped. Deborah suspected embarrassment led him to such a pretence, for she knew Father hated being less than whole.

His eyes rested on all of them in turn, assessing them. "Who is wearing silk?" he said.

"I am, Father," Mary said, stepping forward.

"Mary? I heard it upon your entrance. You still have that ugly dog? I can smell him."

Mary had first found Max when he was an injured stray living off rubbish on the streets of London. The legacy of his hard years was one ear which had been bitten in half, and a patch of white fur missing from his back. But Mary loved the odd-looking creature as if he were her child.

"Max has had a bath just a month ago," she protested.

"And Anne, I hear you still hobble like a cripple," Father continued as if he hadn't heard Mary.

"I c-c-c—"

"No, do not respond; I haven't the patience. Deborah, I suppose your idiotic grandmother hasn't bothered keeping up with your lessons. I expect you've forgotten all your languages. Your Hebrew?"

"No, indeed, Father," Deborah said, stepping forward quickly. "For even when Grandmamma hasn't the time to help me —"

"Hasn't the wits, you mean," Father mumbled.

Deborah took a breath before continuing. "Indeed, Father, I have read every day in seven languages."

"Come then. Show me."

Deborah felt her face grow warm and her heart speed a little. "*Ro'lsi He'Horim V'Hinei Ro'lasim.*"

Father's face was set in stone. "And what am I to do with that sentence? Have you forgotten everything I taught you?"

Deborah felt the pit of her stomach hollow out.

"*Ro'lsi He'Horim V'Hinei Ro'lasim,*" Father said, correcting the pronunciation.

"Thank you, Father. I am sorry."

"I hardly count it your fault. Liza, fetch Mrs Milton. It is time the girls met their new stepmother."

Liza hurried out, leaving the three of them standing there, still damp from the rain, their trunks at their feet.

"Have you been well, Father?" Deborah asked. "It has been so long since we had word of you."

"I've been well enough," he said, not managing even the ghost of a smile.

"And your writing? Have you published anything of late?" Mary asked.

He didn't answer. This was one of his most unnerving habits: if he didn't feel a question was worth answering, he simply remained silent. The girls stood without speaking for another moment or two before Liza returned with a young woman who had white-blonde hair, pale eyelashes and a bulbous nose.

"I'm here, John," she said.

"Betty, meet my daughters."

The girls introduced themselves in turn, and Betty took

36

their hands briefly, recoiling from Max's attempt to lick her.

"A dog!" she exclaimed. "Does he bite?"

"No, he's the gentlest, good boy," Mary said.

"I *hate* dogs," she said.

"Does not the youngest resemble me?" Father said.

Betty fixed her gaze on Deborah. "Why, yes, John. The likeness is remarkable."

Deborah smiled. Her father had never actually seen her — he had been blind before she was born — but so many people had remarked upon the likeness that he must have formed a picture of her in his mind.

"Where are we to stay, Father?" Mary asked. "Only, our clothes are damp and we should like to unpack our trunks."

"There is a room to share at the top of the stairs," he said. "It has a large closet which Deborah may take as her own room because she is the smallest."

"Father, Deborah is now five inches taller than me," Mary complained. "She's almost taller than you."

Deborah was secretly pleased at this display of favouritism, though she knew Mary hated to share a room.

"I have made up my mind," he said. "And the room will suffice you until we can decide what to do with you."

"D-do with us?" Anne ventured, and Deborah could see her whole face concentrated on not stuttering. "Are we n-not to stay with you?"

Betty hurried forward. "Come along, girls. I'll take you to your room."

"Deborah," Father said before they left, "do you still have a fair hand?"

"Why, yes, Father," she said, "but not as fair as Mary's. Her handwriting is the envy of all of us."

"Go now, and change into dry clothes. We shall speak again over supper."

Betty led them up the rickety stairs — narrow and steep — to the second storey.

"Here is the withdrawing room, and Liza and I sleep over

behind those curtains," she said, indicating around her. The wall hangings were faded and ragged, the chairs old and chipped, but the room was clean and bright. It smelled of fresh whitewash and was free of the dust and grime which Deborah was used to at Grandmamma's house.

"And where does Father sleep?" Mary asked mischievously.

"In the very chair in which you just saw him. He finds the stairs hard to climb without his eyes to assist him. And besides, I'm sure you are familiar with how early he likes to rise."

Mary rolled her eyes. "Deborah is the same. Up at dawn, spectacles perched on her nose, reading a book."

"I'm studying to be a physician," Deborah offered.

"Idiot. Women don't become physicians," Mary said.

Betty favoured Deborah with an indulgent smile. "You really are your father's girl. Come, let me take you upstairs."

The instant Betty's back was turned, Mary had kicked Deborah gently in the back of the knees. Deborah impishly flicked a curl away from her sister's ear.

"Here it is," Betty said.

The attic room was very dark, with old, faded wainscoting, grey curtains, and bare floorboards. A large posted bed, two candlestands and an oak dresser were all the furnishings. The fire had been lit, and it filled the room with a warm glow. Mary placed Max on the floor and examined the bed while Anne stood stiffly by the dresser. Deborah went to the window to peek between the curtains, and found herself looking at the house across the street from them, at this height only two feet away. If she looked down she could see onto the Walk. A cart rolled slowly up the hill, leaving deep tracks in the mud.

"Draw the curtain!" Betty squeaked, and Deborah spun round to see her new stepmother advance.

"Why? What's wrong?"

38

Betty twitched the curtain shut. "'Tis a new moon."

Deborah shook her head in confusion. Over Betty's shoulder she could see Mary trying not to laugh. "A new moon?"

"'Tis bad luck to see a new moon through glass."

Deborah vaguely remembered hearing this superstition before. "Oh, I see. Fear not, I shan't look at it." Mary smothered a giggle.

Betty turned away and gestured around her as though nothing had happened. "We intended to buy some rugs ere you arrived, but then your father heard of some second-hand ones from a friend's house," Betty said. "They should come sometime this week. Your father hasn't as much money as he once had."

"I'm sure we'll be perfectly happy here, Betty," Mary said, flipping open her trunk and pulling out dresses and ribbons and combs at random.

"Deborah, your closet." Betty showed her to a door, through which lay a narrow, windowless room. A small bed with a dirty white spread had been set up in it. "Now I see you, I think the bed may be too small."

"No, no. I think it will be fine," Deborah said, although she could clearly see it wasn't true. It was a child's bed, and the way her limbs kept growing she couldn't imagine that it would take her full length. But she was so gratified that Father had singled her out for special attention that she didn't mind.

"I shall leave you to settle yourselves," Betty said, heading for the stairs. "When you come down for supper we shall talk of our . . . plans."

"Thank you, Betty," Deborah called to her new step-mother as she left. The instant Betty was out of the room, Anne's lip started to jerk up and down.

"What is it, Anne?" Deborah asked.

"She d-d—"

Mary led Anne to the bed. "What's wrong?"

"She d-doesn't like us."

"What makes you say that?"

"They're p-planning to g-get rid of us."

"Nonsense," Mary said. "Father only just sent for us. Oh, Anne, you really have too wild an imagination."

Anne fell silent, and Deborah wished once again that her oldest sister wasn't afflicted with such a dreadful stammer. Sometimes important things went unsaid, simply because she couldn't manage the words.

"Death! I'm so tired," Mary said, flopping down on the bed. Max scrambled up next to her. "Deborah, check under the bed. Has she given us one pot or two?"

Deborah flipped up the blankets and checked. "Two."

"Good, I hate to share." She turned on her side, looking at her sisters. "Is Betty not the ugliest woman you've ever seen?"

Deborah couldn't help herself, she began to giggle violently. Anne smiled guiltily.

"'Tis a good thing Father is blind," Mary continued, and in an instant they were all convulsed with laughter.

"I don't think she liked Max," Deborah said.

"Well, that is bad luck. Wherever I go, he goes."

"You'd b-better keep him out of her sight," Anne said. "She might p-poison him."

"I'll poison her!" Mary exclaimed, still in high spirits and laughing. "For I'd sooner see my father's ugly wife dead than my sweet little champion."

Anne gasped as though winded, then said in a low voice, "Sister, you should n-n-n—"

"Never say such things, I know."

"You should never wish somebody d-dead," Anne finished quietly, casting her eyes down.

"Oh, go to," Mary replied. "You've put us in a fine sober mood to have supper with Father. Come, we're expected downstairs."

*

A large wooden table in the kitchen was laid out with bread, cheese, and a tureen of potato soup. Liza served Father first, and Anne watched him as he ate without spilling a crumb. For a blind man, he had always been unnaturally capable of looking after himself.

"This soup is bland, Liza," Mary said as she tested hers.

"Mary," Father said, "there is nothing wrong with the soup."

"But it tastes —"

"I think it tastes good, and so it is good."

Anne ventured a sentence, terribly aware that she had barely said a word yet to Father or his new wife. "I think the soup is n-n-nice."

Father fixed her in his blind gaze. "N-n-nice?" he said, imitating a high girlish voice. "I'm g-glad you th-think so."

Anne dropped her head, sucked in her bottom lip.

They ate in silence for a few minutes, then Betty said. "Mary, Anne. You are both fond of clothes and fabrics are you not?"

Anne dared not answer. Mary, her mouth half full of bread, squeaked. "Fond of? I *love* dresses." She swallowed loudly. "Anne has no interest though. Can't you tell?"

Betty smiled a smile which didn't quite reach her eyes. Anne saw her hand steal out to tap Father's lightly.

"Go on then, Betty," he said.

"No. You should tell them."

Father wiped up some soup onto his last piece of bread, ate it, dusted his fingers and sat back in his chair. "We have plans for you, girls."

Anne's lips moved to form the words, "What kind of plans?", but no sound would come out. Deborah jumped in for her. "Plans, Father?"

"Deborah, you are to stay here by me and take my dictation daily, and read to me. My last amanuensis has lately left for Cambridge, and Betty has no languages. It will have to be you."

"I should be pleased to, Father."

41

"And what of us?" Mary said, her jaw set in challenge. "What plans for the ugly sisters?"

"Mary, I can see neither you nor Anne, and know not if you are ugly," Father said evenly.

Betty jumped in. "A lacemaker in Surrey has need for two apprentices and —"

"What!" Mary gasped. "You want to send us out as apprentices!"

"Your father hasn't enough to support you all," Betty started. "He hasn't —"

"Is this your idea, *Mother*?" Mary said caustically.

"Mary, I have made up my mind on this issue," Father said in his implacable way.

"Fine, then," said Mary. "If you've made up your mind."

Anne glanced across at Mary, curious. Why was she giving in so easily? This was not Mad Mary.

"Yes, he has," Betty said.

"And the lacemaker in Surrey knows we are the daughters of Milton?"

"Yes, I expect so," Father said, a slight frown turning down the corners of his mouth. "Why do you ask?"

"Oh, 'tis nothing really. Only, I should imagine they'll be mightily surprised when they see Anne."

Anne turned an uncomprehending gaze on her sister.

"What do you mean?" Father asked. His fear of the opinion of others was his weakness.

"Well, can you imagine? The great Milton, autodidact, revered thinker, linguist, poet, defender of the Good Old Cause . . . I'm sure Anne — with her lame legs and her stutter — I'm sure she will give them something to talk about." Mary had reached a hand under the table to squeeze Anne's, as though the small sign of affection was enough to banish the sickening disillusionment of hearing her sister speak of her in such away.

Father frowned. Betty began to say, "I'm sure nobody will —"

"No, Betty. Let Mary speak."

"Father, she's an idiot. Certainly, I could be there to look out for her, make sure she doesn't say or do anything too stupid, but I can't make her appear normal if she's not. And people may wonder, how did the great Milton father such progeny?"

Deborah's hand now crept under the table and grabbed Anne's fingers in her own. Anne shook off both her sisters and pressed her palms under the table. Mary's words stung like fire. She wanted to stand up and say, "I *will* be a lace-maker's apprentice. And I will show all of you what I am capable of." But she knew such eloquent displays were beyond her.

"And if you keep Anne here," Mary continued, "you'll have to keep me. For Deborah will be busy working for you, and somebody has to take care of Anne. Why, she can barely fend for herself she's such a simple."

Anne could read on Father's face that he believed every word. To him, possessed of such a fiery intellect, of course she would seem to be touched in the head. Of course he thought her a simple, for she could barely read or write, and knew not a single other language like her sisters. But that was only because she had never been taught, because everyone had assumed that she had less than half her wits.

Betty turned to her husband. "John —"

"Mary has a point," he said quietly.

"But we haven't enough for —"

"We have enough, Betty," Father said. "And we certainly have room for them."

"Now you make mention of room, Father," Mary started, "I wonder if I might swap with Deborah and take the closet. Only she's so very much taller and . . ."

She trailed off when she saw how Father stared at her, his lids jerked up wide to reveal his unseeing eyes. "You have said enough," he said quietly. "Deborah will sleep in the closet. You will share a bed with your sister. You will be her

43

constant companion, and you will ensure that I am not embarrassed by her, for it appears you are staying in London."

Mary nodded, squeezed Anne's hand under the table, a little gesture of triumph. "Yes, Father."

Mary had seen it a thousand times before. Anne could only express her anger in mute, teary looks of accusation. She flung herself on the bed and gazed up at her sisters, words forming but not making it past her lips.

"Oh, you know I don't mean the things I say," Mary said, her guilt making her impatient. Deborah moved about the room, stoking the fire and stripping down to her shift for bed.

"Then you sh-sh—"

"I know I shouldn't say them. But he was about to send us off to Surrey. To split the three of us up."

"I would have gone. I would have p-proved to you that I'm not useless."

"Nobody thinks you're useless." Deborah joined them on the end of the bed. "Mary and I know that you are clever and thoughtful and wise."

"I hate it. I . . ." Not another word came out of her mouth. She sat there, her mouth popping open and closed, tears running down her cheeks. Mary locked her arms around her sister and squeezed tight.

"I love you, Anne. Please, Annie, don't cry. We'll stay together this way."

Deborah leaned forward and stroked Anne's hair. After a few moments she began to calm and pulled out of Mary's embrace, sitting up and palming tears from her cheeks. "I want us to stay together," she said softly.

"And we shall. Come, no more tears," Mary said. "Let's all squirm into this bed together — yes, you too, Deborah — and tell riddles until we fall asleep."

"I have a riddle for you," Deborah said as she wriggled

into bed between her two sisters. "Why on earth did Father marry Betty?"

They giggled, even Anne.

"She's a witch!" exclaimed Mary. "An ugly old witch."

"She has such a b-big nose," Anne said.

"And her face is so pink and shiny," Deborah added.

"And as for those silly superstitions! Max not allowed under the table because it is —"

"Extreme bad luck!" her sisters chorused, laughing.

"Well," Mary said, making herself comfortable on her side between the dusty blankets, facing her sisters, "she certainly wasted no time trying to rid herself of us. I hate her already."

"Me too," said Deborah. "If I were granted a wish right now, from a genie, I would wish her sent to Surrey to be apprentice to a lacemaker."

Mary scowled. "Surrey is a pretty place. I would wish her dead."

"Mary, no!" cried Anne.

"Oh, here again," Mary said. Anne's righteousness was so tiresome. "For goodness sake, I don't *mean* it, Anne."

Deborah leaned close to Anne, touched her cheek lightly. "What is wrong sister? You are pale."

"A very long time ago, I wished someone d-dead and . . ." She fought with her words for a few moments. "And it d-did indeed happen."

"Are you talking about Johnny again?" Mary asked. For some reason Anne had always blamed herself for the death of their baby brother Johnny, when they were little more than infants themselves.

Anne nodded.

"Oh, Annie. You are too soft. You were only a child. And though you may have wished him dead, 'twas not your fault he died. He grew sick, as so many babies do."

"B-but it was my fault," Anne whispered in the firelit room. "It was."

"You were a tiny little girl," Mary said, reaching for her hand.

Anne pulled away.

"Really, Anne, why do you have this fixation about Johnny?" Mary said impatiently. "Did you poison him?"

"No!" Anne cried. Then softer, almost under her breath, "No."

"Then what —"

"If I tell you," Anne said, "you are not to wish B-Betty dead ever again."

Mary's curiosity was aroused. "Certainly."

"No, swear. Swear on the grave of our d-dear mother, that you will never wish Betty, or anyone, dead."

"I swear," Mary said, imbuing her voice with as much solemnity as she could muster.

"And Deborah?" Anne said. "Do you sw-sw—"

"I swear, Anne," Deborah said. "What great secret is this that we must swear on Mother's grave?"

"'Tis a secret about Mother," Anne said.

"Then tell us," Mary said, trying not to sound impatient. Anne was far too serious. In fact, it was frightening her. The room was very dark and empty compared to their bright, cluttered room back at Forest Hill.

"Just ere D-Deborah was born, Mother grew ill. Remember, Mary?"

She did remember, though she had only been four. It was the first great terror of her life, seeing Mother so pale and walking with such a stiff gait. "Yes."

"She t-told me something. She t-took me aside and told me something about what she had d-done to make sure we would be safe. If she d-d-died."

Mary waited while Anne drew her breath. Long sentences were difficult for her. Deborah looked apprehensive, all wide watchful eyes. Mother had died three days after Deborah was born. Mary felt such pity that her younger sister had never known Mother's warm hands

46

and soft eyes, and the safety of her embrace.

"She had been to a wise w—" She struggled over the consonant. "A wise woman. The wise woman summoned for her a g-guardian angel. To watch over us. M-Mother gave me the instructions to c-call upon him, should we be in danger or p-p-pain."

"An angel?" Deborah asked.

Anne had drawn pale at the remembrance, which made Mary curious. She had heard of such magic, but had never expended much energy on wondering if it were possible.

Anne nodded. "She made me repeat the summoning over and over, until I g-got it right. Within two weeks, she was d-dead." She fell silent a few moments, and the only sound was the crackling of the fire, and the faraway noises of carts rolling over cobbles. Anne drew a great breath. "Johnny was always Father's favourite."

"I remember," Mary said.

"And when Mother died . . ."

"Father all but forgot we existed," Mary finished for her. "You and I, and tiny Deborah. He talked only of Johnny, and what a fine man he would become."

"Y-yes."

"Go on," Deborah said. "What happened?"

"I was jealous. One night, when everyone was asleep, I c-crept out of bed and went to Johnny's crib. And I summoned the angel."

"You weren't imagining it?" Deborah asked gently.

Anne shook her head, her lips pressed together to hold back tears. "Oh, no. 'Twas more real than anything I've ever s-seen. He was t-taller than a man, b-beautiful, wise and knowing."

Mary was momentarily speechless, her imagination swelling. Anne, she knew, was incapable of insincerity. Could this be truth? "You called an angel? *Our* angel?"

Anne nodded.

"What was his name?"

Anne continued as though she hadn't heard. Her voice had dropped to a whisper. "He asked me how he c-could serve me, and I said that I wished my brother d-d-d—"

Deborah touched Anne's cheek with her fingertips. "Oh, Anne. You were just a child. Perhaps you dreamed it."

"It was not a d-dream."

"What did he say?" Mary asked. "Did he say he would kill Johnny?"

"He said my wish would be g-granted." She choked back a sob. "Johnny died the next day."

"How did you summon him?" Mary asked. "Was it hard? Would he come again? What words did you use? Magic words or ordinary?" Somehow she understood that these questions were distressing Anne, but she could not stem their flow.

"I cannot tell you, for I don't remember," Anne said. "I was too small."

"Yes, you were small," Deborah said. "So you mustn't feel guilty. Perhaps you dreamed it. Or if it were true, perhaps the angel meant that Johnny was already sick. Angels don't go about killing children."

"No, of course not," Mary said. "Anne, you simply *must* remember the summoning. What was the angel's name? How about the wise woman?"

"I remember n-n-nothing!" Anne said, her voice quavering. "Do not ask me again, sister."

Mary stared at her, astonished. How was she expected to sleep, knowing that her mother had provided them with a guardian angel whom they could command, and that Anne could not remember how to call upon him? "Anne, you must remember. I shall die if you don't remember."

"Nobody will die," Deborah said dismissively. Sometimes she was so reasonable she seemed she might be the eldest rather than the youngest; especially now with Anne flushed and damp from crying. "'Tis the fancy of her childhood. The angel is not real."

"He is real," Anne said. "I sw-swear that he is real."

"Then we must call upon him, we must —"

"Mary, no," Anne said. "The w-words are erased from my memory. I vowed never to use them again, and so I shall not."

"But —"

"Mary," Deborah said. "Why don't you take my bed tonight, and I shall sleep by Anne."

"I merely want to know —"

Anne began to sob in earnest. Deborah gave Mary a gentle push. "Go to, no more talk of angels and dying. Sleep, and all will be well again in the morning."

Mary reluctantly climbed out of the bed. She grabbed Max from where he slept in front of the fire, and went to the closet. He wriggled into bed beside her, a warm bundle of love in her arms, and she smiled down on him in the dark, kissed the top of his little head as he drifted off into dreams. Sleep didn't come for her, however. Her mind was too full of the possibilities. Her very own angel, and Anne determined not to remember a single word of the summoning!

Never mind. She had time and she had patience and, somewhere in this city, perhaps the wise woman still worked her trade. "I shall find her," she said quietly, as her eyes drifted closed. "I *shall*."

2
The House of Woe

In a flash of white fur, Max took off across the road.

"Max! No!" Mary raced off after him, down an alley between two shops where the dog had seen a rat.

Anne turned to Deborah. "I know not why she won't tie him. Then he couldn't get away."

"She won't tie him. She says he doesn't like it."

"He'll have himself k-killed."

Mary dashed out of the alley with Max wriggling in her arms, right into the path of an approaching carriage.

"Mary! Look out!" Deborah cried.

Mary jumped back and the carriage rolled past down the hill.

"He'll have them both killed," Anne said.

Mary crossed the road to rejoin them. "Safe and sound," she said, smiling. "Come."

It was late in the afternoon on their second day in London. Anne had decided on a walk to explore the new neighbourhood, and her sisters had joined her. After descending the narrow muddy hill of Artillery Walk, they were now crossing the main street towards the fields. But these fields were nothing like the vast, sunny spaces near Grandmamma's house. Anne could see more dark streets and houses on the other side, as though they were jealously crowding out the open space. Mary released Max and he went running, barking joyously, across the clipped grass.

"So these are the Artillery grounds?" Mary said, gazing

around her. "Where are all the soldiers?"

"I expect they aren't here all the time," Deborah replied.

"I *like* soldiers," Mary said.

"As long as they're grey old generals," Deborah said.

"I suppose you'd like them if they could woo you in Latin at five in the morning with spectacles on."

"D-don't bicker," Anne said. She hated to hear her sisters fight. They could be so cruel to each other and, as far as Anne could see, they already had enough enemies without turning against each other. Father always so full of criticism, Betty wanting to send them away, and Grandmamma with her barely disguised disdain.

Mary flopped down on the grass, a splash of crimson against the green, and Max came running back to lick her face. Then he was off again, chasing imaginary rabbits.

"You really should tie him, Mary."

"He doesn't like to be tied. Look at that cloud. It looks like Betty's face."

Anne and Deborah sank down on the ground next to Mary. "No it d-doesn't. It looks like an elephant."

"Betty looks like an elephant," Deborah said.

"Except her arse is bigger," Mary added. "'Tis a wonder it doesn't swallow the pot when she goes."

"Mary!" her sisters chorused together.

"Do you know she is twenty-four?" Mary continued, as though she hadn't heard. "Liza told me."

"And how old is Father now?" Deborah asked. "Six and fifty? It seems you and our new stepmother have something in common, Mary: a taste for older men."

"They can't possibly be lovers," Mary said in a mock-serious voice. "For Father can't see where to put it."

"Mary, you're outrageous," Deborah said, choking back a laugh.

"Death, I am! I revolted myself," Mary said, giggling. "You're right to admonish me, sister. Mad Mary has finally gone too far."

They lay in the grass for a few minutes, listening to the sounds of the city closing around them: carriages and street vendors and builders; the creaking of nearby windmills. Max, tired of playing by himself, returned to Mary and dropped a stick in her lap. She sat up and threw it for him, and he raced off again.

"Anne," Mary said quietly.

"Yes?"

"Have you thought any more about the summoning for the angel?"

Anne felt her whole body tense against the question. She sat up. "No," she said. "And I shan't. You should p-put the whole thing out of your mind, for it was many years ago and the angel p-probably has other young charges now. We are n-nearly grown women."

"But why can you not remember? Didn't Mother make you repeat it over and over?"

"Can you remember every n-nursery rhyme of your childhood?"

"I can remember some. The important ones. Come, Anne, it is important."

As soon as the pressure was on, words failed her and she became angry. And then the anger locked up her voice tighter still, leaving her with nothing but a mouthful of frustration. "I . . . y-you sh-sh —"

"Leave Anne alone, Mary," Deborah said. "You're upsetting her."

Mary stood up and stalked off, muttering darkly under her breath. She joined Max on the other side of the field. Anne watched them for a while, as they ran and played together. Then Deborah said quietly, "She'll lose interest in the idea soon, don't worry."

Anne didn't reply. Her tongue still felt incapable of forming words.

"And you really must let go this notion that you are responsible for Johnny's death."

"I cannot," Anne said in a whisper. Although Deborah was determined not to believe her, Anne knew what she had seen and heard. Far from seeming unreal, it was the most vivid memory of her childhood. Even her mother's face was blurred from her recollection now. But the angel, with his fierce beauty and his soft voice, was seared into her imagination.

"Look!" Mary shouted, motioning towards the road behind them. Anne turned to look. An elaborate carriage was approaching.

Mary ran towards them, skidding to her knees on the ground. "Do you see that carriage? Why, 'tis so rich and fancy it must be the King's!"

"The King, Mary?" Deborah said, exasperated. "Why on earth would the King be trundling around near Mooregate?"

"He does sometimes come out in his carriage. I have heard he does."

"On special occasions, with a full retinue and liveried servants, and people crowd the streets to see him. That is not the King."

Mary's face fell into disappointment.

"Come, let us return home." Now conversation had turned elsewhere, Anne found it easier to speak. "It will soon be supper t-time." She was always conscious of incurring Father's anger by being late.

"Yes, I suppose we should," Mary said, standing up and brushing grass from her skirt. "Max. Here, Max." The little dog trotted up, the stick still hopefully clasped between his jaws.

They made their way across the street and back up the hill. The houses were dark and narrow around and above them, blocking out the sun. Walking uphill always troubled Anne. Her hips felt more out of balance than usual.

"I'm so disappointed that I didn't see the King," Mary said.

"You might see him another time," Deborah said.

"I should like it if the King loved me," Mary continued, a sly smile on her face.

"He's too young for you," Deborah replied coolly, refusing to be baited.

"If we had an angel who could grant wishes, I would ask him to make the King love me and —"

"Don't!" Anne shouted, stopping in her tracks and turning on her sister. "I asked y-y-y—"

Mary looked horrified. Clearly she hadn't expected such a violent response. "I'm sorry, Anne, I'm only making a joke."

"D-don't." Already her tongue was letting her down. She wanted to say so much more. *Sister, if you love me, don't mention this again, for it terrifies me all the way down in the pit of my soul.* But all she could say was, "Don't."

Mary fell silent. Deborah took Anne's arm. "Here sister, let me help you up the hill."

"I c-can manage," she said, trying to shrug off her sister's help. Deborah, who always seemed to be able to sense Anne's needs, steadfastly held on, supporting her the last few steps to the house. Once inside, Mary mumbled an excuse about finding food for Max, and Father called for Deborah, so Anne found herself ascending the steep staircase to their room alone.

She sat on the floor near the dresser and opened the lowest drawer, carefully pulling out folded scarves and ribbons, making her way to the bottom where her first prayer book was kept. The book seemed so small now, but when she had it from her mother it had seemed enormous, the largest book she had ever owned. She opened the cover and found the woodcut portrait of Jesus on the first page. Her fingers traced the beloved lineaments of his face, his loving eyes, his forgiving smile, and she felt the familiar pull between peace and yearning. If she met him, he would heal her. She knew this for a certainty, and for this reason had been in love with him since first learning of his sacrifice and his forgiveness and his unbounded love.

Anne held the prayer book to her nose, hoping to smell the lingering fragrance of Mother in its yellowed pages. Nothing but dust and years. She flipped it open and found between its central pages a folded piece of paper. It was safe here: Deborah wouldn't dream of touching Anne's possessions, and Mary would have no interest in a prayer book. Anne carefully removed the letter and smoothed it out, glanced over the lines her mother had written.

Dearest Anne,
To summon Lazodeus, who will watch and
protect you . . .

She didn't need to read the words; the summoning was imprinted forever in her brain, as much as she hoped to forget it. Her eyes scanned down to the bottom of the page, where the name of the wise woman was written carefully in letters made large enough for childish eyes. *Amelia Lewis, Leadenhall Street 251.*

Perhaps she was no longer there. Nearly fifteen years had passed. Perhaps Amelia Lewis was dead by now.

Anne refolded the paper. If it wasn't such a dear reminder of her mother, she would have thrown it away. But here it was: a letter addressed solely to her, not a trifle to share with her sisters. It was far too valuable to consign to the fire.

She hid it inside the prayer book, and buried the book below layers of clothes. Safely away from Mary's inquisitive eyes.

Routine made its mark upon their lives as the first and second weeks passed. Deborah would arise early and sit with her father, writing his letters and reading to him from the Hebrew bible; Anne would help Liza with the washing or daydream on a seat in the tiny back garden; Mary played with Max and found a new reason each day to dislike Betty. They squabbled over the dog; over the dusty old rugs Betty had arranged for their bedroom; over how much firewood was being used; over how many biscuits Mary ate. They squabbled over whether it was bad luck to leave shoes on the west side of the door, or to eat bread burned on top, or to wash on Lord's Day. It seemed Betty had a superstition for every occasion. Each new day presented Mary with an opportunity to exchange words with her stepmother. But they wisely kept their fights away from the ears of Father. Betty probably knew as well as Mary how he disdained pettiness, how his fiercest exasperation was aroused when he was bothered by domestic trivia.

Early in June Betty was called away to visit her sister, and on the same day that she left a letter arrived for the girls.

"What does it say?" Mary asked, peering over Deborah's shoulder. Anne and Father had already heard its contents.

"Uncle William is in London, staying with friends near Temple Stairs," Deborah said. "He has asked us to come and spend the week with him. Particularly Mary."

"Uncle William!" Mary said, shuddering. Even though he was her mother's brother, Mary detested him. At Grandmamma's house he had always tried to get her alone, or made excuses to press his body near hers.

"Do I take it you don't want to go?" Father asked. "For I can write and tell him I can't spare you."

Mary was about to open her mouth to say yes, when it occurred to her that Uncle William might know about the wise woman Mother had consulted. She hesitated.

"No . . ." she said, "perhaps it would be nice to have news of Grandmamma."

Anne looked around shocked. "B-but Uncle W-w-w —"

"I should like to go, Father."

Father fixed her with his stern, blind gaze. As always it unnerved her. "Then you shall go, and you shall take your sister Anne."

"I d-don't want to go, Father," Anne said.

"Uncle William is not kind to Anne," Mary said.

"It matters not, Mary, for you told me that you would be your sister's keeper and so you shall. But Deborah, I cannot spare you. Not as Betty is away."

"I'll stay then," Deborah said willingly.

Irritation prickled. How was Mary to ply Uncle William for information about the wise woman when sad-eyed Anne was nearby? But then, knowing Uncle William, it wouldn't take long for the lecherous old devil to contrive for them to be alone.

Deborah awoke just before sunrise. Ever since childhood, she had always woken at the same time, as though her body sensed the start of the day. Her closet was still dark, but she knew that outside the sun was making its way towards the horizon; the sky was lightening, the stars fading, the birds beginning to wake. And Father was waiting.

She rose in the shadowy darkness and moved past her sisters' empty bed to the dresser, choosing a dark blue dress. She shivered and thought about pulling on a shawl, but Liza would have risen half an hour earlier and stoked the fire for Father before heading back to bed. Deborah combed her hair, then descended the stairs and made her way through the quiet whitewashed withdrawing room and down to her father's study.

He heard her approach. "Deborah, you are late this morning."

"Sorry, Father," she said, even though she wasn't late. The sun was not yet above the horizon. The firelight was the only light in the room and it glinted off the brass fire irons hung on the dogs. Father was still rumpled from sleep. She picked up the shell comb which lay upon the mantelpiece and began gently to comb his hair and then straighten his shirt. His rug still lay over his knees, and she took it from him and folded it aside. She had never been able to comprehend how he slept straight-backed in the chair every night, but Father always prided himself on his austerity. He interpreted austerity as a sign of strength.

"That's enough, that's enough. I have a special project for you to work on today, Deborah," he said, resuming his erect aspect, his head slightly tilted to the side.

She replaced the comb and moved to the desk. His desk was adjacent to the fireplace; an elaborately carved piece of furniture Father had owned since childhood. "Certainly, Father. Is it Latin? Greek?"

"No, it is English. It will be the greatest poem in the English language."

Deborah found her writing tray on top of the desk, next to the inkwell and the bronze-inlay human skull in which Father stored his pens. She selected one and checked its point. "Poetry, Father?" Deborah had so far only taken letters, or worked on her father's prose tracts about politics and religion.

"A poem in the style of Virgil, or Homer. I have been composing it for some time, but I am now ready to arrange it into a clear form. Retrieve the pages in the second drawer."

Deborah did as he asked. In the drawer she found a tied collection of papers covered with the writing of his previous assistant. Across the first page, *Adam Unparadised* was written.

"May I read it, Father?" she asked.

"I insist that you do," he said. "Read it aloud to me, from the start."

She returned to the short stool before him and made herself comfortable. As the sun rose and weak sunlight made its way into the room, as Liza woke and brought them bread and tea to break their fast, as Father sat listening with an expression wavering between smug self-satisfaction and artistic distress, Deborah read. The poem told a story of angels and paradise, God's love and man's temptation. In places it was beautifully written, in others awkward enough to make Father cringe. The narrative was disjointed, jumping from one scene to another with little attention to continuity. But Deborah knew they were the bare bones of something which would eventually be magnificent. She had worked with Father since childhood; when he was ready, he would make her read the same lines, the same passages, over and over, effecting tiny changes until they were perfect.

When she had finished, the sun was full in the sky and her throat was hoarse from reading.

"What do you think?" Father said quietly.

"My opinion, Father? Why, I am only your daughter."

"What do you think?" he repeated, more urgently.

"It is extreme splendid," she said, immediately knowing she could impress him with more than praise. He valued a considered reply, even an intelligent criticism. Although his vanity was appeased by those who toadied to him, his intellect always cried out for dialogue.

"But is it worthy of an epic? Will it eclipse Virgil?" he asked.

"It am certain it will, when you have finished it. Only . . ."

"Only? Only what? Have you a criticism?" His head was cocked to one side, almost in a defiant gesture.

"Father, the title speaks of Adam being unparadised. But was not paradise lost to us all?"

He nodded. "Yes, yes. I have been unhappy with the title. I shall think upon it. Good work, Deborah."

"Thank you, Father," she said, positive that she must be glowing with pride.

"We will start work on it tomorrow morning. No, the following morning, for tomorrow is Lord's Day. I have plans to add more drama: the war in Heaven, the casting out of the rebel angels. Magnificent and thrilling. Now," he said, as though suddenly embarrassed that he had revealed too much of himself, "we shall continue with your Greek lessons."

"Father," she ventured, "I am hoarse from reading. Could we not take a walk instead? It is a beautiful day."

"A walk? Yes, I suppose we could. I suppose it matters not that Betty is away."

"Certainly not, for I can guide you just as well." His embarrassment, Deborah knew, stemmed from the fact that he had to hold her hand to walk with her. He was not given to any physical demonstrations of affection. Deborah could count in single figures the number of times they had touched more than accidentally. Ignoring his discomfort, she helped him into his coat and hat and led him out onto the Walk.

"Which way, Father?" she said.

"There is a churchyard, a mile or so to the west. It is very peaceful."

"Come then." She took his hand in her own, momentarily surprised by how aged it was. Her Father always seemed to her ageless, some marble-skinned god of wisdom. They walked down the hill towards the main road. He strode along with characteristic self-possession, his affinity with the city lending his blind footsteps an almost arrogant confidence.

"Be my eyes, Deborah," he said. "Tell me what you see."

She veered left and they walked under dark, overhanging jetties. "I see a tobacconist, and a butcher, an inn with the sign of a bull upon it." She scanned for the details that would satisfy his imagination. "I see a warm haze over the city, and here we are about to pass a gentleman with . . ." She broke off as the gentleman moved into earshot.

When he was past, Father said impatiently, "What about him?"

"With a silver nose, Father," she said quietly. "He must have suffered syphilis."

"Was it a fancy nose? Or plain? What kind of man was he?"

"Plain-shaped, but embossed. He was dressed in wealthy clothes, but they were dirty."

"A syphilite on a downturn," murmured Father. "What else do you see?"

"The nightsoil cart approaching. Let us cross the road away from the smell."

"The churchyard should be nearby on the left."

"Yes, Father. Come with me." She led him across the street and down another dark hill to a walled churchyard. She let go of his hand for a few moments to open the gate, then they entered.

"Go to the newest graves, Deborah. Oh, I can feel the sun on my face."

"Yes, the sun is shining, and there are many trees around. Here, we stand at a gravestone."

"Whose is it?"

She read from the inscription. "John Edward Cross. Born 1589, died 1663."

"Who else?"

Deborah remembered this game from childhood. Father wanted her to find an unfortunate who had been born the same year as him. She scanned the graves nearby. "Yes, I think I see . . . Let us approach a little closer."

"Yes, yes."

She led him further into the churchyard. "Here we are. Philip Pettigrew. Born 1608, died 1659."

"1659!" he exclaimed. "Ha, he did not make it far."

"Not in comparison to you, Father."

"Indeed not, but I have always been of a strong constitution."

"You must be, Father, for here is another. Andrew Benjamin Olson Parkes. Born 1600, died 1661."

"And here am I only a year younger and still as healthy as a horse!"

"Would you like me to find you some more, Father?"

"No, for I know there will be too many. I am glad that you are with me, Deborah. Your sisters are not worth much, but you are a good child."

"Thank you, Father," Deborah said, aware that she should perhaps defend Mary and Anne, but too pleased with his praise to ruin the moment.

"I think you are right about my poem," he said, his red-gold hair glistening in the summer sun. "It needs a new title."

"Father?"

"I think I shall call it, *Paradise Lost*."

It wasn't until after supper on the third day that Mary spied her chance to be alone with Uncle William. The owners of the house, Sir James and Lady Aileen, had decided on an evening walk. The sun was still in the sky, the long shadows drew out along the street, and the heat of the day had eased. She had sent Anne with them and purposed to stay behind with William, feigning a sick stomach.

"Sister, can you go and take little Max with you," Mary had said. "He would love the exercise, and I am too ill to walk."

"If you wish," Anne said, surprised, wondering at Mary being alone with detestable Uncle William. "Only I shall have to tie him."

Tie Max! The thought almost brought tears to her eyes as she remembered it now: finding a soft rope, making a loop for his little head, ensuring it wasn't too tight. All the time Max whimpering as if to say, "Mary, why are you tying me?". Still, he seemed happy and eager enough as he trotted off with Anne, who limped after James and Aileen. They were kind people, and Mary was certain they would walk slowly to accommodate her.

Almost as soon as the sound of their feet on the cobble-stones had faded into the distance, Uncle William had sidled up to her on the wooden bench under the window.

"Mary, Mary, you're so pretty." His hands were already reaching for her. Up close, she could see his hair was dirty and tiny white flecks clung to the strands. Two of his teeth near the front were rotten and the hair in his nose abundant.

"Uncle William, please. Come not so close. I'll call the servants."

"And I shall send them away," he said. But he leaned back a little, chastened, eyeing her cleavage. "You have such nice duckies. May I touch them?"

"I need some information about my mother," she said.

"What information? And what's in it for me?"

"Was my mother superstitious?"

"Aye."

"Did she consult a wise woman here in the city?"

Uncle William cocked his head to one side. "What's in it for me?"

Mary picked up one of his hands and pressed it to her left breast, on the outside of her dress. "Did my mother consult a wise woman here in the city?"

William squeezed hard enough to bruise her. "Aye, she did. I think she was a friend."

Despite her discomfort, Mary was excited by the information. Perhaps she would be commanding her own guardian angel soon. "Do you know anything else about her? Her name? Where she lived?"

William's eyes grew cunning. "I should like to suckle you, Mary. I should like very much to see your duckies and suckle them."

Mary sighed in exasperation. "Take your hand away, Uncle William." And when he didn't comply she said more forcefully, "Take your hand away, or you shall get no further with me."

He withdrew his hand. She unhooked the front of her bodice and opened it to her sheer undershirt. Uncle William's bottom lip hung loose and wet as he ogled her. "Now, what do you know?"

"More," he said.

She wriggled down her undergarments and let her breasts free. He reached for her.

"No," she said, her arm fending him off. She sprang up from the chair and stood in front of him, breasts bare. "Now, what do you remember about the wise woman?"

"She lived on Leadenhall Street."

"Anything else?"

He shook his head and made to lunge at her. She side-stepped him and quickly refastened her clothes. "If you remember no more, then you get no more from me."

"It was so long ago," he wailed. "How am I supposed to remember which wise woman your mother knew?"

"If it is important enough you'll remember." She stood primly in front of him as he watched her, his mind turning over the problem.

"And if I do remember? What do I get?"

"Everything," Mary said without hesitation, for she knew she would never honour the bargain. "You get me. But only if I verify the information as accurate, so don't go making anything up."

"Very well. Very well, I shall find out, you'll see. Within a month you'll be lying beneath me."

Mary sniffed. "Find me the information first." She turned towards the stairs. "Until then, nothing."

Betty was back by the end of the week, and Deborah felt an unexpected jealous tug when she saw her father and new stepmother go walking on the first evening of her return. She watched from the window in her room as Betty led Father to the bottom of the street and then around the corner. She turned her back to the window. Father seemed to love Betty in his own gruff way, and Deborah supposed she should be glad that he had found happiness.

She descended to her father's study. Liza was out at the markets, so she had the house to herself until Father and Betty, or her sisters, returned. She relished the solitude — nobody to disturb her thoughts. Father kept a collection of old books in trunks in the corner of his room. Deborah flipped open the lid of the top trunk and pulled a stack into her lap. The sheer weight of them — pages upon pages of people's thoughts — swelled like a promise in her hands. She wanted so badly to be like Father, to know many things and understand where they belonged in the scheme of the cosmos. She wanted especially to understand the workings of the human body, to know the secrets which made it move and breathe and think, so that she could use them to heal. Imagine finding a remedy for plague, for gout, for Father's blindness. The magic of healing was to her far more thrilling than Betty's superstitions or Anne's delusions of angels.

She chose one of the books — astrology and the humours — and sat back on the floor to read. Liza's return didn't disturb her, nor did the noise up and down the street of carts and vendors. When she finally did look up, it was because there was a commotion just outside the front door. She could hear a woman shrieking, a dog whimpering, and above it all, her sister Mary losing her temper vigorously. Deborah put the book aside and hurried to see what was happening.

"He bit me!" This was Betty, shouting, red-faced, her hand pressed to her bosom.

"'Twas only a nip."

"A dog's bite is extreme bad luck!"

"You ought not have strook him, you cruel, cruel witch." Mary clutched Max hard enough to break bones, tears welling in her eyes. Anne tried to spit out words, but her tongue was tied.

And Father, caught amongst it all, was looking very rattled. "Quiet, quiet," he said, and his head darted this way and that as though he wished he could see if a crowd had gathered to watch the disturbance. His detractors knew where he lived, and would waste no time in passing on the news of the domestic furore they had witnessed, making him a subject for jokes.

65

"That dog is not coming into my house," Betty cried, and reached out to seize Max.

"No, you shan't touch him!"

For a few brief seconds they wrestled over Max, until Mary aimed a kick at Betty's shins and she overbalanced, started to fall, knocked Father . . .

Deborah was with him in an instant, steadying him. Betty fell directly on her buttocks in the mud and Mary began to laugh hysterically. Deborah couldn't endure the bafflement on Father's face, the embarrassed rage over his near-fall, and quickly hurried him inside. "Stop it," she said harshly to Mary and Betty as she passed.

In a moment she had him sitting in his chair. "Is all well with you, Father?"

"Yes, yes, I'm well enough. What kind of nonsense is that?"

"I'll stop them. Wait here calmly." She went to the door. Anne was helping Betty up and Mary was still laughing.

"Please, please, don't argue here on the street. Can't you see you're embarrassing Father?"

Betty huffed and marched inside. "That dog is going," she said over her shoulder. "Your father will make you give him up."

"Indeed he will not!" Mary cried, racing after her.

"Don't upset Father any further," Deborah said. Anne limped in, offered a crooked smile. Already Betty and Mary were in with Father, demanding he hear their cases. "Welcome home, sister," Deborah said to Anne.

"This will end b-badly."

"I fear the same."

They joined the others in Father's study.

"John, the dog bit me. He's ugly and he smells, and I don't want him in this house any longer."

"She's lying. He nipped her gently, that's all. Why, there is not a drop of blood spilled."

"A dog's bite is a bad omen no matter how hard or soft.

66

And who's to say he won't bite harder next time?"

"He's a good, gentle boy."

"He's a dirty wretch."

"Stop it!" This was Father, and his eyelids were raised as though he were staring them down. "I have had enough. How dare you both bother me with such rubbish?"

Betty was contrite, Mary clutched Max desperately.

"John, the dog must go."

"Father, please, let him stay. I love him so much."

"And so I am to decide? Will all fighting stop once I have decided?"

"Yes," Betty said confidently.

"Father, he's just a —"

"Will all fighting stop?"

"Yes, Father," Mary said, tears streaming from her eyes as she pressed Max into her chest. She obviously expected the worst.

"I wish to ask good counsel," Father said. "Ere I make my decision, that is."

"Counsel of whom, John?" Betty asked.

"Of the only other person in this household who has any sense. Deborah? Step forward."

Deborah drew a quick breath. "Me, Father?"

"Yes, yes. Tell me, what do you think I ought to do about this dog? Is he a biter? Should we send him out on the street?" At this Mary flinched.

"I . . ." Deborah began. Was this some trick? Was he testing her loyalties?

"Deborah? Child? Speak. What shall I do?"

She went with her conscience. Father would expect that of her. "Max does sometimes nip, Father, but only gently. Usually as a sign of affection. He's never hurt anyone."

"He hurt me!" Betty exclaimed.

"Wounded pride doesn't count," Mary said.

"I think," Deborah said more confidently, "that if Mary promises to keep him away from Betty, she should be allowed to keep him. He's her dearest friend."

"Hm," Father said. "Is this right, Mary?"

"Yes, Father, he's the dearest, sweetest —"

"While I believe you should be more discriminating about your friends, I cannot see why I should put the dog on the street if you promise to keep him away from your stepmother."

"Oh, I promise, I promise," Mary said.

"But John —"

"Be reasonable, Betty," Father said. "Did you never love anything so much as Mary loves the dog? Mary, Max can stay."

"Thank you, thank you." Mary was nearly laughing with relief.

"Liza will have supper soon," he said gruffly. "You had best change into your house clothes."

Mary practically danced out of the room, Max under one arm, her travelling case under the other. Deborah and Anne followed in procession up the stairs. As soon as they were in their room, the door closed behind them, Mary enclosed Deborah in a rapturous hug.

"Oh, thank you, sister. Thank you for making him take my side."

"I merely offered him rational advice," Deborah said, extricating herself from Mary's affection. "And you *will* be careful to keep Max away from Betty?"

"Yes, of course. For his own safety, the dear little thing. You should have seen how hard she strook him. Oh, I can't bear to hear him yelp like that."

With a bang, the door burst open and Betty stood there, her face flushed with anger. Max ran to hide under the bed.

"It were meet for you to knock," Mary said, barely concealing her smirk. "We may have been dressing."

"Don't you . . ." Betty fought with her anger.

"Mother? What have you come to tell us?" Mary said. Deborah kicked her heel lightly, tried to will her not to be so bold.

"You needn't be so smug, Mary Milton," Betty said. "He is fonder of me than of any of you. I shall be rid of that dog, even if it means I have to be rid of the three of you." She turned and slammed the door behind her.

A few heartbeats passed in silence, then Mary whispered darkly: "If she hurts Max, I shall kill her."

"S-sister —" Anne started, a pale hand reaching out.

"Oh, shut up, Anne," Mary said. "You're becoming tiresome."

3
The Fatal Trespass

It was October before Betty tried for revenge. Throughout the noisy London summer she waited and watched, observing her stepdaughters carefully. Deborah, she would have to suffer to stay. John was fond of her, and she was a good scribe. Betty had poor spelling and no languages. No matter how often she offered to help, John always turned her down. But the dullard, Anne, she knew he would lose easily, and he seemed to have no attachment to Mary either. She felt confident that she could persuade John to send them away, provided she made it easy for him. So, as the leaves began to fall from the trees and the mornings grew colder, she wrote to the lacemaker in Surrey again, and weaved her gentle lie. Within a week, she had a reply. She took it to John, kneeled beside him and pressed his hand in her own.

"John? I have news."

"Yes, Betty?"

"My friend the lacemaker in Surrey has written. He still has need for two apprentices. I thought Mary and Anne could —"

"We discussed this earlier in the year," he said dismissively.

"Please, John, allow me to read what he has said."

"Go on, then."

She unfolded the letter and read. "'Dear Betty, We should be very pleased to take to apprentice Mr Milton's daughter and her simple friend.'"

"What? What did he say?"

"He thinks Anne is merely Mary's *friend*," Betty said. "He goes on to commend Mary's kindness in taking responsibility for a cripple and says it reflects well on her father. He doesn't know that Anne is your daughter."

"But they are sisters, and they look like sisters."

"No, they do not. Mary is much rounder, Anne's face is more angular. John, you haven't seen them since they were children. I assure you they are quite different."

"Hm."

"Well?"

"Betty, they've settled in now. They are my children," he said, then added in an embarrassed mumble, "As much as they bother me sometimes."

Betty felt as though her stomach had filled with air. "But, John, you wanted them to be sent away as much as I did."

"That was six months ago, Betty. They're part of the household now. It wouldn't be fair on them."

Fair on them? Betty wanted to shout, *What about me?* Then the seed of an idea came to her. "John, I wonder that they don't take you for a fool."

He bristled. "What do you mean?"

"John, they have sold some of your books." In fact, Betty had sold a half dozen of his books, old ones from the bottom of the pile, to pay the pie man.

"What? Are you certain?"

"Not certain, but there are several missing." She leaned in close to deliver the final blow. "They have taken advantage of your blindness."

He fell silent with a thoughtful twist to his lips. Betty held her breath, afraid he might see through her ploy.

"John?"

He sighed. "I cannot decide, Betty. If the lacemaker still wants them, and if I need not be bothered any longer with it, then perhaps they should go. A trade will ensure their security in the future. But Deborah will stay."

"Yes, John, of course."

"For while I'm unsure whether the eldest two have the cunning to sell my books — and I'd just as quickly blame Liza and give her nought more than a beating — I know for a certainty that Deborah would stand by me."

"I share your certainty," Betty said, though she suspected her envy may have tainted her voice.

"Write to him, then," John said. "They shall make good apprentices."

Anne stood on the threshold of the Church of St Giles at Cripplegate, reluctant to move out into the cold autumn morning. It was the first Lord's Day of November, and a light haze of mist clung to the rooftops. She shivered and wished she had brought her muff. Her hands grew cold so easily. She glanced behind her. It wasn't just the cold which made her reluctant to leave the church. In there, she was one of God's perfect children, not despised for her faults: Jesus smiled at her and her heart was at ease. Out here she was a cripple and a simple. A fat woman bumped her from behind, so she limped out of the way and joined her sisters on the street.

"Oh, your poor hands," Deborah said, taking Anne's hands in her own and rubbing them. "Look you, they're quite red and blotched."

"Put them in your placket, Anne," Mary said. "Nobody will mind."

Anne inched her fingers into the pocket at the top of her skirt.

"Where are Father and Betty?" Deborah asked.

"They were speaking to Master Allard when I left," Anne said.

"Well, I wish they would hurry, for I should like to be inside by the fire with Max in my lap," Mary said.

An elderly man in rich clothes walked past, and Mary smiled at him sweetly, eyelids fluttering.

"Morning, Miss Milton," he said.

"Morning, Sir Wallace."

When he was out of earshot, Deborah asked, "A new conquest, Mary?"

"Not yet. Maybe."

"He must be ninety."

"He's less than fifty."

"Here c-comes Betty," Anne said, as their stepmother walked from the church, spotted them, and strode over confidently.

"Where's Father?" Mary asked.

"He'll be along shortly," she said smiling. "He's discussing theology with Master Allard. I wanted to speak to you girls."

"What about?" Anne asked, suspicious.

"Your father and I have changed our plans. Anne and Mary, you will be going to Surrey after all."

"Surrey? What's in Surrey?" Mary asked, but then realisation dawned. "What? The lacemaker?"

"And you needn't think to manipulate your father with all that nonsense you tried last time. I have put paid to those concerns. He has left it solely up to me, and it has all been arranged. You are to join the lacemaker directly after Twelfth Night."

Anne tried to speak but couldn't. Even Mary was too shocked to find words for arguing.

"I'm going inside to fetch your father," Betty said, turning to leave.

Deborah watched her go, then turned to her sisters with an anxious expression. "This is awful."

"What do you care, lickspittle? You get to stay here," Mary said.

Anne couldn't bear to see them fight. "Please —"

"But we'll be split up. I'll be lonely."

"I'll be a lacemaker! 'Tis far worse. Apprenticed out like some pauper."

"How far away is T-twelfth Night? Two months?"

73

"Yes," Mary said. "Do you think it is enough time to reverse this business? To convince Father he's making a mistake?"

"P-perhaps."

Mary rounded on Anne. "You have let me down. You have let us all down. I have kept quiet about this for months now, in consideration of your feelings, but now you must consider mine. Mother gave you the responsibility of our guardian angel, who was charged to protect us if adversity such as this arose, and you have made a decision on behalf of all to keep him from us."

Anne was startled, made so guilty she almost blurted out the summoning. But then, in her imagination, she could suddenly see Betty pallid and unmoving, just as Johnny had appeared that awful morning. And she knew she could not be a party to it. "I c-can't r-r-r —"

"Oh, don't stutter like an idiot!" Mary roared, and stormed off.

Anne dropped her head. Her hands were quite frozen by now, and she inched them further under her skirt, pressed them against her warm shift.

"I wish it were true," Deborah was saying. "I wish there were a guardian angel to protect us and keep us together."

"Th-th—"

Deborah smiled down on her sister. "Anne, leave it be. I am not so gullible as Mary. We are nearly grown, and we cannot expect to stay together much longer."

An enormous surge of feelings was caught in Anne's throat: guilt, love, desperation. All of it remained trapped behind her tongue. It was her curse to have so much to say, to explain, to *express*; but to be doomed to silence.

As the afternoon drizzle turned to rain, Mary walked under the jetties on Leadenhall Street. She went slowly, looking for any evidence that a wise woman might live nearby. She considered knocking on every door, but the street was long

74

and narrow and dark, and she was aware that night was descending. A man burst out of one of the houses and walked briskly past her.

"Excuse me," she said, "do you know of a wise woman living in this street?"

"Women can't be wise," he muttered, not breaking his stride.

"I mean . . ." She watched him walk away. Hopeless. Why couldn't Anne co-operate? Didn't she realise how important this was? Mary didn't want to be a lacemaker in Surrey; she could imagine nothing worse. If she bided her time, laid the right bait, she could marry a rich widower and live a life of extravagance. Sir Adworth's wife could die soon, for instance, and he could send for her. Men didn't like to stay unmarried, she knew, and Adworth adored her immoderately.

Darkness was closing in so she turned for home. Anne may have been quick to accept they would be split up, apprenticed out like ragged boys, but Mary wouldn't accept it. She was determined to thwart such a destiny.

"Don't worry, Max, Mary will be home soon." Deborah lit the candles in the iron holder on the dresser and gave the little dog a pat on the head. He had been fretting for an hour, trotting from the bedroom door to the window and back. She turned to Anne, who sat despondent on the bed.

"Anne, don't look so distressed." She settled next to her sister.

"I'm n-n—"

"You will enjoy lacemaking, I'm certain. And you will be good at it. You have always been clever with your hands."

"M-Mary is very angry with me."

"Mary is too bossy for her own good."

Anne gave her a shy glance. "And I shall miss you, Deborah."

"I shall miss you, too. You aren't to worry, Anne,"

Deborah said, smoothing her hair. "It will all work out. Would you like me to comb your hair for you?"

Anne nodded. Deborah went to her drawer and pulled out her boxwood comb, and returned to sit by Anne. She carefully unwound the tight bun and eased Anne's hair down around her shoulders. Anne never fussed with her hair as Mary did, and Deborah thought the tight style far too severe for her.

"You should wear your hair loose," she said, pulling the comb through the dark strands. "It looks pretty."

"'Tis too straight," Anne replied. "You're so gentle, Deborah. Mary always tugs."

"Mary hasn't the patience for anyone but her dog." Deborah ran the comb in careful strokes. She could feel Anne begin to relax, her shoulders easing forward, her hands becoming still in her lap. When just the two of them were together, Anne's stammer nearly vanished.

Liza brought their supper and left, and still Anne sat motionless in the firelight while Deborah tended to her hair. Deborah wondered if a physician would feel such a sense of gratification, easing people's sorrows, aiding in their comfort.

Suddenly the door flew open and Mary was there.

"Did you enjoy your solitary walk, sister?" Deborah asked, dropping the comb and advancing towards the supper tray.

Mary walked quickly towards the window. "Girls, I discovered something while in the street downstairs."

"What is it?" Deborah asked, picking out some cheese.

"Never mind about supper," Mary said, "this is much more exciting." She lifted the sash and pushed the window open, beckoning to them. They crowded about the window with her. Deborah could feel a cool autumn breeze on her cheeks as they looked down into the street. Max whimpered for attention near their ankles.

"The shop next door is boarded over. It has closed down. I checked from the garden and the street, and I can see no lights in any of the windows. I believe 'tis empty."

"And?"

"There is a ledge, between this window and the empty house."

"And?"

Mary turned crossly on Deborah. "Death! Don't be a stupid baby. It means that I can have my own room after all."

"M-Mary, you're not thinking of —"

"Keep an eye on Max." She hoisted her dress up around her thighs.

"Be careful, Mary," Deborah said. "Are you sure the ledge is stable?"

"It d-doesn't look very w-wide."

"Oh, stop fussing." She sat on the windowsill and swung her legs around. "Hold my hand, Anne, while I test the ledge."

Anne grabbed her around the wrists, and she carefully found her footing on the ledge below.

"You can let go now," Mary said. "It is stable." She began to inch her way along the ledge. Deborah leaned out the window to check her progress.

"Don't fall, Mary, for I know not how I would explain that to Father."

"We can't have you being out of favour with Father," Mary replied caustically, her voice nearly carried away on a passing breeze. Deborah saw her stop and fiddle with the neighbouring window.

"Aha!" she called. "'Tis unlocked. I'm going in."

"Don't be long."

Mary disappeared into the window, then leaned out again and waved. "It is enormous! And all mine."

"Is it not cold?"

"Yes, but there's a fireplace, and somebody has left some old mats in here. Come and see."

Anne and Deborah exchanged glances.

"I doubt that I'll manage," Anne admitted. "You go."

Deborah nodded. "I shall look and return directly." She picked her skirts up and slid out the window and onto the tiny ledge. From up here, she could see all the way to the bottom of the street and the trees waving along the edge of the Artillery grounds. She took a huge gulp of the fresh autumn wind, relished it on her bare legs, almost laughed at herself for being so uncharacteristically liberated.

"Come, Deborah, the ledge is perfect secure." Mary leaned out her window and beckoned, an enormous grin on her face.

"'Tis cold out here." Deborah inched along the ledge towards Mary, who caught her hand and helped her inside.

"Look at you, Deborah, your eyes are shining. Enjoying the mischief?"

Deborah glanced around. The big dark room was empty and cold, the wooden boards bare but for three sad, thin mats. "'Tis large."

Mary indicated the door opposite the window. "I've tried the door. It must be boarded on the other side."

"We'll have to come here by daylight to see it properly."

"I shan't wait for daylight. I'll bring back candles and coal after supper, and those old hangings Betty intended to throw out."

Deborah turned to Mary, considering her in the dark. "You're serious then? About having your own room?"

"Of course I'm serious."

"How will you get Max across here?"

Mary frowned. "I shall make a little sling for him, bind him against me. He'll be frightened, though."

"And where will you sleep?"

"On the floor. I'll bring some blankets over, start a fire." She frowned, and Deborah doubted she would ever actually spend a night here.

"Mary? Deborah?" Anne called querulously from the window.

"Just a minute, Anne," Deborah replied. "And what will you do when the shop is let again, and somebody wants to live here?"

Mary shook her head. "Anne and I are only here until Twelfth Night anyway. And if that is so, if Father and foul Betty are determined to send us away, then I shall not care what trouble I cause. Why, I might invite Sir Wallace up here for an illicit exchange."

"Mary, you shouldn't endanger the reputation of all of us," Deborah remarked, feeling her temper rise. Mary's flightiness and rages she could live with, but not her unchaste excesses.

Mary punched Deborah playfully. "'Tis little wonder you're the only daughter Father wants to keep by him. You are so virtuous. Sir Wallace is probably too infirm to climb up here anyway."

"Mary?"

"Yes, Anne, we're coming!" Mary cried.

"Be easier with her," Deborah said as they moved towards the window.

"As soon as she tells me how to summon our guardian angel, I will be easier with her," Mary huffed. "Until then, she's a traitor to our family, to us."

Deborah followed Mary back to their attic room. Her sisters were both determined to believe this guardian angel story, but surely such things didn't exist outside of nursery rhymes. They were no longer children. Mystical beings wouldn't take care of them; they had to rely upon themselves.

"Mary! You have a letter!"

Her sister's voice came from deep in the house. Mary was kneeling on the grass in the tiny garden, combing tangles out of Max's coat. "Who's it from?" she called. Max wriggled this way and that, whimpering intermittently. "Shh, Max, sit still. It doesn't hurt."

"Uncle William."

Mary turned. Deborah stood in the doorway holding the letter out to her.

"Uncle William?"

"Do you want me to throw it straight onto the fire?"

"No, no. I've asked him for some information." Mary stood and Max instantly fled inside. "Here, give it to me."

Deborah passed her the letter. "What information?"

Mary tapped Deborah's forehead with the corner. "Don't be so curious." She picked off the seal and quickly scanned William's uneven handwriting.

> *Mary,*
> *I have found the address of the wise woman your mother knew. Her name was Amelia Lewis and she lived at Leadenhall Street 251. Now, even if you don't find her there, if she is dead or has moved, you must honour your part of our bargain. Next time we find ourselves together, I expect to receive what I am owed.*

Mary squeaked with excitement. She folded the letter hastily and grabbed Deborah's hand. "Come walking with me."

"Where?"

"To Leadenhall Street."

"What's on Leadenhall Street?"

"Just come with me."

"Should we ask Anne if she'd like to walk with us?"

"No, just you and I."

"Mary, you're acting strangely."

"I'm mightily excited," Mary said, then leaned in close to whisper, "I know where the wise woman lives."

Deborah's brow furrowed in puzzlement. "Mother's wise woman?"

Mary nodded. "I can barely keep my skin on, Deborah."

"I'll come with you, but you should not expect to find anything there."

"Come, we'll go over the garden wall so nobody sees us."

Mary led Deborah via a back route down to Mooregate, then across the city until they reached St Peter's on Bishop's Gate Street. The tall smooth trees in front of the church stood deep in piles of shed leaves. A brisk wind gusted up Cornhill, making the leaves rattle against each other.

Deborah shivered. "Where are we?" she asked.

"We're here," Mary said.

"She lives in St Peter's?"

"No, she lives at Leadenhall Street. Number 251."

"Then why are we standing here? Why are we not walking up Leadenhall Street?"

Mary turned to her. "I think I'm frightened."

Deborah laughed out loud. "You're not frightened of anything."

"Anne is so determined that it would be wrong to call the angel back."

"So you really believe Anne's story?"

"Don't you?"

Deborah shook her head. "I am uncertain. I find it impossible to imagine us commanding an angel."

"Then why is Anne so affected by the idea? If it is not true?"

"Perhaps she dreamed it."

Mary grabbed her hand. "Deborah, when we speak of the angel, Anne becomes pale and shakes. Does any dream of your childhood affect you so fiercely?"

Deborah considered. As a child, she had often dreamed of being publicly decapitated: the filthy, screaming crowd, the cold block beneath her cheek, the bite of the axe. It had terrified her when she was young, but now it hadn't the power to affect her. "I suppose . . ."

"Sister," Mary said, her voice solemn, "what if it is true?"

A cold twist of fear moved in her stomach. She hadn't considered for a moment that it might be true. "I . . . I know not."

"Do such things exist in the world? If we can believe in

God in his Heaven, can we not believe his angels are here on earth?" Mary placed her hands on her sister's shoulders. "What power might such a creature have to heal? What might he teach you of physic and the working of the body?"

A sudden wave of anticipation washed over Deborah. "Perhaps . . ." Some of the most respected writers on natural philosophy had mentioned communing with angels. If it was right for them, it should not be wrong for her.

"There is no harm in trying to summon him. Can we not believe in more than can be seen? Can we not believe in magic?"

Deborah nodded slowly, feeling her excitement grow. "The whole hidden universe . . . he may be able to tell me of it."

"Let us find her."

They walked quickly up the street. The traffic was heavy, and carts were parked along the way. The strong smell of horse sweat and dung filled the air. Deborah stepped carefully over the filthy cobbles. In the distance, somebody played a tune on the harpsichord. The solemnity of the music seemed out of place on the dirty, crowded street.

"There!" Mary exclaimed, pointing to the last house in a row. It was constructed of black wood and was unusually narrow, as though it had been built on the corner almost as an afterthought. The front path was laid with old straw and two gaunt trees bent over the front door, their pale branches a severe contrast against the dark wood. A shingle hung from the front, an eye inside a triangle.

Mary pressed a hand to her chest. "My heart is fit to burst. I do not know if I'm more terrified than excited."

"We need not be terrified, I am sure. Mother wouldn't have done anything foolish, would she?"

"I know not. I was only little when she died. And knowing the rest of her family, Grandmamma and Uncle William . . ."

Deborah laughed. "Oh, pity us, for that is the line

from which we must draw our inheritance."

They giggled for a moment, then turned to face the house together. "Come, then," said Mary, "knock at the door."

"You knock. This is your idea."

Mary squared her shoulders and moved down the path, Deborah following close behind her. She had heard tales of witches, crones with the devil's eyes in their heads. Mary lifted her hand and knocked. In a few moments, the door opened a crack and a hunchbacked old woman with a black veil over her hair peered out.

"What is it?" she asked in a heavily foreign croak.

"Are you Amelia Lewis?" Mary asked.

She shook her head. "I'm Amelia's maidservant. Is she expecting you?"

"No."

"She doesn't see anybody new."

"We aren't new, though. At least, our mother was one of her clients. Can you ask her if she'll see us?"

"What are your names?"

"Deborah and Mary Milton, daughters of Mary Milton late of Petty France," Deborah said. "It was many years ago, but she may remember."

"Wait here."

The maidservant closed the door, leaving Mary and Deborah standing between the two slender trees in the autumn chill. Mary tried a smile. "I wonder what she looks like."

"I thought the crone was her."

"As did I. Just like a picture of a witch."

The door opened again and a blonde woman appeared on the threshold. This was no crone. Although she was, perhaps, as old as Father, her dark eyes were sharp, her face pretty, her hair glowing brightly. Even her teeth were still whole. She wore a black dress, deeply plunging in the front, and black ribbons in her hair. Deborah assumed she was in mourning, possibly recently widowed.

"Good day," Mary said, "are you Amelia Lewis?"

"Yes, I am. You are the daughters of Mary Milton?"

"Yes. I'm named for my mother," Mary offered.

Amelia fixed her eye on Deborah. "And you are named for the Hebrew prophetess."

"I know not."

"Ask your father, he will tell you as much. Come in to the warm." She ushered the girls in and led them to a dark withdrawing room where a tiny fire crackled in the corner. The furnishings were rich: velvet chairs, embroidered tapestry hangings, wool rugs, silver candlesticks. The lushness inside contrasted dramatically with the poor appearance of the outside of the building. Scattered about the place, as though they were beautiful accessories to the room, were seven cats. And yet the house didn't smell of cats, it smelled of rosewater and lime.

"Please sit down. Would you like biscuits? Gisela has been cooking all morning."

Deborah settled among velvet cushions. She saw Mary's fingertips brush the soft material longingly. "No, thank you, Mrs Lewis. This is a fine home," Deborah said.

"Call me Amelia. I am not and have never been married."

"Never been married?" Mary blurted, "but you're so . . . beautiful."

"My beauty was not the problem. The lack of it in others was."

"I thought these were your widow's weeds," Deborah said, indicating the black dress.

"Oh, these are certainly the clothes of bereavement," Amelia said with a frown. "I am mourning my lost youth."

Deborah didn't know if she should laugh. But Amelia didn't appear to be jesting.

"Ma'am . . . Amelia, do you do so well from your trade that you can afford such a magnificent house and a maid-servant?" Mary asked.

Deborah glared at her sister for being so forward, even though she wanted to know the answer herself. She had

84

never seen such rich objects, and the very idea of an independent woman living this way was astounding to her.

"No. I had a large inheritance from my grandfather, and Gisela works for me out of love. I cured her of the plague, ten years ago." Amelia sat opposite them in a grand, stuffed chair and took a cat in her lap.

"You can perform physic?" Deborah asked, her curiosity piqued.

"Hush, Deborah, we are not here to be nosy," Mary said with a mischievous smirk.

Amelia leaned forward. "Time enough later for questions. How may I serve you, girls?"

"Do you remember our mother came to you, ere Deborah was born?" Mary said.

"I have never forgotten anything, ever," Amelia said. There was no indication that she spoke anything other than seriously. "She asked for a guardian for you and your other sister . . . Anne. Why is Anne not with you? Has she died?"

Mary and Deborah exchanged glances. "No, Anne is well," Deborah said.

Amelia drew her eyebrows together. "She doesn't know you're here. She doesn't want you to be here."

"Did you guess that or do you . . . know?" Deborah asked. She had heard that some wise women could read thoughts.

"I guessed, Deborah Milton," Amelia said, a pale hand stroking the cat lovingly. "You look at each other furtively, you feel guilty."

"Anne is afraid," Mary said. "She thinks that the guardian angel killed our little brother."

"Angels are not so base," Amelia replied.

Deborah felt a wash of relief, and realised that under deep layers of her thoughts, Anne's fear had affected her. "Yes, of course," she said.

"She only recently told us about our angel," Mary said. "And now we are under threat."

"And you want to call upon him. I see."

"Is he still ours?" Deborah ventured. "Or do they only look after children?"

"No, he is yours for life, until the last one of you dies."

"Can we have the summoning, then?" Mary asked.

Amelia pressed her graceful hands together. "Let me consider it for a few moments."

"But Mother paid for it, did she not?" Mary said. "You *have* to give it to us if we ask."

Amelia turned a gaze on Mary that was akin to how she might consider a carpet bug. "My dear, I don't *have* to do anything. I'm Amelia Lewis."

"I apologise for my sister," Deborah said. "She's very excitable."

"The problem is this," Amelia continued, as though she hadn't heard. "The angel is supposed to serve all three of you, but your sister Anne does not want him called. So what I shall do is give you a summoning in which all three of you must partake. It will then be your role to convince Anne to join you."

"Convince Anne! But she'll never agree to it," Mary moaned.

"If she never agrees to it, then you'll never see your angel," Amelia said. "But 'tis important that the three of you work together. Do not treat the bonds of sisterhood lightly." She rose, dropping the cat gently on a nearby cushion. They were the most docile cats Deborah had ever seen, not like the mad creatures at Grandmamma's house, always running terrified from whomever approached. "Now wait here, I will go to my study and write the new summoning."

"But . . ." Mary started, then decided better of it.

Amelia left the room in a swoosh of black silk. Mary leaned forward, shaking her head. "This is pointless. A summoning which Anne must be a part of? We will never be able to use it."

"We will try our best," Deborah said. "I must see this angel

86

with my own eyes. I must ask him how I may best help mankind."

"First worry how we convince Anne to help us."

"So far only you have tried to convince her," Deborah said. "She may listen to me."

"Yes, perhaps. She expects my attempts to manipulate her, but she does not expect them from you."

Amelia returned with a piece of paper in her left hand. She blew gently on the ink and once more sat across from them. One of her cats put his nose in the air and she leaned down to receive its kiss. The paper drew Deborah's curious eyes.

"Is that the —?"

"The summoning? Yes." She blew on it once more then handed it to Mary. "You must speak the incantation together. That is the only thing I have specified. You may change the wording if you like, but be very careful."

Mary scanned it quickly then passed it to Deborah, who read the instructions with awe.

"I have left out the name of the angel. That is for Anne to tell you. You say his name instead of 'angel'. As long as you have his name, he must obey you."

"Do you have any advice on how we might convince Anne to join us?" Mary asked.

Amelia smiled. "Words, Mary Milton. There is no more powerful force in the universe. Choose your words carefully, and the world will be in your hands; choose them poorly and . . ." She spread her hands and shrugged. "Still, 'tis growing late and you must go."

Within moments, the girls found themselves once more out on the cold street. The sun was sinking and birds were wheeling high above, finding their way home before dark.

Deborah clutched Mary's hand. "We could command an angel."

"Anne is all that stands in our way. If it were only we two . . ."

"Mary, don't imagine dear Anne out of our lives," Deborah said. "We'll convince her, we'll find a way."

Anne said no a hundred times before the end of that week, and a hundred more the next. She reached such a frenzied state of stuttering and blinking that Deborah eventually told Mary they had to stop and leave her be a while.

"But how can we?" Mary groaned. "This is all, this is everything to me."

"We are making Anne so anxious I fear for her health. No, we must stop and think and find another way to solve this problem."

But Deborah could think of no solution, and began to accept that her learning must come from books as it always had. Anne's awful fear that the angel would harm or kill someone was an impassable monolith. Despite Mary's occasional pleading, Deborah refused to allow the subject to resurface.

One evening close to Christmas, while Mary was in the street looking for Max, Anne slipped into the bedroom and sat on the edge of the bed.

"What is the matter, Anne?" Deborah asked. She stood in front of the curved glass which they all shared, combing knots out of her hair. In the reflection, she could see Anne's downcast eyes, the twisting of her hands. Fresh candles burned in the candlestands by the bed.

"You have not mentioned the angel for some t-time now."

"Your anxiety was too much for us," Deborah said. "We have all but given up hope."

"Why do you want t-to summon the angel? Knowing what he d-did to Johnny?"

Deborah put the comb away and turned to Anne. "I don't believe he killed Johnny, Anne. Amelia herself said that angels do not kill."

"And you believe her?"

"Angels, Annie, angels." Deborah perched on the edge of

the bed next to her sister. "Like the angels you adore in your hymn book."

"He did not resemble those angels. He was not ... serene."

"Not serene?"

"Not like the angels in pictures."

"Are you saying he was not an angel?"

Anne's lip twitched a moment. "I suppose he was. Just not as I have d-dreamed of angels." She fell silent. Deborah could hear Mary calling to Max downstairs on the street. Eventually, Anne turned her face upwards. "You must hate me."

"I don't hate you."

"M-m-m—"

"Mary doesn't hate you either."

Anne nodded. "You must t-try to understand me, Deborah. What if M-Mary wished Betty dead? And the angel took her at her word? What if she wished an illness upon Father? Or me? I have lived with such a g-guilt for so long — that my actions k-killed a loved one. Do you not wish to avoid such a burden?"

Deborah stared at Anne, listening to her protestations clearly for the first time. "Your sole concern is that the angel will injure or kill someone?"

"Yes, of course. For what other concern can there b-be?"

Deborah thought of the summoning, of Amelia's words. *You may change the wording if you like.* Was it possible that Anne's fears could be allayed so easily?

"What is wrong, Deborah?" Anne said, and Deborah realised she hadn't spoken for nearly a full minute.

"Anne," she said slowly, "we can make the angel's summoning dependent on a promise that he will injure nobody."

"What do you mean?"

Deborah leaped up and searched in Mary's top drawer for the summoning. She clutched it in her left hand as she sat down again, noticed her heart speeding. "The only condition Amelia has specified is that we speak the incantation together. But we can change the wording. Look you." She pointed to the last line and Anne peered at it, reading slowly. "We can say in here, *only if he injures nobody.*"

Anne frowned. "I d-don't know."

"Anne, please! We have to try this."

"How do we know he'll do as we say?"

"He is at our command. He must obey us."

Anne stared at the summoning, her brows drawn tight together.

"Oh, please, Annie, please. This way we'll stay together. Betty's plans for us will be foiled and nobody will be hurt." Deborah could hear footsteps approaching. Mary chastised Max as she brought him up the stairs. Mary's arrival would surely shatter the intimacy she had cultivated with Anne. Deborah willed Mary away. Her own breathing seemed very loud and she told herself she mustn't grow too excited.

Suddenly, Anne dropped to the floor, pulled open her drawer.

"Anne, what is it?"

"Naughty Max, naughty boy." Mary was directly outside.

Anne thrust a prayer book in Deborah's hands and backed away. The door flew open.

"He was all the way down in the park!" Mary said. Her hair was damp and her dress was muddy. "I was mightily worried."

"I must help Liza with supper," Anne said, slipping out the door and closing it behind her. Deborah glanced from the door to the prayer book to Mary.

"What's the matter, Deborah?" Mary asked, dropping Max and untying her cap.

"I don't . . ." She opened the prayer book, flicked through the ageing pages. A folded piece of paper slid out. She smoothed it, read the lines written upon it; lines her dead mother had composed. Then she caught her breath.

"Deborah? Answer me. What is wrong?"

Deborah looked up at her sister in the dim light of evening. "Lazodeus."

"What?"

Deborah turned the piece of paper around to show Mary. "Our angel finally has a name. It is Lazodeus."

By Christmas Eve they had learned their parts. The house smelled of the fresh evergreen branches which Betty and Liza were pinning up over all the doorways. Betty was in such high spirits that she didn't even blink when Max went barking through the house, overstimulated by the trees inside and the hot biscuits Mary had been feeding him as Christmas treats all day.

Mary chased him through the kitchen, laughing. He yapped, wagged his tail in a frenzy. Just as she was about to pick him up, he took off again in the other direction. Towards Father's study.

"Max, no!" she called as she saw his little white tail disappear around the corner. She raced after him, burst into the room to find Father holding out a hand to Max, having his fingers soundly licked.

"I'm sorry, Father," Mary said.

"I thought you were supposed to keep control of the dog in the house. You will upset Betty." Despite his words, he didn't seem genuinely angry. Mary found her father a mystery most of the time.

"I'm sorry," she said again, scooping Max up into her arms and scurrying out. Perhaps she could wish the angel to make Father more generous, more loving. To all of them, not just to Deborah who was clearly his favourite. Now that Anne had insisted on a clause that the angel injure nobody, it would be safe to make all kinds of wishes.

Max yapped, not as sobered by the exchange with Father as she had been.

"Come, Max. Calm yourself."

He licked her face and she felt the familiar, happy wash of feeling. Dear little Max. "After supper, Max," she whispered, close to his fur. "After supper, I shall wish our angel to protect you always."

Over supper, she glanced between her sisters, hoping they were clever enough not to give away on their faces what a momentous act they were to perform tonight. Anne stuttered and stammered her way through the meal with her head bowed and her hands shaking, but Mary doubted anybody would notice a difference from her usual anxious jittering. Deborah was cool. Any excitement Mary showed could be attributed to Christmas. As Liza cleared their things away, Mary shot back in her chair.

"Oh, I'm so tired. I'm going straight to bed."

"Me too," Deborah said.

Father turned his unseeing eyes on them, a slight frown drawn down between his brows. But if he suspected something, he said nothing. "Goodnight, then," he said. "We shall go to church in the morning, so don't sleep too late."

Goodnights were exchanged. Mary raced up the stairs. She and Deborah were the first to the bedroom, Anne limped in a few moments later.

"I wish you weren't so excited," Anne said, "for I am t-terrified and certain we are doing the wrong thing."

"Anne, you agreed to go through with this," Mary said. How dare she cast her pall of malcontent over the proceedings?

"Only because b-both my sisters begged me," Anne replied, glancing from one to the other.

"And because we promised to make it safe," Deborah said, taking one of Anne's hands in her own. Mary wondered that Deborah could be so patient when Anne was such a moaner. "Don't forget that, sister."

"I haven't time for this," Mary interjected. "You agreed, and now we are proceeding, and I shan't spend another breath on the preliminaries." She scooped Max up and shut him in Deborah's closet so he wouldn't be frightened, then kicked over the mat to reveal the triangle they had white-washed on the floor earlier in the day.

"Take your places, sisters," she said. "Soon we shall command angels."

4
Between Worlds and Worlds

Deborah slid the dresser in front of the door, made certain it couldn't be opened, then took her place at one of the peaks of the triangle. Anne reluctantly limped into position.

Mary extinguished the last candle and found her way to her place. "We must wait a few moments for our eyes to adjust to the dark," she said. "I want to be sure I stand in the correct position."

A minute passed, the only sound in the room their breathing. Far away in the distance, a bell tolled the hour. Revellers in the street below burst from a house and went on their way, their voices trailing away on a winter breeze.

"Our lives will change forever," Anne said, and something about the weight of her words in the dark sent a chill through Deborah's bones.

"Don't talk such nonsense, everything will be fine," Mary said. She glanced at Deborah, who could see trepidation in her eyes. They both sensed the truth in Anne's statement.

No stopping now. They linked hands.

"Lazodeus, angel of the fifth order," Mary began. Her sisters joined in.

"Come to us this night, stand within this triangle and, under a solemn vow that you will injure nobody, appear to us. Come, Lazodeus, that we may command you."

They held a collective breath. Nothing happened.

"Once more, let us repeat it," Deborah said.

"Lazodeus, angel of the fifth order . . ." Again and again, their voices soft in the dark spaces, the chant going around three, four, five times.

On the sixth repetition, light glimmered weakly along the edges of the triangle. Deborah's heart hammered under her ribs. Her excitement was almost choking her.

"Lazodeus, angel of the fifth order . . ." Seven times, and suddenly it all happened. Light shot up in bars towards the ceiling, creating a brilliant white cage between them. Deborah's heart jumped as though it might stop altogether. As they intoned the last line, "Come, Lazodeus, that we may command you," a sucking sound filled the room. Then, as though being pulled from the air, a male figure appeared within the bars. He cried out in pain.

The girls' voices trailed off. Their hands were firmly linked, and Deborah could feel her sisters' perspiration, their anxiety in their desperate grasps. The room was suddenly very quiet.

Deborah licked her lips and tried to swallow. "Are you Lazodeus?"

"Yes," he said, turning to her. She caught her breath. He was easily the most beautiful creature upon whom she had ever gazed. Under arched brows, his eyes were blue-green, brilliant and clear, and fringed thickly with black curling lashes. His dark chestnut hair fell to his shoulders, and gleamed in the uncarthly light. His face was exquisite, with wide cheeks and rounded jaw; his clean-shaven complexion flawless but for the white crevices of two deep scars, one across his left eyebrow and one on his top lip. His skin was ivory, smoothly extending across a body the like of which Deborah had only seen in sculptures; not on the barrel-bellied men she passed every day on the street. He was entirely naked, taller than anyone she had ever met, towering over the three of them. But there was more to his beauty than merely the collection of these physical characteristics. Such a clarity seemed to freshen her eyes while looking upon him, a sharp focus which made the rest of the room seem dull and fuzzy.

Mary gulped. "Are you an angel?"

"I am an angel."

"Anne, is this the angel you remember?"

"Y-y-y—"

"My name is Lazodeus. Please, let me out of this prison."

"How . . . how do we do that?" Deborah asked.

"Ask me to join you in your world. I'm caught between at the moment."

Deborah and Mary exchanged glances. Anne had screwed her eyes tightly shut and Deborah could see the gleam of tears on her cheeks.

"Very well," Mary said, "Lazodeus, join us in our world."

With a flash of white light, the bars disappeared and Lazodeus remained in the middle of the room, now fully clothed. He wore a plain black tunic, buttoned closely over a lace-edged black shirt, black breeches and black leather boots to his knees. The glowing bars were gone, but Lazodeus, despite his sombre clothes, glowed faintly, lending a cast like luminous moonlight to the room. Deborah dropped her sisters' hands and palmed her eyes. She was beginning to feel as though events weren't real, as though she may be dreaming.

He bowed deeply, then said, "How may I serve you, sisters?"

"Be at our command," Mary said boldly. "Always."

"That I am. I am your guardian. But you have called me for a reason?"

"Our stepmother wishes us sent away as apprentices; make sure it doesn't happen."

"But harm nobody!" Anne cried, suddenly finding her voice.

The angel turned on her. "I am an angel. I do not harm anyone."

Anne gaped at him in terror.

Deborah had expected an angel to be more patient. "Please, don't lose your temper with our sister," she said.

He shook his head. "It is difficult to come through the worlds. It causes me great pain. Forgive me, I am not myself."

"Here, sit down," Mary said, leading the angel to the bed. He sat heavily with his face in his hands, breathing slowly. He wore a large silver ring, set with a black stone, on his left hand. A long scar ran from the base of his thumb up to his middle finger. Mary looked urgently towards Deborah.

"Would you . . . er . . . would you like a drink of wine?" Deborah asked.

He looked up. "No, I neither eat nor drink mortal provisions."

"What can we do to help you?" Mary said.

"There is nothing you can do. Every time I make the transition it will cause me tremendous pain. Unless you wish to keep me always by you. But I suppose, as I have not heard from you in fifteen years, that I am to be consigned back to my own realm."

"No, no," Mary said, recovering far quicker than Deborah was able. "We didn't know about you, you see. Anne never told us. If you want to stay with us and watch over us, you can."

"But where will he stay?" Deborah asked. "We can't keep him up here in our room."

The angel burst into loud laughter. Deborah looked at him in hurt puzzlement. It seemed he mocked her.

"I can be with you, and not be in the same sphere of existence," he said. "I require no bed, no fire, no fancy hangings . . ." He indicated around him with a gesture almost disdainful. "You only have to tell me to stay."

"Then stay!" Mary cried.

"All three of you must agree." He turned his blue-green eyes on Deborah. "Deborah?"

97

"Are you sure you are an angel?" she asked.

"I am certain." His gaze was very steady.

She considered a few beats.

"Please, Deborah," Mary said.

"I command you to tell me the truth," Deborah said.

"I am an angel," Lazodeus said confidently, an amused smile twitching the corners of his mouth. For the first time, Deborah liked him. "I swear that I am an angel, Deborah Milton."

"Very well, stay. Anne?"

They all turned to the eldest sister. She said nothing.

"Anne Milton," Lazodeus said, "you must understand this: I am incapable of inflicting physical harm on anyone. People injure people, angels do not."

"But Johnny . . ."

"If you wish me to stay, then you may command me to explain his death to you," the angel said.

Anne hung her head.

"Anne, please," Mary said, taking Anne's hand in her own and squeezing it. "Please, Anne. We can command him away again. Can't we, Lazodeus?"

"I am at your command." He bowed his head.

"Stay," Anne said quietly. "Stay with us."

Lazodeus's shoulders sagged with relief. "It is agreed. Now, you wish me to ensure that your apprenticeships do not eventuate?"

Mary's voice was excited. "That's right. Anne and I are to be sent away to Surrey as lacemakers — our stepmother is responsible."

"I will fix it this night."

Mary clapped her hands together in glee. "And can you make Father kinder? And protect my dog, Max? And can we have some nicer things in here? Velvets like Amelia's place?"

Lazodeus laughed again, this time louder, and Deborah feared he would be heard downstairs. "Mary Milton, you should ask to be cured of your greed. I cannot change your father, your dog is your responsibility, and do you not think your stepmother would notice if your room was suddenly filled with velvets?"

A creak on the stairs. Betty was on her way up.

"Quick! Go!" Deborah said, racing to the door. "Betty has heard you."

"No, don't go!" Mary wailed. "Stay and do as we say."

"I shall go, but you may summon me again."

A knock on the door. "Girls?"

"Just a moment, Betty," Deborah called.

"Another summoning? With the triangle and the chanting?" Mary asked.

"No, now you have asked me to stay close by, it will be easier. You don't have to be together. Just close your eyes and say my name as a whisper. I will hear you, and I will come." He touched Mary's cheek lightly. "Goodnight, Mary."

"Goodnight, angel."

Betty was trying the door. "What's going on in there? Have you barred the door?"

Lazodeus turned to the others. "Goodnight, Deborah. Goodnight, Anne. I look forward to knowing you better." The white glow around him began to intensify. With a mock-solemn bow, he disappeared, leaving them in darkness.

Betty pounded on the door. "Open this door at once. I can hear what's going on in there."

Deborah raced to the door and pushed the dresser back. She pulled the door open and Betty strode in.

"Where is he?"

"Who?" Mary asked, with a look of obviously feigned innocence.

"I heard a man's laugh."

"No, 'twas merely Anne coughing," Deborah said. "She has a chill. Look you, she weeps for the pain in her chest."

"Then why is the fire not stoked? 'Tis freezing in this room." Betty lit a candle from her own and went to Deborah's closet, and flung the door open. Max scurried out.

"This is the only man we have in our room," Mary said, scooping the little dog up. Betty recoiled as he tried to lick her.

"I heard a man's laugh, and then a man's voice. I'm not an idiot." She stalked to the window and pulled the curtains. Threw open the sash and looked down. "Did he go out the window?"

"'Tis a long way to jump," Mary said, stifling a laugh.

Betty turned and glared at them. "You think I'm a fool. You think I'm a halfwit like your stupid sister." She indicated Anne with a wave of an impatient hand.

Mary squared her shoulders. "You are a fool. Anne is a thousandfold smarter and kinder than you."

Betty took two steps forward and stood nose to nose with Mary. Max whimpered and cringed into Mary's arms.

"In twelve days, you will be gone," Betty said. "You need not feel superior to me."

Mary opened her mouth to retort, but Deborah kicked her. "I'm sorry if we have disturbed you, Betty," Deborah said, "but as you can see 'tis only the three of us up here. Perhaps you heard a voice from outside. There are some loud revellers in the street."

Betty sniffed. "Lie your lies, girls, I don't care. I shall be rid of you two soon enough." She turned to Deborah. "Don't make me plan to rid myself of you withal."

She left, slamming the door behind her. The three sisters exchanged glances, the excitement of the night overwhelming them. As one, they burst into laughter, though Anne's cheeks still ran with tears.

Betty's first Christmas as Mrs John Milton was chaotic. First, the argument with the girls on Christmas Eve. Did they think her a fool? She had heard a man's voice, a man's laughter. Where they had hidden him was still a mystery to her, but she knew they had been entertaining him in their bedroom. She hadn't told John — he would die with the humiliation. Then Christmas morning, very early, the message had come from the Powells in Forest Hill: the girls' grandmother was mortally ill, and she had requested Mary to join her immediately. Of course, Betty was glad to see the annoying girl leave, but there had been such a tumult of weeping and pale faces and shaking limbs that even John had been moved. The house had been plunged into a darkly sombre mood.

But on Boxing Day, the worst news of all had come.

The letter looked innocent enough: she had expected something from the lacemaker in Surrey, a confirmation of the details for the girls' arrival. When she tore the letter open, though, it was vastly different from what she had expected. After the usual formalities of inquiring after her and her husband's health, he had written:

Although I have promised to take on Miss Mary and her friend Anne as apprentices from Twelfth Night, I now find I have to refuse them. On Christmas Eve I was visited by an angel who warned me that should I employ them, my family and I would suffer greatly. It is not for me to question the word of God's messengers, nor to put my family at risk.

Betty read it twice, trying to comprehend it. An angel? She felt a chill thread through her body, for this was surely an omen. Bad luck would attend upon this.

But then she began to grow angry. Yes, bad luck was already in attendance because this meant the girls would stay. Angelic visitations? Why would an angel carry tidings of a pair of draggle-tails like Mary and Anne Milton?

She screwed up the letter angrily and threw it towards the

fire. It bounced off the hearth and clattered into some hanging pots.

"What's going on?" John called from his study.

Betty meekly picked up the letter, placed it among the flames, and joined her husband.

"I have had a letter from the lacemaker in Surrey. He believes he has had a religious vision warning him not to take Anne and Mary."

John repressed a chuckle. "A vision? About my ungrateful daughters?"

"'Tis no matter for laughter."

"I am not laughing." Still, a pull at the corner of his mouth.

"We can make him take them, you know. He breaks the law, for he made a promise."

"Betty —"

"Or we can find them another apprenticeship. Surely not every lacemaker in England is foolish enough to believe a drunken dream is a religious vision."

"Betty —"

"I can write to my sister in Suffolk, see if she knows anyone who —"

"Betty!" he roared, and she took a step back in shock.

"John?"

"Maybe they are meant to stay with us."

"What do you mean?"

"Maybe my daughters are meant to stay with us."

"But —"

"I have had enough of this to-ing and fro-ing; they will not go. Accept it. The Lord works in ways which are impossible for us to understand. But perhaps He wants them to stay here, by their father."

Betty glared at him, knowing that he couldn't see the depth of her anger. "Very well, John," she said, and she heard the strain in her own voice, the breath trapped behind her teeth. "I shall endeavour to get used to them being here."

Impossible.

By now, she despised them all.

"Anne? You look so pensive."

Anne glanced up from where she sat in the chair under the open bedroom window, gazing down into the street. Deborah wore her spectacles, which made her pretty face owlish. Evening grew close and long shadows crept across the room. Anne's nose was frozen from the cold air.

"I'm thinking about G-Grandmamma." It was a lie, and Deborah probably knew it. Grandmamma had never been kind to Anne. No, she was thinking about Lazodeus, and had thought about little else since Christmas Eve.

Deborah touched her hair gently. "Would you like me to light a candle?"

Anne nodded, watched her sister go about lighting a candle and stoking the fire. The light in the room changed from grey to amber. Deborah returned to close the window. "Father wants me to read to him and a friend this evening. Would you like to come down and listen?"

"No, I think I shall sit here by myself and think."

"Don't think too much, sister," Deborah said with a smile. "Thinking can be a dangerous occupation." Anne watched her go, then turned back to the window. She sighed and leaned her forehead against the crisscross lines of lead. Her distorted reflection looked back at her from the uneven diamonds of glass, and she closed her eyes.

On Christmas morning, after the news of Grandmamma had come, Mary made them swear not to call the angel until she had returned, and Anne had agreed readily. Deborah had considered and then, in her typical fashion, judged that it was a fair request.

So why couldn't Anne get the idea of summoning Lazodeus out of her head? She hadn't wanted him anywhere near them before Christmas Eve, and yet now she wanted very badly for him to return.

She opened her eyes and glanced around the room. Shifting shadows chased each other across the dark walls. *Be honest. You know why you want to see Lazodeus again.* He had spoken of Johnny's death; he had promised to explain what had really happened. Could he lift her burden of guilt? Or would summoning him again be dangerous? She dare not ask Deborah to help her, because she would insist they wait until Mary's return. But when Mary was home she would dominate affairs with Lazodeus, and Anne would never get a chance to ask him. At least, not alone.

And she wanted very much to be alone with him.

Anne realised that her heart was beating rapidly. Did her heart know something about her intentions? This wasn't like her at all. She was the safe one, the *scared* one.

The guilty one.

She crept to the door and opened it, leaned her head out and listened hard. Voices far below in Father's study, none of them clearly distinguishable. She had perhaps an hour before supper. She closed the door, leaned her back against it and took deep breaths. Easier just to leave it be. Easier not to call him.

But with just one word, she could finally know the truth about Johnny.

With just one name.

She closed her eyes. Tried to make the word come. Curled her tongue to form the L. A dammed flood of desperation waited behind it.

"Lazodeus," she breathed. She felt a presence appear next to her and dared not open her eyes.

"Anne?" His voice was kindly, affectionate.

"I'm frightened," she said.

A warm hand touched her cheek. "Open your eyes."

She did so, and was alarmed at how close he stood. Tentatively, she lifted her gaze to see his face. He smiled at her. His eyes were a deep clear aqua.

"What do you want from me, Anne?"

"I . . ."

"You do not trust me."

Anne stared at him mutely.

"Let me earn your trust." His fingers touched her lips fleetingly. "Say something."

She shook her head in puzzlement.

"Do it. You will see why."

"What shall I say . . . Oh!" As she spoke the words tumbled freely. "Oh. Oh, I can speak. I've never . . . I can speak." It was the most incredible sense of liberation, and of imminent danger, as though thoughts could now escape from her without her consent. "I can speak. I can't believe it." She sang a few lines of a tune Mary always sang, then realised her voice was off key and stopped, laughing, pressing her fingers to her mouth.

"It is not permanent," Lazodeus said. "I'm sorry, but that is not in my power at the moment."

"Will it ever be?" she blurted.

"Perhaps, eventually." He smiled. "For now, you must be satisfied to feel this effect only on occasion, and those occasions only when I am with you."

"Do not say that, for I shall want you with me all the time," she said, then checked herself for her boldness. "I mean . . ."

"You called me for a reason?" He shifted his weight so he leaned with his back against the door. His stance was so casual. She had always thought angels would be proper and mannered.

"Why do you have no wings?" she found herself asking.

He spread his arms and considered his black sleeves. "If I appeared to you in my true form, it would be too much for you."

"Would I go blind?" She thought of Father.

"No, not blind. Mad, perhaps." He dropped his arms. "There are some things mortals are not meant to see."

"I'm frightened by you," she said, once again without

knowing she was going to say it. Was this what it meant to be able to speak easily? Was one always expressing one's feelings without due consideration? She had to learn to be more reserved in her use of language.

"You are my commander. You are in control."

She appraised him. Strange feelings brewed inside her; feelings she did not recognise.

"What is it you wanted to ask me?" he prompted.

"Did I kill Johnny?"

"No."

"Did you?"

Irritation briefly crossed his countenance but was soon gone. "No. No, angels do not kill."

"Then how . . . ?"

"You wished him dead, and I said to you, 'your wish will be granted' because I knew he was already ailing. I tried to explain this to you, but you were far too small to understand."

A tide of relief swelled up through her body. She found her knees suddenly weak. "Oh," she said, beginning to crumble, "oh."

He caught her and led her to the bed. She found herself sobbing, shaking. He kneeled in front of her, her hand caught in his and she noticed he was smiling.

"Mortals cry when they are happy," he said. "I love that about them. We all love it."

"All the angels in Heaven?" she managed to say through her tears.

"All the angels everywhere," he replied.

She tried to compose herself. "For my entire life," she said, "I have thought it my fault that Johnny died."

"No. You were so little, Anne. I remember it so clearly. You were a beautiful child, so innocent and serious. I was enchanted by you."

Anne felt pleased with herself, though she knew her vanity was foolish. "Really?"

"Yes. You were not capable of anything so base as killing your brother. It is not in your nature. You know it is not."

She nodded. "You're right. You're right."

He stroked her fingers. His other hand brushed a limp strand of hair from her cheek. "You suffered for so many years, when all you had to do was call me. I hope you will never be so hesitant to call me again."

Her eyes met his, and she found herself unable to look away. "No," she whispered. "I shall not hesitate."

Footsteps approaching.

"That's Deborah," Anne said, pulling her hand from his. Why did she feel guilty?

"You don't want her to see me here?"

"We promised Mary —"

"I'll go." He stood, then reached down and his fingers grazed her shoulder. "But do not be afraid to call me again."

"I'm not afraid," she said, and she meant it.

He disappeared and a few moments later Deborah entered the room. Anne was certain her guilt would be acutely apparent, but Deborah was absorbed in her own distress.

"What's the matter, D-Deborah?" Anne said. The frustration of jammed words returned.

"Father is so disappointed in me," Deborah said, and she sat down on the floor cross-legged and started to cry, her long honey hair falling forward to cover her face.

At moments like these, Anne was reminded that Deborah was barely more than a child.

"Father is always d-disappointed with me," Anne said.

"He said my Italian was monstrous. Monstrous! And I've been practising so hard," Deborah said through sobs.

"Was he angry with you? Did he shout?"

"No, his voice was very cool and quiet, and I feel . . . I feel . . ." More tears.

Anne lowered herself to the floor next to Deborah. "There, hush now. Father can be cruel."

"No, he is not cruel. He is right! Italian is my worst

language, and it is one of his favourites. I should have worked harder. Oh, I wish that I could please him better."

"Father is p-perfect p-pleased with you."

"It is not enough, I cannot do enough." She began to compose herself, to wipe away her tears. "I must practise harder, that is all. I shan't come down for supper. I'll stay up here and read and read until I get it right."

"Are you not hungry?"

She shook her head, and her hair glimmered in the firelight. "No. You go down. Liza has spit a chicken. They are expecting you. Tell them I feel ill, tell Father I feel ill. Haply then he will think my illness was at fault." Deborah stood and helped Anne to her feet. "I must go and practise."

Deborah disappeared into her closet and as Anne prepared herself for supper and left the room, she heard her sister's voice, repeating over and over, "*Nel mezzo del cammin di nostra vita mi ritrovai per una selva oscura ché la diritta via era smarrita.*" Anne mused upon how Deborah dared be disappointed over her inability to pronounce a foreign language correctly, when Anne could barely manage her own.

But then, perhaps, Lazodeus could eventually fix that problem. She would do almost anything to make that dream come true.

Father had been silent for a long time, and Deborah was almost nodding off in her chair. It was still dark; the only light in the room came from the fire and a weakly burning candle at her left hand. Outside, a delicate scattering of snow had fallen, settling in feathery drifts across the street. Father's great poem was spread out around her — sheets of paper in neat piles. She suppressed a yawn.

"I can hear you," he said. "Do you find this tedious?"

"No, Father."

"Women are too easily distracted from a task," he said irritably. "That is why they cannot be great scholars."

"But, Father, I —"

"Read me back what I wrote yesterday."

She shuffled the papers, looking for the page. This week had been a trial of patience, as they rearranged Father's poem into distinct books. She had read the same pieces over and over as he decided where to fit them, made sketchy notes about what would fill gaps. He planned another two books yet, but had not begun to compose them. When she found the right page she started reading. Raphael was telling Adam about the war in Heaven. She finished and Father remained silent. His ability to be completely quiet and still was unnerving.

"Father," she ventured after a while. "What do you know of angels?"

"Is that a criticism of my work?"

"No, no. I mean, how have you learned so much, and do you know all there is to know about them?"

"I have been reading of angels for many years, from arcane texts and modern theology: Plutarch, Zanchy, Psellus, Fludd, Pictorius, old Hebrew stories, many, many sources . . . Why? Do you doubt my ability to write of such things?"

"Father, no. You have misunderstood my curiosity. I have an interest in angels, and wish to know more of them. Perhaps I could ask you a question about them."

"Certainly."

"Are there guardian angels?"

"Some scholars believe there is a guardian class of angels."

"Do they come to our world?"

"They watch over us from their own world."

"But can they come to our world?"

"I am unsure." He frowned, and she knew that he hated not being able to answer her question. She also knew that he would never fabricate an answer.

"Are all angels good?"

"Angels are the Lord's emissaries."

"So, all angels are good?"

He considered a moment. "We could quibble here over the meaning of a word."

"How so?"

"Angels who are fallen are not good."

"Devils?" Her heart stopped.

"That is a misnomer. In truth, they are still angels and consider themselves so. Even Lucifer is an angel. He was God's favourite archangel. His name means 'bearer of light.'"

"Are they bad?" she managed to say. "These fallen angels?"

"They are God's adversaries. They are vain and weak and stupid, and they are interested in the sin of men."

"Are they dangerous?"

"I'm sure you may deduce that for yourself, Deborah," Father said. "Now, return to the task at hand. Read me the last ten lines again."

It took her a moment to compose herself, and then she started reading. Her mind was not on the lines in front of her, however. Instead she thought about fallen angels. Could Lazodeus be one of them? He certainly didn't fit Deborah's fantasy of an angel: he seemed too impatient, too worldly. Father had said that fallen angels were interested in the sin of men. With growing unease, Deborah wondered if they were also interested in the sin of young women.

5
So Spake the False Dissembler

Finally, Mary had to admit she was angry with Grandmamma. The old woman was ill, yes, but she was not dying. Mary should have known that it would be just Grandmamma's fashion to turn a minor ailment into a terminal illness, to get her family to rush about her as though she sat at the axis of the firmament. She missed Max madly, but he was safe with Deborah; Uncle William could not be trusted around the little dog. Ordinarily she wouldn't mind. She would be grateful that Grandmamma was feeling better each day, and grateful for a break from her father and Betty and even from her sisters. Deborah with her disapproving looks, and Anne with her patience-trying stammer. She would ordinarily enjoy the time sitting in Grandmamma's chamber, reading the old woman stories, and being smugly aloof to Uncle William who hung hopefully about the door a few times a day like a weevil hangs to a flour sack.

But these were not ordinary times.

Lazodeus, her angel, waited for her. And the longer Grandmamma's convalescence took, the longer she would be without him.

Grandmamma stirred in her sleep and Mary glanced over from where she sat by the window. Would she wake and demand more fish pie? More reading? But no, Grandmamma's enormous bosom shuddered with a long breath then settled back. Moments later, her gentle snoring continued. Mary faced the window and watched afternoon shadows creep across the fields.

"Are you trying to kill her?"

Mary turned to see Uncle William standing in the doorway.

"I beg your pardon?"

"With the window open like that."

"'Tis only open a crack."

He bustled in and closed the window, his armpit directly above Mary's face. She held her breath until he moved away.

"How is she today?"

"Feeling better, still tired." Mary glanced at Grandmamma. "She was never desperately ill. She certainly wasn't dying. I know not why she sent for me."

Uncle William smiled a crinkled smile. "Perhaps I sent for you."

"What?"

"Perhaps I writ up the letter you got."

Mary sniffed. "You can't write, Uncle William."

"Perhaps I paid someone to write it for me."

Mary narrowed her eyes. "I would be very angry if that were the case."

He shrugged. "You made a bargain with me, I kept my end of it. Perhaps I thought it was about time you kept your end."

Grandmamma stirred and snuffled. "Mary?" she called weakly.

Mary ducked past William and went to her. "Grandmamma, are you feeling better?"

The old woman had opened her gooey eyes. "A little. Has Ruthie made another fish pie?"

"I can go and ask her."

"Please."

"Grandmamma. Do you think I might be able to return to London soon?"

112

Grandmamma's face took on a mournful aspect. "Not yet. I am still so unwell."

Mary nodded, then turned to check on William. He was gone.

All afternoon and evening she tended to Grandmamma, then after supper she returned to the room and bed she was sharing with Ruthie, the servant. It was a tiny, musty room under the stairs. The room she had once had with her sisters was now boarding two of Hugh's friends. As always, the house was too full.

She unpinned her hair and struggled with her dress. Ruthie was nowhere in sight. She poked the fire then hung the iron, stripped down to her shift and moved to the glass above the dresser to brush her hair by firelight. Movement in the glass caught her eye and she whirled around.

William.

"Hello, Mary." He slunk out of the shadows, wearing a long housecoat.

"What are you doing here?"

"What do you think?"

"Ruthie will return any moment."

"No, she won't, for I have paid her enough to stay away for the whole night."

"Well, you should expect nothing from me, for I am tired from tending to your mother all day."

"I expect everything from you, Mary." He advanced towards her and dropped his robe. Underneath, he was completely naked. "Come on. Let's start with a little suckle."

Mary shuddered. "I'd rather suckle a snake."

"You made a promise," he said petulantly.

He had her backed up against the wall. She eyed the door, but he was watching her. "There's no escape, Mary."

She was beginning to believe he was right. She closed her eyes and cringed as he pressed into her, felt his erect penis stabbing her in the stomach. If only Lazodeus wasn't back in London.

Or was he? He had spoken about living in a different sphere. Did that mean he could be in two places at once? William was slobbering on her neck. She knew for certain she didn't want to pay this debt to her lecherous uncle.

"Lazodeus," she whispered.

"What did you say?" William asked.

Nothing had happened. No valiant angel to her rescue. "Hellfire," she said.

William stood back. "Cursing at me is not going to help. Come, remove your shift."

She considered running away, though she doubted she would make the door before William caught her. She was judging the distances when William suddenly yelped.

He rubbed his buttock.

"What's the matter?"

"I think something bit me. Come on, waste no more time." Then he yelped again, and spun round. Mary noticed two red welts on his buttocks.

"Ow." His head jerked violently to the left as though his hair were being pulled by an invisible assailant.

"William?"

He turned to her. "What's happening?"

Suddenly, he doubled over in pain, clutching his privates. "Oh, oh God."

Mary put a hand over her mouth to cover her smile. "Whatever is wrong, Uncle William?"

"Don't laugh, you witch. What have you done? Put a spell upon me?"

"No. How ridiculous."

"Then what is happening to —" His invisible antagonist kicked his legs out from underneath him and he landed in a heap on the floor. His voice became shaky with fear. "'Tis an evil spirit! Make it stop, Mary!"

"I cannot. I do not know what's happening to you

either." Laughter was barely contained under her words.

"Ouch." Another pull of the hair, and Mary noticed that William had pissed himself with fear. A great pool was spreading beneath him and he sat mournfully in the middle of it, looking as though he might cry. She could no longer hold back, and let herself double over with laughter.

"Stop it!" he cried. "Whatever you are, stop it!"

"No, don't stop it," Mary said through her laughter. "I'd like to see more!" Lazodeus did not heed her. He allowed Uncle William to return to shaky feet, pull on his housecoat and run away, muttering about evil spirits and witches. Mary screamed with laughter as the door slammed shut behind him. A moment later, the angel materialised.

"Death! That was the funniest thing I have ever seen."

Lazodeus considered her with a smile.

"I thought you weren't supposed to injure anyone," she said, her laughter easing.

"I didn't injure him. I scared him. I was very gentle."

"I wish you had injured him. I wish you'd pulled off his prick and thrown it out the window. That would have been a million times as funny."

"Mary Milton, you are cruel," he said, but it was not a judgement, just a statement.

"'Twas Mad Mary, angel. And she's only cruel to those who deserve it."

They stood considering each other for a few minutes. He had the most beautiful face she had ever seen, and she had to remind herself that he was an angel, so of course he was beautiful.

"Is everyone as beautiful as you in Heaven?" she asked.

"There are angels far more beautiful than me," he said, smiling.

"And do you call it Heaven?"

"We have many different names. Heaven, Elysium, Pantheus."

"They are all *our* names. What does God call it? He made it."

He tilted his head slightly. There was something mesmerising about watching him move, like watching flames flicker, or waves tumble. "God calls it Home."

"In English?"

"In every language."

She was fascinated. "Will you stay and talk with me for a little while?"

"I'm at your command."

She flopped down on the thin bed. "I suppose it is beneath you to clean up William's pool of piss?" she said, giggling.

"Are you commanding me to do it?" He seemed unsurprised.

"No. I expect Ruthie will clean it in the morning. But sit with me on the bed. That is what I command you to do."

He did as she asked. She was entranced by the faint glow emanating from his skin. Her fingers itched to touch him, to feel that silky flesh. He sat close, their arms almost touched, and she felt acutely aware of how little she was wearing.

"So," she said, fixing him in her gaze. "What kind of things can I command you to do?"

"Almost anything."

"Almost?"

"I would advise you against some things. If I thought they would bring you into danger ... Remember, I'm your guardian angel and my first instinct is to protect you."

"And your second instinct?"

He lifted his shoulders slightly. "To give you pleasure."

She smiled slyly. "I know what would give me great pleasure," she said.

"Yes?"

"To lie with the King."

He laughed, and she felt herself blush. "What's so funny?"

"What kind of pleasure would that bring you?"

"The pleasures of love," she said, moving a few inches away from him on the bed.

"You know nothing of love's pleasures. You lie with men because you feel it makes them weak and you strong."

"That is a kind of pleasure."

He dropped his voice. "Do you even know what bodily pleasures are available to you?"

"Bodily pleasures?" she said, a warm, unwelcome wash of embarrassment rising across her face. "Aren't angels supposed to recommend against such things?"

"God created pleasure, all pleasure. God *is* pleasure. The feeling of being in His presence is unmatched."

"But aren't there laws against fornication, in the Bible?"

He leaned close to her. "Laws may only bind the being who allows himself to be bound."

She watched him for a moment, his clear eyes, his perfect skin. Felt the flesh on the back of her neck prickling. "What kind of angel are you?"

"Angel of the fifth order," he said evenly. "Guardian class."

"And you live in Heaven?"

He smiled. "I live in London. Thanks to you and your sisters."

She thought of Anne and Deborah at home, about the promise she had begged of them. She had broken that promise herself. "Have my sisters called you?"

"No."

"Do you like them better than me?"

"No."

"Even Deborah? She's so clever and beautiful."

"I am moved by neither mind nor beauty. I am moved by spirit."

"Do I have spirit?"

"You wish to be compared to your sisters?"

She looked at him coyly. "Perhaps."

He reached out a hand and gently touched the bare skin on her throat. "You interest me more than Deborah and Anne."

A frisson of triumph shivered over her. "Honestly?"

"Honestly." He withdrew his hand. "Your command?"

"You won't let me lie with the King?"

"That request may be beyond my ability at present."

"Then I shall have to think upon it some more. I want to be a good commander, a worthy commander."

"If you have nothing more to ask . . ."

"No. Not now."

"Then I shall go."

"I know! Get me home to London. Soon."

"You shall leave tomorrow morning. Goodnight, Mary."

"Goodnight, angel."

He shimmered and disappeared. Mary climbed into bed and pulled the covers up almost to her chin. She felt strangely melancholy now he was gone. She pressed her hands into her face and felt that it was still warm. An unusual fluttering feeling nagged at her, low in the stomach. Was this desire? Was this what she made all those rich, powerful men feel for her?

She had seduced many; it had been her game, her delicate display of might. Yet, not one of them had been an angel. Seducing the King suddenly seemed a half-measure.

Late on the evening before New Year, Deborah was in Father's study, sorting the piles of paper and readying herself for the next day's work. He was growing more and more demanding in his anxiety, as the story took shape and became a real collection of words rather than a grand idea existing only in his imagination. She wrote for him some mornings until her hand ached, and then spent the afternoons reading back to him. Deborah found it endlessly frustrating to watch Anne come and go as she pleased, helping Liza cook biscuits and daydreaming in the garden, when she was constrained to work so hard.

Deborah tied a ribbon around a pile of notes for book ten, then stood to stretch her legs. She had lit every candle in the candelabra for her reading, but now extinguished all except one. The study was peculiarly empty without Father there. He and Betty had gone to visit friends near Holborn Bar and weren't expected back until the morning.

No, it wasn't emptiness she felt, it was relief. Spending so many hours a day in Father's company, when nothing she did was quite perfect enough for him, was wearing her down. It was also wearing her down worrying about Lazodeus's intentions. She longed to talk to her sisters about him, but Mary was still away, and she dared not frighten Anne by mentioning the angel.

She would have to ask Lazodeus herself, she knew that. But she and her sisters had made a pact not to call him and so she wouldn't.

She sharpened the quills and refilled the inkpot. Somewhere in the house she could hear the sounds of Max's little feet running about, of Liza moving upstairs. Why did she feel so disconsolate and lonely? She had a good home, a vocation, a brilliant father, a good mind, a guardian angel. It was more than most women could ever aspire to. She walked to the window and idly touched the keys on Father's harpsichord. He still played beautifully, even though he couldn't see. Monteverdi was his favourite, and he often spoke of having met the composer in Italy many years ago. She closed her eyes and tried to imagine Father as a young man: gifted, spirited, rebellious, with smooth skin and silken hair. She longed for such a young man for herself one day. If she couldn't find one, then she would be loathe to marry at all.

A clatter and a commotion outside drew her attention. It sounded like a carriage had arrived, so Mary must be home. Deborah was relieved. She needed to speak to somebody about her concerns.

"Hello!" Mary called from the doorway. "Where is everybody?"

"I'm in Father's study," Deborah called in response.

Mary rounded the corner and dropped into Father's chair, her red skirts frothing. "Lord, I'm so tired. Where's Father?"

"He and Betty are out with friends. They won't be home until tomorrow."

"What a lovely surprise I shall be for Betty on her return," she said, smiling her characteristically wicked smile.

"I'm glad you're back, sister," Deborah said, "for something is troubling me mightily."

"What is it?"

Deborah sat on the little stool in front of Father's chair, from where she usually took his dictation. "It is about Lazodeus."

"What about him?" Mary had adopted a studied informality, which stirred suspicion in Deborah. Had her sister been in contact with the angel?

Deborah weighed up how to word her concerns. Mary waited. "I'm not sure what his intentions are towards us."

"To protect us," Mary said quickly.

"Did he not seem to you less than angelic?"

Mary drew her eyebrows together in irritation. "How would we know? Who can really know angels until they meet them?"

Deborah considered. There was some sense in her words.

"What's all this about, Deborah?" Mary asked.

"Lazodeus seemed to me more worldly than an angel should, and Father says that —"

"Father! You've told Father about him?" Mary half rose from her chair, but Deborah put her hands up to placate her.

"No, of course not. But Father knows much about angels. He says that even fallen angels, those who have been cast out of Heaven with Lucifer, still call themselves angels. That they are vain and proud and interested in the sin of men. I suspect Lazodeus might be from among them."

"You have to ruin everything, don't you? You have to know better than us and ruin everything."

"Mary, I —"

"What's g-going on?"

Deborah turned to see Anne standing at the door to Father's study.

"Anne, Deborah is saying monstrous things about our angel," Mary said.

"About Lazodeus? What things?"

"Come in and close the door," Deborah said. "We don't want Liza to hear us bickering about this."

Anne did as Deborah asked. "Liza is upstairs in the withdrawing room. She won't hear us."

"We must be careful. We are meddling with great powers."

"Tell Anne what you told me," Mary said.

"I merely said that we need to find out what kind of angel Lazodeus is. Even angels who are fallen may call themselves angels."

"You mean d-devils?" Anne said, her cold hand reaching out for Deborah's wrist.

"We need to know, Mary," Deborah said. "And we can know simply by asking him."

"Very well," Mary said with a determined nod. "Call him, ask him."

"Are you agreed, sister?" Deborah said to Anne.

Anne nodded. "Yes, you may call him."

"Very well. Lazodeus, come to us," Deborah said, keeping her voice deliberately steady; madness lurked in the expectation that Lazodeus would come. She was having trouble getting used to such an incursion of the supernatural into her rational world.

He appeared before them in a moment. He wore the same clothes as the first time, looked handsome and healthy. He bowed deeply. "Good evening. I wondered when I might hear from you again."

Both Mary and Anne had fallen silent, so Deborah took charge. "Lazodeus," she said, "I command you to tell us what kind of an angel you are."

"Guardian class, fifth order," he said smoothly.

She licked her lips, glanced from Mary to Anne.

"Lazodeus, are you a fallen angel?"

An ominous silence reigned, and the longer it extended, the more Deborah's skin felt cold across her bones. The flame in the last candle sputtered and died, leaving for illumination only the fading embers of the fire and the eerie glow of the angel's skin.

"Lazodeus," she said again, and her voice was strained. "I command you to tell us whether you are one of the army of the fallen. I command you."

"You don't understand," he said softly. "Please, please . . ."

Deborah took a cautious step backwards. "What are you?" she breathed.

"Please don't banish me from the sight of you. You can't understand, because of all you have heard of us, all of the half-truths and the myths, which have nothing to do with what we really are. Nothing."

"We shall not b-banish you," Anne said quickly.

"Anne! If he is a fallen angel, he has an interest in our sin."

"No, no, you misunderstand us. Everybody misunderstands us." His eyes became sorrowful, and Deborah was surprised at the tug it caused at her core — a primal anguish, like seeing a child hurt. "Please, please, listen to me. I shall tell you the whole truth, unfettered, from my heart. But don't banish me yet."

Mary jumped up. "I propose we listen to Lazodeus. There can be no harm in listening."

"Very well, we shall listen," Deborah said. "But only if he tells the truth."

Lazodeus indicated that the girls should sit. Mary took Father's chair, Deborah lowered herself to the floor, and Anne sat on Deborah's writing stool. Lazodeus stood by the mantel, waiting for them to settle. The brass pot hanging inside the fireplace gleamed dully, so ordinary among these extraordinary circumstances. Deborah willed her heart to slow.

"We are all angels," he said, "and that is what we shall always be. But there was a war in Heaven. Lucifer and his supporters, fully one-third of the angels, were cast down. Lucifer was a good angel, God's favourite angel, but through a misunderstanding, through jealousy and rivalries between the archangels, he was wrongly accused of conspiring to rule in Heaven." Lazodeus shook his head. "If God only knew how it hurts us to be so far from his presence, how we could never wish to overthrow him."

"Are you a d-d—" Anne couldn't finish her sentence.

"No, I am not a devil, and nor do I live in Hell. Our abode is called Pandemonium. It is a great cave, lit by many fires to keep away the dread cold. It is nothing like the representations of Hell which you mortals produce. We spend our time there in eternal contemplation of how we may once again win God's favour and return to the realm of Heaven. I am an angel and always will be so, and I *beg* you, I beg you to understand and not to turn me away, for I love the presence of mortals and it is my small consolation in this eternal misery."

"Well, I shan't send you away," Mary said with a sniff. "I believe you. It makes sense when you think of it. God always seems so mightily bossy."

"Have you lost your wits, Mary?" Deborah said. "How can we trust him?"

Mary and Deborah glared at each other for a moment in silence. Then, breaking the quiet with her tremulous stutter, Anne said, "I t-t-trust him."

"As do I," Mary said quickly. "I trust him."

Deborah looked from one sister to the other incredulously. "He is fallen from Heaven."

"Deborah, what if he's telling the truth?" Mary reasoned. "What if innocent angels really are living in that ghastly cave longing to return to Heaven? How can we send him back there?"

Deborah threw her hands in the air. "No. I shan't hear of

this, not until I have had enough time to consider. Lazodeus, you shall go. We shall ask you to return when we are of one mind about your attendance on us."

Lazodeus bowed, and once again his eyes took on a sorrow so keen that Deborah almost called her words back. But that made no sense. She was determined to reason this out, to think about it clearly and thoroughly before she endangered herself and her sisters.

"No, don't go!" Mary cried, leaping to her feet.

"Your sister speaks wisely," Lazodeus said. "I hope I shall see you again. I shall dream of you always."

Deborah had the distinct feeling that the last line had been intended specifically for her, and a tendril of discomfort curled into her stomach. He shimmered and disappeared, leaving the room almost in full darkness.

Mary turned on her angrily. "You are the youngest; what makes you think you can dictate what we do?"

"I am clearly the wisest, for your immortal soul is at stake."

"My immortal soul! Listen to yourself. He just told us the truth."

"Why are you so quick to believe it?"

Mary fell silent. Anne stood awkwardly, and looked down upon Deborah on the floor. "I have b-been t-taunted, and I have been t-taken for a fool all my life. But I am not going to be t-told what to do by you."

Deborah thought she had misheard. By the time she realised that Anne had indeed sided with Mary, she had been abandoned by both her sisters. She sat for a few moments alone by the dying fire, trying to make sense of what had just happened.

She remembered Anne's words from Christmas Eve, "Our lives will change forever." But Deborah hadn't expected their lives would change so soon. They had known Lazodeus just one week, and already they were divided.

6
Can it Be Sin to Know?

"Ah. I thought I might see you back here again." Amelia Lewis stood aside and let Deborah in.

"Thank you, Amelia. I have questions."

"I knew the instant I met you that you would be the one to ask the questions. Please, come through to my withdrawing room."

Deborah could hear Gisela, the old maidservant, coughing loudly in the kitchen. She almost tripped over a cat as she stepped into the withdrawing room. The smell of the place — faintly citrus, faintly floral — seemed heavenly after the stinking street outside, where filthy melting snow ran rubbish over the cobbles, washing the entire city in waste. She sat in a deeply upholstered chair and leaned back against the velvet cushions. A large ginger cat approached and put his front paws on her lap.

"Sunday wants you to pick him up," Amelia said.

"Sunday?" Deborah said, lifting the cat into her lap.

Amelia gestured around. "They are all named for a day of the week. As I had seven, it seemed appropriate." She fixed Deborah in her gaze. "Now, tell me why you are here."

"Lazodeus is a devil."

Amelia recoiled. "Don't use such a word."

"You told us he was an angel, but he lives in the underworld with Lucifer. He admitted as much."

Amelia sighed and shook her head. "The trouble is that most people haven't the slightest idea about the spirit world, so they believe the superstitious rubbish that they hear in churches and they never experience the full exercise of their power. I had thought you would be different, Deborah."

"Me? Why?"

"Because you are brilliant like your father. You question things, you make connections, you think think think, all the time, thinking."

"Really? That is your opinion of me?" Deborah was pleased in spite of herself.

"It is not an opinion, it is a fact. I see such a light of intellect within you . . . I feel you may even surpass your father for learning. In the right circumstances."

"Surpass Father? 'Tis not possible." The cat in her lap miaowed loudly, and she realised she had been squeezing him too tightly. She relaxed her grip and he jumped off and padded away.

"I assure you it is possible. One generation is often exceeded by the next."

Deborah's imagination was captured by Amelia's words: to surpass Father in learning? Was it wrong even to dream of such a thing? She forced herself to remain unmoved, to stay upon the path she had come here to explore.

"Amelia, I have so many questions."

"Then ask them."

"May we start at the beginning? Could you tell me how it all happened? How my mother could afford such a luxury for her daughters as an angel? For surely, would not every man have one were it so easy to acquire?"

"Your mother did not pay for her angel with money. I owed her a favour. It is a great deal of work and time to call an angel, and it is very detrimental to the caller's health."

"Why did you owe her a favour?"

"She saved my life." Amelia pulled one of her cats into her lap, her fingers working gently through its fur. "I was set to hang for witchcraft."

"For witchcraft?"

126

"Actually, for murder, but I had been accused of murdering through bewitchment. I was residing at Stanton St John at the time, and I knew your mother well. She provided information at the assizes which made it clear I could not have murdered the man, and I was set free. When she came to London, we contacted one another and I promised her I would repay her." She smiled a mischievous smile. "I did, by the way."

"Repay her?"

"No, I did kill the man."

Deborah felt her breath catch in her throat. "What?"

"He deserved to die. But fear not, he is the only person I have killed and I have no regrets, and nor would you if you had been in my circumstance."

"What was your circumstance?"

She scooped up the cat, cradled it like a baby. "Yes, I think Deborah Milton might understand," she said to her cat, in the kind of voice one might use with a small child. She looked up at Deborah again. "I have never married, and nor have I ever lain with a man. I have no desire for it. Men are beasts."

Amelia Lewis suddenly grew immense in her estimation. "Yes, yes, it's true. Mary gives up her body indiscriminately. What gain is there for the soul, for the mind, in that?"

Amelia nodded. "Then you will understand. This man, the man I killed, attempted to defile me. When thwarted, he threatened to return and complete the task." She laughed lightly. "One should not threaten Amelia Lewis. He was dead in forty-eight hours, a strange pox which no doctor could explain. I did it, and I am glad. And I am glad withal that I did not hang for it, for he was not worth dying for."

For all it was a breach of one of the Ten Commandments, there was a certain Old Testament justice in Amelia's story. "How may I be like you, Amelia? How may I avoid the curse of marriage?"

"You are little more than a child. Marriage is not yet a

threat to you. In the meantime, you must work to become independent. You must develop your mind, and exercise the powers which are now available to you."

Deborah felt her excitement die a little. "You mean Lazodeus?"

"What are your misgivings?"

"He lied to us. He told us he was an angel."

"And so he is."

"A fallen angel."

"The politics of Heaven are not for men to understand."

"Is he a demon?"

Amelia smiled. "A demon is something quite different. The Greeks believed demons were benevolent spirits. Socrates had one, you know."

"But aren't demons evil?"

"Nothing in the universe is evil. Demons are merely spirits." She paused, then said, "Spirits that may be commanded."

"It sounds wrong."

"It is a great tradition, and divers great and learned men command spirits. It is a pity so many women are scared away from the science. But women are often scared away from what will make them powerful and wise."

"I would be powerful and wise, I would be a great natural philosopher and physician, but I do not want to command spirits."

Amelia sniffed. "Because you are afraid."

"Because it is wrong."

"Forget what you have heard. Learn anew."

Deborah felt the start of a curious longing flicker to life inside her. *Learn anew.*

"Lazodeus has divided us."

"That is your fault," Amelia said, and Deborah was surprised by her frankness. "You are not listening. Your heart knows that he is telling the truth when he says he is not evil. But you are so full of old ideas that new ones cannot make their way in. You may never surpass your father in wisdom unless you reach beyond what you already know."

"Amelia, I fear for our souls."

Amelia put her cat aside, leaned across and touched Deborah's hand. "Lazodeus does not want your soul. It is safe, as are the souls of your sisters. Enjoy yourself, exercise your power, find your independence."

"I know not —"

"And nor will you ever know if you don't learn."

Deborah's hands clenched and unclenched in her lap. She suddenly felt very young. She wanted to trust Amelia because she liked her: Amelia was intelligent and strong and unconventional. Deborah had never met another woman like that.

"Deborah, there is a great tradition among male magicians of taking on an apprentice."

Deborah looked up.

"Would you like to be my apprentice?" Amelia continued. "I could teach you about the unseen world. Perhaps then you would not feel so afraid of Lazodeus."

The idea filled her with wild excitement. Then she thought of Father, of how desperate she was to make him proud. She said soberly, "No. My father would not want that."

Amelia drew her eyebrows down together. "No? I thought you wanted to learn."

With a great effort, Deborah rose from the couch. "I should go. I have stayed too long and my father may need me."

"I will be kinder to you than your father is."

"Good day, Amelia."

Unsurprised, Amelia stood and showed her to the door.

"Thank you for answering my questions," Deborah said as she stood in the threshold to the dirty winter day outside.

"You will return," Amelia said with confidence.

Deborah didn't reply. She walked out into the street and turned towards home, vowing to herself that Amelia was wrong. She would not return.

Anne was supposed to be helping Liza with the mats, but instead she was taking a few blissful moments of solitude up in her bedroom. Mary and Deborah, uneasily reconciled after their disagreement, had gone walking. They had been surprised that she did not want to join them. But more and more, she relished being alone. Being alone meant she could think about Lazodeus.

She sighed and lay back on her bed. The quiet hung around her like a promise. She closed her eyes and remembered the feeling of speaking easily. "I can speak," she said aloud, for she rarely stammered when she was on her own. Still, the words didn't come easily, as though her mouth were a mechanism with jammed parts. She drew deep breaths, aware of the rise and fall of her chest, of the mellow heaviness which lay in her limbs.

His face. Those lips, so magnificently expressive. Those eyes, so clear and bright. How could Deborah suspect for a moment that he was anything less than a good angel? He was the most beautiful thing she had ever seen. Beauty of that magnitude could not be evil.

And his body. She opened her eyes suddenly. Crazy emotions raced around inside her. Was this love? She would like to be able to ask Mary, who had been in love so many times. But it felt so private, so sore and sweet. She feared to ruin it by speaking of it.

She rose and went to the mirror over the dresser, examined herself. She had always despised her appearance. Her crooked gait and her stupid twitching face made her feel like a grotesquerie. But now, with her face at rest, perhaps she was not so ugly. She looked very much like Mary, though not as plump and merry.

Anne had long believed that she could be herself, with all her faults, and angels would still love her. Now she had met one, it seemed all she could think of was how he might judge her. She leaned close to the mirror. Her eyes were bright, her teeth were still good. Perhaps her chin was too pointy. Perhaps her hair was too severely parted, too fine and straight. She touched her face with her fingers. Her skin was soft. Had Lazodeus noticed this when he had touched her cheek? Had he thought about her soft skin afterwards?

As minutes ticked by she gazed at herself in the glass. Gazed for so long she almost couldn't identify herself any more, as though she had dissected herself into unrecognisable parts. Her lips; were they inviting? Mary's lips must be inviting, for there was no shortage of people who wished to kiss her. And Anne's lips were almost identical.

What would she look like to someone intending to kiss her? Would such a close view deform her into a monster? She leaned her forehead against the mirror and looked at her dark eyes staring back at her. Pressed her lips against the cool glass and watched herself. Would Lazodeus find her beautiful if he kissed her?

The door suddenly flew open and Anne hastened away from the mirror. Liza stood there, hands on her hips.

"Your father has said you must help me with the mats."

"I am sorry. I f-forgot."

"I told him you must have forgot, but he's angry."

"He th-thinks I'm an idiot anyway. I c-c-can hardly fear his anger."

"Don't talk such nonsense. Come."

Anne left the room with one last glance at the mirror. Once again she was limping, twitching, stuttering Annie. Nobody would ever love her. Least of all an angel.

"What are you doing, Mary?" Anne said sleepily.

Mary turned from where she stood near the window and put a finger to her lips by the light of the candle she carried with her. "Shh. You'll wake the whole household."

Anne propped herself up on an elbow. "Close the window, 'tis cold."

"I'm going next door to my secret room."

"You'll freeze."

"I took coal over this morning, and some old rugs."

"Be c-careful."

"I promise I shall scream mighty loud if I fall," Mary said.

"D-do not even make such a joke," Anne said, settling back under the covers.

Mary hoisted one leg and then the other out the window, turned and said goodnight to Anne, then made her way along the ledge. It was not as easy with only one hand to steady her, but the ledge was sturdy and her feet were sure. Once in her secret room, she took a few minutes to light the fire and assess the room.

The rugs were dismal and threadbare. Even the light of the fire hadn't the power to cheer the room. She sank to the floor, depressed. In her imagination, the secret room was full of the rich fancies that Amelia owned. In reality, it looked like a pauper's home.

She stretched her hands out to the fire and sighed. Perhaps she should have dressed properly, instead of coming in her shift. The room was cold, and taking a long time to warm up. Still, she was alone, away from her sisters, and ready for adventure. Ready to try a seduction.

"Lazodeus," she said, "come to me."

He appeared, and Mary marvelled that something so magical could happen so quietly. It seemed the whole world should rise and applaud at such a wonder. She smiled at him.

"Good evening, Mary," he said.

"Do you like my new room?"

"No. It is very cold and colourless."

"Can you fix it?"

He sat down next to her. "Maybe." Almost instantly, the fire began to roar, the temperature in the room began to rise.

"What about some cushions? Some tapestries? Like

Amelia Lewis's house. I suppose they were provided for her by you or an angel like you?"

"I know not how Amelia Lewis furnishes her home."

"Do you mean you won't do it?"

"Is that why you called me? To command me to produce little comforts?" He sounded impatient.

Mary was taken aback. "No. I merely wanted to speak with you."

"Your sisters do not know you've called me."

"Anne wouldn't mind, I'm sure. Deborah is still deciding whether or not to trust you, but I already trust you. So I don't see why I shouldn't call you." Still, a guilty feeling lurked in the back of her mind. Deborah would prefer it if Lazodeus only attended them all together. She had explained to Mary on their walk that afternoon, that her greatest fear was the three of them being divided over the angel. Mary had assured her that it wouldn't happen, and yet here she was speaking with him by herself, hoping that she may enjoy some forbidden intimacy with him.

She pushed the guilt aside. She was braver than her sisters, and they all knew it. Brave enough to deal with Lazodeus directly.

"Forget about the furnishings," she said. "I only wished for a nicer setting in which to entertain you."

"You are entertaining me?" he asked, smiling. "Am I not supposed to be entertaining you? I am your servant, at your command."

"I want you to be our friend, not our servant," she said. "In fact, I command it."

"Your sister Deborah would be appalled to hear such a thing."

She waved a dismissive hand. "Oh, Deborah is such a baby, really. She may be Father's favourite for being clever, but it does not equate with being wise."

"A very wise thing to say," he said, and Mary felt herself blush with pleasure.

"What would we speak of?" Lazodeus continued. "What would we do, now we are friends, rather than servant and mistress."

"We could speak of intimate things," she said boldly. "We could undress each other." This very offer had worked so many times for her, that she was stupefied to see him shake his head.

"No, Mary. That is not for us to do."

Disappointment sank down inside her. Fool, for thinking that an angel would be so easy to seduce. "But why not?"

"Because you want such intimacy for the wrong reasons."

"I want to please you."

"And what of your pleasure?"

"It would please me to lie with you."

"The pleasure you take from your lovers is cruel. It is about defeating them, not about loving them."

"Love is a word fatigued through use. Besides, I can command you to do it." She warmed to the idea.

He leaned very close, his nose almost touching hers, the warmth of his body seeking out her skin. She felt vaguely frightened but was unsure why. "You can no longer command me, Mary Milton. For you told me not five minutes past that you would now have me for friend rather than servant."

"But I meant . . ." She had meant exactly that. Her heart picked up a quick rhythm. "So I can no longer tell you what to do?"

He shook his head. "Nor your sisters for you did say 'our friend'? From now on I may listen and help you, because of the love I bear you all, but I may say no whenever I please." His fingers brushed her shoulder. "Mary, there is a delight in skin touching skin which you do not yet know," he said. "Are you not curious?"

Nothing was going to plan. She had imagined their exchange so differently. He would be like all the others she had known — the offer to use her body would be quickly accepted, clothes would be removed, some childish grunting would follow and then she would be the new queen of his angelic body, the object to which his thoughts always returned, the constant topic of his conversation, the sole aim of his labours. Instead, he was no longer her servant and she felt threatened, as though she teetered on the brink of a chasm.

"I . . ."

He leaned away suddenly. "When I think you are ready to know the true pleasures of the flesh, I shall call upon you again. Until then goodbye, *friend.*"

"Go then," she said, turning her face away. "I don't care if you go for I —" She stopped abruptly as she looked around and saw he had gone.

The empty room suddenly felt very cold.

The next morning, Mary took a brass candlestick across to her secret room as though that one small object could counter the dingy appearance of the place. As she climbed in the window, she gasped with astonishment.

The room was full of velvet cushions, thick fur rugs, rich curtains, ornate lamps and candlesticks, gold-threaded tapestries, paintings, pottery and statues. She stood in the middle of it for a moment, taking it all in. Then she began to laugh.

This kind of luxury was the least a girl who had once commanded angels could expect.

"Mrs Milton, may I speak with you?"

Betty glanced up from her embroidering. She sat in a weak sunbeam in the whitewashed withdrawing room. Liza stood in the doorway, shifting from foot to foot like an anxious dog. "Of course, Liza, what is it?"

Liza looked furtively behind her then approached Betty. "I have been waiting for an opportunity to speak privately, while nobody else is nearby."

"What's all this about? What secrets are we sharing?" Betty asked, putting her embroidery ring aside. Secrets made her nervous.

"I want to show you something, but I . . . that is . . . you aren't to be cross with me for not showing you earlier."

"What is it?"

"Here." Liza suddenly dropped to her knees and folded back one of the mats.

"You want me to join you on the floor?"

Liza made a motion for her to be quiet and beckoned her over. Betty's curiosity was piqued. She knelt on the floor next to Liza. "What am I looking at?" she whispered.

"See . . ." She indicated a knot in the floorboard. "I realised a few months ago that I could do this." She pushed her smallest finger under the knot and it popped out, leaving a perfect hole about an inch across. Liza pointed down and mouthed the words, "Look you."

Betty leaned over and peered through the hole. She could see directly into John's study. He sat in his chair listening to Deborah reading to him. Betty flinched and drew back, indicating that Liza should reseal the hole. When the mat was returned to its place, Betty grabbed Liza by the arm. "What is all this about? Have you been spying on my husband and me?" She felt unsafe and exposed.

"No, no, I swear I . . ." Liza hung her head. "Sometimes I look to see . . . when he's on his own . . . to see if he keeps his eyes open or closes them."

"What an abominable display of disrespect!" Betty exclaimed, pinching the maidservant by her ear. Memories of all the things she may have done in full view of Liza rushed into her mind. Had Liza seen her take the books to sell? Or witnessed the lifeless conjugal relations between her and John? Or noted every undignified movement she had ever made when certain that nobody was watching her?

"Wait, ma'am, wait! I need to tell you what I saw."

Betty released Liza's ear, and looked at her suspiciously. "What did you see?"

"On New Year's Eve. When you and Mr Milton were away."

Betty suddenly became excited. "The girls? The girls did something?" Something heinous, something awful which Liza would attest to. Then John would have to send them away.

"Yes, the girls. They were entertaining a gentleman."

"A gentleman! I knew it! How long did he stay?"

Liza suddenly dropped her head again. "Ma'am, I . . . 'tis impossible . . ."

"What? What's impossible? They are capable of anything, those minxes."

Liza took a deep breath and met Betty's eyes. "Ma'am, he disappeared into nothing. I swear, one instant he was there and the next gone. Like . . . magic." Her voice trailed off to a whisper, and Betty realised the young woman was terrified. Her face had drawn chalk white.

Betty felt a sudden chill glide over her body. "Rubbish, Liza," she said without conviction. "Men don't disappear suddenly, they use doors." Christmas Eve: she had heard a man's voice, without doubt, but when she went in only the three girls were in the room.

"Ma'am, I saw it with my own eyes. I swear, 'tis the Lord's truth. And I heard some of the things they were saying, things about angels and devils and Lucifer himself."

"Lucifer?" Betty said. Her voice didn't sound like her own. A strange, excited fear had taken hold of her. But she had to remain calm and take her time, for if she made a hasty accusation, John would think badly only of her and refuse to hear any more on the issue.

"Ma'am, 'tis true."

Betty brushed her hands on her skirt. "Liza, you were right to tell me. I want you to keep an eye out for any more appearances of this man."

"If the girls catch me spying, they'll beat me. Especially that Mary."

"For every beating you get from them, you'll receive a threepence from me."

Liza sighed. "Yes, Mrs Milton."

"You may go now. Thank you."

Liza backed out of the room. Betty returned to the couch and caught up her embroidery ring, picked idly at the stitching. Were the girls really involved in something so very dangerous as sorcery? If that were the case, would John throw them out, have them charged, disown them? What would he do to them?

She shivered as another thought occurred to her. If she told their father, what might they do to her?

Betty fell sick with a winter chill in the second week of January, throwing the whole household into chaos. A sudden icy-cold snap had gripped London, laying the streets with thick snow. Betty moaned from morning until night about the cold. Deborah had never known someone make such a fuss of such an insignificant illness; her demands were endless. Mary wisely stayed out of the house all day, preferring to take refuge in her secret room. Because she wouldn't take Max with her — "it would frighten him too much carrying him across the ledge" — he was bored and restless and under foot. Liza ran back and forth, her cheerless eyes fixing on Deborah and Anne as she told them tonelessly that Father had ordered them to help chop and net vegetables for cooking, or wash the bed covers, or fetch coal, or find Betty's favourite nightcap, which it was implied one of them had stolen.

On a visit to the study to find a book to read to Betty, Deborah was surprised to see Father pacing the room. He knew precisely where each item of furniture was, and walked as confidently as a man who could see the obstacles around them.

"Father? Is everything well with you?"

He turned and took a moment to find her with his sightless eyes. "Why? Do I look unwell?"

"You seem . . . impatient." He was always impatient, and Deborah had to stop herself from adding, "More so than usual."

"Betty has been ill for three days and I have not been walking," he said petulantly, almost as though he suspected Betty had fallen sick on purpose.

"Father, 'tis freezing outside. I nearly turned to ice going out to fetch the coal."

"Nevertheless, *solvitur ambulando*."

Deborah smiled. *It is solved by walking.* She wondered what problem he wished to solve. He hadn't dictated to her for nearly a week; clearly he had reached an impasse with his great epic.

"I can walk with you, Father," she offered.

"I think that is for the best. Ask Liza to show you where my winter mantle is."

Deborah felt a wonderful sense of freedom as she ran upstairs to tell Liza that she and Father were going out. Out of the house, which was too warm because Betty insisted every fire in every grate should be roaring to compensate for the chill which had taken hold of her chest. Out with father — *solvitur ambulando*. She returned downstairs to find him waiting by the door, patiently, like a small child.

"Here," she said, handing him his gloves.

He tried the left one on his right hand, but just as she reached to help him, he pulled it off with a look of self-disgust. Would that she were blind to that expression. Gloves fitted to the correct hands, he held his arms out for his mantle and hat. Deborah pulled on her own heavy winter cloak and hat. She couldn't use a muff for Father would need to hold her hand, so she found a pair of mittens and opened the door.

The first blast of icy air sent Father back two steps. "Just a short walk, eh, Deborah?"

"Yes, Father. Just a short one."

The stuffy house behind them, they linked hands and walked down the hill. At the main street, he said what he always said, "Be my eyes, Deborah."

"The sky is perfect grey, it is barely daylight. I see lanterns burning in windows, diamond patterns of light on the snow."

"The snow is deep," Father said, lifting his feet high. "Hold my hand tightly for I do not wish to trip."

"I shan't let you go, Father. Here, walk this way, for someone has shovelled the snow into a pile on that corner." She led him across the street. "The trees are paler than the sky. The branches are bare and damp and seem to shiver in the wind."

"I can hear them. Is there anyone else around?"

"Not for yards. I see a woman with a basket. I think she is selling potatoes, but she is dressed very poorly for this weather. She must be cold. Do you want to go to the cemetery?"

He shook his head. With his free hand he wrapped his scarf high up over his chin. "Just around the block. 'Tis very cold, though I find the fresh air invigorating."

"Me too, Father."

"Let us practise our languages. Describe the world to me in Italian."

Her breath caught in her throat. "Italian, Father? It is my worst language."

"It should be your best for it is my favourite. What use are these languages to you beyond conversing with me?"

Deborah felt a wave of pity for him. He possessed so much knowledge, was so fluent in so many languages, but had hardly anybody with whom to share his mind. The King's return to London had signalled Father's withdrawal from the public world and, now in retirement, blind and submerged in the tedium of domestic life, he had few avenues for his great intellect. She was vastly disappointed with herself for not making Italian her chief area of study simply because it did not appeal to her as much as the strange secret sounds of Hebrew, or the sweet complexities of Greek.

"Go on, then, what do you see?"

What do you see? Deborah looked around desperately. Houses. *Case.* Trees. *Alberi.* He had taken her by surprise and she found herself straining for the most basic of sentence constructions. *Vedo . . . Vedo . . .*

"Well?"

"Forgive me, Father. I am used to reading and translating the language, but to compose in it is more difficult. A moment, please."

"Disregard my request," Father said abruptly. "I should not have even bothered teaching you, for one tongue is enough in any woman's head."

"No, Father, I will try. I am simply not as confident as you."

"I said to disregard it. I wish to return home." He did not speak angrily. In fact, his voice was devoid of any emotion. This emptiness cut her to the quick, made her feel desperate and wretched.

"Father, be not angry with me. I do try. I'm weak, I'm stupid."

He remained silent, and she knew that no matter what she said between now and home, what questions she asked, he would not say another word. It was his way of dealing with those he considered to be vastly beneath him.

She scuffed along through the snow next to him, wondering what she wouldn't give not to be so very low in his eyes.

7
Devils to Adore for Deities

Four months had passed since Mary had last seen Lazodeus, and still he remained uppermost in her thoughts. As the snow melted and she sat in her velvet room alone, she thought of her angel. As the first buds began to sprout on the trees in the park while she played with Max, she thought of her angel. As she bickered with Betty, as she berated Liza for spying on her, as she sat down to take dictation from Father while Deborah rested, as she made polite conversation with Betty's cousin Anthony, who had come to stay and didn't look like going any time soon, she thought about nothing but her angel. How dull, how very dull life had become.

And now, as she let Sir Wallace lift her skirts and bury his bone in her, she remembered Lazodeus's promises regarding the pleasures of the flesh. She looked around her. They stood together in an alley behind Sir Wallace's home. It was very dark and the wall behind her was rough. A long way off she could see daylight, and people passing on the street. Wallace grunted loudly in her ear.

"Oh, Mary. Mary, you are so beautiful."

She smiled to herself. His jewellery rattled as he bumped against her, and the large red feather in his hat tickled her cheek. Wallace had eight servants. Eight! What kind of power would it be to command eight people.

Then Mary cringed as she remembered she and her sisters had once commanded an angel. And it was all her fault they no longer did. Not that she had mentioned this to either Deborah or Anne. Deborah had refused to summon Lazodeus until she knew for certain he meant them no harm, and Anne had meekly gone along with her. Neither of them were aware yet that Lazodeus had taken leave of them.

She had tried to call him, of course she had. But he had not come. Tears and rages hadn't helped, nor had reasoning, nor had pleading. He was gone, and his absence had caused her to lapse into a profound state of melancholy, which was something she had never suffered from before. Usually it was for Deborah to be introspective, or for Anne to be gloomy. A great well of feeling swelled inside her, a feeling which could only be dispelled in one long, unknowable syllable. Until she could learn what that syllable was, she just repeated over and over, *Lazodeus, Lazodeus, my angel.*

Wallace was almost achieving his peak. Mary brought her mind back to the business at hand, but contemplation of Lazodeus had caused her to realise how old and how ugly Wallace was. Rather than her usual rush of excitement as his face reddened and his calls became more bestial, she experienced a disgusted recoil. As he pulled himself out of her to soil her thighs, she shrank against the wall.

"Oh, oh, oh!" he cried. Then sagged against the wall with a great sigh. "Oh, Mary. Mary, Mary."

She patted his arm, smoothing over her skirts.

"Oh, Mary, you are so beautiful," he said, relacing his breeches. "Come to me next Thursday. My wife is going away. Come inside the house, and I shall love you amongst the riches of my bedroom. You can choose yourself a ring or a bracelet from my wife's jewellery box. My Mary deserves better than a dark alley."

Here was the offer she had long waited for: taken inside, laid down among satin and velvet, adorned with jewels . . .

"I am uncertain."

"What?" He stood back, surprised.

"I shall see what I have to do. My father keeps me very busy."

"Your father? That shabby antique?"

"Nevertheless, I . . ." She could not finish her sentence.

"'Tis the best offer a girl like you can hope for," Wallace said.

"Then maybe I shall come."

Wallace shrugged. "Suit yourself. I must go."

He rearranged his clothes, smoothed the feather on his hat, and turned away from her. She stood where she was for a moment, watching him slip through the back gate into his walled garden. At length, she started down the alley for the street. Summer had come early; a hot wind blew down Little Woodstreet, making her eyes dry and sore. She passed a man vomiting, deftly stepped around him, wrinkling her nose against the sour smell of his stomach. A family of street cats scattered as she approached. Thunder rumbled in the distance.

Why hadn't Wallace's promise of rings and bracelets thrilled her? She felt a sudden barb of anger against Lazodeus. Before he had come along, her life had been far less complicated. She had certainly never felt such an emptiness, such a chaos of yearning and listlessness.

Thunder sounded again. She eyed the horizon and saw heavy black clouds advancing. She hurried her step. Max hated storms. She couldn't bear the thought that he would be frightened and think she had abandoned him.

To feel abandoned was the worst kind of misery.

Anne could not remember ever despising anyone so much as she despised Anthony.

It wasn't simply his odious personality, a rival for his cousin Betty's. It wasn't simply his revolting appearance: he had a body like two pillows tied together, a drooping, overly moist bottom lip, and eyes sunk back into shadows. No, by far his most detestable characteristic was the way he had installed himself as joint master of the house. And Father, clearly starved for educated male company, allowed him to do whatever he wanted.

"Anne! Come here at once, girl," he bellowed from Father's study. She limped in as fast as she could. Father sat in his usual position by the fireplace, Anthony opposite him in a comfortable chair he had taken from the withdrawing room.

"Can't you move any quicker?" he asked.

She attempted to answer but found her mouth wouldn't even produce the start of a word.

"Never mind, stupid cripple," he said dismissively. Then, articulating loudly and clearly, as though she were a child, "Can you fetch me a cushion. Not one of those small ones from the withdrawing room. Fetch me a pillow. The one from your bed will suffice."

"B-but —"

"Fetch me a pillow!" he roared.

Father sat unmoving and unmoved, his unseeing eyes turned towards the tiny window.

Anne nodded and backed out. She hurried up the stairs and stopped at the curtain which sealed off Betty's room. She peeked around the curtain, saw the room was empty, and quickly grabbed a pillow. If anyone should have Anthony's arse imprinted on her pillow, it should be Betty. She had invited him, she cooed and fussed over him, bragged about his recent education in Italy, and gloated every time he shouted one of the girls down about something.

It would all have been bearable had Lazodeus answered her calls; but it had been months now since she had last seen him. She supposed it was her ugliness and lameness that had driven him away. As she advanced down the stairs, she could hear Anthony complaining loudly.

"What is taking the girl so long? She would have been better off drowned at birth than to live and prove such a vexation to her family."

Anne heard Father's voice, softer, and paused outside the door to listen. Was Father defending her? Her heart rose a little in her chest.

Anthony's laughed pierced through the wall. "That's right, that's right," he said, in response to Father.

"We didn't realise there was anything wrong with her until she was two years old, and by then it would have been murder. Besides, her mother was fond of her."

"Women are so weak."

"But I didn't expect the child to live. When her mother died, I did consider sending her off to another family. One that perhaps could see to it that she met an accident."

Again, Anthony roared with laughter. Anne suddenly had trouble breathing. She knew Father bore no special love to her, but to hear that he had considered killing her . . . She slunk into the room and held the pillow out.

"And about time," Anthony said. "Now I want you to . . . wait, where are you going?"

"I c-c-can't —" she started to say, as Anthony grasped her around the wrist.

"You c-c-can't wh-wh-what?" Anthony said, enjoying the game.

"Let me g-g—"

"What, Anne? What? Let you giggle? Let you graze? Let you gasp? What are you trying to say?"

"F-Father, t-tell him to l-l—" Her tears fell freely now.

"Anthony, let her go. A woman's tears put me at the end of my patience. Go, Anne. Stop wailing, you fool." At least he had the decency to turn his face away guiltily; perhaps he realised she had heard him.

As Anthony's fingers left her wrist she hurried out of the room, knowing that her uneven gait did not allow her a dignified withdrawal. His laughter followed her. "Is that the best you can run? Lucky there is not a bear chasing you!"

"Leave her be now, Anthony," she heard Father say as she headed for the stairs. But it was too late, for now the pain and humiliation were shuddering up through her body and she heard the guttural sound of repressed sobs echoing around the staircase. She lumbered up to the bedroom, relieved that Deborah and Mary were not around to see her in such a state, and buried her face in the bed. She sobbed and sobbed until it felt she might shatter to pieces. Why had God suffered her stupid, broken body to live? Was He not merciful? Surely it were mercy to have destroyed her before she could breathe and see the stars and know the feel of sun on her skin. Surely it were mercy for her not to have known such a glimmering of love for an angel; an angel who was so revolted by her that he had broken his promise to be commanded, and beat a hasty retreat.

"Why, why, why?" she found herself saying, over and over. She could feel a trail of drool from her mouth to the rough covers, and wiped her lips with a shaking, damp palm. She sat up and shook her hair out of her eyes. Her face was hot. She caught sight of herself in the glass and began to cry anew. Ugly, so ugly. Not beautiful and clever and honey-haired like Deborah; not round and bow-lipped and alluring like Mary. She pressed her face into her palms and wept like a child.

Something brushed against her hand and she looked up, startled.

"Lazodeus." Her heart suddenly doubled its rhythm.

"Anne, I cannot bear to see you cry."

"Wh-what . . . Where have you b-b-b —"

"Sh, sh. Wait." He placed a finger over her lips, and for a brief, perfect moment she could taste his skin, sweet and hot.

"Now, speak," he said.

"Where have you been?" And the words came freely tumbling off her lips.

"I have been away."

"I thought you were supposed to protect us. I thought we were your commanders. But you haven't come when I have called and I have been so desperate."

"I wanted to come, I really did, Anne."

"Then why?"

"Mary has made a terrible mistake."

"Mary? You have spoken with Mary?" The barb of jealousy was swift and sharp.

"A long time ago now. It was she who dismissed me from my duties."

Anne looked at him bewildered. "How? How is that possible?"

"She commanded me to be your friend rather than your servant. I had to grant her command and so it was."

Anne shook her head. "'Tis not possible that she should be so foolish."

"And yet she was. But be not angry with her. She did not understand what she asked. She is not as wise and thoughtful as you."

She felt a smile come to her lips in spite of herself. "Oh. Well . . ." She paused, attempted to regain her composure. "So you are no longer our servant?"

He knelt down in front of her. "I am, I am. But not by command, not by decree. I am your servant for the love I bear you, but as I am not assigned to you through an enchantment any more, it is not possible for me to come whenever you call. I have other duties. But I shall try. Anne, I do not wish to see you cry. I shall try harder to come when you need me."

When she needed him. But she had needed him so often and so desperately in the past few months, and he had ignored her pleas. She turned her eyes down, felt another small shudder of a sob ready to shake her chest.

"Anne, what is it?"

"You have not come. So often I have called —"

"I explained —"

"But how can I trust you? How can I trust you to watch over me when you have been so far from me for so long?" She tilted her face up to him again. Every perfect feature was somehow more exquisite than she had remembered it.

His eyes narrowed slightly. "You question my trustworthiness?"

It hurt to see him offended. "No, I just —"

He put his finger to her lips to silence her again. The touch was all too brief, seemed to leave a burning imprint on her skin. "Very well, Anne Milton. I shall show you why you should trust me. Though it will cost me dearly, though the powers above me in Pandemonium may punish me severely —"

"No! I don't want you to be hurt. I will trust you."

"Anne, I can make it so that you can always speak without hindrance."

She held her breath. "I . . . How?"

"Through angel magic. But we are not supposed to alter so vastly the state of mortals without due permission."

"I don't want you to be punished for my sake," she said, infusing her voice with as much sincerity as she could manage. You must not —"

Suddenly he grabbed her by the upper arms and pulled her against his chest. Before she had a chance to savour the moment, he had pressed his lips hard against her own. Sweet, blissful touch. He parted her lips with his tongue, and her body seemed to break its own bounds, to float outwards into the universe. Then a second later it was over.

"It is done," he said, pulling away from her.

A moment passed before she could speak. "What will happen to you?"

"I know not. But it will go better for me if I return immediately and tell what I have done."

"Then go. Go quickly, for I will suffer with guilt until I see you returned to us, safe and whole."

He smiled. "Feel no guilt, Anne. It was all my pleasure." His attention was suddenly drawn downwards as though he may have heard a supernatural voice calling him from below the earth, and Anne felt a moment's chill apprehension.

"Goodbye," he said. "I promise to return as soon as I may."

"Goodbye," she said, but he had already disappeared.

She slumped back on her bed and closed her eyes. Licked her lips to see if she could still taste him. It wasn't a kiss, it was only magic, and she shouldn't read anything more than his concern as her guardian into it. But the way he had spoken of his pleasure . . .

She opened her eyes and said out loud, "Anthony Minshull, may you die of a pestilence." The words came as easily as breathing. Now all she needed was the courage to say it to his face. The power to speak did not necessarily equate with the power to speak out.

Deborah was enjoying a few quiet moments of solitude in Father's study — he and Betty and Anthony had gone walking. She opened the trunk and began searching through for the book she had been reading the previous day. Here, Jerome Zanchy's *De Operibus Dei*; a modern text on angels Father had used early in his research for the poem. She found her place and began to read.

This had been her world for the last few months. Reading voraciously, everything she could find about angels and the spirit world, so that she could make the right decision about Lazodeus. The further she delved the more surprised she became: much evidence existed that the command of spirits was not evil, that fallen angels did not necessarily endanger one's soul, that a long and great tradition of men dealing with ethereal beings preceded her.

Men. Not women. She thought of Amelia's words again and they stung. Was she flinching from it because she was a woman? Was her caution really just misplaced timidity?

Still, she would not rush her decision. Mary had long since stopped nagging her about making up her mind, and Anne seemed happy to go along with her for as long as it took to decide what was right.

She sat back on her feet and sighed. All the reading in the world was not going to tell her what to do, not really. And she owed her sisters an answer very soon. She was far too young to have such a responsibility of choice thrust upon her. Why, she knew girls of her age who had barely put away their poppets.

Outside a heavy rain began to fall, and she expected the three of them back home any moment. Liza and Anne were in the kitchen, and Mary hadn't been seen all morning. Presumably she was doing whatever it was she did in her secret room. Deborah dreaded Anthony's return. Not because he was cruel to her like he was cruel to Mary and Anne — no, he took Father's lead and was more patient with her. She dreaded it because Father had chosen him to be his eyes; Deborah had been all but relieved of her duties as scribe and reading companion.

And he wasn't even as clever as she was! That was the killing blow. For all that Anthony had spent time on the continent, he certainly hadn't used his days in learning the languages. She knew for a certainty that his Italian was far worse than hers, but Father never mentioned it. Not once.

She heard a scuffle and a whimper from up the stairs, and put the book aside to investigate. The whimpering grew louder, frantic, and she hurried to the withdrawing room to find Max with his paw jammed firmly between the bottom two stairs.

"There, Max, there," she said, gently easing his paw free.

He yelped, but was soon freed. She put him on the floor and watched him limp a few paces, then sit down with his paw held out, quivering.

"Oh, you poor, dear thing. Is it sore?" She collected him into her arms, but he wouldn't be consoled. He needed Mary. "Come, then, little fellow. We shall find your mistress, shall we?" She stood and headed up the stairs, closed the bedroom door behind her and went to the window.

"Mary? Mary, come home. Max is hurt."

No answer.

"Mary?" she asked again, louder.

Curious. Mary normally responded instantly. Deborah looked at Max. "Where is she?" If she had gone walking, she would have taken the dog. Deborah leaned out the window and looked across. "Mary? Is everything well with you?"

Perhaps Mary was ill, or injured. Deborah gently set Max on the bed — he trembled still, but she suspected it was more from fright than from pain — and returned to the window. She hadn't been in to Mary's secret room since the night she had first seen it. Mary had become very possessive about it, forbidding them to enter, and in any case, the walk along the ledge did not appeal to her. She assessed it now, the rain dripping onto it.

But if Mary were hurt . . .

She hoisted her skirts up and gingerly climbed out. Edged along to the window and grasped the sill firmly in her hands. Curtains. They hadn't been there before. And they looked like rich brocade, not secondhand rags. She parted them and peered in, her sister's name poised on her lips.

"Oh, my God!" she exclaimed instead when she saw the room. She clambered in and landed on a pile of wine-red velvet cushions. Mary was nowhere in sight. She advanced into the room. Burnished candlesticks were positioned around the room, thick hangings in white and gold adorned the walls, and everywhere were cushions piled high in different colours, rich fabrics. "Oh, my," Deborah said, touching one of the wall hangings, feeling its soft friction slip between her fingertips. She admired a gilt-framed landscape on the wall, and a marble statue, about two feet high, of a young wood nymph. Where on earth had Mary acquired all these fine things? One of her rich suitors? But then how did she carry them up here? She had no access except via the ledge. How could she have brought all these cushions up through the house and out the bedroom window without being noticed?

Then the answer struck her. Lazodeus. It was just the kind of thing Mary would command an angel to do. She felt her cheeks grow hot with anger. They had agreed, they had all agreed to wait, to weigh the situation, to be rational, not impulsive.

She marched to the window and hoisted herself out onto the ledge. She could hear somebody moving about in the bedroom and stopped to peek before she went in. It wouldn't do for Betty or Liza to find out about the secret room. She had expected to see Anne, but instead it was Mary, slipping off her shoes and taking a tiara out of her hair.

"Mary, where have you been?" Deborah asked.

She looked up guiltily as Deborah slid in the window, then said, "Where have *you* been? I didn't give you permission to go into my room."

Deborah's eyes widened in astonishment. Mary was wearing an exotic pendant with a large blue stone, and four different gemstone rings. "Where did you get these jewels?"

Mary sniffed and tossed her hair back. "I've been with Wallace."

Deborah felt a vast weight of tiredness. Why on earth did Mary prostitute herself like this? "And was it worth it? Was it worth your dignity to acquire these jewels?"

"Don't be silly. I have no dignity," Mary said, pulling off the rings and placing them side by side on the dresser. "And you still haven't told what you were doing in my secret room."

"Max was hurt and —"

"Max? Where is he?"

"He must have grown tired of waiting for you."

"Was he hurt badly?"

"No, no. He merely twisted his paw and pined for your sympathy. I went to look for you and instead found a room full of expensive things. Would you care to explain?"

"Wallace sent them to me."

"You're lying."

"Well, who else?"

Deborah nearly said Lazodeus's name, but stopped herself. It was not right to assume Mary was lying. She owed her a chance to explain. "How did you get it all up there?"

"'Twas a surprise. He acquired a key and took it all up through the front of the building."

Deborah considered this. Maybe it was true. Everyone knew where the Miltons lived, and Wallace may well have the power to acquire keys to empty houses. She suspected rich men might do as they please most of the time. "I see. And how many times have you had to lie with him to gain such treasures?"

"None of your business."

"'Tis hardly an efficient method of earning. You should hang out a shingle, Mary, set a price and stick to it."

Without warning, Mary stood up and slapped her. Deborah took a step back in shock. Her face stung.

"Don't you say that to me."

"I . . ." So many times before Deborah and Mary had argued over this point, but Mary had never become violent.

"So what if Wallace is an ugly old man? So what if they're all ugly old men? What does it matter to you? What does it matter to anyone?"

"Mary, if I hurt you I —"

"You make a habit of hurting me, and I already hurt so much." Mary's voice quivered a little, then she set her jaw against tears and said, "Father was looking for you. He and Anthony have plans for a poetry reading and he wants you to help. Sounds like a waste of everybody's time, but I expect you'll be there with your eager face and your foul spectacles."

"Mary, I'm your sister. I bear you no ill will, so bear me none."

Max came trotting in, and Mary bent to scoop him up. "Dear Max, where does it hurt?" The little dog put out his paw, as though he understood Mary's question. Deborah decided it best to leave Mary alone a while so her temper might cool. She had never seen her so angry, so passionate, before. In truth, it frightened her.

Anne chose suppertime the next day to make her debut as the reformed, clearly spoken woman she had become. In the meantime, she kept her head down and spoke to nobody, afraid that the power to speak would leave her if she dared to boast that she finally possessed it.

But it was with a measure of confidence that she took her seat at the table that evening. Liza had laid out bread and jams and cheese and salted fish. Betty was preparing Father a selection of morsels when Anne took a deep breath and said, "Mary, I would be most grateful if you could pass me the butter."

It seemed everyone stopped what they were doing and stared at her. Father, an uncertain frown on his brow, said, "Deborah?"

"No, Father, 'tis Anne," she said.

Mary passed her the butter dish, wide-eyed.

"Anne, you speak so clearly," Deborah said.

"I believe that perhaps I have outgrown my old stammer."

"Overnight?" Mary said, her eyebrows raised suspiciously.

"Yes. Last night I dreamed that I could speak clearly, and this morning I awoke and it was so." Anne turned her eyes downwards, concentrating on the bread in front of her.

"Why, the other day you stammered like a fool," Anthony said.

"Yes, Anthony, and maybe your taunting finally made me ashamed enough to stop. For that, perhaps, I owe you thanks."

Anthony laughed out loud. Father leaned forward. "Speak again, Anne, for I can barely distinguish you from Deborah."

"What would you have me say, Father?"

"Ah, yes. Your voice is softer, less certain. I shall be able to tell you apart after all. Well done, child." This was the first time her father had ever bestowed his regard upon her, and it stunned her into silence.

"Yes, well done, I suppose," Mary said, scowling.

Anne knew Mary suspected Lazodeus, of course she did. But torture wouldn't drag from Anne the truth about her newfound clarity of speech. She and Lazodeus shared a confidence, and that felt sweet and secret. She glanced at Deborah, who was picking at her food. If her youngest sister suspected that the angel had been involved, she hid it well.

Deborah lay awake for a very long time. She had heard Mary and Anne arguing in whispers for the first half hour after retiring. Mary demanded that Anne confess to having called Lazodeus, Anne rejected the accusation repeatedly, and finally Mary had given up and mumbled something about it being "possible, I suppose" that Anne had spontaneously discarded a lifelong habit.

Deborah refused to believe it. Now she suspected that both her sisters had contacted Lazodeus and tried to hide the fact. But the only way to know for sure was to ask the angel himself.

And this is what she told herself as she crept silently from the room and down the stairs, out through the kitchen and into the garden. She told herself that she was calling Lazodeus to command him to tell whether either of her sisters had been in contact with him, in spite of the solemn vow they had made to wait upon Deborah's investigations.

If, while she was in his company, she asked him a few questions about angel magic, there was no harm in it. It did not mean she was ready to take his side, and forgive him for lying to them about what he was.

It had been a hot day, but now Deborah felt a shiver of

gooseflesh across her back and arms. Above her, the half moon shone dimly on black trees. A cat crept along the stone wall which divided their house from the one behind it. The garden was tiny, no bigger than her closet, but she would be less likely to be heard out here.

She took a deep breath and said, "Lazodeus, I command you to come."

In the next instant he was there, and she had to admit she enjoyed that power.

"Mistress Deborah," he said, bowing low, "what would you have me do?"

"Only tell the truth. Has my sister Anne been in contact with you?"

"Yes."

"And you cured her stammer?"

"Yes."

"And have you also spoken with my sister Mary?"

"Yes."

"And you filled her room with rich objects?"

"Yes."

Deborah shook her head, exasperated. "I don't believe it! We had an agreement."

"No, you tried to force an agreement upon them."

She studied him for a few moments. A church clock in the distance struck three chimes. Was it that late?

He met her gaze evenly. "What do you want, Deborah Milton?"

"Want?" The question threw her. "I . . . I know not what I want."

"I can give you whatever it is you want. Do you want pleasure? I can give you pleasure."

"Pleasure is not pleasure if it is bestowed so easily," she said, stepping back. He suddenly felt too close.

He narrowed his eyes slightly, as though trying to read into her mind. "What is it, then?" he asked. "What do you want?"

"Why are you so concerned with giving me what I want? Will my wish be granted in exchange for my soul?"

He looked as though he were trying to cover a smile. "Your soul?" Then he began to laugh. "Is this why you fear me? You fear that I will take your soul?"

"The soul's fortune is not a matter to be laughed about," she said, standing her ground even though he had inched forward.

"Deborah, you misunderstand me. You misunderstand us. All the fallen angels . . . we are misunderstood."

"Yes, yes, as you have tried to explain ere now."

"I am your guardian. I am your protector."

"You are a liar."

"I have never lied to you. I told you I am an angel and so I am." His voice rose and his face grew angry.

"You are not very patient for an angel."

"Forget what you have heard of angels — fallen or otherwise."

"You ask what I want. I want to know if it is safe to talk with you. I command you to tell me."

"It is always safe."

"And there will be no ill consequences, for myself or my sisters, in pursuing such occult knowledge of spirits and demons and fallen angels? I command you to tell me the truth."

"No ill consequences. None at all."

She fell silent for a long time, contemplating.

"You will grow old if you wait to be entirely sure, Deborah. Nothing is given to us as a certainty." He reached under his tunic. "Here, if you desire to know what your sisters do when you are not with them, use this." He pulled out a small looking glass, embedded in carved stone with a short handle.

"What is it?" she said, warily taking it from his hand.

"It is a scrying mirror, a shewglass. Magic. Go on, look in it."

158

She looked in it, but only saw her own face in the moon-light. "I see nothing unusual."

"Ask it where your sisters are."

Curious now, she leaned close to the mirror and said, "Show me Anne." A mist crept across the mirror, and a vision appeared. Anne, sleeping, curled up on her side.

"Now, pass your hand over the mirror to clear the vision."

She did as he said, and the image disappeared. She realised she hadn't breathed for nearly a half a minute. "I cannot accept this," she said, thrusting the mirror out to him. "I do not wish to spy on my sisters."

"Not just your sisters. Anyone. Your father. Your step-mother. Anyone."

She held out the mirror. "I don't want it. Not until I have made up my mind."

"I cannot take it back."

"Then I shall break it."

"It can only be broken by magic as it is a magical device. Deborah, why are you turning away from this power? Did you not want your life to be extraordinary? Did you not want to know of physic and natural philosophy?"

"Yes, yes, I want those things, but I do not wish to pay too dearly for them. And until I am sure of the price, I will not commit myself."

"Keep the mirror. I can argue with you no longer. Unless you have something else to command me to do, I will take my leave."

"Certainly, go. And take this with you." She held out the mirror one more time. He smiled, then vanished without another word.

"I shan't keep it," she said aloud, even though she was now alone in the garden. Though perhaps it would be prudent to hide it somewhere, in case someone less respon-sible found it.

She crept back into the house and up to her closet. She

wrapped the mirror in an old shift and hid it under the bed, then climbed between the covers.

Sleep would not come. Her mind was in turmoil. The angel, under command, had assured her she was safe; Amelia had admonished her for her fears; her sisters were so certain that Lazodeus was genuine that they had dealt with him secretly.

As dawn broke, she found herself unwrapping the mirror again, laying it in her lap and gazing at her reflection in its gleaming surface.

"Show me Father," she said. And there he was, sitting upright in his chair, eyes closed. But he was awake, she knew. He would have woken with the first birdsong. He was probably thinking, planning his epic in his head. She gazed at his face, thought about all that he had taught her: languages, philosophies, art and poetry. Not the key to the secrets of the universe, and yet . . . perhaps it was enough. She passed her hand over the mirror and wrapped it once more. She hid it securely and vowed not to open it again, climbed into bed and, at length, slept.

8
Flesh to Mix with Flesh

Mary had not seen Deborah all morning, so had assumed she was up early working with Father. When she crept into Deborah's closet to borrow a ribbon, she certainly didn't expect to see her younger sister still lying in her bed.

"Oh, Deborah, forgive me. I assumed you were up and gone."

Deborah sat up sleepily. Her face was puffy and her eyes half-lidded. "So, here is my false sister Mary."

"False? What do you mean?"

"I have two false sisters. You have both lied to me, you have both betrayed my trust, for each of you has spoken with Lazodeus."

Mary feigned innocence. "I know not what you mean."

"The decorations in your secret room, Anne's easy speech. These were granted by the angel."

"That is not so," Mary said, although it confirmed her suspicion that Anne had contacted Lazodeus, damn her. "Wallace gave me the velvets."

Deborah waved her hand. "You needn't lie any more. Lazodeus himself told me."

An awful, hot jealousy grasped her heart. "You have spoken with him?"

"Yes, I have, though you aren't to think I called him for any other reason than to explain your betrayals to me."

"You called him and he came?"

"Yes, why do you gape so? You called him, Anne called him, why should I not call him? Is he not my angel also?"

"But . . . he is no longer ours. We no longer command him."

"What do you mean? You make no sense."

"I . . . He told me we no longer command him."

A moment of distrust crossed Deborah's face. "But he responded to *my* commands."

Mary shook her head. "It cannot be. I made an awful mistake. I commanded him to be our friend, instead of our servant."

Deborah glared at her. "Say you are joking, Mary. Say you did nothing so dangerous as to relinquish our command."

"He said he will still serve us, but as he wishes, rather than as we instruct."

"Then he may have lied to me. All of those questions I commanded him to answer truthfully, he may have lied to every one."

"No, no. He is not a liar."

"I cannot trust the angel. I think that perhaps it were better if none of us ever attempted to make contact again."

"He does not respond to my calls anyway," Mary said, dropping her head. Why? Why had Lazodeus come to Anne and Deborah and not her? Was he punishing her? Did he like her least? A deep well of anger began to boil within her.

"I think I shall rely upon my usual sources for knowledge," Deborah was saying. "I think I will live without the dubious knowledge that Lazodeus offers."

"Oh, so you shall rely upon Father? A useless, blind relic?"

"At least I may trust him. At least he behaves consistently."

"I do not care to listen to such nonsense. I am going to my secret room."

"And may you spend some time in there contemplating what you have done, how you have betrayed us, how you have let ambition come between the bonds of sisterhood."

"Don't be so pious, Deborah. It is unbecoming in a

162

woman of your young age." Mary walked out with purpose, determined to shout and scream and rage until Lazodeus turned up. She fed Max a biscuit from her drawer, then left him behind to go to her secret room. She centred herself on a rich oriental rug and called, "Lazodeus. Come to me." Nothing happened.

"I said come to me. I command you to come!" Her voice grew desperate. "I know that in the last few days you have been commanded by both Anne and Deborah, so you must also be commanded by me!"

A long silence followed, and Mary felt a sick whirlwind of anger rising up inside her. She picked up a candelabra and hurled it at the fireplace. *Crack*. The noise was satisfying. She threw another. "Damn you, Lazodeus. Come to me!" Her voice rose to a shriek. "Come, angel. Be at my command." She began to pick up the cushions and fling them about, tear them with her hands, kick them and stomp them into the floor. "Where are you?" she shouted. "Damn you, where are you?"

Already her rage was diminishing. She sank to the floor among the cushions and wailed. "I hate you, angel. I hate you," she said, and naming the awesome swell of emotions that she felt seemed to help. "I despise you, I . . ."

She trailed off as she noticed movement near the ceiling. A long curtain of gold cloth which she had not seen before, was gently unfurling. "Lazodeus?" she said, hope rushing back into her heart. "Are you here, angel?"

The curtain fell to the ground with a soft whump. She watched it with expectation. Something moved behind it. "Lazodeus?" she asked again, quieter, hopping lightly to her feet.

No answer.

"Who is there?" she said, and her voice wavered slightly.

A man's hand appeared around the edge of the curtain. He wore a gem on each finger. Mary took a step back. If not Lazodeus then who was it?

A man with a long black wig drew the curtain back and stepped out. He was tall and imposing, with a small moustache, dressed in fine gold and blue clothes.

Mary gasped, fell immediately into a curtsy. She had seen him in many portraits. "Your Majesty." When she dared look up, the King was approaching her, his finger held to his lips in a gesture to be silent. She stood straight and waited for him, her heart beating wildly. Had Lazodeus finally decided to grant her request? Did that mean he was nearby, watching? She glanced quickly about the room, but was soon distracted by a brush of the King's fingers across her shoulder.

"Your Majesty, I —"

He pressed his finger against her lip. Said, "Shhh." She curled her tongue around his finger and drew it into her mouth. He caught her around the curve of her back and pressed her against him. How was this possible? Or was anything possible for Lazodeus, with his angel magic? If so, she had been a fool to let him go. The King found her lips with his, pressed hard against them, his moustache bristling against her soft skin. He groaned softly, and she felt a swooning sensation of power. The King, the mightiest man in the land, groaning at her charms. She felt a laugh bubbling on her lips, allowed it to spill over. The King drew back and smiled at her, then indicated she should undress.

He stood back as she unlaced her bodice, slipped it over her head, loosened her skirt and stepped out of it to stand proudly in her shift. He raised his hand to encourage her to continue. As he did and his cuff rode up over his wrist, she thought she saw a red, scabrous patch on his arm. She hardly gave it a second thought as she wriggled out of her shift and stood naked in front of him. A cool breeze crept in the window, making the curtains in the room dance slowly, and bringing gooseflesh up on her skin. The King admired her with a hungry gaze. He stepped closer, taking the weight of her breasts in his hands. A guttural sigh escaped his lips.

"For your enjoyment, Your Majesty," she said in spite of his charge to remain silent.

"On the floor," he whispered, and his voice was low and strange, almost a croak. "And say nothing else."

She lowered herself to the floor and lay back among the cushions, allowed her knees to fall apart slightly, teasing him with the sight of her quim. He gazed down upon her, and his face was a mask of violent longing. She ran her hands over her breasts, inviting him. He knelt next to her, and she reached up for his jacket, trying to push it from his shoulders. He flicked her hand away and shook his head. Instead he loosened his member from the front of his breeches, put a knee either side of her shoulder and forced himself into her mouth. She gagged at first, and then caught his rhythm and watched his face above her. His eyes were closed in ecstasy. She put her hands up to cup his buttocks, and felt that his skin was rough and scaly. Did he have some skin disease? Is this why he didn't want to undress? Why, this was perfect: she had learned something about the King that perhaps none but the closest to him knew. Her hands crept around to the front of his tunic, eased out his shirt and slid her hands under it. The skin on his belly was rough, and so red it frightened her. She hoped he wouldn't pass this illness to her. He fought her hands back down and pinned them at her sides. This was uncomfortable and tiresome. She tried to take pleasure in his pleasure, but wished for him to make love to her in the usual fashion. At least that felt like someone was holding her, appreciating all of her instead of just a single orifice. She closed her eyes, bored, to await his climax. He began to grunt loudly, then the grunts turned to moans, then to yelps. She opened her eyes to watch him, but when she saw what knelt above her, a shock went to her heart.

It was no longer the King. It was a scarlet, scabrous thing, a man-sized toad in fine clothes, its eager face a twisted confusion of bug's eyes, cat's mouth, goat's beard, pig's snout. Had she not had its member rammed so firmly down her throat, she would have screamed loud enough to shatter the earth. As it was, she choked out a shocked grunt, and brought her teeth down hard on its flesh. It yelped and immediately withdrew, clapping a clammy hand over her mouth to stop her screaming. She struggled against it violently, but it had her pinned down.

"Don't scream, Mary," it said in the horrible, whiskery croak that she had taken for the King's whisper earlier.

But all she *could* do was scream, even though her cries remained trapped beneath its palm. Horror was shuddering up through her body in furious tremors. She had forgotten the King, the angel, the whole mess. Escape was everything. She strained against the creature, kicking her legs savagely and trying to turn her head. Seconds drew out into infinity and her heart felt as if it might burst with terror.

"Mary, be calm." Another voice. She looked around wildly. *Oh, thank God, thank God.* It was Lazodeus. The creature released her and cringed away from the angel. She drew her breath to scream but this time Lazodeus dropped his hand over her mouth. "Shh now, Mary, shh. Don't scream, or your sisters will come running in here." He lifted his hand slowly and she drew a great breath.

"What is it? What is that thing?"

Lazodeus turned to the creature and with a gesture of his hand, it disappeared. He returned his attention to Mary. "You must be calm. I will explain all, but first be calm."

She nodded. An unbearable pressure built up behind her eyes and she began to sob. Lazodeus cradled her in his arms, shushed her softly. The horror of the last few minutes, the dashed hopes of the last few months, all weighed upon her like a millstone. As she clung to him damply, she sobbed and sobbed until her body shook. Slowly, she became aware of the marvellous warmth of his body, the achingly gentle movements of his hands as he stroked her hair. Her skin prickled, and she suddenly felt unbearably vulnerable in her nakedness. She sat up, pushed him away and crossed her arms over her breasts.

"I am sorry," she said. "Forgive me, I should dress."

"Mary, do not be ashamed. I have known you since you were a child. Your nakedness is no disgrace."

"I feel strange," she said, and as she said it she knew it for one of the profoundest statements she had ever uttered. "I do not know how I feel." Sweet, aching, empty. "You make me feel strange."

He collected her in his arms once again, pushed her hands away from her breasts and tentatively reached out his own hand. Gently, his index finger caressed a nipple. She gasped. A tremor fluttered up her thighs. "Do you like the strange feeling, Mary?" he asked.

She nodded, her eyes glued to his.

His hand trailed down, down. Her belly twitched as he grazed it. He leaned in and kissed her above the navel, below the navel. His fingers descended. Mary felt her breathing become shallow. What incredible pleasure as he deftly found his mark between her legs.

"Oh," she said, for all other words had been robbed of her.

"Lie back. Let me show you."

She felt unsafe, her self-control slipping through her grasp, the world beneath her listing slowly to one side. He pushed her back among the cushions, stretched out at his full, spectacular length beside her. His full lips descended over one nipple, his fingers moving deliciously inside her, long hot strokes which created tingles and spaces of pleasure which she had never known existed. Too late she realised that this may be what she made her lovers feel, that Lazodeus may be taking from her the very power she took from them. Too late. She was cresting a wave which was rushing to shore; all she could do was abandon her body to its fate. An incredible, shuddering pleasure-pain shot up inside her. She felt herself moving with it, collapsing over it. It lasted a few moments and then died away, leaving her buzzing lightly with warm satisfaction.

Lazodeus sat up and grabbed her shift, laid it gently over her. "Is this angel magic?" she gasped.

"Mary, it is merely the pleasure of the flesh, as I have told you. Do you not enjoy the receiving of it far more than the giving?"

"I shall never give it away again." She reached up to touch his face, her addicted fingers finding solace in the warmth of his skin. A frown touched his brow.

"What is it?"

"I am sorry about the demon."

A cold tickle of memory eroded her pleasure. "That ghastly thing. Where did it come from?"

"Ethereal beings communicate in many different ways. Some demons have the power of insight. I can only imagine that it was privy to one of our discussions, where you begged to lie with the King. It took advantage of your heart's wish. A heart's wish can be a dangerous thing to name."

"Is it gone forever?"

"I banished it. It won't return."

She snuggled her head against his chest. "I'm so glad you came. What would I have done?" And then quieter, remembering the pain. "I thought you must hate me."

"No, I do not hate you."

"You came to Deborah and to Anne."

"They needed me. You have not needed me until now."

She pulled away, shook her hair from her eyes. "That is untrue. I needed you desperately."

He smiled, and once again Mary was fascinated by the faint unearthly glow which rose from his skin. "I am the judge of your needs, Mary Milton. That is my role as your guardian."

"Even a fallen guardian?" she asked, teasingly.

The smile faded. "Be not so glib, Mary. Every day I lament my fallen state. Every day, all of us long to be restored to God's favour."

His admonition, gentle as it was, brought tears to Mary's eyes. "Oh, oh. I'm sorry, I did not mean to . . ."

"Shh, Mary," he said, dropping a gentle kiss on her forehead.

"I do not know why I'm crying," she said. "I feel so strange . . . so different."

He sat up and looked down on her. "Mary, you are not to tell your sisters of what has passed between us today."

She shook her head. "No."

"They will judge you, and perhaps judge me. They would not understand for they are not like you." He touched her bottom lip with his index finger. "Can we not just keep this secret between you and me?"

"Of course."

"One little secret will surely not be noticed in a universe so large."

"Of course. I will not say anything." She was unduly flattered that an angel should want to share such intimate secrets with her. "But, Lazodeus, do you not wish to sample your own pleasures with me?" She smiled in what she hoped was an inviting fashion.

"Mary," he said softly, tracing an idle pattern on her skin. "I am sorry, truly. But ethereal beings take no pleasure in lying with mortals. It is not for us to do that."

Disappointment nearly brought her to tears again. But she told herself not to be such a snivelly mouse and forced a smile. "You will not wait so long to attend me again, Lazodeus?"

"Attend you?" he said, the corners of his mouth turning up wickedly. "Or make love to you?"

"Either, both," she said shrugging.

"Are you expected home any time soon?"

She shook her head. "I argued with Anne last night and

Deborah this morning, so neither of them will have the least care for where I am or what I do."

"Then, let us spend the morning exploring your newfound pleasures."

Impossibly, the sweet ache was starting all over again.

"Do you want me to show you, Mary?" he asked.

"Yes," she said, and the thought of surrendering to him no longer frightened her. It liberated her. "Oh, yes."

9
Like a Black Mist Low Creeping

Candles blazed from every surface, Father played the harpsichord to accompany Betty, and Deborah had never known a party could be so much fun. She had attended birthday parties as a child of course, but this, a real, adult party with loud-voiced men and laughing women, was something new to her.

Anthony had arranged it, of course, and she found it hard to hate him when she saw how much pleasure he brought to Father. Their planned reading night had escalated into this event; men had invited their wives, the withdrawing room had been cleaned and decorated, the harpsichord brought upstairs. All the windows were open to let in the light summer breeze, but it grew very hot and humid in the room. To Deborah, a number of glasses of wine past prudence, the steamy ambience simply added to her pleasure. She had even taken the time to pin her hair up in a fashionable style — the back wound around with beads and the sides falling in long curling tendrils — and to squeeze into one of Mary's less bold dresses. Whenever she moved she was aware of the bounce of curls and the rustle of blue silk. It made her feel quite grown and womanly.

"How drably these women dress," Mary commented wearily, as the three of them stood together with their backs to the window.

"You more than make up for all of them," Deborah

commented, glancing at Mary's scarlet and gold gown.

"Thank you. I believe I look splendid," Mary said with a smile.

"Did Lazodeus bring you that?" Anne asked softly. Her pupils were very round and dark. Deborah had still not grown accustomed to her speaking so easily.

"No, I had it from Grandmamma years ago. I've never had an opportunity to wear it ere now. Besides, I wouldn't order an angel to bring me dresses."

"You ordered him to bring you cushions," Deborah said.

"When we could still command him," Anne added.

Mary sniffed. "There's no point in being sour about it."

"And why should we not be sour?" Anne asked. "You took it upon yourself to —"

"'Twas a mistake!"

"Don't interrupt me while I'm speaking," Anne said.

"You wouldn't be able to speak at all if it weren't for the angel," Mary countered.

"Stop it," Deborah said.

"What does it matter if we no longer command him?" Mary said glibly. "Anne has her heart's wish: she speaks without impediment. I have my heart's wish: a roomful of luxury. Deborah has her heart's wish: to stay as dull as she ever was."

"It is dull to hear the same jokes told again and again," Deborah replied. "So our angel is gone; perhaps 'tis a good thing." She meant it. With Lazodeus no longer at her command, temptation was out of her way. Not that she had stopped thinking about Amelia Lewis's offer of an apprenticeship in magic. She had begun to consider whether she could trust a mortal woman more than she could trust a fallen angel. "Listen, doesn't Father play marvellously?"

"He does," Mary conceded, "but Betty sings extremely poorly."

"She sings like a cat on a fence," Anne added.

Mary laughed. "I'm surprised to see Father enjoying

himself so much. I didn't know the old Puritan had it in him to be so gay."

"I've always told you he's not a Puritan," Deborah said.

"Those two are," Anne said, indicating a soberly dressed couple who stood by the door. "They have refused all drinks, even to Father's health."

Mary turned to look at them. "Perhaps they are smellfeasts."

Anne shook her head. "No, Quakers don't barge into parties uninvited."

"They are guests. Father has many interesting and divers friends," Deborah said. "It simply demonstrates how impartial and tolerant he is."

"Tolerant!" Anne snorted.

"Yes. He even has friends in Italy who are Catholics, to whom he writes weekly."

"He is not so gracious to the Catholics on Leake Street."

"'Tis politics, not prejudice," Deborah replied firmly.

"Deborah, don't defend him on every count," Mary said. "He is human, you know. He does piss and shit like the rest of us."

"Mary," Deborah said, suppressing a laugh, "sometimes you are so coarse."

She smiled smugly. Anne giggled into her glass.

"Oh, go and sing, Mary," Deborah said. "I shall turn mad if I have to hear Betty murder one more note."

"No, I shan't. I hate singing."

"But you have such a pretty voice."

"Yes, sing, Mary," Anne said. "For all our sakes."

Mary needed little encouragement to take the centre of attention. She approached Father, who turned his ear to hear her request, then nodded enthusiastically and dismissed Betty.

"Are you angry with Mary?" Anne asked.

Deborah turned to her sister. "Angry? About Lazodeus?"

Anne nodded.

"I'm unsure. Perhaps I am just relieved." Deborah took Anne's hand. "Why? Are you angry?"

Anne nodded again, more fiercely, and her eyes welled with tears. "Oh yes," she breathed, "I'm unspeakably angry."

"You can speak now."

Mary had started singing, and a group of people had gathered around. Deborah glanced over, then returned her attention to Anne.

"I feel 'tis so unfair," Anne said, dabbing her eyes quickly with her knuckle.

"Anne, I hope you have not developed feelings for the angel which you cannot manage."

"No, no. I suppose I am just sick of people making my decisions for me. I feel I have no control over my own life."

"Very few people feel in control."

"Look at her," Anne said, indicating Mary with a wave of her hand. "She is so independent, so forthright. Nobody ever tells her what to do."

"That is not the case, for she has to abide by Father's decisions."

"She is never here! If he cannot find her, he gets us to do her chores. She is a free spirit."

"Not forever, Anne. None of us can be free spirits forever. We shall have to marry, to bear children, to grow old and infirm." A twinge pulled in her stomach. She desperately wanted to be different from that. Go to the continent; practise medicine; understand natural philosophy. Or be like Amelia: independent, powerful, wealthy, and beautiful even in her old age. But this was not the destiny for which Father was preparing her, was it?

Mary finished her song and started another to enthusiastic applause. Two of the couples had started to dance in the cramped space; the evening had grown almost raucous.

"I wish I could dance," Anne said.

"I will dance with you."

"I'm a cripple."

"We shall dance unevenly then. Come." Deborah pulled on her hand.

"No. I would feel too conspicuous."

Deborah dropped her hand and smiled. "How strange it is to hear you speak so fluently."

"How strange it feels," Anne replied. "And now I shall use my powers of speech to bid you goodnight."

"You are going to bed?"

Anne indicated around her. "Each of these people, at one time or another, has visited with Father and looked upon me disdainfully. I do not wish to keep their company."

Deborah allowed Anne to go, and went to Liza to refill her cup. She was feeling a little woozy, but contentedly so. With Lazodeus out of their lives, she and her sisters were drawing close again. It was more like other, innocent times.

"Deborah, come here, child." This was Father calling her. She hurried over to his side. He had left the harpsichord to a doughy woman in a blue dress, and stood among a group of men by the curtain which separated the withdrawing room from Betty's bedroom.

"Yes, Father?"

"I am telling Thomas and Cyriack about your command of languages. Would you demonstrate?"

She felt her chest puff up proudly. "Of course, Father. What would you have me do?"

"Can you recite a little bit in each?" He turned to his friends. "It is remarkable," he said to them. "You won't credit it."

Deborah took a deep breath to sober herself. She felt very clear and very confident as she launched into a few lines of Greek, of Spanish, then Latin, French, Italian (she even surprised herself how well she managed the first lines of *Inferno*) and, finally, Hebrew. The men gathered around spontaneously applauded, and Father looked very pleased with himself.

"Well done, child," he said. "You may go now."

"Is there nothing else I can do for you, Father?" she asked, disappointed that she was being dismissed so soon.

"No, go and help Liza."

She was not going to help Liza, not tonight with a party spinning around her. Father had turned back to his friends, and she desperately wanted to hear if they would keep talking about her skill in languages. She hesitated a moment, then crept behind the curtain into Betty's bedroom and tiptoed up to where Father stood on the other side. Hidden behind the draping fabric, she heard one of the men in mid conversation.

". . . truly remarkable," he said. "And she's quite a beauty."

When Father replied, there was a frown in his voice. "She's only a child."

The men laughed, and Deborah heard Anthony's laugh among them. He must have joined them. "John," he said, "if you could see her you wouldn't call her a child."

"You should be careful," a man with an affected voice said. "She'll catch a cavalier's eye."

Deborah felt suddenly self-conscious. She was too tall, too big.

"Lock her up like the Italians lock up their daughters," Anthony joked. "'Tis something we could learn well from the Catholics. Women are far too free in London, wandering about unfettered."

"Your Mary sings like an angel," a man with a plain, forthright voice said.

"Mary and Anne have both been a great disappointment to me," he said, and Deborah felt the guilty pleasure of his favouritism again.

"I concur that Deborah is a credit to you," the affected voice said. "How does one train a woman to do such things?"

"By the same method one trains a dog: patience and rewards," Father replied. "For, like a dog, learning is not instinctive for a woman."

A hollow space opened up in her stomach.

"One can develop her appetite for knowledge, though," Father continued.

"How?" Anthony asked.

"Let us return to dogs. What is it that a dog wants above all?"

"Food," offered one.

"No," said Father.

"His master's favour," said Anthony.

"Precisely. One must manipulate a woman's innate desire to please the important masculine figure in her life. So a husband should teach a wife, but first a father should teach a daughter."

"I knew a fellow who trained a cat to ring a bell every time it needed to shit," Anthony boomed, laughing.

"Surely not! Cats cannot be trained."

"As easily as any other creature. Dogs or horses . . . or women."

More laughter. Deborah sank to the floor, her face working to fight back tears. Was this how her father really saw her? Nothing more than a cleverly trained animal, a credit to his ability to exploit her sense of loyalty? She sat very still and listened further, but now their conversation had turned elsewhere. She waited half an hour, and they did not return to that topic. All her enthusiasm for company had evaporated, so she took herself to bed with heavy feet.

Deborah lay, eyes open, reliving the conversation over and over. She felt such keen disappointment. Despite his impatience, his sometimes cruel sense of humour, she had always trusted that Father loved her and even respected her. Trusted that his pride was for her achievements, not his. How could he say that she had no instinctive love of learning? It had been all her care for as far back as she could remember.

But then, was that because Father had developed her appetite for it, as he had suggested to his friends? Was it true, then, that it was to his manipulations she owed her cultivation? She flipped over on her side and groaned; couldn't bear the thought. Was she even the person she believed she was? Her whole identity seemed on the verge of shifting sideways.

She sat up, ran her fingers through her hair, upsetting her hairstyle. Should she wake Anne and talk to her? No, Anne had suffered a lifetime at the hands of Father. She would be unable to understand how it felt ever to have imagined his respect was hers, let alone to learn that respect was a fantasy.

Breathe deeply. Think rationally.

Perhaps it was not as bad as she thought. Perhaps he had said something contradictory after her departure. *Of course, when I speak of women's learning, I mean women in general. Some, like my daughter Deborah, have such aptitude born to them, and these women should be lauded.* She tried to imagine Father saying it: how his face would move, how his voice would inflect. But the fantasy would not form for her, kept falling apart, and he would say instead that women could be trained like animals, and did not know themselves.

She heard the door to the bedroom open and she hoped it was Father, come to apologise. Vain hope. Drawers opened and closed, and she realised it must be Mary, coming to bed. Of course. Father had never been up here; he didn't like the rickety stairs. And even if he knew he had hurt her feelings Father would never apologise. He occasionally admitted he was wrong, but he never said he was sorry for it.

When she heard Mary and Max settle and the room fell quiet once again, she began to wonder where Father was now, to whom he was speaking. The sounds of the party had died off, and she assumed that most, if not all of the guests, had gone home. She still had Lazodeus's scrying mirror, why should she not use it? Just to see if Father was even now telling his guests he had been wrong to say such things earlier. If he did exculpate himself and she never heard it, she would have to carry this wound around inside her needlessly. And using the mirror did not necessarily mean she had taken Lazodeus's side: she still thought him untrustworthy and reserved her decision about whether any more attempts should be made to contact him.

She reached under her bed for the wrapped package, drew it out and hid under the covers. The mirror glowed dimly under her blankets. "Show me Father," she said.

Instantly, the image washed over the surface. He sat with Anthony, and she could see his mouth moving but couldn't hear him speaking. "Let me hear him," she said. Faintly, as though heard from far away, the voices became clear.

"How soon, then?" Father was saying.

"In the next day or so, John," Anthony replied. "And you'd do well to do the same thing. Reports have it many are already dead, and this hot weather is expeditious for the spread of such an illness."

"I shall be sorry to see you go," Father said, and after that evening's insult, her father's unmitigated affection for Anthony — an ill-educated oaf — cut her deeply.

"I shall come again, haply next spring. Until then, you still have your daughters."

"Yes, yes. Deborah is a good scribe, and not a bad reader."

Her heart lifted, and she knew it was coming: the disclaimer she wanted to hear.

"Did you know that Robert Entwhistle's wife has a lover near Ludgate?" Anthony said. Damn him for changing the topic.

"I did not know. Does he know?"

Anthony nodded. "He allows it, for it is rumoured he has no interest in women."

Father laughed and Deborah passed her hand over the mirror, returning the dark and the quiet. Gossip; that was what Father and Anthony did when nobody was around. And Father had the nerve to suggest that women were base and unintellectual. She wrapped the mirror and jammed it under her pillow, rolled over and kicked at her blankets.

A single thought plagued her. *I have been so sorely let*

down. How to prevent it happening again? How to prevent this terrible feeling that she did not even know herself, or her reasons for acting as she did?

"Amelia," she said softly. And in the dark, a resolve was formed.

Betty stood at the end of the alley, looking across at the Baileys' house. No sunlight shone between the jettied houses, and the muddy street smelled of stagnant water. The tiny windows were dark and looked back at her like empty eyes. The Baileys were Catholics, and it was Father Bailey she was particularly interested in.

Too much time had passed since Liza had seen any evidence of the girls dealing with spirits, so much that Liza had begun to doubt what she had seen previously. "Perhaps 'twas just a man," she had said last night when Betty had drawn her on it.

But a man — one glimpsed months ago by a spying maidservant — was not reason enough to order the girls to leave.

She needed somebody who could tell her — and later, John — what the signs of spirit possession were, to know for sure if the girls were dabbling where they shouldn't be. And who better to provide that information than an exorcist?

So why was she hesitating? Was it because she could already hear John's voice in her ears, deriding such Papish nonsense? Then she remembered the party the previous night: the way Mary had upstaged her with her singing, and the thorn of rage quivered again. She had to rid herself of them.

With purpose she crossed the road and knocked loudly on the door. A grey-haired woman opened it.

"Yes?"

"I need to see Father Bailey."

"Come in, child."

Betty followed her in, looking around. The rooms were dark and cramped with heavy, carved furniture. On every surface were idols: crosses, statues of Mary, pictures of Christ.

"Lettice? Who is it?" a male voice called from upstairs.

"A young woman to see you," the grey-haired woman called in return. "Come down." She turned to Betty. "My brother takes time to respond. Please sit down. I'm Lettice Bailey."

"I'm Betty Milton," Betty replied, perching on the edge of a hard chair.

Lettice's eyebrows shot up. "Of the Artillery Walk Miltons?"

"Yes. I am John's wife."

"Well, I am very surprised to see you, as I'm certain my brother will be. I shall be interested to hear your reason for coming."

"I would rather wait and speak directly to Father Bailey," Betty replied, and Lettice conceded with a nod.

Father Bailey took his time. Betty sat on the hard chair, growing more and more anxious, for nearly half an hour passed before he descended the creaking stairs and approached her. He was older than his sister, stooped and white-haired, with only a half dozen rotted teeth in his warm smile.

"Good morning," he said.

"Good morning, Father Bailey. I'm Betty Milton —"

"John Milton's wife," Lettice added quickly.

Father Bailey hid his surprise well. "And how do you require my assistance, Betty Milton?" he asked.

"I need to ask your opinion on . . ." Betty glanced at Lettice, who was gazing at her eagerly. "Father, may we walk? I would speak with you privately."

"Certainly. Wait here while I fetch my coat and hat."

Betty waited another ten minutes while Father Bailey pottered around looking for his coat and hat, and Lettice glared at her icily. When he was finally ready, he led Betty out into the street and down an alley to a walled garden. "I often come here to gather my thoughts," he said, opening the gate and indicating a fallen log under the giant spreading arms of a tree. "Please, sit down."

Betty sat on the log, certain that Father Bailey would not be able to lower himself to the seat successfully. But he was surprisingly nimble for a man his age.

"Now, tell me."

"I must tell you all this in the strictest confidence. John has enemies, and I do not want this information to fall into their hands."

"I swear in Jesus's name I shall not breach your trust."

Betty hesitated, then decided to proceed. "I have reason to believe that my stepdaughters are involved in the calling of spirits."

"I see."

"The maidservant saw them with a man who then disappeared into vapour. I know it is hard to believe but I —"

"It is not hard to believe. Protestant girls may easily be tempted by the devil."

"All I need from you at present is some information on how I could determine if the girls were possessed. Then I can decide what to do about it."

"It will be obvious from their behaviour. Are they rude? Aggressive? Incontinent?"

She thought of Mary. "One of them is, yes."

"Do they possess books of spirits and magic?"

"I know not. The youngest is always reading, but I believe they may be her father's books."

"Reading intensely is very dangerous for young women. They are best not taught to read."

"As I was not," Betty said proudly, then realised that a Catholic was not a person to impress. "Go on."

"If they come by gifts or powers which seem to be beyond their reach —"

"Yes! The eldest has just began to speak clearly after a lifetime of being simple."

Father Bailey shook his head in frightened awe. "Mrs Milton, you have devils in your house."

Betty felt a cold shiver crawl across her skin.

"Do not wait another day ere you have somebody drive them out. I can come this afternoon if you wish —"

"No! I have to discuss all this with John. Tell me, Father Bailey, would you be willing to speak to John, to tell him what you have told me and help me convince him that the girls are involved in necromancy?"

"Certainly, if that is what you want. But I know of John Milton, and I believe I can imagine his response to my presence and my advice."

Betty smiled. "I believe I can, too."

"Better to have me come and drive the devils out when he is not there, and then the problem would be solved."

But it wouldn't be solved, because Betty didn't want the devils driven out so much as she wanted the girls driven out. Cause to evict them was the reason she had come here, and yet now her superstitious heart clenched against the fear of evil in her home, even if so far it was confined to the girls' attic room. "I'm unsure at the moment how to proceed," she said. "Give me time to think it over and I shall return to ask your good advice."

He shook his head. "Do not take too much time, Mrs Milton," he said. "Evil has made its way into your home. It already has three young women. You may very well soon become its next aim."

Amelia Lewis's house was in chaos when Deborah arrived the next day. Gisela showed her into the withdrawing room, but all the cushions and tapestries were gone, the cats were gone and piles of books covered the floor. Amelia sat in the middle of it in a pool of black silk, sorting pamphlets and letters.

"Amelia?" Deborah said.

Amelia looked up. "Hello, Miss Milton."

"Where is everything?"

"I'm leaving London for a while. A great sickness approaches. It is not safe for me or my cats to be within the city walls this summer."

"You're going away?" The timing was impossible; Deborah had only just developed the courage to come to Amelia. "For how long?"

"Until the sickness has passed. Gisela is understandably anxious, and I feel the need to protect my own is greater than the need to help with a cure."

"But —"

"But what?" Amelia said, putting aside a sheaf of papers and cocking her head. "Why have you come to see me?"

Deborah moved towards her and lowered herself to the floor between two stacks of books. "I want to be your apprentice," she said softly.

Amelia smiled. "Wonderful. I'm delighted."

Deborah looked around shyly. "So, if you go away . . ."

"No, no. You can still be my apprentice. Here . . ." She leaned over to select two heavy books from a stack, and handed them to Deborah. "Learn everything in these, and when I return to London, I will give you the demon key."

Deborah was momentarily stupefied at the idea of learning everything in the enormous books. She flicked through a few pages of one: they were covered in tables and charts. Then she realised what Amelia had said. "What's the demon key?" she asked.

"It is the tool with which one controls spirits. You'll need it."

"I am afraid, Amelia," Deborah said. She thought it wise to be honest.

"Fear is your enemy. It will stop you from being who you truly are. Now go. You and your family should leave the city

184

too. Tell your Father, he is a wise man. He'll know it is safer to go."

"What sickness is it?" Deborah asked "And how do you know?"

"I know because I have seen the signs ere now," Amelia replied. "Don't treat my warning lightly. The plague is coming."

"Damn Anthony."

He had caught Mary going up the stairs — on her way out the window and into the secret room to meet with Lazodeus — and told her he had a message to be delivered to Trinity Lane urgently. Never mind that Trinity Lane was practically down at the river; never mind that she had other plans. Never mind that it was stinking hot and the last thing she wanted to do was to wander around all day looking for Anthony's damned friend's house. She had to go, because when she tried to refuse, Father's voice rang out loud and clear from his study. "Mary, you *will* take the message."

So she did, and now she was disoriented, wandering back through the city. She'd lost her way around Bow Lane, where an upturned cart blocked the road and a crowd of eager people had stopped to see if the driver's injuries were fatal. She had tried a shortcut, too preoccupied with thoughts of Lazodeus to concentrate properly, and now she had no idea where she was.

No idea at all.

"Damn Anthony," she said again. Lazodeus only came to her once a week, but when he did he bestowed upon her pleasures of an intensity she had never dreamed possible. The feeling was so addictive, that she sometimes tried to create the same pleasures by herself. But it was never the same.

She picked her way around a pile of horse dung and headed towards the light at the end of the narrow street. Mary considered herself a woman these days. Even with all her previous lovers, she had felt girlish and callow. But now, she carried herself differently, knew herself to be more mature, wiser. Deborah had noticed. "You have grown very calm in the last weeks, sister," she had said.

Very calm. Very satisfied.

She stopped and looked around her. No familiar landmarks. She heard the bells of St Paul's in the distance, oriented herself on the sound and began to walk again. She found another alley and turned into it.

An awful stench hit her nose, and she immediately pulled out her kerchief to cover her face. Only death smelled that bad, and the smell was laid over with smoke. She began to regret taking this shortcut. As the lane meandered further into darkness, she noticed that some of the doors had red crosses painted hastily on them. Plague crosses. Sickness had been through this area. A fire roared in the middle of the alley, the city's attempt to burn off the illness.

"Miss! Miss!" She looked up and saw a young gentleman beckoning to her urgently.

"What is it?" she asked.

"You should come away. Fourteen people are dead and the city hasn't been to collect the bodies yet."

She hurried her step, squeezed past the fire — unbearably hot on a day which was already steaming — and broke free out into the open air again. The gentleman took her arm and led her up towards St Paul's Churchyard.

"Is it very bad?" Mary asked. Her fear of the plague was acute: as a child, she had seen a young prostitute lying in a gutter, freshly dead, the enormous poisonous sores disfiguring her beautiful face and body. "Will it spread?"

The gentleman nodded. "The heat has made it much worse. Many people are leaving the city." He dropped her arm and tipped his hat. "Good day."

"We live outside the city, at the Artillery grounds."

"It is spreading very fast. They are collecting all the dogs and cats within the walls for slaughter."

"They're killing the dogs?"

"And the cats, yes. Go home, get out of the city."

Mary turned and began to run. If they were killing the dogs within the city walls, then it would take no time for them to start killing dogs everywhere else in London. She had to get Max out.

Sweat was trickling in uncomfortable lines between her breasts, across her stomach, down her face, when she arrived home. Flustered and panting, she went straight to Father.

"Father!" she exclaimed, falling at his feet. "Father, we must leave London."

"Leave? What is wrong, Mary?" Bless him, for once he wasn't harsh with her. He could hear the keen desperation in her voice.

"The plague. It is claiming dozens of lives and they fear it will spread."

Anthony, who stood by Father, touched his shoulder. "I'm telling you, John, the girl is right."

Mary couldn't swear it, but it seemed to her that Father looked frightened. "I am uncertain —"

"Father, please. We shall all die horribly." Especially Max. They would cut his throat and let him bleed to death on the back of a cart.

"Do you have somewhere you could go?" Anthony asked.

"Thomas Ellwood spoke at the party of friends in Chalfont: the Fleetwoods. They have an empty cottage."

"Don't waste time, then. Arrange it soon."

"Yes, Father, please."

Father drew his brows down. "You are suddenly very wise, Mary."

"Father, they are killing the dogs within the city walls."

"Ah, the dogs. You still love Max imprudently, I see. That is more like the nonsense I expect from you." He considered a few moments. "I have no desire to die from the plague," he said. "Fetch Betty. We shall make our plans."

"Thank you, Father," she said, breath returning to her lungs.

"Keep the dog inside until then."

"He shan't leave my bedroom."

"Go and tell your sisters."

Mary was so relieved as she climbed the stairs, that she almost forgot Lazodeus. But then the little anxieties came. Could she continue to dally with him if she had no secret room? She almost wavered, but then Max ran out to greet her, tail wagging, affectionate tongue seeking out her hands. She pressed him to her breast, felt his little heart beating hard next to her own. Nothing felt as good as this. She would simply trust that things would work out with the angel, somehow.

Two nights after Mary spoke with Father, the girls were packing to leave London. But it wasn't the leisurely packing which Anne remembered from leaving Grandmamma's: no carefully selecting dresses, laying them gently, rolling ribbons and boxing hair clips. Instead there was a hasty grabbing and shoving, a rush to seize as much as possible in the short time before their conveyance came.

The illness had spread wildly within the city walls, and only yesterday the first death outside the walls occurred. And it was just two streets from their home. Anthony left immediately. Father and Betty had desperately tried to arrange a carriage, only to find that the huge exodus from London had tied up nearly every carrier in the vicinity. Finally, just that evening, they had managed to acquire the services of a man who had an uncovered cart. He waited downstairs for them. Anne was not looking forward to the journey: uncomfortable, exposed, a full night's travel. But it would be endured. They had all learned to fear the plague since childhood. Nobody wanted to die in that manner.

"There is a storm coming," Deborah said from the window.

"Just what we need," Mary muttered. "A downpour."

"Deborah, why are you not packing?"

"I have everything I need in that trunk," Deborah replied.

Mary stood and picked up Deborah's trunk. "'Tis the weight of an elephant. What do you have in here?"

"Books."

"Any dresses? Or will you read naked?"

"I have two dresses, and I wear one. That should suffice me."

Anne tied up her trunk and joined Deborah by the window. Thunder rolled far away, and the sky fluttered with white light. The day had been hot and steamy, and the absence of the sun had barely cooled the world down. In the distance, she could hear a bell ringing, and a lonely voice calling, "Bring out your dead."

"Look," Deborah said quietly, pointing down at the street.

"I can see nothing, it is too dark."

"Over there. 'Tis a searcher."

Anne looked, then caught sight of a man in a hood and a bird's beak. "I wish they would not wear those masks. They look like creatures from a nightmare."

"They have cleansing herbs in the beaks. If they did not use them, they too would die. I dream of one day wearing such a mask, of tending to the sick."

"What is he doing on our street?" Anne asked.

Once again, lightning fluttered, and the girls saw clearly that he was painting a plague cross on the door, only four houses up from them. Anne's stomach hollowed.

"'Tis so close," Anne said.

"Yes," Deborah breathed.

"What if we are already sick?" Would Lazodeus protect them? Or was he out of reach, now that he had taken a burden of punishment to let her speak again?

"Oh, stop it you two," Mary said as she tied her trunk. She picked Max up under one arm and marched to the window, pulled it shut. "We are leaving immediately. This time tomorrow we shall be in the country air and

189

nobody is going to get sick, and nobody is going to die."

"Though we may get drenched," Deborah said, as more thunder rumbled, closer by.

"A small price to pay," Mary said. "Are you both ready?"

Deborah went to her trunk and bent down to check the laces. Anne turned once more back to the window, but now could only see her reflection in the tiny panes.

"Anne?"

All of them heard his voice at once. Anne turned to see him standing very close, casting no reflection in the glass. Beyond his shoulder she could see her sisters: Deborah angry, Mary plainly jealous.

"What are you doing here?" Deborah asked caustically.

He put his back to the window so he could see them all. "I have come to ask you to set me free."

"Set you free? But we no longer command you," Mary said.

"That is correct. However, remember when you first pulled me through into your world, I asked you to have me stay nearby?"

They all nodded.

"I want you to let me go, so that I may deal with others. A great sickness sweeps the city: thousands upon thousands will die. There is much work for ethereal beings at such a time, and I cannot serve unless you set me free."

Anne's heart seemed to liquefy in her breast. The idea of losing him forever was unbearable, but his desire to be free to serve other poor souls was moving, thrilling.

"What kind of work do you do when thousands die?" Deborah asked.

"Ever suspicious, Deborah," Lazodeus said. "I will only say once more that I am an angel, no matter what you believe me to be."

"I think it mightily noble," Anne said. "And of course we'll set you free, if that is what you wish."

"Will we ever see you again?" Mary asked mournfully.

"Yes, of course. When you return to London, I will find you again. I have grown attached to you, all of you."

Anne knew the comment was directed to her. For once, she felt a wave of triumph: Mary clearly adored Lazodeus, but he showed her no special attention at all.

"Will we be long away from London?" Anne asked.

"I know not. The decision is with your father."

"And will any of us die of the plague?" Mary asked.

"No. In fact, I shall ensure that your journey out is safe. Not a drop of rain will touch you, not a breath of wind will chill you. But you must let me go."

"Go," Deborah said with a shrug. "I care not."

"I care, but I will let you go," Anne said softly. Lazodeus smiled at her, and the sweet, churning discomfort of love swelled inside her.

"Yes, go," Mary said. "But do not be too far from us."

"I am your guardian. Fear not. We will all meet again." With that, he disappeared.

"Good riddance," Deborah said, hefting her case with two hands.

Mary looked as though she might make a cruel comment, but restrained herself. Anne wearily picked up her trunk. "They are waiting for us," she said.

Anne thought there was a certain melancholy excitement in their flight from the city. Father, Betty, Liza, Deborah, Mary and Max, and herself all crowded into the back of a dirty cart, with trunks uncomfortably stacked around them in the light of the plague fires. The smell of the horse, the grimy face of the driver, the unsteady rocking as they rumbled down the Walk past the plague crosses, the bonfires burning against the foul air, and the cries of the dead collectors. The sky flashed and rumbled, but no rain fell as they travelled out of the city. Just as Lazodeus had promised.

"It will rain," Father said, and Anne noticed that he clutched Betty's hand very tightly. "We shall be soaked."

"It will not rain." This was Deborah, leaning over and touching Father's free hand firmly. "I promise you, Father, it will not rain."

Anne turned her head, watched the road disappear behind them, occasionally lit by faint lightning. The illness may drag on for months; how long would it keep them away? She imagined herself, sitting in the house at Chalfont waiting interminably for the plague to run its course, yearning and yearning for the company of a being she should never have fallen in love with. The long summer stretched out in front of her like an endless, empty road.

Empty of love. Empty of angels.

An Interlude

Not for the first time, the old woman began to cough violently. During the telling of her story she had coughed in such a way half a dozen times, then recovered and continued. I waited, but when she finally drew breath again she fell silent.

"Is there more?" I asked. I wanted very much to hear more.

She shook her head. "Not now. Not now, Sophie. I am tired. You will have to come back."

I snapped off my tape recorder. "This evening? Tomorrow?"

"No, not that soon." The old woman cast her gaze towards the bookshelf. "Sometimes I am so weary."

"When?" I asked, and noted with curiosity that I sounded desperate.

"A week and a day," the old woman said. "Not before."

"So next Thursday? Next Thursday is okay? Can I come in the morning?"

"The same time as today. Mornings are hard for me. Go now. Can't you see I'm tired?"

Of course I could see she was tired — slumped in her chair with her eyes cast down — but I held on to the hope that she would continue. She didn't. She turned towards the window, and said nothing more.

"I'll see you next week, then," I said.

She didn't answer. I went down the squeaky stairs, and out into the street. An afternoon breeze had picked up, and it cleared my head of the stuffy heat in her room.

As I walked back to Old Street, I began to feel empty and despondent. It was unusual for me to feel this way: in my opinion, melancholy was reserved for those who haven't enough to occupy themselves. But melancholy was how I felt. A vague yearning had started deep in my stomach. I didn't feel like going home, I wanted to ramble a little while. I changed trains a few times, watching the ebb and flow of business people and tourists as they came and went, and I finally came above ground at Covent Garden. I wandered down to the market and eyed the goods on display, but saw only expensive rubbish. The warm sun kissed my shoulder, and it only reminded me of how long winter can be sometimes. A beautiful, slender soprano sang 'Danny Boy', but her sweet voice hadn't the power to move me. I thought, *I am in London — flower of all cities — and it all means nothing*. I reasoned it must be the lack of Martin in my life, but then even the thought of Martin, even imagining having him back again, did not seem enough, could not soothe my melancholy. Say we reunited — time would still march on, age me, kill me, and what had I really done? What had I done with my life that meant anything or changed anything or could make any difference to the way I felt now? My existence struck me as a hollow illusion. But somewhere, somewhere deep in the past, glimmered a memory of lost happiness, some perfect satisfaction which had slipped through my fingers. I didn't know what it was, but I ached for it like a teenager aches for first love.

I walked home through hot, crowded streets. Mrs Henderson called out to me as I was about to let myself into my room.

"Sophie, a man dropped this off for you." She held out with both hands a black, zipped bag. I took it from her. Neal's spare laptop.

"Thank you, Mrs Henderson."

"Is he your boyfriend?"

"No."

"Because I charge extra if two people sleep in your room, so if he stays over you have to —"

"He's not my boyfriend. I said he's not my boyfriend. I don't have a boyfriend."

Mrs Henderson took a step back, and it was only then I realised how angry and impatient I must have sounded.

"I'm sorry," I said. "I've had a bad day."

"I haven't sorted the mail yet. I'll leave it on the hall table."

"Thank you."

I let myself into my room, placed Neal's laptop on the bed, and grabbed a towel and some fresh clothes. I stood under the shower a long time, letting the water run over my head as though it could wash out this unwelcome depression. It couldn't. I returned to my room, picked up the laptop, and sat on the bed. I unzipped the case, and a folded letter looked back at me. I groaned. *Please, no declarations of love. Not today.*

"'Dear Sophie,'" I read aloud. "'Here is the computer I promised you. Please don't feel uncomfortable about accepting it as a gift.'" I didn't. "'I know you don't have much money, and I'd like to help out, because I sense something very special about you. Love, Neal.'"

I wondered how long he had agonised before writing "Love, Neal." Had there been other drafts of this letter; ones which ended "Regards, Neal", or "Sincerely, Neal", or even just "Neal"? If I wasn't feeling so sorry for myself, I might have felt sorry for Neal, unwittingly helping me out with the tools I needed to expose his and his colleagues' foolishness. I fiddled for a few hours copying old files onto a disk and loading them up on the new machine, testing the keyboard, changing the settings, anything to distract me from the empty feeling. It was early evening when my stomach growled, reminding me I hadn't eaten since breakfast.

I pinned up my hair — greasy — pulled on a light jacket, and headed out. I collected my mail from the table in the hallway and stuffed it in my bag to read later.

The Bishop's Gate had become my local. It was a nice pub, in the old-fashioned way; it was small, they knew my name, and they let me run up a tab. On that evening, it was particularly crowded. I ordered a pork pie, a plate of chips and gravy, and a pint. As I turned around to scan for a spare space, an elderly couple vacated a corner table. Perfect. I sat down with my beer and pulled out my mail.

The first sip of beer didn't numb the melancholy, and I wondered just how many sips it would take. I knew I'd drink as much as necessary to anaesthetise myself, to drive away the despondency, to forget the sound of the old woman's voice. A week and a day. It seemed an eternity away.

I opened the letter from my mother. I scanned it quickly, decided to save it until later. The second and third envelopes were bills, one of them overdue. I took a couple more gulps of my beer, and signalled to Laura behind the bar to bring me another with my dinner. The fourth and fifth letters were addressed in my own handwriting: responses from literary agents to the queries I had sent out about the book.

My dinner arrived. I lingered over breaking the seals.

Dear Ms Black, thank you for your letter. I regret to inform you that . . .

Dear Sophie, We appreciate you considering our agency in submitting your query, but unfortunately . . .

I crumpled them up, one then the other, and stuffed them into the ashtray. I played disconsolately with my chips. Once again, this was unlike me. I usually handle rejections brilliantly: stepping stones across the river to success.

The first taste of food made me ravenous. I devoured the pie and chips in minutes, washing them down with more beer.

More beer. That's what I needed. Laura was already on to it: another pint arrived at my table as the plates were cleared.

"You look like you could use it," Laura said.

"Thanks."

She weaved off between tables, clearing glasses and plates. I reopened Mum's letter and began to read.

"'Scuse me?"

I looked up. A short man with slicked-back hair stood in front of me, pointing hopefully at the spare seat. "Is this seat taken?" he asked.

I noticed the square bulge in his pocket. "Can I have a cigarette?"

He drew out the packet and offered me one, lit it for me as he sat down.

"I'm Dave," he said.

"Sophie," I replied, dragging. Gorgeous, perfect headspin.

"What do you do?"

For a moment the question made no sense. Nobody had made small talk with me in a long time. Then I caught his meaning. "I'm a journalist. You?"

"I clean windows." He pointed at my near-empty glass. "I'm going up to the bar. Can I buy you another beer?"

I picked up the glass and drained it, handed it to him. "Make it a vodka."

Drunk, drunk, drunk. I stank of smoke and I was bumping into things like a toddler. I couldn't remember if I'd let Dave feel my arse, or if he'd just asked if he could. Either way, I'd laughed at him, and he'd withdrawn all cigarette and vodka privileges immediately after. Even Laura looked disapproving as I stumbled from the Gate at closing time, promising to pay my tab the next day when I was sober enough to sign a cheque. I found my way home, peed for what seemed like half an hour, then blissfully, blissfully peeled off my clothes and dropped into bed.

Quick emotional check-up: no, not depressed. Not wishing till it hurt to return to the old woman's place and hear more. Just tired — weary to the bone — and drifting on a wave of drunkenness into a sleep which seemed like catatonia.

Maybe half an hour later — not long, I know that much — I began to drift upwards into consciousness again. I could hear her voice echoing in my ears, and I yearned for her. I yearned for her company, the strange stuffy smell of the room, the story, all of it. I yearned and yearned and it hurt me so much that it woke me up. For the first time, I wondered if Neal and Deirdre and the others could be right: if it was possible to put a spell on someone through telling a story. Then I sat up, fully awake, and knew that drunkenness was leading me to stupid conclusions. I got out of bed to start transcribing the tapes.

The second day was worse than the first, and the third was worse than both. I would have done anything to fill the emptiness growing inside me. I began to spend money recklessly. I went out for breakfast, lunch and dinner, drank whole pots of coffee, bought donuts to take home with me, bought cigarettes which I smoked quickly and desperately. I consumed so many toxins I made myself sick. I spent those two afternoons lying flat on my bed, nursing nausea and dizziness, hopelessly trying to name the thing that would make me feel better. But I could not even begin to imagine what it was that I was so keenly missing. I felt moderately better when I sat down to transcribe the tapes, but it was a shadow of satisfaction, really, like imagining sex rather than engaging in the real thing.

By the fourth day, I was motivated to act. I was certain I'd go crazy if I didn't at least try to do something constructive. I did what I do best: research. I read all about Milton. I even read parts of *Paradise Lost*, though it was hard going for a reader accustomed to the rhythms of Ruth Rendell. I discerned this much from my day's research: Milton did indeed have three daughters, one of whom was lame and simple. They were reportedly at odds with him often. He was blind, and he did dictate his writings to them; not much information was available about his daughters, and certainly no suggestion of a guardian angel, fallen or otherwise, had made its way into the mythology. I walked home from the library in a light summer rain, letting my hair get soaked, almost enjoying the smugly sympathetic glances of the umbrella-ed class. Yes, they could tell I was miserable, maybe the most miserable person to walk along Euston Road in its entire history. Perhaps naively, I started to explain my depression as a delayed effect of splitting with Martin. I had spent all these weeks feeling numb, trying to feel nothing, and now it had overwhelmed me. It was that simple. Somehow, spending time with the old woman, hearing a story about love and loyalty, had cracked open my heart and let the hurt into the rest of my body.

My reaction to Chloe's phone call that evening surprised me. She asked me over for a special dinner party with the Lodge members the following night. When I got off the phone, I was practically elated. Perhaps, because the Lodge was the first place I'd heard about the old woman, Neal and the others had grown more attractive in my estimation. Certainly, I felt none of the usual bored resignation about attending a Lodge meeting. The twenty-four hours until dinner couldn't go quickly enough for me.

But a low point first. The following day, the day of the dinner party, I spent my last thirty pounds — which I'd been saving to buy a new printer cartridge — on a bottle of wine and more cigarettes. When I came home to change for dinner, I sat on my bed for a long time considering what I'd done in the last few days, realising I now had no way of earning more money because I couldn't print out the half dozen articles I had on the computer. I sobbed, but only once, then collected my breath. I promised myself not to think about it, not until after Thursday, not until after I'd been back to see the old woman. Until then, nothing mattered. I would live like nothing mattered.

Consequently, I was already drunk when I turned up at Neal and Chloe's, half an hour early. The pain in my heart had become unbearable, and being in company promised to help me decompress a little. Chloe answered the door. She wore an apron over a peach twinset.

"Sophie, you're early," she said, but there was no impatience in her voice.

"I'm sorry, I was bored," I said, trying to appear sober.

"Come in, come in. You can always drop by if you're bored."

I followed her into the kitchen. "Can I help with something?" I asked, dreading her saying yes. I was not a good cook at my soberest.

"No, no, it's all under control. Neal!" she called, going to the doorway of the kitchen. "Sophie's here."

He was with us in seconds, buttoning up his shirt, pink-faced and smelling of aftershave. "Hello, Sophie." He gave me a quick peck on the cheek, and I noticed my heart was beating faster. Of course, one way to fill the emptiness would be sex, but I had avoided thinking of that until now. But with Neal? What about Chloe? What about my standards? I stepped back, the careful soberness of those who know they are close to being exposed making my words and movements precise.

"Hello, Neal," I said, not meeting his eye. These invisible urges are always perceptible whether we admit it or not, and he had sensed my body's sudden openness. He gazed at me hopefully while Chloe chopped carrots behind us.

"Would you like a drink?" he asked.

My brain said no, but the head it lived in was nodding. "Sure," I said.

"Red wine or white?"

An old school friend's voice came back to me: don't mix your drinks. "Red, thanks."

Soon I was furnished with a glass of wine and the three of us were sitting around the table while dinner — smelling deliciously of garlic, butter and onion — cooked in the oven.

"You said you were bored, Sophie," Chloe asked.

"Yes, I can't seem to get my head together to study these last few days," I said.

"You should drop by the shop if you're bored," Neal suggested. "We could always go for a coffee."

"I've started smoking again," I admitted guiltily. "I'd stopped for a couple of months."

Chloe frowned. "I have asthma. You won't be wanting to smoke here, will you?"

"No, I didn't even bring them with me. I know how anti-social it is. And it's so expensive. Today I spent my last few quid on cigarettes. I don't know what's wrong with me." I was talking way too much — far more than I wanted to — but the emptiness required it. For my entire career, I had relied on the stupid neediness of other people to drive them to talk too much. I didn't like it happening to me.

"We can loan you some money, if necessary," Neal offered. "Can't we, Chloe?"

Chloe's smile didn't quite reach her eyes. "Of course. Do you want some money?" I saw her glance at Neal, and realised she knew he had a crush on me. I wondered how many times previously his wandering libido had come to her attention.

"No, I expect I'll manage."

"Sophie, you don't seem yourself," she said softly, and now the genuine care was back in her voice. "Are you a little down about something?"

"Everything," I blurted, and gulped the remains of my wine.

"Let us refill that for you," Neal said. "Is it about this ex-boyfriend?"

"He's not really my ex. That is, I still consider him my partner. The break is only temporary, I know it is."

They exchanged the fool's-paradise glances, as I knew they would.

"We can introduce you to some nice men," Chloe said. "If you'd like some male company, nothing serious." She fetched the wine from the kitchen bench and brought it to the table, sliding into a chair opposite.

"Chloe, I'm sure that's not what Sophie wants." Not what he wanted either, I knew.

"Thank you, but no," I said. "I'm fine, really. Just a bit melancholy."

"It happens to all of us, dear," Chloe said refilling my glass. I was heading into dangerously drunk territory.

"What brought it on?" Neal asked. "Because a feeling always starts with a thought."

A chime on the doorbell had Chloe springing out of her seat. "Excuse me, that's probably one of the other guests."

Three of the other guests, actually: Marcus and Mandy, who I had now picked for a couple, and Deirdre behind them. Chloe ushered them in ahead of her, clucking about wine and entrees and poor Sophie who was feeling a little depressed. Mandy sat her bony body next to me, big-jawed Marcus offered Chloe a bunch of flowers, and Deirdre . . . well, Deirdre took one look at me and shrieked.

"Deirdre, whatever's the matter?" Chloe said, rushing over.

Deirdre glared at me, her left eye fluttering like a shutter in a breeze. "Where have you been?" she said. I was drunk, so this frightened me.

"What do you mean?" I asked. My mouth grew dry.

"Where have you been? What have you heard? How much? Is it all over?"

"Deirdre, you're making no sense and you're frightening poor Sophie," Neal said.

Deirdre turned to him and shook her head. "It's us who should be frightened of her. She's been to see the Wanderer."

The upshot was I was kicked out. Politely, of course. Chloe was practically in tears as Marcus and Deirdre insisted over and over that I had to leave. I was a danger to them. I had brought the compulsion with me. I could not be trusted to keep it to myself. I was to have no further contact with them until they had worked out what to do about me. I threw the last of my wine down my throat, got up unsteadily and attempted a dignified exit. Neal offered to show me out, but I said it wouldn't be necessary.

He followed me, of course, Deirdre calling out behind him to be careful. When we were clear of the building he pulled me over and pressed my back against the window of a closed shop.

"What? What is it?" I asked impatiently.

"How did this happen?"

"I didn't believe you. I wanted to know what the old woman's story was."

"You didn't believe us?"

"Sorry."

"No, we should be sorry. You were so new to it all, Deirdre came in, and she had been touched by the spell. It was still with her and it transferred to you. Tell me the truth. Why did you go to see her?"

"I just wanted to."

"You had to? You felt compelled?"

"A little," I agreed.

He ran his hand through his hair and groaned. "I feel so guilty. It's our fault — it's Deirdre's fault. We exposed you to this, so we're going to have to help you get out of it. How much have you heard?"

"Some, not all of it."

"You can't go back."

I groaned. "I'll die if I don't go back."

"Much worse will happen if you *do* go back."

"I'm so confused. I have never felt so bad in my life."

"Don't worry, I'll speak to the others. We'll take care of it.

Just promise you won't go there tonight. Promise me."

I didn't tell him it was impossible for me to go there tonight, that I still had three days to wait. "I promise, I swear."

He shoved his hand in his pocket and pulled out his wallet. "Let me give you some money."

"No, there's no need," I said with absolutely no conviction.

"I insist. It's our fault, it's all our fault, and we'll take responsibility for it."

He offered me sixty pounds, which I took and put in my bag.

"It will be all right, Sophie," he said. "You're not to worry."

I flung my arms around him and for a surprised moment he held me close. I would have taken him home then and engaged in hours of intense sex, ultimately meaningless and certainly not the satisfaction I craved. But, as I suspected, he preferred to have his affairs in his imagination. He resisted my kiss, left me smacking my lips against empty space.

"Sophie, I have to go," he said regretfully. "The others will be worried and they might come looking for me. But don't worry, we'll help you."

I nodded, tight-lipped, as he turned and walked away. I saw him disappear into his building, and I sagged against the window and I cried. His offer of help when I felt so helpless was more than my sad heart could bear.

It is interesting to me, now, to note how much time passed before I accepted that my melancholia had anything at all to do with the supposed curse of the Wanderer. But then, one can believe something for a long time before one will say it out loud, even form a coherent thought about it. *I believe I am under a curse.* Those words did not organise themselves into a sentence in my head for a very long time, and certainly not directly after being shrieked at by Deirdre and offered money by poor, bumbling Neal. As I walked home I swore at them all for fools, and for having put the idea in my head that a curse would come over me if I talked to the old woman, for certainly I was downhearted and suggestible, and that's why I had fallen into this depression. As I sat on my windowsill, chain-smoking, I reasoned that Deirdre had had contact with the old woman herself, and that was how she knew I had been to see her; and she had used that information to frighten me. As I lay in bed, kicking at the covers then pulling them back on, I decided Chloe had put her up to it because she knew Neal fancied me, and all the sweetness and concern were just a front for darker feelings.

As I sat up at three a.m. and finished transcribing the tape, and read some more of *Paradise Lost* and skimmed through another biography of Milton, I felt a little better — just a little. And I didn't know why, though I felt vaguely frightened.

When I awoke at ten o'clock the next morning, I fought with my impulses for around ten minutes, then got dressed and walked down to Soho for breakfast at a patisserie. I was cramming my face with apple danish and strong, strong coffee, when I looked up and saw a familiar figure on the street outside. Marcus from the Lodge of the Seven Stars. He saw me look at him, and ducked away. Strange. But then, perhaps I had been mistaken.

In any case, I barely thought about it for the rest of the day, being so taken up with my growing despondency. It was only later that evening that it became important.

I couldn't return to the Bishop's Gate because I owed them so much money, so I walked down to a pub on Tottenham Court Road. There was a big uni crowd, and I felt a bit old and a bit ordinary amongst all the bright young things from University College. The pub was much trendier than my usual preference; odd jazz music played, people drank cocktails and spirits, the decor was in stark, unexpected colours. I nursed a beer in the corner for most of the evening and didn't make eye contact with anybody. Then, when I left at closing time, there he was again: Marcus, lurking across the street. And I knew that they were watching me. This was Neal's grand idea for helping me: to watch me until I attempted to go to Old Street, and then stop me seeing the old woman.

I was annoyed. I walked right up to him and said, "Are you following me?"

"Sophie, what a coincidence to see you here," he replied, grinning his square grin. "Do you want me to walk you home?"

"What's all this about?"

"We're trying to help you."

"I'm going home now, and I don't need an escort."

"I'll come with you and make sure you get there safely."

He walked alongside me, asking me occasional questions, but I maintained an aggravated silence.

"Goodnight," he said, as I turned the key in the front door lock.

"Goodnight."

He watched me go inside, then took off. I showered and got ready for bed, wondering why they thought it was safe for me to be left alone overnight. But then as I went to the window to draw the curtains I saw, in a car parked across the road, Deirdre sipping from a thermos. She must have pulled the short straw for the first night shift.

Surely they wouldn't keep it up for the rest of the week? Surely they couldn't stop me from actually going to see the old woman? I was furious with them for being so certain I was in some kind of supernatural trouble, because their conviction — a conviction that led to them giving up sleep and taking out a twenty-four hour watch on me — frightened me to death.

The pressure built and built and built. The urge to return to the old woman and hear the rest of the story felt like unerring instinct. And it was still two days before I could return. I could not have felt more desperate had I been a week without food or water. I woke up distracted, depressed. I cried at cat food commercials in Mrs Henderson's television room. I smoked until my coughing threatened to split me in two. On Tuesday I started drinking at ten in the morning.

The strangest thing was that, despite my attributing the depression to post-Martin break-up, I had all but forgotten him. It was not his face which I imagined at night, his voice or his smile. It was the old woman I fantasised about — the image of her silhouetted against the dusty sunlight — and I felt lost and forlorn in her absence.

My resentment against Chloe began to build to dangerous levels. It was her jealousy that had made all this happen: she had plotted with Deirdre and the others to scare me half to death and make me think I was under a curse, and in my fragile emotional state it was working. This was just the kind of psychological torture that the Lodge — their heads so full of stupid ideas about magic and the universe — would dream up. My conviction that Chloe was behind it all was magnified by the fact that I never once saw Neal on watch. If I had been thinking straight, I would have remembered that Neal was the only one of them with a full-time job, and that I didn't really know who was watching me half the time. They tried, for the most part, to sink into the shadows.

It was late afternoon, the day before I was to return to the old woman, when I stepped out to buy something that might help me sleep. I was determined to go to bed even before the sun went down, and to sleep through what promised to be the longest and most agonising night of my life. I bought some herbal sleeping remedies at Boots, and then a bottle of wine with which to wash them down and improve their effectiveness. I was shoving these items into my bag when I caught sight of Chloe watching me from inside an electrical shop. A dull rage began to throb inside me, and I wondered just how far she would go, how far she would follow me, and what she would do to stop me.

I hurried up to Goodge Street station. The lift was beeping and I got in; the door closed just as she arrived. On the platform, a train was waiting. I stepped on, but then the train didn't move for a minute and I saw Chloe get on in the next carriage. I changed at Euston and she followed me, and I knew I was going to Old Street, and she probably knew too and was panicking. It would have been so easy to lose her, and I felt smug and relieved, because they couldn't really stop me. The closer I came to the old woman's residence, the more the pressure began to lift, and I felt light-headed.

I saw Chloe on the platform at Old Street, and I broke into a run and sprinted away from her, up City Road as fast as my legs could carry me — which was significantly faster than her — to Bunhill Fields burial ground. Then I crouched behind a headstone and waited, waited.

Chloe appeared a few moments later, puffing, dashing through the cemetery. She didn't see me, and I sprang out and pounced on her with a loud, "Ha!"

She shrieked, and I laughed. She tried to laugh too, but it was uneasy, and I think she knew my laugh was hysteria and not amusement.

"What are you doing, Chloe?" I asked, no longer laughing.

"I —"

"You've been following me. All of you have been watching me and following me, but do you see how easy it would be for me to get away from you if I wanted?"

"Sophie, we're only trying to help."

"Help? By putting stupid ideas in my head that scare me half to death and make me depressed and crazy?"

She gazed at me like a trapped bird for a moment. A light wind moved in the treetops and a threesome of tourists walked by.

"Sophie," she said softly, "if you feel depressed and crazy, that's not because of us."

"Yes, it is. You and Deirdre hatched this between you because you can't stand that Neal fancies me. Yes, that's right, I've noticed too. You've preyed on the fact that I'm lonely and vulnerable and you've put this idea in my head and now I can't get it out." My voice shook and I started to cry. Chloe tried to touch my shoulder.

"Don't touch me," I said, shaking her off violently and taking a few steps away.

"Sophie, you feel this way because of the curse. And the only way to make it better is to fight it, and not go back. Because if you hear the story until the end, things will be much worse."

"How could I feel worse than I feel now?" I sobbed. "I hate you for what you've done to me."

"I haven't done anything, and if you look in your heart you'll see that. I think you know, deep down, what's really going on here."

"Don't give me your stupid new age crap. How stupid do you think I am? As stupid as you? Do you realise what idiocy you lot go on with? Do you realise how ridiculous you all look?"

I saw Chloe glance over my shoulder and spun round to see Neal approaching. I looked back at Chloe.

"I called him from the station," she said apologetically.

"Come on, Sophie, we'll give you a lift home," Neal said as he came closer.

"I don't want to go home." I wanted to sit right there, in the cemetery, as close as I dared get to the old woman, because I feared if I turned up at her place early she may refuse to see me ever again.

"It would be better if you fought it, Sophie. Why don't you have lunch with Chloe, take your mind off it? Our treat."

"All right," I said, because they didn't know it was impossible for me to return to the old woman yet. "All right. You're both right, I have to fight it."

Neal put an arm around me, and Chloe let him. They bundled me into Neal's car, and drove me away from the cemetery. The hideous anxiety began to clutch at my stomach harder and harder the further we drove. I began to whimper as we pulled up outside a cafe near the British Museum.

"You girls have a nice lunch together," Neal said. "I have to get out to Greenwich this afternoon."

"Goodbye, darling," Chloe said, leaning over to give him a kiss. She helped me out of the car and Neal drove off.

"Don't worry, you've done the right thing," Chloe said as we walked into the cafe. "The first refusal is the hardest. Next time you feel like going back, it will be easier to resist."

I didn't reply. I didn't really have the energy. I was half-drunk, exhausted, strung out, hadn't washed my hair in four days, hadn't changed my clothes in two, and was completely out of control of my emotions. I was weeping, and didn't even realise it until Chloe handed me a tissue. Chloe sat me down and went to the counter to order for both of us. I put my head in my hands, leaning on the table as though it were the only thing holding me up.

"Sophie? Sophie Cabrel?"

I looked up. A well-dressed man in his mid-thirties stood in front of me, and it took me a moment to recognise him. Terry Butler, a friend of Martin's.

"Oh, hello," I said, straightening up, self-consciously pushing my hair out of my eyes. "Terry, isn't it?"

"Are you all right?" he asked. "You look unwell."

"I am . . . I haven't been . . ." I began to weep again, and I knew somewhere in some other consciousness that this was bad, very bad, because Martin was supposed to believe that I was happy, healthy, hearty and doing just fine without him.

"Can I buy you a coffee?" he asked. "Perhaps you can tell me what's wrong."

"I'm with a friend," I managed, pointing at Chloe, who was returning. "I'll be fine, don't worry."

"Hello," Chloe said, looking curiously at Terry.

I introduced them and they exchanged greetings.

"I'll be on my way then," said Terry, holding up a paper takeaway bag as evidence. "Sophie, I'll say hello to Martin for you."

I tried to smile but couldn't, so I grimaced at him as he left, then slumped onto the table.

"It will be all right," Chloe said, patting my hand. "Don't worry."

I knew that. I knew it would be all right. Because tomorrow I would be with the old woman again.

* * *

I didn't realise how foolish I had been until the following day, the glorious promising day of my remedy. My adventure with Chloe, leading her all over town, bragging about how easily I could lose her had, of course, made them twice as vigilant. Exactly twice. When I peeked out the window in the morning, there were Marcus and Mandy. Waiting, chatting to each other, no doubt ready to grab me if I went out the front door.

"Damn," I said. "Damn, damn." I paced the room. I had planned to leave mid-morning, lose my guardian on the underground, and come up at the Barbican because they would be expecting me to go through Old Street. I knew that by the time I was in the old woman's building, they wouldn't come near me. They were too afraid. Deirdre had wanted me thrown out of the dinner party on Sunday because she feared contamination. There was no way they'd break in and grab me once I was there.

Still, I'd rather they didn't even know.

I dressed and made a tentative trip to the bakery for breakfast donuts. Marcus and Mandy flanked me as soon as I left the building.

"How are you feeling?" Mandy asked, her anorexic chin trembling in fear as she assessed how much weight I'd managed to put on in just a week.

"Terrible," I said. "Just awful."

"But you did it," Marcus said encouragingly. "You refused to go back yesterday, and that must mean you're feeling more able to keep refusing."

"It does, it does," I said. "I'm just getting some food, and then I'm going back upstairs to work all day. Take my mind off it."

They seemed to accept this. I suppose it was easier for them to accept it than to continue worrying about when I'd make my break for it.

I took refuge once again in my room, the curtains drawn tightly. At mid-morning I peered out and saw Neal and Art had relieved Marcus and Mandy. My palms were wringing wet, and I trembled all over. I should go soon, I should be on my way soon. She was expecting me. If they stopped me, would she refuse to see me another day? I gasped at the thought, suspected I might die if that were the case. I had to get out of the building some other way.

I went to the bathroom and pushed open the window to assess it as an escape route. It would be a tight squeeze, but I could fit. The drop was fairly steep, but there were two drainpipes running side by side; their curves would make good footholds. From there, I could disappear up the alley, come out near Euston Road, and walk down to Great Portland Street for a train.

Shaking with fear and anticipation, I returned to my room to gather my things. Tape recorder, fresh tapes and batteries, notebook. I caught sight of myself in the mirror over my wash basin and barely recognised myself. None of this mattered. Nothing mattered but the knowledge that I would soon be in her company. I took one last glance out the front window — Neal and Art were sitting on a fence talking — and went to the bathroom.

I limped all the way from the Barbican to the old woman's house, on account of a four feet fall from a slippery drainpipe. I barely felt the pain, but knew by tomorrow my ankle would swell and I would be in tremendous pain walking on it. The thought of tomorrow, though, was an alien one to me, like the thought of one's own mortality. Yes, it would happen eventually, but for the present it hardly seemed possible.

She was waiting for me, eyes fixed on the doorway. "Sophie, you've come back."

"It's been agony," I moaned, closing the door behind me. "Friends have been watching me. I hope they don't come up here."

"They won't. Not once I start talking. It will keep them away."

"What's happening to me?" I asked as I set up my tape recorder. "Why do I feel so terrible?"

"I warned you when you first came."

"You didn't tell me it would hurt so much."

She shrugged. "I warned you. That was the extent of my obligation."

"It doesn't matter," I said, sitting on the floor, then giving up on any pretence of propriety and stretching out full-length on the bare boards, on my back, waiting for her voice as an exhausted woman waits for sleep. *It's coming. Sweet, sublime relief.*

"Where was I?" she said.

"The plague."

"Oh, yes. They left London. And they were away for many months. Around a quarter of London residents were afflicted and died. It was the worst plague in living memory."

And so — thank the Lord — at last she spoke.

10
Who Could Seduce Angels?

Mary raced into the kitchen, Max running at her heels, and stopped short. "Death! It smells terrible in here!"

"What did you expect?" Deborah said, stacking coal into the fire. "It has been locked up for nearly a year."

"Locked up with a dead rat in the chimney," Mary muttered, scooping Max into her arms and pressing him against her face. Six months without a bath and he smelled better than their kitchen.

After a long bumpy journey, the family had finally arrived home to the house on Artillery Walk. While her sisters, Father and Betty had brought in the trunks and opened the windows, Mary had spent ten minutes running up and down the street seeing which of their neighbours were still alive. And checking, of course, if anyone had moved into the house with her secret room. Luck was still on her side.

"Well, Mary?" Father said, leaning on the table. "Who is alive and who is dead?"

"The two old people on the corner are dead, the Whitlocks lost four of their children, everyone from the house adjacent to Greene Lane died, and the three houses directly across are still vacant — I suppose they haven't returned from the country yet."

"I hope we haven't returned too soon," Father muttered.

"But we've been away so long, Father," Anne said. "We

had to come back or we would have forgotten what London looked like."

"Are the Baileys still there?" Betty asked Mary.

"Who are the Baileys?"

"The Catholics on Leake Street."

"I didn't walk that far."

"Go back and check. I'd like to know if they're still alive."

"Do it yourself," Mary said. "I've better things to do." Mary had long since dropped any pretence of being polite to Betty, and Father had long since given up admonishing either of them for their bickering. "I'm going up to check our room," Mary said.

"Wait for me," Deborah said.

"I'll race you to the top of the stairs."

They both ran off, and Mary felt a twinge of guilt that Anne had to limp so slowly behind them. But excitement at being home was too much for her; Max yapping merrily around their feet, she and Deborah chased each other up the stairs.

Their room was exactly as they had left it, though dustier.

"We shall have to give all the rugs a good beating, and turn all the beds," Deborah said, inspecting her closet.

"I'm going to the secret room," Mary said.

"Good luck," Deborah said. She was on her hands and knees, feeling under her bed.

"What are you doing?"

"Just checking if something's still there."

"Watch Max for me?"

"Of course. But don't be too long. Betty will get suspicious."

Mary threw open the window and hoisted herself out onto the ledge. She could see clearly down into the Walk: the boarded-up houses, the fading plague crosses on doors. An air of emptiness still clung to the street. They had heard reports of the enormous numbers of people who had died, but the illness had run its course, and slowly the refugees were starting to return. By midsummer, she expected, all would be as normal.

And Lazodeus, hopefully, would be back.

Her first shock was that the window of her secret room was open. Had it stayed open all this time? Obviously it had, for the rugs and cushions near it were mouldy with rain damage. She kicked them aside and moved further into the room. Dust took the edge of brightness from her cushions and hangings. She shook a red curtain half-heartedly, sneezed from the dust which emerged. Her eyes itched and she rubbed them vigorously. Lying down among the cushions, she closed her eyes and did what she had known all along she would do the instant she was back.

"Lazodeus? Can you hear me?"

She hadn't really expected him to arrive, but she was disappointed when he didn't. Not a day had passed in the country cottage when she did not long for him. Rather than waning, her yearning had grown stronger every day. She squirmed in her bed at night, next to her sisters, longing for the intense pleasures he had taught her. On many occasions she had walked out into a secluded field, lay among the long grass and given those pleasures to herself. One particularly fortunate week, she had found a local boy willing to attempt learning the methods. But neither solution was really satisfactory. It was the angel she longed for, his divine face, his thrilling presence. What could she do to make him come?

She sighed, flipped over on her stomach and sneezed again for the dust. It was bliss to have some space to herself. The house at Chalfont was small and there had been little chance of avoiding her family. In summer and spring it was fine enough to go out of doors; all three of them had often left the cottage in the morning, went their separate ways and did not return until supper. Whenever they were inside, Betty seemed determined to harass them, especially Mary whom she particularly despised. Mary found, though, that she almost relished being Betty's enemy. She bathed in Betty's loathing almost as indulgently as Deborah bathed in Father's approval.

No, that wasn't right, for Deborah no longer seemed so eager to please her father. She had changed in those months away. Physically, she had grown to full maturity, and — damn her eyes — she was the most beautiful of them by a large margin; a young woman for whom heads turned as she walked by, but with absolutely no interest in men and their attention. But it was in matters of the heart that Deborah had changed the most. She no longer toadied around Father hoping to impress him. She would go out in the morning with two enormous books under her arm, find a tree to sit beneath and read all day. Mary had looked into the books once, when Deborah was sick in bed, and found that they were books of magic and astrology. It was all too much like mathematics for Mary's liking, and just so typical of Deborah to reject Lazodeus and then go looking for magic in a book.

The worst part of Deborah's growing indifference to their father was Father's growing irritation with all three of them. Without Deborah to displace his paternal affection onto, he had begun to accuse all of them of being ungrateful, disloyal, cold-hearted and disobedient (much to Betty's joy). If Betty could read and write well, he would most certainly have sent them away by now. But his great epic — that interminable trial of patience he called *Paradise Lost* — needed scribes, and Father, not clever with money at the best of times, had to rely on his daughters for his dictation.

Boring, old, blind, waspish Father. Healthy as a horse, though. Wouldn't die any time soon.

Mary picked herself up and headed for the window. She should rejoin her family, help to set the house up again. There was nothing much for her in the secret room anyway. She wondered how long she would have to wait for Lazodeus's return. A brief moment of cold fear swept over her when she allowed herself to imagine that he may never return. But no, she couldn't believe that. To believe that was to lose all hope. For without him, she knew, she would surely die.

Deborah knocked vainly on Amelia's door for five minutes, then had to admit that the older woman wasn't home. She turned and scanned her surroundings. The two slender, bent trees were heavy with leaves and a blackbird hopped among them, watching her warily.

So Amelia had not yet returned to London, and Deborah could not gauge her own disappointment. She had spent all the time away at Chalfont poring over the books, learning the endless lists of correspondences and mathematical formulae as keenly as she had once learned every remedy in the *Pharmacopoeia*. Now she wanted to put her new knowledge into use. Now she was ready to be Amelia's apprentice.

She felt overwhelmed, unsure what to do, so she sat on Amelia's doorstep and put her head in her hands. The long months of their refuge from London had changed her in many ways, but she was still at her core the same person. She would weigh the situation up carefully, and decide what her next course of action would be. Perhaps she should spend the time until Amelia's arrival revising what she had learned. She could leave a note, asking Amelia to send word when she had returned to London. And she would not experiment with anything magical — the scrying mirror, for example — until she was safely under Amelia's tutelage.

The blackbird took to flight as she stood and walked past it, back onto the street. But as she began to walk away, she saw two figures approaching in the distance. One tall, elegant lady and a hunched hag. Amelia and Gisela.

Despite herself, Deborah began to wave madly.

"Amelia!" she called. "You're home!"

Amelia waited until she was closer to respond. "I've only been out at the markets."

"I thought you weren't yet returned to London."

"I've been back since Christmas. And you?"

"Father was over-cautious. So many died." She remembered her manners and nodded her head at Gisela, who was carrying a sack. Gisela smiled a crooked smile and walked on ahead of them.

"I've learned everything I can from your books," Deborah said. "I know you will be pleased with me."

"Come inside, then. The cats will be happy for a fresh lap to sit on."

The walls inside had been newly whitewashed, the candlesticks had been polished to a fine gleam, and all the rugs and cushions had been beaten back to their former glory. The cats lazed in soft places. Richly coloured curtains were drawn against the daylight, and candles glowed in the dark.

"Where have you been?" Amelia asked, clearing a space to sit.

"Out in the country. All living on top of each other. Betty nearly drove us mad." Deborah picked up a cat and sat down.

"And your Father?" Amelia said, eyes gleaming. "Has your relationship with him improved?"

"My relationship with my father is not what it was," Deborah replied, and she still felt the tingle of cool regret. "He is not what I thought he was."

"Most of our idols have clay feet. You'd do well to remember that," Amelia said. "So, you believe you are ready for an apprenticeship with me?"

"Yes, haply."

"I will have to test you."

"I anticipated you would."

She leaned forward, and Deborah got the distinct impression that Amelia expected her to fail.

"What is the highest emanation on the Tree of Life?"

"Kether," she said. The question was too easy; a trick question to mislead someone feigning knowledge. She may as well have asked the first letter of the alphabet.

"The twenty-fourth angel of the Decanates?"

This was more the question she expected. "Uthrodiel," she answered without hesitation.

Amelia suppressed a smile. She was surprised, impressed. Deborah felt pride swelling inside her, for she knew she could impress her new teacher even more. Every day for months she had gone out to the forest and studied the books assiduously.

"And his sign?"

"The scorpion."

"Hmm," Amelia said. "Very good. So far . . ."

"I'm ready for more."

"Who is the ruler of the ninth hour of the day?"

"Vadriel."

"His numeric value?"

"Two hundred and fifty-two."

"Which demon is represented by a lion with a donkey's head?"

"Valefor," she said, and to obviate further questions: "He is ruled by Venus, cadent by day."

"And would you call on Valefor if you wished to find something stolen?"

"No, for Valefor teaches thieves. I would call upon Andromalius."

Amelia leaned back and clapped once. "Ha!"

"Are you pleased with me?"

"You have an exceptional memory."

"I studied very closely."

"But does the whole system make sense to you? Or are they all simply unrelated facts?"

Deborah paused over this question. "I understand the system, the chain of correspondences, but I do not believe that all the knowledge of the universe is answerable to the system."

"And why do you think that?"

"Because there are more angels and more demons than we have names for. Lazodeus, for instance, the guardian you called for my sisters. He is not accounted for."

"He's a fallen angel, probably of a lower order. He has no specific function. But you're right, Deborah. The system, the charts and tables, cannot account for everything. There is much still mysterious to us, and in the mystery lurks the power." Amelia stood. "You have earned the demon key."

Deborah felt a shiver of apprehension, even though she had believed until this moment that she had come to terms with the aspects of magic which relied on spirits. The word "demon" still frightened her. Some old associations were hard to shake off. "Is it safe to use?"

"I'm safe, aren't I?" Amelia snapped, going to a cabinet and pulling open a drawer. "You really must stop being so frightened, Deborah. Fear makes us weak."

Amelia's words were like a slap, and Deborah vowed not to show such weakness in front of her new mistress again. She waited while Amelia drew from the cabinet a silver box. She sat and passed the box across to Deborah.

"Go on, open it."

Deborah sprang the catch on the box. Inside lay a tarnished silver bar with a small loop on the end, through which a chain was threaded. "It doesn't look like a key at all," she said.

"A key? Oh, I see what you mean. It has nothing to do with locks. Pull it out and I'll show you."

Deborah, baffled, pulled the key from its box and held it up. Amelia took it in her long fingers. It spun slowly on its chain. "Gisela," she called, "bring me a cup of water."

Deborah sat, transfixed, watching the demon key spinning between them. Gisela hurried out with a cup of water then retreated.

"Now, Deborah, an experiment. If I wished to turn this water into wine, who would I call upon?"

"Haagenti."

Amelia nodded, then focussed her gaze upon the demon key. "Haagenti, I call upon you with this key as your commander, turn this water into wine."

For a moment, nothing happened, but then Deborah realised a sound was gathering around the key. A sweet music, more delicious than anything she had ever heard, began to emanate from the dull silver bar. It tingled in her ears, and she thought of intricate cobwebs silvered with dew, or the finest sugar woven into delicate shapes. And yet, there was something wicked, forbidden, seductive about the music. Only five notes sounded, and then it fell silent.

"What was it?" she asked.

"The demon key. It is music, Deborah. The spirits have always been very fond of music. Here, drink this." Amelia handed the cup to Deborah, who warily put it to her lips. It was no longer water; it was the sweetest wine.

"You did this?" Deborah asked.

"Yes."

"Could I do this?"

Amelia handed over the demon key and shook her head. "No, not fully, not as an apprentice. You can call on the particular demons, but you will only be attended by their apprentices. The fresher you are to the craft, the weaker the demon you are assigned. It is an unreliable science for the first few years. And still, many years later, I find weaknesses in my own craft." Amelia shifted to the seat next to Deborah, and helped her fasten the chain around her neck. "You may take this home and experiment with it. Call upon the demons who can explain astrology and geometry to you, and let them teach you now."

"I'll still be your apprentice, though?"

"Oh, yes, of course. You can come to me once a week and I shall answer your questions, in return for which you can fulfil small tasks for me."

Deborah fingered the tarnished silver rod on its chain thoughtfully. She wanted very badly to ask, *Is my soul in any danger*? But she would not disappoint Amelia by doing so. Instead, she asked, "Is there an angel key?"

"I have no angel key," Amelia said guardedly.

"But does such a thing exist?" She wondered how much infinitely sweeter the sound of angels' music would be.

Amelia leaned back. "It is a foolish man who attempts to command the angels."

"Is Lazodeus not an angel?"

"He is fallen. He is disconnected from the pure source."

"From God?"

"Whatever you like to call it."

Deborah's curiosity was piqued. "What would I have to learn ere I could be granted an angel key?"

"Learning will not help. There is too much danger involved."

"Danger for my soul?"

"For your life. One must be almost at the point of death, and when an angel comes to assess the state of your soul, one must seize the angel and demand the key. Nothing is worth that kind of danger."

"Because one could die?"

"Yes, and because angels do not like to be commanded, and because angels may grant favours but ask for a repayment too great for an individual to bear."

"What kind of repayment?"

"It matters not, Deborah. The angel key is not something with which you should concern yourself. Perhaps when you are an old woman, with nothing else to live for, you may attempt to experiment with angel keys. But a girl of your age need not even think upon it."

Deborah nodded, persuaded. "That makes good sense."

"You are a sensible girl."

"When you speak of angels, I perceive that you believe they are not all good."

Amelia waved a dismissive hand. "It is often the purest beings who can be the cruellest."

223

"Lazodeus said that the war in Heaven was unfair, that he and the other fallen angels were unjustly expelled from Heaven."

"While the religiously intolerant would be appalled to hear such a thing, I believe it may be true. I have never dealt with angels directly, but I know others who have, and they testify to a cruel, unforgiving streak. Good, by definition, Deborah, must be entirely good. To preserve such purity of purpose involves a certain blind severity."

Deborah pondered this for a few minutes. Amelia returned to her own seat and said, "Now, I have answered your questions. It is time you performed your duties for me."

Deborah looked up brightly. "Anything," she said. She looked forward to helping with magical experiments, writing from dictation as she did with Father.

Amelia smiled. "Go to the kitchen and help Gisela pluck a turkey for dinner," she said. "'Tis not all mystery and glamour."

Anne could imagine no better time for her purpose. Mary was out walking Max; Deborah had disappeared that morning and was not yet returned; Betty and Liza were at the markets; and Father never ventured upstairs. She was alone for the first time since they returned to London and she could wait no longer. She had to see Lazodeus.

She stood tall in the middle of the room and closed her eyes. "Angel, Lazodeus, will you come to me?" He would come, of course he would.

She opened her eyes. He did not come.

"Please, please, please," she whispered. Did he not know what great distress it had caused her to be separated from him for so long? "Can you at least give me a sign that you are nearby?"

Anne strained her ears for a whisper, glanced around for the lightest movement of the hangings. This was unbearable. She flopped onto the bed with an arm over her face, wanted to weep until she died. Had she known that love would be so painful, she would have guarded her heart more carefully. Too late now. Far too late for prudence.

The door burst open and Mary came in, carrying Max under one arm. Anne sat up with a start. "I thought you were out walking," she said, and reminded herself she need not sound so guilty.

"We only got as far as the kitchen. Liza has baked sugar cakes — want one?" Mary offered her a hot biscuit with her free hand. Anne took it while Max sniffed it desperately.

"No, Max," Mary said. "You've already had three."

"Three? What will Liza say? Are there any left?"

"She should not leave them out upon the table unattended to cool if she doesn't want them stolen. Not with Mad Mary about," Mary said, gently placing Max on the floor. "So, what is wrong with you?"

"Nothing is wrong with me," Anne replied. She still wasn't accustomed to how easy it was to lie now that she didn't stutter so badly. She took a bite from the biscuit.

"When I came in, you were prostrate upon the bed in a gesture of despair." Mary flung her arm over her forehead in a melodramatic impersonation. "In which vale of tears do you wander, sister?"

"None. I assure you I am perfect content," Anne replied.

Mary sat on the bed next to her, and passed her another sugar cake. They ate in silence for a few minutes, then Mary said, "Do you ever think about the angel?"

Anne shook her head. "No. You?"

"No."

"Why do you ask? Are you thinking of calling upon him?" The jealousy would be too much to bear. Anne felt her face flush at the thought. More than anything, she wanted Lazodeus only to herself.

"No, it is just that we haven't discussed him for so long. The whole time we were away —"

"We didn't speak of him. I know." Because it was too

secret, too intimate to share with her sisters. Especially with sisters who were rivals: Mary because of her obvious erotic interest; Deborah because of her fresh beauty. "But he is little use to us now we cannot command him."

"I expect you are right. I expect that we would gain nothing from his attendance now." Mary would not meet her eye. Anne watched her closely. Did Mary really care for the angel no longer? It was one of her dearest wishes. But . . .

"Anne, perhaps it would take all three of us in partnership to call him again anyway. We had to let him go so he could help others."

"I'm afraid . . . I suppose that is true," Anne said. "And Deborah would never agree."

"It matters not. We do not want to call him again, do we?" Mary said, tossing a curl over her shoulder.

"No. We do not."

Mary lifted herself off the bed and stretched. "I'm going to get more sugar cakes. Want some?"

"I shall be down anon."

Mary nodded and left. Anne sat and pulled her knees up under her chin. Mary was most certainly right. All three of them would have to work together to summon Lazodeus, and she desperately didn't want to share the angel with her sisters. What to do, then? Wait and hope that he came back of his own accord? Tempting, so tempting. He *must* feel the same way about her as she did about him. For love could surely not be so one-sided. The universe could not be so cruel.

11
Foul Distrust and Breach Disloyal

All through the long months at Chalfont, Betty had watched with satisfaction as John's heart turned against his daughters. Now, one week back in London, with space between them all again, the urgency of his resentment was dissipating. They were useful to him: Deborah was good with languages, Mary had a fair hand, and Anne helped Liza with the chores. He hadn't enough money to hire scribes and extra servants, and Betty — despite her attempts to improve — was simply not literate enough to be of great use to him.

So Betty had sent Liza in search of what evidence she could find to employ against the girls, any one of them. She had not shed her conviction that the girls were dallying with spirits, even if they had not done a single thing to suggest it was true for nearly a year. Sometimes, when Betty worried that Liza had invented the scene which had so inflamed her imagination, she reminded herself of Father Bailey's words — not so frightening now at a distance of many months — but enough to keep her vigilant. *You have devils in your house.*

She sighed and paced from the window to the couch and back. Deborah sat in the garden below, reading. Mary and Anne were out collecting a turkey pie, so Betty had sent Liza up to investigate their bedroom. She leaned her back against the window frame. The room was bright with morning sun and fresh whitewash. Even so, she did not like this house as much as the one at Chalfont. She could never quite get used to the city, though John loved it unreservedly.

Liza burst in, brandishing a book. "Ma'am, I may have what you need," she said breathlessly.

Betty hurried over. "What is it?"

"A book, but it looks wicked, ma'am."

Betty seized the book and began to flick through the pages. Strange designs, tables of information and, here, invocations for spirits. She remembered Father Bailey listing such a book as a sure sign of necromancy. "Aha!" Betty cried. "I have them. Whose is it?"

"It belongs to Miss Deborah, ma'am," Liza said. "'Twas under her pillow."

"Good work, Liza. I shall take it to her father immediately."

"There's something else, ma'am. I found this under her bed." Liza drew a bundle from her apron, and unwrapped it to reveal an elaborately carved mirror. "I wondered why she hid it, and then it occurred to me she might have stole it."

Betty took the mirror and laid it on top of the book. There was something sinister about the stone carvings around the mirror; something grotesque and overwrought. But then, perhaps she felt that way because of the book about spirits, because she was frightened by it all.

"Thank you, Liza. I shan't be needing you for a while. You may take a few hours off."

Liza nodded and left the room, untying her apron. Betty took a deep breath and marched down the stairs to speak to John.

He stood by the window, his hand resting in a sunbeam, listening to the birdsong outside. As she entered, he turned to face her.

"Who's there?"

"Betty," she said.

"You walk with more purpose than usual, Betty. I did not recognise your gait. I thought it may be Mary."

"Mary and Anne are at the pie shop. I have something of great importance to discuss with you."

"Go on."

"I believe that Deborah is communicating with evil spirits."

The corner of John's mouth twitched, and she realised he was suppressing a laugh.

"John, 'tis true! You must not let your cynicism allow evil to happen in this house. I have here a book, filled with descriptions of demons and spirits, and ways that one may invoke them. Do not let your blindness make you ignorant of what those girls are doing."

The smile faded and he became very serious. "I wish you would not refer to my blindness to support your arguments."

"I'm sorry, John," she said dropping her head.

"Bring Deborah in here, and we will question her about this book."

Betty swelled with triumph. She placed the book and the mirror carefully on John's desk and hurried to the garden to find her stepdaughter.

Deborah glanced up through her ill-fitting spectacles. "Are you looking for me, Betty?"

"Yes. In fact, your father is looking for you. He wishes to question you about a certain book which was in your possession." Betty's reward was the sight of Deborah's pretty pink face drawing pale.

"What do you mean?"

"We have found a certain book, about which your father wishes to question you," Betty said again, grabbing her by the elbow and dragging her to her feet. "Come, girl, 'tis time you explained yourself."

"Ow, let me go."

Betty pulled Deborah through the kitchen roughly. "I've known for a long time there's something not quite right with the three of you. How involved are your sisters? Was it magic that made Anne's stutter disappear?"

"What are you talking about? The surgeon at Chalfont said it was common for such an infliction to disappear at adulthood. Magic? Betty, are you mad?"

"You protest too fiercely for someone who claims innocence." They reached John's study and she pushed Deborah ahead of her. "Explain to your father what you have been doing." Deborah stumbled into the study, then gathered herself and stood tall in front of John. He had taken the book and the mirror and sat with them in his lap. Deborah's eyebrows shot up when she saw the mirror, but she was soon composed again.

Betty wondered if it was more than a stolen mirror. Was it a magic mirror? She had heard of such things and it caused a darting fear: bad luck, extreme bad luck. John fingered the grotesque carvings on it idly.

"Deborah, your stepmother has found items in your possession which we would like you to account for," John said.

"Certainly, Father. What questions would you have me answer?"

"First, this book. Betty tells me it has information in it about demons and commanding spirits."

"That is true, Father. But it contains information about angels withal. You write of angels, and I wished to know more of them. I found the book in the house at Chalfont, and have been reading parts of it ever since."

"You brought it back to London with you? That is stealing. Colonel Fleetwood may miss it."

"I assumed he would never return from America. Now the King is restored, it were dangerous for him to come back."

John nodded, finding this statement reasonable.

"But John," Betty complained, reminding herself to try harder not to whine, "'tis a guide for necromancy surely."

"No, I assure you," Deborah said, turning to Betty. "Divers good men and proper have an interest in such things which is critical rather than practical." She moved to

John's chair and knelt beside it. "Father, I know my place. I know it is not for women to be involved in such things as how the universe works and which beings may people it. I assure you that my interest was solely derived from working on your *Paradise Lost*."

John stroked the cover of the book and was silent for a few moments. "I believe you," he said at last.

"I do not!" Betty cried.

"Betty —" John began.

"No, John. The book should be burned. There is far more in it about demons than angels."

"We cannot burn it, for it belongs to Colonel Fleetwood," Deborah said and, damn her, produced a triumphant smile that John would never see. There had been a time when Betty felt fondness for Deborah, but now the girl was becoming as insolent as Mary.

"Well, what about this mirror?" Betty asked, knowing it sounded lame.

"What about the mirror?" Deborah shot back, success making her bold. "It is a gift for me from my mother's mother. Why should a mirror prove aught about my behaviour? Or is my vanity a pressing issue in this household?"

"Why was it hidden? If neither of these items are proof of your wickedness, why were they both hidden?"

Deborah did not have an immediate answer, and John noticed.

"Deborah?" he said.

"I hide the mirror because Mary covets it. The book was under my pillow because I was reading it in bed this morning."

"John," Betty appealed, "at least let me confiscate them."

"Certainly. A good idea. Betty will take your mirror and your book, Deborah —"

"But they are mine."

"Do not interrupt me!" John roared, finally reaching the end of his patience.

Deborah set her jaw but did not say another word.

231

"Betty will take these items into her possession for your own protection. If you wish to use either of them, especially the book, it shall be with our supervision."

"Yes, Father."

"Now go," said Betty.

Deborah turned and narrowed her eyes at Betty, her expression pure hatred, but her voice as sweet as spring. "Certainly, Mother. I entrust the items to your safekeeping." She tossed her red-gold hair and left.

Betty waited a few minutes before turning to John. "I think you have done the right thing, John," she said, picking up the book and the mirror.

"Betty, you may be happy with the outcome of this dispute, but I want you to shake off any ideas that my daughters — especially Deborah — are involved in necromancy."

Betty did not answer immediately; she was considering the mirror. But she could see no evidence of magic, only her own reflection. How would such a device work? She shook her head: such curiosity could only be troublesome.

"John," she said quietly, "I think that you are too forgiving of the girls."

"No, I am not. I believe they are ungrateful and unkind. But they earn their keep."

"I have spoken to someone who says that such a book is a sign of the devil; who says that rude and aggressive behaviour — like the girls all display from time to time — is a sign of possession by spirits."

John frowned. "And who would say such a thing to you?"

"I . . ."

"Betty?"

"Father Bailey on Leake Street."

"A papist? You dare to quote to me the words of a superstitious idolater? Betty, you do not know me well enough if you think I can be persuaded by such a fool. You have undermined your case enormously."

"I'm sorry, John, I —"

Suddenly John gasped, his hands clutching the chair arms so hard that his knuckles turned white. "You told a Papist about affairs in my home?"

"No, John, no. I assure you I was speaking of generalities, not specifics."

"Still, he may now suspect something of us. Betty, how could you be so foolish? Do you not value my reputation?"

Betty hung her head and felt her face burning with shame. She was an idiot for ever mentioning Father Bailey. She should have been satisfied with the day's small victory.

"Take the book and the mirror and keep them safe," John said dismissively. "When Mary gets home, send her in for some dictation."

"Yes, John," Betty said. "You can rely upon me."

"No, I cannot," he said. "I can rely upon nobody." She detected real sadness in his voice, and her guilt caused her to gather her things and leave quickly.

Betty took the items to her room. She would not endure the presence of the book and the mirror in her home for long. In a day or so, when this dispute was forgotten, she would take them to the exorcist so he might destroy them. She would see how clever Deborah would solve *that* problem.

Deborah lay on her side on her bed, idly fingering the demon key. She had not used it yet. It had seemed imprudent, almost disrespectful, to experiment with it until she had a purpose. Was this not a good purpose? To seek the return of stolen belongings?

She sighed and rolled over, holding the metal bar in front of her to gaze at it. How could such a small piece of metal cause her so much apprehension? But she had to use it at some time: she couldn't just own it and never use it. That would be foolish, that would be fearful, and Amelia had already made it known how she disdained such fear. If she used it today, and if she were successful, it would prove to

Amelia that she was serious, that she was worth more to her new mistress than for her services in the kitchen.

"What to do, what to do?" she murmured to herself. She didn't need the book returned for her own purposes: she knew it from cover to cover. But it belonged to Amelia, and to confess that she had lost it would disappoint her mistress greatly. Deborah had always been uncomfortable under the weight of a disapproving gaze. And the mirror — she wanted it back. Betty could not be trusted with it.

She closed her eyes. Return of stolen belongings. Andromalius. Deep breaths. Nothing enormous, nothing to insult the universe, just a few words.

"Andromalius," she said. "I call upon you with this key as your commander. Return my stolen belongings."

The wondrous sound began to gather around the key, and then five clear notes rang out, more mellow than summer fruit. She felt a quick rush of excitement bubbling up through her, and found, with surprise, a laugh upon her lips. The thrill quickly subsided, and she looked around almost guiltily, suddenly frightened somebody may have seen her abandon herself to the feeling.

Did that mean it had worked? Amelia had suggested it may take some time to make the demon key work properly for her. When could she expect a result?

But then, perhaps the result didn't matter as much as the fact that she had exercised her new power. Amelia, she hoped, would be proud of her.

Betty could tell instantly that Lettice Bailey was not happy to see her. Clearly, her previous reluctance to share gossip had caused offence.

"Yes?" the exorcist's sister said imperiously, barring access over the threshold into the house.

"I'd like to speak to Father Bailey, please."

"Does your husband know where you are, Mrs Milton?"

"Is Father Bailey home?"

Lettice turned away from the door with a derisive glare and called her brother. Betty waited by the door, turning the package over and over in front of her. The mirror and the book. The longer they stayed in the house, the more uneasy she became. She knew the exorcist could dispose of them safely. But as she waited for Father Bailey to arrive, she began to regret coming. Lettice was right: John would despise knowing she was here. But John didn't believe that the book was evil. Betty did, and she wanted it as far away from her as possible.

Finally, snow-haired Father Bailey arrived. "Mrs Milton, I am so pleased to see you again. Is it regarding your previous problem?"

"Yes, Father. May I come in?"

Father Bailey led her inside the dim room. Lettice appeared with her maidservant, tying on her hat and pulling on gloves. "You needn't worry, Mrs Milton, I shall be going to market with the girl. I shan't hear a single secret word."

"Please don't leave on my account," Betty said, with little sincerity.

"No, 'tis better that we have privacy," Father Bailey said. "Take a seat, and I shall open a window, for it has grown very stuffy in here."

Betty waited while Lettice and her girl left and Father Bailey opened a window. A light breeze blew in, making the wall hangings dance gently. Betty saw motes of dust float by on a weak sunbeam. She tried to relax. Father Bailey sat opposite her, smiling through his rotten teeth.

"And so you are returned to London?" he said.

"Yes, and the problem with the girls appears to have worsened. Especially the youngest, the most learned one."

"These are the dangers of teaching girls. What have you brought to show me?" He indicated the package she clutched upon her lap.

Betty passed the package to him. "I found these in the youngest girl's closet."

Father Bailey's wrinkled hands carefully folded back the cloth. First he picked up the mirror.

"I am uncertain if it is a forbidden object," Betty said quickly, "but it seemed odd that she hid it."

Father Bailey nodded, his lips pressed tightly, deepening the lines which ran vertically from his mouth. "Oh, it is an instrument of necromancy for certain. The design is fiendish."

"That's what I thought," Betty said, excited finally to speak with somebody who took her seriously. John was too much of a cynic for his own good.

"Let me show you," Father Bailey said. Unexpectedly, he lifted the mirror and slammed it down on the corner of his chair with a crack. Betty anticipated that it would smash into pieces, and felt a sudden twinge of guilt at breaking Deborah's possession. It didn't break. Father Bailey held it out for her to inspect. The glass was not even cracked.

"Evil," he said, "protects itself."

"Then how can we destroy it?" Betty asked, aghast that she had even handled such a sinister object.

"I can destroy it, fear not." He put the mirror aside cautiously, then turned his attention to the book. "Ah, you did well to bring this to me. It is a book of necromancy."

"Deborah defended herself by saying that it was a long and honoured tradition for men to read about spirits and angels."

"No man does it for any reason other than personal gain, despite what he says. Or she. It is always wicked."

"Then we should destroy it too?"

"Without question."

"She said it belongs to somebody else; a well-respected friend of my husband."

"She lies. It belongs to the devil. We shall stoke the fire and return it to his care. It would be most negligent of us to allow it to circulate in this world, especially in the hands of a young woman." Father Bailey stood and walked to the fireplace. Betty watched as, despite the heat of the day, he stacked it with coal and lit it. His movements were frustratingly slow and meticulous. The longer she was away from home, the more lies would be necessary to cover her absence. She hoped she could at least be back in time to take John on his afternoon walk.

"Very well," he said at length, happy with the low flames which now burned in the grate. "Pass me the mirror first."

Betty stood and took the mirror to him, laid it in his withered hands. He mumbled a few words of Latin, and Betty looked around nervously. What if somebody dropped by, somebody who knew her and reported back to her husband? She realised she was sweating: the warm day and the fire conspiring with her anxiety.

Suddenly the mirror flew up in the air and then rattled to the ground a few feet from them.

"Did you do that?" Betty asked, but could tell from Father Bailey's shocked expression that he hadn't.

"It does not want to be blessed or burned," he said in a harsh whisper. "There are demons protecting it."

"Demons? Here?" Betty's heart sped.

"Pass me the book," he said, indicating where it lay on the chair.

She didn't want to touch the book. "I . . ."

"Pass me the book," he said sternly.

She reached for the book and, to her horror, it spun away from her and landed on the floor. "How does it move like that?" she gasped.

"Evil moves it," Father Bailey said grimly. He turned away from the fireplace with purpose and marched first to the book and then the mirror, picking them up firmly. Once again, he tried to say a Latin blessing over them. First the book, then the mirror shot out of his hands to lie on the hearth. Betty felt a sudden bolt of courage galvanise her, and she stepped forward to kick the book towards the fire. It slipped out from under her, unbalancing her and sending her crashing to the floor. As she fell, she bruised herself painfully on the chair.

"Never mind, Mrs Milton, it will take more than a demon to defeat me," Father Bailey said, and a little fleck of spittle escaped the corner of his mouth. "Gather the objects and wrap them once more. I shall deal with them later, when I have all the proper instruments of exorcism around me."

When Betty hesitated, he said, "Go on, Mrs Milton. They will not hurt you. Not now our intentions have changed."

Betty bent to pick up the mirror and the book, and both of them were inert again. She wrapped them in the cloth she had brought with her and passed them to Father Bailey.

"Good. Now, if you leave them with me, I shall take care of them."

"Thank you, Father," she said, relieved that she would never have to see the objects again.

"Your problem now is far more serious."

"My problem?"

"These are only the symptoms of a greater sickness in your household," he said. "Your stepdaughters are dabbling in necromancy. The house should be properly blessed. I shall have to come in and drive the demons out."

Betty squeaked. "No!" she managed to say. "Oh, no, Father. My husband would ... well, I'm certain you can imagine my husband's reaction to such a suggestion."

"Mrs Milton, what is more important? Your husband's anger or your soul's health? And his soul? And those of your stepdaughters?"

Betty stopped herself from saying that she would gladly see her stepdaughters burn in hell. Instead she said, "You'll have to let me think about it."

"Do not take too long to think, Mrs Milton. This is very serious."

"I know, I know," she said, backing out. "I must go. I shall be missed."

"Do not let your upbringing send you to damnation. We are the one true faith, and we still have the only sure remedy against demons."

"It is all impossible at the moment, Father Bailey. But my husband is talking of going away for a little while soon. Perhaps I can conspire to stay behind."

"You must do something. And quickly. Ere matters develop beyond my capacity to contain them."

Betty nodded. "I must go," she said again.

"Do not be foolish."

"I shall not," Betty said, but as she let herself out and found her way home, she wondered over and over again if she would be foolish. If she would ignore the Father's warnings and let her fear of John stop her from driving out the evil in her house.

It took two weeks before anything happened, and in the meantime Deborah did not use the demon key again. But finally, late one evening, she returned to her closet to find the book and the mirror lying neatly upon her bed, just as though someone had lain them there carefully. She picked up the mirror, traced the grotesque carvings with the tip of her finger. Why had Lazodeus given this to her? If his sworn purpose was to use his magic to protect them — a magic they were all forced to relinquish when Mary had unwittingly released him from their command — why give her a scrying mirror? What were his intentions, and where was he now? She had neither seen nor heard of him since the night they had left London.

She passed her hand over the mirror and said, "Show me Lazodeus." The mirror remained blank. She tried again. Had the mirror ceased to work?

"Show me Betty," she said. The mirror gleamed back an image of Betty sifting flour in the kitchen with Liza, her sleeves rolled up and her cap pinned on crooked. So it still worked. She passed her hand over the mirror's surface, thoughtful. It didn't work on the bestower of the mirror. For a reason? Could one not watch an angel? Or did the angel, as she had always suspected, have something to hide?

A knock at the bedroom door had her hurriedly hiding the book and mirror under her bedclothes. Liza's voice: "Miss Deborah, your father needs you for dictation."

Deborah poked her head out of her closet. "I'll be down in a minute," she replied.

Liza left, closing the door behind her. Deborah pulled out the book and mirror. She had hidden her other book deep within her trunk, and now, wrapping the objects carefully, she buried them among her clothes. As an added measure, she pulled out the demon key and held it up in her right hand. "Bael, I call upon you with this key as your commander. Protect my belongings from the eyes of those who seek them."

As the beautiful music rang out, she once again felt a thrilling power streaming through her. It took her a few moments to recover herself before she went downstairs to work with Father.

"You took your time," he said sourly, as she gathered up her writing tray and sat across from him.

"I apologise, Father. What would you have me do?" The long poem was becoming more and more of a trial as he dictated pages, deleted them, and dictated them again. Because Mary was also working on it, there was confusion about where they were up to at any given moment. Father repeatedly said it was "almost finished," but as far as Deborah could see it had never been more of a mess.

"Mary should have left it at the right place. Read me the first lines you have in the pile."

Deborah picked up the sheet and read, "So spake th' Eternal Father, and fulfilled all justice . . ."

"Yes, yes, keep reading."

Deborah read for a few pages, and Father was very pleased

with himself, almost cheerful. When she had finished the section, he sat back smugly. "I'm mightily delighted with it, Deborah. What do you think?"

"It is masterly, of course," Deborah said, and it was not false flattery. "But Father, may I ask you something?"

His mouth tightened. "Certainly."

"How do you write so confidently of angels and our first parents, when you were not there to witness these happenings?"

Father considered the question, pressing his pale fingers into his chin. "Why, Deborah, I had never considered such a question."

"Do you believe what you write is fact, Father?"

"I believe it is a version of the truth. I could not continue to write it if I did not believe that. It would seem pointless, the babyish meanderings of a wild imagination."

"But you have never seen the face of Adam; you have never heard Raphael speak . . ."

"And yet I have such conviction that what I write is real and living." He chuckled, perhaps a little nervously. "At least, I did feel that conviction. Until you asked me about it."

Deborah leaned forward. "Perhaps there is an alternative to this story. The angels being thrown out of Heaven; Lucifer; Hell."

"All my reading points to the accuracy of my story; all my instincts declare it also." He drew up tall, suddenly remembering his pride. "I have been destined since birth to write this work. That calling alone ensures that what I write must be of truth, albeit poetic truth."

"Of course, Father," she said, sharpening her quill. "Shall we proceed?"

Anne was combing her hair, Mary stretched out across the bed scratching Max's belly, when Deborah came upstairs to bed late that evening. Mary watched as Deborah hesitated for a few moments in the threshold of her closet, glancing between her two sisters.

"What's the matter, Deborah?" Mary asked.

Deborah walked across to their bed and sat next to her. "I want to talk to you both very seriously."

Anne turned, her comb in her hand. "About what?"

Deborah patted the bedspread. "Please, come and sit down."

Anne, suspicious, laid her comb on the dresser and joined her sisters. "What is this all about, Deborah?" she asked, and Mary could see the vague fear in her eyes. "You sound so serious. Is it something bad?"

"'Tis serious, but not bad. At least, I don't think so."

"Go on, then," Mary said.

"I want to call the angel back."

Mary gasped loudly. "Lazodeus? *You* want him back?"

Anne shook her head. "Deborah, I am so surprised. Why? You wanted to be rid of him."

"Only until I could decide for certain what we should do about him. I have thought about it at great length —"

Mary snorted, and Deborah glanced at her annoyed.

"I have thought about it at great length, and I have decided that we are in no mortal or spiritual danger from Lazodeus, and there are a great many questions I should like to ask him. I expect that because the three of us sent him away, only the three of us can effect his return."

Mary recalled her earlier conversation with Anne. She turned to her older sister. "Anne? Do you want to see Lazodeus again? Or do you find the idea tiresome?"

Anne's feigned nonchalance would have convinced nobody. Her fingers practically trembled as she pushed her hair away from her face. "I suppose we could call him again."

"Let it be done, then," said Deborah. "I want to waste no more time, for I am still full of silly fears and may change my mind and disappoint myself."

"How do we do it?" Anne asked.

"The same as the first time. Remember? The triangle and the chant."

Mary took a deep breath, certain her pounding heart could be heard by her sisters. "Yes, I remember. It was so long ago, but I still remember."

"Bar the door," Deborah said. "I shall outline the triangle with charcoal."

Mary leaped to her feet, trembling from feet to fingers. Tonight she would see the return of her angel.

12

Warring Angels Disarrayed

He arrived as he had the last time, naked inside a cage of light. Without having to be asked, Anne said, "Lazodeus, join us in our world." The bars disappeared and he tumbled to the ground, in his familiar outfit of layered black. All three of the sisters hurried to help him at once. But, to Mary's shock and disappointment, it was Deborah's hand he took, and Deborah upon whom he leaned when he stood.

"Are you unwell?" Mary asked lamely, her hand brushing his glowing skin as Deborah led him past her to the bed.

"I shall be well enough in a moment," he said, sitting down with his head in his long, pale hands.

Deborah crouched before him, looking at him closely. "I have many questions to ask you."

"Deborah, let him catch his breath," Anne said from behind her.

Lazodeus looked up, a smile playing at his lips. "Questions, Deborah? Have you decided to trust me?"

"I've decided to listen to you. Tell me about the war in Heaven. Tell me how it is that you and the other fallen angels were expelled."

"Deborah, just let him be!" Mary said, stepping in and pulling Deborah away from Lazodeus.

"No, no, all is well. I am nearly recovered," Lazodeus said. "But will you want me to stay by you this time? Or will you be sending me back as soon as I've answered these questions?"

"Stay," Anne said quickly.

"Anne, don't forget we cannot command him any more," Deborah said prudently.

"But I would still help in times of trouble," Lazodeus replied. "If I could."

"I should like you to stay," Mary said, hoping that Lazodeus could read through her pretended casualness to the burning desire at her core.

He gave her a smile. "Should you, Mary? That is comforting."

Mary felt a hot flush seep up through her body.

"Stay then, for I don't care," Deborah said. "But tell me of the war in Heaven. I want to hear it from someone who was there."

"All of you sit down, then," Lazodeus said. "We shall make ourselves comfortable. We won't be disturbed, will we?"

Mary glanced to the door. "Nobody can gain entry, and Betty rarely bothers us after supper. But you must speak quietly so she cannot hear us."

"Certainly," he said smoothly. "Now, let me begin.

"The war was caused by a series of misunderstandings and betrayals. It may be hard for you to comprehend the politics of angels, for you have been raised to believe that angels are good and forgiving, that God has no follies, that all are merciful and peaceful. But all of these ideals are attributable to the Son."

"The Son? You mean Jesus?"

"Yes. For he is mild and merciful, and he is God's representative on earth. But the truth is that angels are beings who are not all of one mind, just as mortals are not all of one mind, and that means there are as regular and passionate debates in Heaven as there are anywhere else. If you can accept that, then the rest of my story will make more sense."

"I have heard that angels are sometimes cruel in their goodness," Deborah said.

"It is true, for any zealot can be tempted to protect their cause without mercy. What is also true is that God, or

Father Infinite as we call him, has a weakness. His weakness is that he loves to love. And that is how this story truly begins. A million angels were not enough for him. He decided that he wanted a child, a son.

"This was in a time before your history. The world was not yet created, and beyond Heaven there was only a void, in which strange creatures, which are long since extinct, resided. We lived on Heaven's plains in five tribes; one belonged to each of the archangels."

"Michael, Uriel, Gabriel, Raphael and Lucifer," Deborah said.

"That is right. Lucifer was then an archangel. And he was Father Infinite's favourite. He was second only to the Father in power and influence, and in beauty."

"What does God look like?" Anne said.

Lazodeus considered a moment. "You could not look upon him direct, but even to see the reflection of his glorious countenance is to experience true fulfilment. He is as a blaze of perfect light, but he never takes mortal form as we do, as Lucifer does."

"But I thought we were created in his image," Mary said.

Lazodeus shook his head. "A misunderstanding. You were created like him in that you love too much, that love is your weakness.

"Lucifer ruled the northern plains of Heaven with a devoted tribe of angels. We were called to gather around Father Infinite's throne, which was on a hill in the central lowlands. And there we all arrived, a million angels arrayed with our ensigns and standards, shining canvasses and flying flags, camped around the hill waiting for Father Infinite's arrival. Such a beautiful sight, so much colour. I still see it in my mind's eye, and a great longing possesses me, for it is all lost to me now."

He shook his head. "Once we had assembled, Father Infinite sat upon his throne and spoke in an excited and reverent voice. He had decided to create for himself a Son, an expression of his love and a being for him to adore. I was thrilled, as were we all, for we knew we too would adore the Son. I cheered with the rest of the crowd, a merry joyous cry of happiness.

"But then Father Infinite said, 'When the Son comes, he shall be the vice-regent of Heaven, and you shall all bow before him. Those who do not shall feel the edge of my wrath, and may find themselves banished to the outer limits of Heaven.'"

Lazodeus paused a moment, reaching for words. "You see, Father Infinite feels so fiercely in love, that he sometimes displays an impatience which is difficult to tolerate. And yet, we loved him dearly and so we accepted his stern warning and rejoiced with him. The day was declared an enormous celebration. We raised our pavilions." He narrowed his eyes as though seeing it again. "For as far as my eyes could see were the coloured banners of the angel tribes and families, bright tents and long tables laid out with angel food. Such a delicious combination of smells and sounds: food, flowers, rain-fresh earth, happy voices and the gentle breeze in treetops. We played music and we danced and we all spoke of the new Son, and when he would come, how he would look, how precious he would be to us.

"But as night fell, and we found our places around fires and inside the pavilions to converse and to sing quietly in groups, a rumour went about that delegations from Michael's tribe and Raphael's tribe had come to see Lucifer. Although I was not a Throne or a Duke or a Principality, I knew Lucifer well, as he had been my mentor when I approached guardian class. A few close friends and I decided to go up to his pavilion to see what was happening. Lucifer's pavilion was very grand, warm compared to the evening chill outside, and suffused with the light and scent of burning candles. There I saw four Dukes, two of Michael and two of Raphael, along with various Seraphim and other important angels from our tribe. They sat upon the thick fur rugs which lined the floor, and spoke — and not in hushed voices or furtive whispers, but openly — about how they felt about the Son being declared vice-regent. It was an innocent conversation, I swear to you, an exchange of feelings and thoughts. One of Michael's Dukes asked Lucifer if he felt particularly affronted.

"'And why should I be so?' said Lucifer.

"'Because you were our vice-regent in Heaven,' the Duke replied.

"'Unofficially,' added a delegate from Raphael's tribe.

"'Yes, unofficially,' Lucifer ceded, 'but Father Infinite never led me to believe anything greater awaited me.'

"'It is a great loss of power for all the archangels,' the first Duke said. 'Though I suppose there is nothing we can do about it.'

"Soon after, goodnights were bade and the delegation left. Lucifer invited us to stay for more food and song, and the rest of the evening passed uneventfully. My friends and I lay down to sleep in Lucifer's pavilion. After a few hours, I woke for some reason — perhaps the noise of more revellers close by — and saw that Lucifer sat awake still in his throne. I rose and went to sit with him.

"'Are you troubled, Majesty?' I asked him.

"'I feel that I have been given a monumental problem to consider, and no time or space in which to consider it.'

"'You speak of the new Son?'

"He nodded.

"'It is not for a lowly guardian such as I to offer advice. Should I wake some of the Seraphim?'

"'Yes,' he said, 'fetch Belial and Asmodeus. I would feel better if I could speak with them.'

"I found the two Seraphim that he spoke of, sleeping outside under the glorious stars. They woke a number of other retainers and high-ranked angels, so that all in all there were seven of us who returned to the pavilion. We sat on the floor around our troubled majesty and listened.

"'Should I be worried about the coming of the Son?' he asked us, when we were all assembled.

"Belial seemed bursting to speak. 'Does it not strike you as strange that he should name a vice-regent and it should not be you, Majesty? Have you not always been the one who sits closest to Father Infinite, there at his left hand? It should have been either you or Michael, but everyone knows you are the Father's favourite.'

"'I am proud,' Lucifer said, leaning forward with his perfect hands cupping his chin. 'I know I am proud and I must guard against pride, but I have been sitting here for hours thinking the same thing. If Father Infinite decided he wanted a vice-regent, he should have given us a chance to argue our case for the role. And then, if he still chose to create a Son and name him so, I would feel more content. But I have not even been given a chance.'

"'What can we do, Highness?' Asmodeus asked.

"'We can do nothing, not surrounded by the other tribes and with Father Infinite still so excited by his new plan. I think we should withdraw back to the North to think upon it further. Perhaps we can arrange a delegation to visit Father Infinite in the coming weeks, while he prepares to create the Son. When the first flush of his excitement has worn off, and he is more like to listen to reason.'

"And the murmur went around that it was an excellent plan, and so on. And we began to pack up right then, for dawn was only a breath away and we had the furthest to travel of all the tribes. But when we started to leave in the early light, angels from other tribes came by to ask us what was wrong. And through ignorance more than design, the rumour arose that we were leaving because Lucifer was angry with Father Infinite, and we were withdrawing to the North in order to cut ourselves off from the rest of the tribes and make it known our outrage. Before long, we found that other angels from other tribes wanted to join us, because they too were unhappy with the idea of an unknown vice-regent. They threw their lot in with us and angered their archangels. Consequently, Michael, Uriel, Gabriel and Raphael sent a messenger to Lucifer: he should return immediately and swear allegiance to the new Son. Their hypocrisy was not lost on Lucifer, for it was the archangels who had originally encouraged him to express his dissatisfaction.

"Lucifer declared his hand would not be forced, that he intended to return home and think about the new developments and would speak with Father Infinite soon. He would not deign to speak with other archangels when the matter did not concern them. With this, he made four powerful enemies. The other archangels, whether they admitted it or not, had always been jealous of Lucifer: his beauty, his intimacy with Father Infinite, the loyal devotion of his tribe. Now they had an opportunity for their resentment to grow into something real.

"Long before we reached our homeland, we realised that fully one third of all angels were now in Lucifer's train. I was amazed to see them, mighty and beautiful, following us to the North. With this large group of supporters, I began to imagine that Lucifer's case would be heard and perhaps even that Father Infinite would agree to make him vice-regent." Lazodeus paused momentarily, as though struggling with an uncomfortable thought. "In all truth, perhaps Lucifer's pride did become too unwieldy at this point. Perhaps he could imagine all too easily what shape his own vice-regency in Heaven would take, and that fantasy robbed him of his undivided reason. We camped on the plains, a day's journey from our homeland, and Lucifer decided to address his followers. He decided to speak out about liberty. This was his fatal error."

"Why?" asked Deborah.

"Because liberty is a word that rebels and radicals use. To justify pride, excess, even cruelty. This dispute was not about liberty, and Lucifer knew it. We all knew it. This was about wounded dignity.

"He had spirits erect him a glittering throne on a hilltop, and all of us waited, gathered around for miles, to hear him speak. He appeared, a vision of great beauty in dazzling white, proud and tall. The love I felt for him, the admiration and longing we all knew, made the air thick around us. I would have followed him to ... well, in the event, I did follow him to the end of Heaven." Lazodeus let his head hang forward.

"Does it make you sad?" Mary asked.

"I cannot express to you the grief which comes from being separated from Heaven — my homeland, the place where I know I belong. I know not if I shall ever see it again, but I would wait beyond eternity for just one more glimpse of those hills and valleys."

Mary considered how much more beautiful he appeared in his distress. She could not remember ever having felt so twisted up inside. Her helpless hands clutched each other in her lap.

"Lucifer waited until we had all fallen hushed. And then he said, 'Fellow angels, we have this day been threatened by the four other archangels, told that we must answer to them, respond to their questions as though we were inferior to them. As though they were our betters. All this follows on from Father Infinite's announcement of his intention to name a vice-regent of Heaven. This vice-regent will not come from among the ranks of the angels, but will be his newly created Son.'

"From the front of the crowd, somebody called, 'You should be vice-regent, Majesty.' And a great cry went up, for that was the love that we bore Lucifer. I wanted to see great honours heaped upon him; I wanted him to be the King of Heaven, because Father Infinite was remote and unknowable, but Lucifer knew me and bore me great love. In those moments, those delicious dangerous moments on the edge of the northern plains, it began to seem possible. I imagined Lucifer replacing Father Infinite, an active, dynamic leader rather than a vague source of passive love. To be in that crowd at that time was to feel as though history, the very history of the infinite universe, was being shaped in my hands.

"Lucifer must have felt it too, for I was close enough to see his beloved face, and doubt suddenly shadowed his eyes. Despite his early strong words, he began to resist the tide that wished to sweep him to power. He said, 'No, my friends. We must open a dialogue with Father Infinite and tell him our concerns reasonably and with love, and he will listen as he always does. My quarrel is with Michael, Raphael, Gabriel and Uriel, not with the Father.'

"'We know nothing about the Son!' a voice called. 'How can we let him rule us?'

"That should have been the moment where Lucifer urged caution, reminded everyone about the loyalty we still owed to Father Infinite. Perhaps he could have brought us under control then, but it was all too clear that Lucifer agreed with the sentiment. He hesitated, and in the space of his hesitation a Principality of our tribe, an angel named Abdiel, began to shout, 'Listen to you all. Rebels! Traitors! Have you forgotten where your true allegiance lies? It is not a matter of whether Lucifer has an argument with the other archangels. It is whether we trust Father Infinite and his decisions. And you do not. Lucifer, for shame. He loves you so dearly and you repay him with such treachery.'

"'If he loves me so dearly, why does he advance his son over me?' Lucifer cried. I heard real pain in his voice. I believe in that moment all was lost, for he sounded so sorrowful, so betrayed, that we all became firm to our purpose. And that purpose became revolution." He looked up, fixed Deborah with a keen gaze. "Do you see now how it was? How our intentions were formed through opportunity and love? Not malice, not pride and vanity and evil design as your mortal race has been told."

Deborah nodded once. "I would like to hear the whole story. What happened next?"

Lazodeus pressed his hands together between his knees. "Violent debate began between Abdiel and Lucifer, between Abdiel and the crowd, and he was driven out. We did not harm him, but he must have felt unsafe as such a barrage of abuse was rained upon him. He returned immediately to Father Infinite while we withdrew to the North, towards our homes. The huge distance between the Palace of Lucifer and Father Infinite's throne began to be a serious disadvantage. We could not get home in time.

"Dark clouds began to gather in the east. Angels do not war, so our tribe did not have weaponry. Yet all the while the other angels were arming themselves. It is true. Father Infinite in his fury gave thunder swords to Raphael and Gabriel and their tribes, and sent them after us.

"They arrived unexpectedly, a huge array of armed angels. We barely had time to assemble, and could only use our angelic powers as defence. Powers which they too possessed, of course. Lucifer took a few close advisers and went out to meet with the archangels. But before a single word could leave his mouth, Abdiel — that filthy traitor — broke from the legion behind Gabriel with a thunder sword, and ran Lucifer through."

"A mortal wound?" Anne asked.

"No, for we are not mortal. But thunder can scar." He touched the white ridge on his own lip. "And it is painful. Very painful. Lucifer fell to the ground in agony. Chaos broke out. I was one of the angels who rushed towards Lucifer, who brought him back to camp and tended to his wound. Outside, the rebel angels — unarmed — attempted to fight the attacking angels. They threw thunderbolts, they created a whirlwind, they raised a howling storm and caused the earth to shake . . . but their foe knew the same magic, and deflected it all harmlessly.

"The united angels advanced towards us, lashing out with

their thunder swords. Not one of us escaped that long day of battle without a scar, and that is how you can distinguish between fallen angels and angels still loved by God. We are scarred upon our ethereal bodies — the wounds show up as dark patches in the light or, when we take mortal form as now, they show up as discoloured ridges on our skin. The luckiest of us took scars to our bodies, but most of us were attacked in the face and hands. There is no doubt that they unleashed their resentment towards Lucifer's beauty in this way." His voice dropped almost to a whisper. "Two Thrones, friends of mine, named Achramelech and Asmadai, were so mangled as to be unrecognisable afterwards. As soon as Lucifer could stand again, we began to retreat.

"When night fell, Father Infinite's legion backed off and camped. Lucifer sent spies to their camp and in the early hours of the morning we heard the awful news. Father Infinite had armed Michael with the Sword of Annihilation."

"What's that?" Deborah asked.

"The one thing that can destroy us. The one thing that Father Infinite promised he would never raise against his own angels. Only then did we realise the full extent of his anger. He wanted to destroy us. You cannot imagine the icy paralysis of terror which gripped us all. Michael would only have to walk among us and wield the sword in an arc, and anyone it touched would cease to exist. As mortals, you are perhaps reconciled to your eventual death. We are not. We recognise it as the most unnatural and horrifying concept upon which we could ponder. None of us wanted to die. Not for Lucifer, not for Father Infinite, not for *anything* did we want to die.

"This changed everything. Everything. Our cause, I knew, was not worth annihilation. Lucifer arranged a hasty gathering of trusted angels and told us he would fall upon the Father's mercy. Nobody argued. I just wanted to go home. I wanted so badly to return to the vast northern plains, the sheer cliffs and foaming falls, the great still lakes and the tall, tall firs. I went back to my camp and, regretfully, but with relief, dozed a few hours away.

"The sun was just making its way over the vast horizon when, in the distance, a rushing sound, like a killing wind, became audible. I shook myself awake and looked up to the east where the dark storm clouds had been gathered since our accidental rebellion. A glimmer against the black, the sound growing more keen, a wind picking up. Then I saw it: the great chariot of the Father, silvered and adorned in a thousand eyes, led by Cherubim. And Michael sat in it, holding high the Sword of Annihilation.

"Screams and shouts broke out around me, and before I knew what I was doing, I was running; we were all running, scattering away from our camp and racing, desperately, towards the north, towards home. We ran and ran as fast as we could. Michael knew we would head in that direction, and he rounded on us, drove us out further and further to the west. Lucifer urged us on, told us to preserve ourselves. One unfortunate angel turned and stood his ground, begged Michael for mercy and was cut down, the blazing light of his existence extinguished in a single stroke. I knew then that there would be no mercy for us, no reasoning or apology would alter our fate. Michael drove us in front of him, throwing thunderbolts and cutting the air with the Sword, so we could hear the deadly whish-whish of its curve and were in no doubt that he intended our obliteration.

"I knew the chase could not last much longer, because we were approaching the crystal Wall of Heaven, the vast, glittering limit of our world. I was in such fear and panic that I hadn't considered what might happen when I arrived there. Michael drove us mercilessly to it and, as I drew close, I could see an opening out into the void; a black eye of nothing gazing back at me impassively. The angels began to pull up, to disarray in confusion. Some turned back, some tried to escape to the north and south, some kept running, and Michael picked a few of us off to remind us what a dire position we were in.

"I kept moving towards the Wall of Heaven. I was terrified of the void, of course. We all were. But at least it was not annihilation. It was an awful nothing, but it wasn't the final nothing. For most of us there was no choice. Lucifer reached the Wall first and the black eye opened and rolled inward, growing until it was an enormous gulf in front of us. Michael had drawn back, hovered above us and waited. Lucifer hesitated.

"'Father Infinite in his mercy has created a new world for you in the caverns down there,' Michael said. His tone of voice made it clear how vexed he was by that mercy. He should have liked to see all of us consigned to the void. 'If you leave now, I shall withdraw and no angel will be annihilated.'

"Of course, it was the best offer we could expect. But to leave Heaven . . . to leave the gentle hills and wild plains, to leave the sweet music of the seasons, to leave the dazzling intensity of the dawn and the soft balm of the twilight . . . how could I leave? How could I ever be happy if I were separated from Heaven and from Father Infinite? Even Lucifer, brave Lucifer, trembled on the edge of the void, the great cloudy nothingness rolling beside him, the crystal wall of Heaven glittering above.

"'Michael, can we not speak with the Father? Can we not throw ourselves upon his mercy?'

"Michael's answer was to raise the sword. 'Lucifer, your name shall no longer be spoken in Heaven. You shall be known as our great adversary, Satan. And I, for one, shall not miss you.'

"Lucifer drew himself up proud. 'If this is true, if I am to be your great adversary, then let it be so. But you, and the other archangels and the Father, shall regret it, for I shall prove to be the most formidable adversary imaginable.' He turned to us. 'Come, my angels. To stay in Heaven is annihilation, but in the cavernous below we shall live and we shall thrive.' With that, he hurled himself into the void.

"I wish I could say that I was as brave, but I, like most of the others, had to be driven through the gap by Michael, bullied and threatened. Still, a few lost their lives, too afraid to move. I took that giant step and I fell, the awful rolling, sick sensation of nothingness spinning through me. I fell and fell, and I began to think that Michael had lied, that no caverns existed and that I would fall eternally. My screams were useless and pitiful in the void. It was too dark to see others and a tremendous loneliness seized me. But soon, my wails grew less because my fall continued and I was hoarse and bewildered. Nine days I fell, in terror and in the agony of uncertainty. But then, finally, voices from below told me I had found the bottom." He crossed his hands over his chest and winced, as though remembering a terrible pain. "The impact of the fall had not the power to kill me, but I lay for a very long time on the cold ground — among the other dazed angels — in shame and in agony, scarred and driven out of my true home.

"When I began to rouse from my daze, and rolled over to look up, the sky had been closed out by the vaulting black walls of a cave." Here, Lazodeus pressed his palms to his face and had to choke back a sob. "Such a despair, such a vast despair which still weighs upon my heart, extinguished all that was light and joy in me. This was to be our prison."

He removed his hands and composed himself. "Every one of us submitted to our misery. We wept and we moaned. The cold was biting and we were sore and scarred. I know not how long we spent in that mad despair, but at length great Lucifer stood — a diagonal scar from his forehead to his chin had not obliterated his great beauty — and said that we must arise, that we must return to our feet, that despair was not our lot; rather, we must proclaim the great cavern our new kingdom.

"When Alathor wailed that our lost kingdom was far greater, Lucifer told him that he would rather be the king of the abyss than a lowly toad in Heaven, answering to the new Son as if he had reason and right to rule us." Lazodeus smiled, a bitter smile. "Of course, once the Son came, we understood that Father Infinite had been right all along. Heaven's King is, indeed, the Son."

"It seems so strange to hear a devil say that," Deborah remarked.

"I'm not a devil, Deborah. As I have told you so often, I am still an angel."

"But did all this — your exclusion from Heaven, your casting down into the abyss — did it not make Lucifer, did it not make all of you hungry for revenge?"

He shook his head. "If you had seen Heaven but once you would know why all we want is to return. But to return for any of us is to be annihilated."

"I thought Hell was supposed to be full of fire," Anne said.

"It is, for it is so very cold at the farther reaches of the void. Immediately, Lucifer used his great skill with fire to create an immense burning lake at the very centre of the cave, and it has burned there ever since. And we have fires burning in every corner, and in every street of Pandemonium, which is our great city there."

"But Pandemonium translates to 'place of all demons,'" Deborah said. "I thought you were angels."

Lazodeus laughed. "Deborah, are you trying to prove me a liar?"

"I simply want to know the truth."

"It is called Pandemonium because it was built for us by demons, and demons live there with us."

"So what are demons?" Mary asked.

"Spirits with one purpose each — elementals who may be commanded by angels. Or even mortals." With this, Mary noticed he turned his gaze upon Deborah and watched her for a moment. Deborah's face was impassive; she merely met Lazodeus's gaze and waited for him to continue. Mary felt the itchings of jealousy. Why was he staring at her so closely?

"Go on," Deborah said.

"We commanded the demons to build us our towers and rooms of state. First a grand palace where Lucifer rules, and then a massive city with tangled roads and tall buildings. But the sun neither rises nor sets on Pandemonium. It is in blackness all the time. And so it was, for a very, very long time, that we heard nothing of Heaven and became resigned to our lot. For centuries I dreamed of the open spaces and sweet music, but soon those dreams faded and I accepted my new home.

"Everything changed when, after long millennia, we heard that Father Infinite was to create a new race, and a new world for them to live in. Again, he did it because he wanted more beings to love. His love is infinite, and insatiable. The wonderful benefit for us was that the new world, the mortal world, was accessible to us. We could travel between it and the cavern, and we saw for the first time in what had seemed forever the rhythms of stars and moons, the blue sky and the open fields — a pale shadow of Heaven's beauty, but such a glorious change from the dark, firelit streets of Pandemonium."

"We know the story now," Mary said, growing bored with this history and wanting to devise a plan to get Lazodeus alone. "Adam, Eve — she ate the apple, now we all get to die. Father's been writing about it and boring us all to death with it of late."

"It was so much more subtle and complex," Lazodeus said, "but I see you tire of my story so I shall draw it to a close. The most important thing you should know is that the moment we saw the mortals for the first time, we fell in love. And no surprise, for they were created for angels to adore and we do adore you, all of you. There is no hatred borne by the inhabitants of Pandemonium towards mortals. We want you all to proceed to Heaven and know its glories too. Your souls are in no danger, from me or from any of us." He directed this at Deborah.

"And Father Infinite sent us his Son."

"Yes, because the mortals were uncontrollable." He chuckled. "Which is something which makes us love them even more fiercely. The Father needed a presence in the mortal world to inspire them. And it is through mortals and the mortal world that we fallen angels hope eventually to be reunited with the rest of our race, and with our homeland. It is a common ground which we share, where we can communicate with angels and prove ourselves to them, by giving mortals pleasure and helping them in times of need. You, all of you, are stepping stones on my pathway back to the echoing northern plains of Heaven. Deborah, if you are looking for a less-than-selfless motive from me, that is all it is." He sagged forward. "I am very tired. I would like to go now."

"Don't go," Mary wailed.

"Of course he shall go, Mary," Anne said, then turned to Lazodeus. "But you will be nearby?"

"Yes, just call my name, as before. But remember, since you have dismissed me as your guardian I cannot be as reliable in my attendance. Deborah, have I satisfied you with my tale?"

"Thank you, Lazodeus."

"Perhaps when I return you could tell me about this work your father is writing?"

"Perhaps," Deborah said, a frown crossing her face for the first time this evening.

"Oh, 'tis as dull as a muddy puddle," Mary said dismissively.

Lazodeus smiled. Mary could not stop looking at the scar on his top lip. Thunder-scarred, driven out of Heaven. It all seemed so distant and unreal. And she cared, of course she did, but she cared more for the feel of those lips on her body.

"Farewell for now, sisters," he said, standing. "I shall be nearby, and I will try to come promptly when you call." With a shivery glimmer of light, he disappeared.

13
The Majesty of Darkness

Even though his light was subtle and diffuse, the room seemed suddenly darker now Lazodeus had gone. Deborah rose and lit a candle, thinking about his story.

"I can't believe he left!" Mary stamped her foot and her dark curls shook.

"You're mightily upset for someone who told me recently she didn't care if she saw him again or not," Anne said, her head tilted curiously.

"Oh, go to, Anne. I liked you better when you stammered."

Deborah weighed in. "Sisters, are we to begin our sniping and fighting again? Are our bonds of love so sorely tested by this creature?"

"I notice you are very calm," Mary said. "You got what you wanted. You used up all our time together having him repeat that stupid story. Always trying to prove he's a liar."

Deborah stood back. "Mary, what interest do you have in Lazodeus? Both of you. Why is it that we cannot mention him without quarrelling?"

Mary seemed to get her feelings under control. She lifted her shoulders casually. "I have no more interest than either of you. I just don't like it when you dominate our meetings with him."

Deborah shook her head. Mary and Anne were both in love with him. It was plain to see, but impossible to believe. "I am tired. My bed awaits. Try to be loving to one another.

261

We are sisters, not rivals." She went to her closet and closed the door behind her. The bed was too short but she was grateful for her private space. She placed the light on the rickety table next to her bed and sat cross-legged on the covers, chin in hand, thinking.

Lazodeus's story was plausible. It was certainly compelling, and easy to imagine how a series of bad decisions and misunderstandings could lead to such a serious breach. But wasn't God supposed to be merciful?

Perhaps not always. She had read the Old Testament, and Yahweh — Father Infinite — was often cruel and unforgiving. Besides, the Bible itself was full of internal contradictions, gaps and weaknesses of representation. Even Father had once urged caution over complete confidence in its accuracy. The hands of too many fallible men had passed over it; the true way to God was via her own conscience.

Could evil from one perspective be foolish reaction from another? Of course it could. She had witnessed enough fights between Mary and Betty to understand diversity of perspective. But the whole world believed Lucifer was evil. Could she side against the opinion of the whole world? Amelia would encourage her to do so, but Amelia did not have her innate caution.

It was tempting to try to see Lazodeus again, now he had returned from his long absence. Deborah scrambled to the trunk at the end of the bed and pulled out the scrying mirror. If she could see him when he didn't know she was looking, he may prove himself to her. Or betray himself to her. She passed a hand over the gleaming surface. "Show me Lazodeus," she said quietly.

Nothing. The mirror continued to reflect her own curious face in the candlelight. Perhaps ethereal beings were not able to be seen in the mirror. She pondered for a few moments, then decided to test this theory. She had most recently called upon the apprentices of Andromalius. Were they able to be seen in the mirror?

"Show me the apprentices of Andromalius."

She should have prepared herself for what such beings might look like: toad-faced, squatting creatures, surrounded by fiery light, wriggling against each other trying to get comfortable. But nothing could have prepared her for where she found them: in the walls of her closet. She gasped and looked around her. The walls seemed ordinary and benign, but when her gaze returned to the mirror, there they were: crammed against each other behind the boards, their softly glowing hides only visible in the scrying mirror. With a shaking hand, she passed her fingers over the mirror again. "Let me hear them."

A soft chittering and snorting began to sound, then she cleared the mirror, not wanting to hear it any more, not wanting to see their ugly wriggling bodies. How was she supposed to sleep in here now, knowing that they surrounded her? Could they see her? She even gave a few moments to the selfish idea of swapping the room with Anne or Mary, but surmised that the beings would follow her. They came with the key, or maybe with the mirror or the books. They were hers. The shock drove all thoughts of Lazodeus out of her head for a while, as she extinguished the candle and took refuge under the covers. In the dark she stared at the walls around her, strained her ears, but could distinguish no sight, no sound of the creatures she knew were there.

Then she began to ponder. If the scrying mirror could see the demons, why couldn't it see Lazodeus? The conviction returned to her as it always did: he was being less than honest, he was hiding himself from her. It was perfect logic. He knew she didn't trust him, he knew that she would eventually be tempted to check on him, so he had deliberately charmed the mirror against finding him.

For all that, he seemed to know things about her that she hadn't told him. Her hand went to the key around her neck as she remembered the keen way he had gazed at her when speaking of men who command spirits. He knew. But how did he know? Was he spying on all of them in some magical way? Or could he sense the key in her possession? Maybe the demons she had used had told him. She knew so little, and yet she was knee-deep in such mysterious power.

What would Amelia say? *Do not be fearful. Be bold.*

She closed her eyes, but took a long time to sleep. Hard to be bold when surrounded by invisible creatures which she could not hope to understand.

It seemed Anne could never be alone. All she wanted was a time and a place to call Lazodeus. Mary had her secret room, Deborah had her closet, but Anne only had the shared bedroom and an opportunity never arose for her. It wasn't as though she could go crawling along the ledge to Mary's secret room for privacy, not with her crooked hip. A week went by, and then another. On one occasion — with Mary out with the dog and Deborah downstairs — she had taken her chance. With a wildly beating heart she had closed the bedroom door and stood in the middle of the room. But before her tongue could even curl around the L of his beloved name Mary had burst in, suddenly bored with the idea of walking Max. Anne was fairly sure it was to prevent her calling the angel.

Finally, she could stand it no longer. Perhaps the old Anne Milton — the one who could barely speak and was afraid of everything — would sigh resignedly and accept it. But she wasn't that Anne Milton any more. She wanted to take the problem into her own hands and solve it. All she had to do was find a place and a time where she could be uninterrupted. On the second Saturday in July, she lay awake very late, until she was certain Mary was asleep. Then she waited a little longer — perhaps half an hour — before creeping out of bed.

It was too risky to dress properly. Mary would be certain

to hear her. So Anne pulled a long cloak over her night-gown, and went barefoot down the stairs.

Because of her limp, she had to be assiduous in her silence. Every step threatened to be a beacon of her waywardness. Carefully, so carefully, she arrived at the front door, opened it with a tiny creak, and set off into the night.

The sunny warmth of the day was faded from the stony ground, but the night was balmy and the air heavy with London smells: faintly coppery, a slightly sick smell of old mud and distant sewage, overlaid thickly with the summery scent of rotting blooms. None of it unpleasant; in fact, vaguely reassuring. She knew where she was when she smelled those smells, they centred her. She hurried down the hill, her limping leg dragging behind her, to the park where they sometimes took Max to play. A thick copse of trees edged the park before it gave way once again to rows of houses. She headed for the trees, and sat beneath them, panting, heart racing, catching her breath. From where she sat she could see the dip of the park, the mist collecting in it. The grass was dewy, but not wet enough to discourage her lying back and looking up at the stars through the branches of the trees. She savoured the wait, the few gorgeous moments before she called his name.

"Lazodeus," she said. "Come to me."

A brief silence terrified her. He wouldn't come. He was too busy looking after someone else, loving someone else. But before the terror could work its way down into her heart, he was there, a soft light in the darkness, kneeling next to her.

"Anne, it is late and your sisters are both sleeping," he said.

"I don't care," she said. "I wanted to see you."

"And you had to come this far from your home to see me?"

"I wanted to be alone with you," she said boldly, then instantly regretted it. "I mean ... there are things that I don't want Mary and Deborah to know."

"Such as?"

"You must tell me how severely you were punished for my sake, for giving me my voice."

Lazodeus smiled and shook his head. "It is all in the past now, Anne. It would not do you any good to know."

"Still, I should like to know." She sat up and clasped her arms around her knees. "I should like to measure fully the extent of my debt to you."

"You owe me nothing, Anne. But if you are determined to know, I was imprisoned for a short time."

"Imprisoned? How long?"

"Only two weeks."

"Oh, you poor thing. I can't live with such guilt. Was it unpleasant?"

"Not too unpleasant, but cold. We aren't allowed our fires in prison."

"I'm so sorry. I should never have asked for such a favour."

"Anne, it is over with. It is not the first time I have been imprisoned. It is hard to behave appropriately around mortals, for we love them so much. Most fallen angels suffer such a punishment at one time or another in Pandemonium."

Anne felt the discomfort of guilt and wriggled against it. "I am so sorry. Can I repay you somehow?"

"Say not another word about it. It is my reward to see how comfortable you now find it to speak. You are a changed woman, Anne."

She felt the smile form on her lips in spite of herself. "In truth?"

"You are so much more poised. Before you left London, you were still like an awkward girl. But now look at you." He took each of her hands in his own and spread them apart. "You have grown beautiful."

She hung her head. "Please, I'm uncomfortable with such flattery."

"It is not flattery, it is truth." He gently released her hands

266

and she folded them once more over her knees.

Her heart seemed to have developed an irregular flutter; it twitched about in her chest like a frog in a box. "I do not feel beautiful," she said, darting a quick glance at him and then looking away. "I feel like the same clumsy, tottering Anne that I always was. Certainly, my mouth is more bold, and perhaps my mind, but I am still constrained by the weaknesses of my body."

"Does that make you sad?"

A breeze fluttered in the leaves, tugging at her hair. "Sometimes. Sometimes I should like to run. Or to dance."

"You can dance with me."

The fantasy flashed briefly before her mind's eye. Enclosed in his arms, moving rhythmically to some exquisite music. But then she dismissed it. In such a situation, he could only become far too aware of her feeble body, her crooked hip, which made her left leg straggle behind her, pushed out uncomfortably. Then, certainly, he could feel only repulsion for her. "I cannot dance, Lazodeus," she said. "Least of all with an angel."

He stood and held out his hand to her. "Anne, you can *only* dance with an angel."

"What do you mean?" she said, eyeing his proffered hand warily.

"Stand, you will see."

She grasped his hand and stood, and her hip was perfectly normal, her leg perfectly mobile. She took a few paces on her own, marvelling at the freedom she felt — like moving through silken water.

"Oh," she said. "Oh, it feels wonderful."

"It is only for tonight, I am sorry."

"I care not. I shall enjoy it for tonight."

He drew her close to him. "Come, Anne, dance with me."

"I know not how to dance. I've never danced." A giddy tide of exhilaration washed through her.

"You merely listen to the music and let your body move you."

"There is no music."

He gracefully rolled his right hand in the air. Instantly, music began to play.

"Where is that coming from?" she said, giggling in excitement.

"It is angel magic. Ask no more questions. Come. Dance with me."

She bit her lip in a last moment of concern, then decided that on such a mad night, with a warm breeze and angel music to accompany them, the only sane choice for a girl to make was to dance. She surrendered her body to the music, and began to move.

His arms closed around her waist, he spun her around, he pressed against her and moved away. Violins and harpsichord rang out joyously on the air, and she expected the whole world to wake and wonder of the gorgeous song which had worked its way into her heart. She danced and she spun and she stretched and she twirled and she *moved* with an aching joy in her bones. Laughter poured from her lips and her eyes were moist with tears. The moon and all the stars laughed with her.

I am in love.

When her legs began to tire, when perspiration was trickling across her stomach underneath her nightgown, when the maddening touch of his angelic hands was too much to bear any longer without opening her heart and begging for his love, the music began to fade and he gently lowered her to the ground.

She took deep breaths.

"You glow, Anne," he said.

"Why did nobody wake? The music was so loud."

"Only we could hear it."

"'Twas divine, truly."

"You dance beautifully."

"I've never danced ere now. Oh, 'twas joy!" She gulped a few more breaths and then sat up straight. "I should go. Mary will miss me."

"No, don't go. I have taken care of Mary. She is enjoying a deep dream from which she will not wake." He touched her hair gently. "Put your head in my lap and talk to me. I love to talk with mortals."

"I . . ."

"Come." He stretched his legs out in front of him and pulled her down. "It is not inappropriate, Anne. Think of me as a loving uncle or father."

"I have had neither," she laughed.

"Let us be alone in the warm darkness a while, Anne. Trust me."

Her fear wasn't that it was inappropriate to lay her head in his lap; her fear was that her heart would burst with such intimacy. She nestled against his thighs, staring up at the starry sky. His fingers twined in her hair. Aching, aching, she turned her timid eyes to meet his. It was too much. Her heart would explode.

I am in love.

"Has Mary called you?" she asked hesitantly.

"Yes, Mary has called me a number of times."

She looked away again. Much safer to gaze at the stars. "Oh."

"I have not responded, however," he said. His hand curled around the top of her head, resting there warmly.

"No?"

"If I tell you something will you promise to keep it between us?"

"Of course, I will do anything . . . I mean . . . I will keep any promise."

"Mary always wants something. Sometimes she is exhausting to be with."

"Yes, yes, she is."

"So I often stay away."

Anne felt a surge of triumph. "I see."

"You must think me heartless. Cruel."

"No, no," she said quickly. "Not at all."

"I much prefer to be with you. Though I suppose I should not reveal such a partiality."

"I shan't take advantage of it. I shall not ask for too many things, as Mary does."

"I know. I know, Anne, that is why I trust you the most."

"You don't trust Deborah?"

He frowned for a moment, casting his eyes upwards. "I know little of Deborah. She is suspicious of me, I suppose," he said.

"'Tis most unfair for her to feel that way."

"Nevertheless, it is how she feels. I accept that." His fingers were moving again, twining her hair and releasing it. "Tell me a little about Deborah."

"What would you like to know?"

"Perhaps you can tell me what drives her? What is at her core?"

Anne thought hard. It was important to answer his question as fully as she was able. "Deborah is excessively loyal to Father. She was always his favourite, and that has long been her weakness, I suppose. Though lately she grows impatient with him at times."

"Why do you think she is so loyal?"

"She loves him."

"Why does she love him?"

"Because he is her father."

"But he is your father, and you bear no love for him. Nor does Mary."

Anne considered this. "She wants to please him. She wants to remain his favourite. When she was tiny, if Father roared at her because she had been naughty, she would cry for days, saying 'poor Father' and so on. Then, she would carefully select a toy from among her favourites: a poppet or a treasured ball, and she would throw it on the fire to punish herself. She would stand there silently, gravely, watching as the flames consumed it, then march in to tell Father what she had done. 'I have given up Molly for my sins,' she would say, or 'I have given up my purple hoop.'

"I doubt that he even remembered what small thing had upset him, and he certainly didn't understand the magnitude of her sacrifice. He would merely nod in a distracted way and go on with what he was doing."

"You say that her obedience to him is waning, though?"

"Yes, most definitely. It is not the same as it used to be. She still pays him the same respect one should pay a parent, but she no longer defends his impatience, or rushes to be his helper."

"Anything else?"

Anne reached for words, trying to articulate the essence of her sister. "She is committed to learning, mainly of physic and natural philosophy. She speaks of one day healing the sick. Again, I think this is to impress Father, but lately I am not so sure. She spent all her time at Chalfont reading under a tree."

Lazodeus nodded, as though considering what she had just told him. A pang of jealousy darted into her heart. "Why do you want to know?"

"I am interested in all of you. I am still, in some ways, your guardian. Though not officially."

"Deborah has always managed to look after herself very well," Anne said. "I believe she is the last person in the world who requires a guardian. Even if she did believe you were a good angel, she would not ask for help. She would probably ask you to teach her medicine."

"What is it your father does that he requires Deborah so much?"

"He is writing a great poem. I have heard little of it, for I cannot write and I am no use to Father. Though I read well enough."

"Mary said it had to do with angels and with God."

"And devils withal, I believe. The story is not nearly so compelling as your tale."

"Hmm. I should like to see it."

"I am uncertain if I could steal it for you," Anne said, suddenly worried that she could not perform the sole request he had so far asked of her. "Father won't let me near his writings."

"No, Anne. Do not worry. It is not important."

They sat in silence for a long time, and Anne closed her eyes and let the sensation of his glorious touch sink into her skin. Perhaps she began to doze a little, but his deep voice roused her. "Anne, the dawn approaches, you should return to your bed."

"Yes," she murmured, trying to open her eyes.

"Ah, hush." He said, gently touching her eyelids with his fingertips. "Dream on, beautiful Anne."

She heard the sounds of birds awakening, felt a slanted beam of sun on her face. Her eyes flew open and she sat up with a start and a gasp. She was in her own bed. Mary, sleepy-eyed, rolled over next to her and grumbled irritably. "What's all that noise about?"

"Nothing," Anne said. "A dream. Go back to sleep."

But not a dream. She had been with him, and somehow he had returned her to her own bed. She lay back and closed her eyes, began to drift off again, dancing in her imagination, spinning and turning with his warm arms around her.

Mary stood on the ledge, her back to the wall, and breathed deeply. Sometimes she took a few moments up here, on her way home from her secret room, to enjoy the fresh air and relive the glorious moments she had just spent with the angel. Her skin shivered as she remembered the hot wax he had drizzled over her, the silk scarves he had used to tie her hands and wrists, and the bold places into which he had slid the warm candle. The aftershocks of passion still ached between her legs.

She looked down. Sometimes she imagined jumping — not because she wanted to die, but because she wanted to feel the sensation of falling. That's how it felt with Lazodeus: falling and falling, abandoned to pleasure. She sighed and leaned her head back. Almost every day since the three of them had summoned him, she had spent precious moments in his company. Almost every day. Some days he told her he wouldn't come; he told her the intensity of her sensation would be doubled on the following day because of his absence. And maybe that was true, but it wasn't the intensity of sensation that she was addicted to any more. It was him she was addicted to, and not to see him was to suffer. She would do almost anything to be near him. And that meant tomorrow she had to smuggle Father's manuscript to the secret room for the angel to read. Though why he wanted to waste their precious time together in such a dull pursuit was a mystery to her.

Gathering her wits, she slipped in the bedroom window. Anne was nowhere to be seen, but she could hear sounds from Deborah's closet. Max came running up to her, tail wagging, and yelped a quick hello.

"Hello, darling," she said, scratching his ears. She glanced up to see Liza emerging from Deborah's closet, staring at her astonished. They spoke at the same time.

"What are you doing here?"

"Where did you come from?"

Mary glanced towards the door and noticed that the dresser had been pushed in front of it to prevent entry.

"Why have you barred our door?" Mary asked standing. "And what do you have in your hands?"

"Nothing," Liza said stupidly. It was plain that she held some of their possessions.

"You are stealing!" Mary strode over and snatched the items from her. An old bronze mirror which Uncle William had once given her in an attempt to seduce her. Two of

273

Deborah's books: a Hebrew grammar and a book of anatomy.

"No, I am not stealing," Liza protested, her skinny arms clutching anxiously around her own waist.

"Then explain why you have these things. This mirror was deep in my drawer. You have meddled with my private belongings. And these books of Deborah's, what do you want with them if not to sell them for money?"

"Where did you come from?" Liza asked again, and Mary finally deduced that Liza was frightened about her appearing from nowhere. She didn't know about the ledge and the secret room.

"Never you mind," Mary said, playing on her fear. "Explain yourself at once, or I'll give you a beating and tell Father to put you out on the street. And nobody will hire you for I shall tell all of London that you are a thief."

"Mrs Milton told me to!" she blurted, giving Mary pause.

"What? Betty put you up to this?"

Liza nodded.

"What did she tell you to do?"

"To look for a magic mirror or a magic book."

Mary looked down at the objects in her hands and could barely contain her laughter. "Magic mirror? Magic book? You clodpoll. This is an old mirror bought cheap at Forest Hill. And these . . ." She held up the books. "If you could read you would see that one is a guide to Hebrew and one is a text on anatomy. These aren't magical symbols, fool."

"I didn't know!" Liza cried, now more concerned about being thought a fool than being caught stealing.

"Why did Betty want to know if we had magic books?" This was new. Betty had been impatient with them about many things, but never magic. Did she suspect? And if so, why?

Liza shrugged, and wouldn't answer.

"You are a dunderhead," Mary said, reaching out to clip

her around the ears. "Take these objects to Betty then, and tell her they are proof of our dealings with necromancy. She will probably give you a beating for your stupidity." She held out the books, but Liza wouldn't touch them. She kept glancing towards the door.

"I suppose you will tell Betty that I appeared from nowhere as proof of my magic?" Mary said.

Liza remained silent. Mary shoved her violently. "Idiot. Tell her whatever you want. But remember, if we *are* magic, then we may put a spell on you."

The servant's face blanched. Mary marched to the door and moved the dresser. "Go," she said. "Go tell Betty that it may be dangerous to spy on us."

Liza scurried out. Mary felt her heart beating rapidly, and the heat of rage burning under her skin. How dare she! Betty had gone too far this time, and she desperately wanted to punish her. Mary closed the door and paced the room. She longed to push her stepmother down the stairs, or break a clay jug over her head, or kick her in the stomach until she spat blood. But she could do none of those things, for laws and magistrates and prisons and gallows existed as deterrents. Besides, attacking Betty with fists and feet was beneath her. Far, far beneath her. For she had an angel who could perhaps vex Betty in undreamed-of ways.

Deborah reluctantly took up the pen and ink as Father waited, a stern frown pulling at his lips. She had been nearly out the door to attend her weekly meeting with Amelia when he had ordered her to return for dictation.

"Can't Mary do it?" she had protested.

"Mary has been luckier than you in escaping the house this morning," Father said. "Liza can't find her anywhere."

Damn Mary and her secret room.

"So, Father, where are we to begin today?" Deborah said. She could feel the twitch of each moment pulling on her attention. By now, Amelia would be wondering where she was.

"Find the lines where Raphael speaks to Adam . . . he says, 'How shall I relate to human sense . . .'"

"Yes, yes, 'th' invisible exploits of warring spirits.' Would you like me to keep reading?"

"No. No, destroy it all, destroy that entire section."

Deborah was amazed. "Destroy, Father?"

"Yes, yes, throw it on the fire, it is all wrong."

"Are you certain you would not like me to read it to you first?"

"No, destroy it. It is wrong."

Deborah carefully scored through each of the pages he referred to, and put them aside. "I have cancelled them through, Father, and will feed them to the flames later."

"Good, good. Now, we shall begin this section again." He leaned in, his voice dropping to a conspiratorial whisper. "I have had the most incredible dream, Deborah, while dozing in my chair just this morning."

"Of what did you dream?"

"Of all the faults in my poem, of scenes heretofore unwritten, of the true majesty of my villain."

"Satan?"

"Yes, for I have represented him as weak and vain. But he was an angel, Deborah. An angel first, and therefore I must restore to him his pride and dignity."

Deborah felt an uneasy sensation of dread swirling into her stomach. "Father, Satan is our adversary."

Father straightened his back. "I need no lesson in theology from you, Deborah. Yes, he is our adversary, but can he not be a worthy one?"

Deborah dipped her pen. "Go on," she said.

Over the next hours, Amelia forgotten, Deborah scribbled as quickly as she could, as Father related to her perfectly Lazodeus's story of the war in Heaven. Father's version was of course more persuasive and compelling than the angel's, wrought as it was in beautiful language and meter. But it was Lazodeus's story with barely a deviation. When he had finished, he sat back with a satisfied grin on his face.

"What do you think, Deborah? Are they not some of the grandest lines I have ever composed?"

"Why, yes, Father," Deborah said, glancing over what she had written with an uncomfortable sense of helplessness. What was she to do? Did it matter that Father had repeated Lazodeus's story with all its biased loyalties? How dare Lazodeus invade her father's dreams?

"You sound unsure. What is the problem?"

"I . . . Father, it reads as though you are aligned with the fallen angels, rather than the ones who remained true to God."

"Does it?" A moment's concern crossed his face. "But I wrote it as I dreamed it. Why would I dream such allegiances?"

"I don't think you have, Father," Deborah said quickly. "Only, your generous and fair nature, your ability to see both sides of any dispute, has led you to be overly charitable. And Father, it is no surprise that a man such as yourself should feel sympathy with rebels. For were you not one yourself, in your youth? The earliest distress of my life was your removal to prison for sedition."

"Hmm." He stroked his chin gently. All was silent for a few moments. "I shall think upon it, Deborah. Leave it as it is for now. When I return from Cambridge I will reconsider."

"Yes, Father."

"You may go. You were in a hurry to be somewhere not long past."

Deborah put aside her writing tray. "Thank you, Father."

"And thank you, Deborah," he said gruffly, turning his chair away. She took the small compliment of his affection carefully. Lately, she had had to guard her heart against the passionate loyalties which Father aroused in her. She wouldn't be hurt by him again. Pulling on her cap and gloves, she headed for Amelia's.

The sweat ran in trickles under Betty's clothes as she and Liza stuffed a fish by the cooking fire. It was too hot to be in the kitchen, but the work had to be done. Pike was John's favourite and, as he occasionally reminded her, if she couldn't cook his favourite dish at least once a week, what was the point of him calling her his wife? She could never be certain whether or not he was jesting when he said such a thing.

She glanced up at Liza. The maidservant sported a purplish bruise on her right cheek which Betty had administered. The idiot had confessed to Mary that Betty had sent her spying for proof of magic. Despite lack of material evidence, she was in no doubt about their guilt. Liza had said that Mary appeared from nowhere, and Father Bailey had sent word that the book and mirror had disappeared from a locked trunk in his home. The situation had become dangerous now. With the girls dabbling in necromancy, what was to stop them turning it against her? Once the animosity she had felt for her stepdaughters was simply jealousy. Now it was fear.

Betty sprinkled flour on the fish and rubbed it in. Sweat tickled where her thighs touched. She wriggled her legs together to ease it. Summer was fully upon them. In a few days, she and John were travelling up to Cambridge to stay with an old friend of his there. The girls had been invited but all had refused. John had secretly confessed his relief: even Deborah was becoming unpredictable.

"Ma'am, how much sugar shall I put in the rice pudding?"

Betty pushed her hair off her face with the back of her wrist. "Why do you never remember a single thing I tell you?" The tickling between her legs had inched higher and was becoming unbearable. This heat would drive her insane if Liza's incompetence didn't first.

"I always get it mixed up with the sugar cakes."

Betty strode over to Liza's side of the large table, measured out the sugar and dumped it into the mixing bowl. She wanted more than anything to be able to scratch herself down below, but her hands were covered in flour.

"Thank you ma'am."

"There's an easy way to remember and that's —" Betty gasped. Suddenly the tickling had become a scratching and she squeezed her legs together tight to relieve it.

"Ma'am?"

Betty reached for a nearby cloth and wiped her hands vigorously. "I have to go upstairs for a moment," she said. As she dropped the cloth she noticed a spider crawling on the floor by the table. "And squash that ere it makes its way into the pudding," she called over her shoulder as she rushed out of the kitchen.

"Squash what, ma'am?" Liza called after her. But Betty barely heard her. She scratched herself vigorously through her skirt, but still the tickling, prickling sensation pestered her. Her private parts and thighs were awash with the feeling. Once within the privacy of her bedroom, she pulled the pot out from under the bed and squatted over it, yanking up her skirts.

Spiders.

The intensity of her scream surprised her, and was still echoing in her ears as her frantic hands moved between her legs. Spiders, dozens and dozens of spiders, crawling around in her pale pubic hair. She brushed at them desperately, but the itch, the awful itch of them, was inside her and she knew it. She shrieked and shrieked as she tried to squeeze them out. A little urine escaped her body and some of the spiders landed in the pot. She plunged her fingers inside herself and roughly scraped her insides. They were on her fingers, crawling up her hands, softly dropping on the edge of the pot and the floor around it.

The commotion outside the bedroom could barely distract her.

"Betty? Betty, are you sick?" This was John, and it occurred to her that her scream must have terrified him if it had brought him up the rickety stairs.

"Ma'am, ma'am!" This was Liza rushing in, pushing through the curtains. "Whatever's the matter?"

"Spiders! Spiders! Look, they're everywhere!" In her shock and distress, she didn't give a thought for her dignity, but stood with her skirts hoisted, showing her naked quim to the maidservant.

"Ma'am, I can see no spiders. Calm down. There are no spiders."

"But they're everywhere!" She scooped up the pot and proffered it to Liza; even as she did, she realised that the itching had stopped, that she could not see a single spider on the edge of the pot.

Liza inspected the pot closely. "No, ma'am, no spiders." She took Betty gently and smoothed down her skirts, led her to the bed. "I think you must be ill."

Betty allowed herself to be led, her mind still aswarm with the hot horror.

"Liza? Is everything well?" This was John, just outside the bedroom curtain.

"Yes, sir. Mrs Milton's taken a nasty turn is all. You're not to worry."

Voices just outside, conferring. One of the girls. Then Deborah spoke: "Betty? Liza? Can I come in?"

Betty was too shocked to answer. Deborah tentatively parted the curtain. "Are you unwell, Betty?"

"She said she saw spiders in her pot," Liza replied.

Betty shook her head. "I know they were there. I felt them."

"It is very hot. Perhaps you are feeling dizzy?"

Betty met Deborah's gaze for the first time, and suddenly a connection snapped into place. The girls were involved in magic, and now they knew that Betty was watching them. This was her punishment.

"Get out!" she screamed. "Get out, witch!"

Deborah's shocked reaction made Betty think twice before saying anything else. "Betty, I . . . certainly, I shall go. I shall help Father down the stairs." In a moment she was gone, leaving Betty staring at the curtain.

"Ma'am, we'd best get you into bed," Liza said, turning down the covers. "You'll need to rest if you're to be well enough to travel to Cambridge on Friday."

The thought of going to Cambridge provided a moment's relief: away from the girls and their magic, safely out of the house. But then she thought about Father Bailey, about how John would never let an exorcist into the house. And she knew she could not go.

"I am most unwell," she said. "Tell Mr Milton to prepare to travel by himself."

14
Discord, First Daughter of Sin

Betty could not remember having been more anxious in her life. John had left, sour and resentful, at first light, urging her until the last moment to travel even though she was ill. The fact that her illness was feigned only served to heighten her guilt. What kind of wife was she, sending a blind man on a long journey alone? Yet, the coachman had been given an extra shilling to keep an eye on him, and she told herself he would be safe. The reasons she had stayed behind were far more urgent than John's brief discomfort.

Some time during the full sun of the afternoon, she had managed to get the girls out of the house, too. Liza had been charged with that responsibility and for once hadn't disappointed. The maidservant herself had reluctantly taken the afternoon off at Betty's insistence. Finally alone, Betty paced back and forth, from the kitchen to the front door, wondering when Father Bailey would arrive. He was already late, and she wanted him finished and gone well before the girls arrived home. The last thing she needed was for them to discover her plans.

She stopped and peered through the window. Footsteps on the street outside caught her attention, but it was only a couple walking past on their way to the main road. She perspired lightly. John was known to so many people. What if somebody saw the Catholic priest arriving at their house? If it were one of John's supporters that would be bad enough. But one of John's detractors with that information could be dangerous.

But what was she to do? There were devils in the house. The girls were witches. And she never wanted to suffer under one of their hideous spells again.

Finally, finally, she could see him advancing up the hill. Her eyes darted about, searching for witnesses. Thankfully, the street was empty. She threw open the door and called out hello.

"Good evening, Mrs Milton," he called in return. He was dressed in a long white robe, and carried a cloth bag.

Betty breathed again only when he was safely inside, away from the eyes of the public. She closed the door behind him.

"Good, then. Where shall we start?" he said, smiling his rotten-tooth smile. "Where are your stepdaughters?"

"The girls aren't here," Betty said.

Father Bailey raised his eyebrows in surprise. "Look you there now! Did you not want me to perform an exorcism?"

Betty's heart fell. "You mean they have to be here?"

"'Tis them to whom the devils cleave. They must be cleansed."

"But they will hurt me."

"Once they are cleansed they will not hurt you. They will kiss you and thank you for saving their souls."

"Can you not cleanse their room?"

"An excellent idea. And then I can come back tomorrow and finish the task. Will you show me where they perform their magic?"

She nodded and led the way. Father Bailey, with his slow, methodical movements, took an age to ascend the stairs. Betty despaired of him working quickly and leaving promptly. And as for him coming back tomorrow to work on the girls — if they suspected an inkling before he arrived, then she dreaded how they would repay her. Perhaps next time it would be snakes instead of spiders. Her throat grew dry at the thought.

Father Bailey pushed open the door to the girls' bedroom and took a step in, Betty close behind him. He lifted his nose and sniffed the air.

"Ah yes, this room is full of evil." He turned to her. "Tell me, Mrs Milton. Did you ever find the book and mirror after they disappeared from my home?"

She shook her head. "No, Father. But I suspect they are in Deborah's closet." She pushed the door open and showed him in.

"The girl has this much private space? Why, no wonder she has turned to necromancy. Young women should be watched more closely. They are predisposed to evil."

He examined the walls and the bed, and Betty wondered when he would start the proceedings. Time ticked by.

"Very well, I shall start here," he said. He reached into his cloth bag and brought out a flask. "Let us pray."

Betty bent her head as he started mumbling away in Latin. It went against everything she had been taught about God and faith, but she complied because she saw no alternative solution. After the Amen she looked up to see he had pulled the cork out of the flask. He began to speak more Latin, and she wished for even a basic command of the language so she could understand what he was saying.

As he spoke he drew crosses in the air and scattered water out of the flask. He spent a long time in Deborah's room, then moved into the main bedroom. More invocations, more crosses, more holy water. Betty had a thousand anxious questions poised on her tongue, but did not make a sound in case he had to start the prayer all over again. Already the evening was growing dangerously late. Elongated shadows drew across the room as the long twilight settled in.

It took less than an hour, but Betty's anxiety had drained her. When Father Bailey declared the room free of demons, she ushered him downstairs as quickly as she could.

"Thank you, Father, I appreciate your help."

"It is my duty, Mrs Milton. But I shall return tomorrow for the girls."

"Father, I fear that they will know you are coming and they will punish me."

"Pray, child. God will protect you."

Maybe, not long ago, Betty's faith could have been strong enough to assist her, but after the incident with the spiders she wasn't so sure. "What time will you come, Father? Early? At first light while they are sleeping?"

"A good suggestion. Expect me at dawn. In the meantime, keep safe. The house is rid of demons, but the girls may bring more with them."

He was out the door, standing in the street. Two passers-by glanced at them. Did they know John? Would they tell? They kept walking without comment.

"Good day, Father Bailey."

"Good day, Mrs Milton."

Betty closed the door quickly and pressed her back against it. Safe for now. Still, her heart hammered in her chest. She prayed that the girls wouldn't find out what she had done.

"Well, I know not why it takes three of us to carry a pie," Mary said as they rounded the corner into Artillery Walk.

"'Tis not as though you're actually carrying anything, Mary," Deborah sniffed.

"I'm keeping an eye on Max, aren't I? Dear boy." The dog trotted happily in front of them.

"I think Betty wanted us out of the house for a while," Anne said, pulling her lame leg behind her.

"That's clear enough," Mary said. "Perhaps she is having a paramour to visit."

Deborah giggled. "Mary, you are the limit." She looked up the hill and saw a pale figure emerge from their front door.

"Wait, is that Father Bailey coming from our house?"

"That dirty old Papist," Mary huffed. "Surely not. It must be next door."

"I am certain it is not," Anne said. "Deborah is right. He was visiting Betty."

They all looked at each other and burst into uncontrollable laughter. "Betty's paramour is a Catholic! How *pleased* Father would be to know," Mary said, nearly doubled over with laughter.

"But think about it, Mary," Deborah said. "Perhaps Betty is secretly Catholic. Can you only imagine? Having to pretend all this time that she's of our faith, and stealing away to confession when nobody is watching."

"That's ridiculous."

"Why else would she have Father Bailey to visit?"

Anne suddenly reached out and clutched Deborah's wrist with a cold, white hand. "Sisters, no. We have it wrong. What is Father Bailey famous for?"

"I have no idea, Anne. Why do you look so pale?" Mary said.

"He is an exorcist."

At once, they all turned to look up the street. Father Bailey had disappeared from view.

"Surely . . ." Mary breathed.

"That stupid trick you played on Betty, Mary . . ." Deborah started.

"Let's get home. Don't let Betty know that we know," Mary said. "Be composed. He can't hurt us, can he?"

"He is gone now, anyway," Anne said.

Mary caught Max in her arms and they hurried home. Deborah thought about the demons living in the walls of her closet. Could Father Bailey get rid of them? And would they come back as soon as she used the demon key again? Her right hand involuntarily went to her neck, to feel the heavy chain there.

"Betty, we're home," Mary called smoothly as they closed the door behind them. Deborah followed Mary to the kitchen while Anne hung back to check in the downstairs rooms.

"Hello, girls," Betty said. Even if she hadn't seen Father Bailey leaving the house, Deborah would have known something was amiss. Betty was positively ashen, and her voice was all strained friendliness, overlying a desperate fear.

"Here is your pie, Betty," Deborah said, placing it carefully on the table.

"Only I don't see why three of us had to go," Mary said. "I thought there must be baskets of food to pick up."

"You must be feeling better if you are up and working," Deborah said.

"Much better, thank you. Liza has the rest of the day off, so I am fixing supper."

"Mary, Deborah," Anne said from the doorway. They turned. "Come upstairs and we shall rest a while ere supper."

Betty's eyes were wide with anticipation.

"We shall return in half an hour or so," Mary said. She smiled a wicked smile. "How cosy, just the four of us for supper."

Betty tried to smile in return, but her anxiety was clearly overwhelming her. Deborah could sense it like a nerve trembling in the room.

Upstairs alone, the girls sat on the edge of the bed.

"I could see nothing downstairs," Anne said. "He has left no signs of his visit."

"But you still suspect he was here in his capacity as an exorcist?"

"I know not. What do you think, Deborah?"

Deborah bit her lip as she considered. She could check instantly, of course, simply by looking in her scrying mirror to see if her demons were still here. But her scrying mirror was a secret as much as her demon key. "Does it matter? He cannot hurt us, can he?"

"I am not certain of that, Deborah," Mary said. "What if

he comes back? What if he tries to exorcise us, and then we can no longer call upon Lazodeus."

Or use the demon key. Deborah stood and paced. "You are right to worry. But how can we know what he plans? Or how to protect ourselves if he returns?"

"Lazodeus could tell us," Anne said confidently. "He will know."

"Yes," said Mary enthusiastically. "Yes, we shall call him."

"Call him, then," Deborah said.

Mary took a step out into the centre of the room and looked up. "Lazodeus? We need to ask your advice. We may be in danger."

A shimmer near the window, then he appeared, dressed in his splendid clothes, all slow smiles and beautiful eyes. "All three of you?" he said. "I am honoured."

But instantly, something was wrong. Perhaps even before he finished his sentence, he pitched forward and barely steadied himself on the windowsill.

"Lazodeus? Are you unwell?" Mary hurried over, Anne limping behind her. They had an arm each within seconds, and had led him to the bed.

"What has happened?" he said, looking around bewildered. "Who has been in here?"

"Do you feel pain?" Anne asked.

Deborah heard the frantic note in her sister's voice, and it galvanised her to move forward. "The exorcist," she said. "He must have blessed the room, and it is making the angel sick."

"No!" Mary shrieked. "We are sorry, Lazodeus. You must leave immediately."

He fell back on the bed, his eyes closed and lay still for long moments.

"Lazodeus," Anne cried, lifting his wrist and patting it roughly. "Open your eyes. What is wrong? What can we do?"

He seemed to gather strength and his eyelids fluttered

open. "I am too weak to leave. I have been crippled by the blessing."

"Oh, what have we done?" Mary sat back and dropped her head forlornly. "What fools we are."

"Will you be well again?" Anne asked.

"I . . ." His eyelids dropped again. His voice came in a soft croak. "I can recover if I rest. But if he comes again, it may finish me."

"Finish you?"

"The exorcist has the power of Michael's sword in his words."

"Annihilation," Deborah said softly.

"We shall keep him away from you. How long will you need to recover?"

"A day, two days," he replied.

"'Tis lucky Father is away," Deborah said. "Though we will have to keep Betty and Liza out of the room."

"You can have Deborah's closet," Anne said.

"No, he can't!" Deborah replied.

"He's sick," Mary said, turning on her. "Have some compassion."

"I do not want Deborah's closet. I cannot move in any case, and you won't be able to carry me. I'm afraid I shall have to lie right here until I am better."

"Fine. We shall sleep on the floor," Anne said.

Already Deborah was shifting the dresser. "We need to keep this door barred. Two of us will have to go down to supper. We can't let on that anything is amiss. And one of us will stay here with Lazodeus."

"I'll stay."

"No, *I'll* stay."

"Anne can stay," Deborah said. For some reason she was unsettled by the idea of Mary and Lazodeus being alone together. Anne was more trustworthy.

"Why are you our commander suddenly?" Mary asked, indignant.

"Please, I must have quiet," Lazodeus said, his hand flying to his brow. Immediately, Deborah's two sisters fell silent, crowded about him, touching him gently and fussing with his pillows. Hopeless. Both of them were clearly in love with him.

"Both of you stay, then," Deborah said. "I shall have supper with Betty alone."

"Tell her we're sick," Mary said distractedly.

"I can think of lies enough, Mary. I trust the angel to your care while I change for supper." Neither of them noticed her disappear into her closet. She quickly pulled out the scrying mirror and passed her hand over it.

"Show me the walls of my closet," she whispered. The demons were all still there, wriggling against each other and chittering their strange language. Father Bailey's blessing was of mixed success then: it had affected the angel mortally, but her demons not at all. She frowned. Amelia might be able to explain it. Deborah's knowledge of ethereal beings was still limited. She hid her mirror once again, and prepared to keep company with Betty for supper.

Deborah had been gone only a few minutes, and Anne was lighting a candle, when Lazodeus lifted his head slowly and called, "Mary, Anne, I need to tell you something."

In moments, they had joined him on the bed. Mary eyed Anne jealously across his prostrate body. Her sister hung on his breaths as though they were gifts to her alone. Mary grudged every second Lazodeus spent looking at her.

"What is it?" Anne asked softly.

"I need to say something that I cannot say in front of Deborah. She bears me no love, and I could not trust her with this information."

"Go on," Mary said.

"The truth is, I will not recover as long as the exorcist still lives."

"What!" Anne cried, aghast. "Say it is not so, Lazodeus. Are we to lose you?"

"I shall kill him, and gladly," Mary said. Fierce anger surged into her chest. "How does he dare to hurt you this way?"

"Mary, I cannot ask either of you to murder for me. Anne," he said turning to her, "how could I request that you cause such harm when I was summoned under an oath to injure nobody. It goes against the very grain of who you are."

Anne set her jaw firmly. "But you cannot die."

He shook his head. "He will return, you know. Without a doubt, he will return. For his targets are you girls. Your stepmother was foolish in having you out of the house when she invited him. Exorcists are more interested in cleansing people than places."

"And when he comes back . . ." Anne started, her eyes wide with terror.

"I shall almost certainly be annihilated."

"But we can't kill him right here in Father's house! Betty would know. We would be hanged."

"I'll kill Betty, too," Mary said harshly. "I don't care. None of them are as important as Lazodeus."

"Mary, you are allowing your anger to speak," Lazodeus said, and she knew it to be true. Actually to kill someone? She could not imagine it. Or at least, she could only imagine it a little. As long as it didn't involve blood and screams and all the sounds and horrors attendant upon death.

"Is there another way?"

Lazodeus nodded slowly. "Yes, there is."

"Tell us."

"If the exorcist is made to . . . fall into a swoon. That is, if he is still alive but can no longer say the words, not even in his mind, that is the equal to his death."

"We shall do that then."

"But how?" Anne wailed. "Is there a poison we can give

291

him? Must we strike him on the head? What if we kill him by accident?"

"There is a way, but it begins to grow complicated," Lazodeus said.

"Complicated how?" Mary asked.

"Your sister has the power to induce a swoon."

"Deborah?"

"She would not want me to tell you this. It is her secret. But she owns a key which can command certain demons to perform tasks for her."

Mary temporarily forgot about the problem at hand. "A secret key? And she has not told us? How long has she had it? Why, the deceitful wench. All along being so righteous about whether or not we contacted you, and she has been involved in necromancy!"

"Do not be angry with her," the angel said. "It is only of late she has acquired it, and I would wager that she has been prudent in her use of it. But now, it is my only hope. My magic will not work because I am too ill. Her magic is all that is left to save me."

"So we need to convince her to use the magic?" Anne asked.

"Don't be a fool, Annie," Mary said. "As if Deborah will deaden the mind of a mortal to save an angel. Especially as she bears no love for Lazodeus. No, we must take it from her. Where does she hide it, Lazodeus? We must find it ere she returns."

"She wears it about her neck on a chain."

"Even to bed?"

"Even to bed."

Mary considered. "I believe I could take it while she slept."

"'Tis our only hope," Anne said. Mary could read the terror in her eyes. That terror made her a strong ally.

"Would you show us how to use it against the exorcist?" Mary asked.

292

"Yes." His eyes fluttered closed. "But now I must rest."

Mary smoothed his brow while Anne sat by, looking on hungrily. "Do not fear, angel. We shall rescue you."

"I shall be forever in your debt," he said with a sigh, and lapsed into a deep slumber.

In the earliest hours of the morning, Deborah was awoken by a soft voice. "Deborah. Sister. 'Tis Mary."

"What is it?"

"May I sleep with you? I am so uncomfortable sleeping upon the floor."

Without opening her eyes, Deborah pulled back the cover. "Of course. Poor thing."

Mary slid into bed beside her. "Thank you, sister. Go back to sleep."

She did, drifting under on that irresistible tide. Time passed as it did during sleep — vaguely. But she had a sense that it had been perhaps an hour since Mary had woken her, when she felt her head being lifted gently off the pillow.

"Mary?" she murmured.

"Shh, now. Just go back to sleep."

The cool touch of metal on her cheek. She stirred, tried to sit up. With a violent tug, Mary pulled the chain over her head. Deborah was wide awake now.

"What are you doing?" The key, Mary had it clutched in her right hand.

"Go back to sleep," she said, this time not soothingly.

"Give that back to me. What do you want with it? It is not yours." She reached out to snatch the key, but Mary was already on her feet. She pushed Deborah roughly onto the bed and ran from the closet, slamming the door behind her.

Deborah leaped out of bed, but Mary held the door firmly from the other side.

"Mary, give my key back." In her just-woken state, she couldn't comprehend what had happened or why. What did

Mary want with her demon key? How did she even know Deborah owned it?

Of course. Lazodeus. She began to beat frantically at the door.

"Mary, return my key. It will not work for you or anyone else."

"Shush, now. 'Tis for the best," Mary said. Then, "Angel, can I use this key to lock her in?"

Lazodeus's voice was faint, but Mary repeated what he said clearly. "Paratax, I call upon you with this key as your commander. Lock my sister in."

Deborah heard five sweet notes, then Mary's footsteps receding from the door. She tried it again, but it wouldn't move.

But how could that be? First, she had never heard of Paratax: the name appeared in none of the books Amelia had given her. Lazodeus must know of beings of whom mortals were not aware. Second, how could the magic work perfectly first time for Mary? She had not trained in the arts, she knew nothing about what she did. Again, Lazodeus must be the answer. He could probably command demons with ease.

And yet he said he was too sick to perform magic. It made no sense.

She quickly lit a candle and felt around in the dark for her scrying mirror. Why did Mary want the key, anyway? And want it enough to lock Deborah in her closet?

"Show me my sisters and Lazodeus," she said, with a quick pass of her hand over the mirror, and its faint glow lit the room. Of course, the mirror would not show the angel. Instead, she could see a view of the corner of the bedroom, where Anne sat on the floor. Mary was not in view.

"Let me hear them."

"You didn't hurt her, did you?" Anne was saying.

"No," Mary said. Deborah supposed she was sitting with Lazodeus. "Don't be silly. It is all for the best, is it not, Lazodeus?"

The angel's voice was not audible, but he clearly offered some words of encouragement, for Anne said, "I know that you are right. When can we expect the exorcist to return?"

So this was about the exorcist. But how could the demon key help them? And why did they not simply ask her for her assistance? She sat on her bed. Her blood boiled. How dare they? And how dare he? What business was it of his if she had a demon key, and where was the loyalty of her siblings if they would so blithely steal it from her?

"I shall stand guard on you all night," she whispered. And hunched over her mirror to watch and wait.

Anne could not remember ever feeling such terror. It seemed barely worth loving, if this was the awful dread attendant upon it. But if Lazodeus died — what then? Nothing. Emptiness. The frozen core of her heart.

She barely slept; dozed an hour here and there. The floor was not comfortable, but the discomfort was a payment she was willing to make for Lazodeus's succour and his swift return to health. Mary, on the other hand, almost seemed to be enjoying his illness. She fussed around him and sat with him and held his hand . . . things that Anne, too, would like to do. But her heart was too sick to do anything more than sit and wait. Any jealousy she would ordinarily feel about Mary, any guilt about Deborah or, indeed, any anger toward the exorcist who had done this to her angel, seemed vastly insignificant next to this hollow, paralysing fear.

Please, do not let him die.

Her eyes were open when the first dim glimmerings of dawn touched the sky. She sat up. Mary had curled asleep next to Lazodeus. The angel's eyes were open.

"Lazodeus?" she said softly, coming to stand by the side of the bed. "Are you still ill?"

He nodded slowly. "Yes, Anne. I'm afraid so."

"We shall do whatever it takes to make you well again," she said, even though she had said it before. She wanted to feel as though she were part of his cure, not just a passive ninny who let Mary take care of everything.

"I know, Anne. I know how you feel."

But did he? If he knew how much she loved him . . . well, he may laugh. Or scorn her. She let her head droop forward.

Mary yawned loudly. "Are you awake, then?" she said to Anne.

"I am, yes."

"Have you checked on Deborah yet?"

Anne glanced guiltily towards the closet. "No. I . . ."

"See if she's still angry." Mary turned and began to stroke Lazodeus's cheek. Anne crept to Deborah's closet door and knocked quietly.

"Deborah?"

"Mary? Let me out of here."

"It is Anne."

"Anne, what is going on? Why are you doing this to me? The key is mine, earned by me for my hard work and learning. It is not fair to take it from me."

"You may have it back as soon as we are finished with it."

"Finished with it? What do you intend to do?"

"I can't tell you, Deborah. But it is for the best."

Her sister began to pound on the inside of the door. "Open this door! Open it at once!"

Anne scurried away, took refuge with Mary at the bed. Lazodeus's glow had begun to fade. Anne felt a cold finger touch her heart.

"He grows worse," Mary whispered. Anne could hear the desolation in her voice for the first time.

"What shall we do? What if the exorcist does not return? Will we have to go after him, to his home?"

Lazodeus shook his head. "He is here. He is in the house already."

"What?" Mary exclaimed.

"He will be up here in moments. Betty is with him. He . . ." Lazodeus sank back on the covers. Anne could control herself no longer; she kneeled over him, her lank hair trailing across his face.

"Lazodeus? Lazodeus?"

"Calm down, Anne, he is not dead yet." Mary stepped off the bed and pulled out the demon key. "I am ready for the exorcist."

A sharp rap at the bedroom door gave her a fright. Mary marched towards it, but Anne caught her in time. "Wait, Mary. We know not what to say. Lazodeus must tell us."

Then a strange mumbling. Anne recognised it as Latin, but couldn't understand it. "He has started the exorcism," she gasped.

"Lazodeus," Mary said, running to the bed. "Wake up, you have to tell us how to overcome the exorcist."

Lazodeus struggled to sit. Before he could say anything, a voice, loud and clear and in English, began to repeat the exorcism. It was Deborah.

"In the name of Jesus Christ, our God and Lord, strengthened by the intercession of the Immaculate Virgin Mary, Mother of God, of Blessed Michael the Archangel, of the Blessed Apostles and all the Saints and powerful in the holy authority of our ministry . . ."

Father Bailey's voice grew louder in response.

Lazodeus groaned.

"Be quiet, sister!" Mary shouted. "Don't make us have to hurt you."

"No, she has no power," Lazodeus said. "She is not ordained in the church. It is the priest who causes me pain."

"Well, she's torturing me," Mary cried.

"Tell us what to say to him," Anne said. "Quickly, ere he kills you."

"We drive you from us, whoever you may be," Deborah continued, translating Father Bailey's words. "Unclean spirits, all satanic powers, all infernal invaders, all wicked legions . . ."

"Lure him in here," Lazodeus gasped. "Then use the key

to command Drachiarmus to make him swoon."

Deborah's voice grew stronger. "In the name and by the power of our Lord Jesus Christ, may you be snatched away. God the Father commands you, God the Son commands you, God the Holy Ghost commands you, Christ, God's word made flesh —"

Mary pushed the dresser aside and threw open the bedroom door. The Latin stopped; Deborah stopped. Anne huddled close to Mary's shoulder. Father Bailey looked back at them in the dim morning light.

"Come in, Father Bailey," Mary said.

"I . . ."

Mary grabbed his wrist and pulled him. Anne leaned across and pushed the door closed.

"The sign of the cross commands you!" Father Bailey exclaimed, forgetting his Latin in his fear. He crossed himself and threw holy water upon them.

"Nobody commands me." This was Lazodeus. Anne turned to see him sitting up in the bed, his unearthly light returned to him, his eyes narrowed in rage: a black angel of unparalleled beauty. She caught her breath. "Girls, deal with him," he said.

Father Bailey's eyes bulged and with a jerk he turned and scrambled for the door. Mary darted in front of him and barred the way, held up the little key and said, "Drachiarmus, I call upon you with this key as your commander. Induce in the exorcist a profound swoon."

Five notes rang out, the same as last night, and Anne felt both enchanted and horrified by the sound of them, as though the pleasures of the music were secretly eroding her soul. Father Bailey swooned to the floor.

Lazodeus leaped from the bed. "You see, I am recovered."

Mary received him in her embrace eagerly, Anne more warily.

"What shall we do with him now?" Mary asked, stepping back.

"Hide him somewhere."

"Will he be well again?" Anne asked, poking him with her toe.

"I don't care," Mary replied.

"I shall remove him to his own home soon enough," Lazodeus said with impatience. "I do not understand your anxiety, Anne. Has he not received what he deserved?"

"It is . . . I . . ." Anne was speechless. She kneeled next to Father Bailey. His eyes were glazed and unfocussed, but he still breathed softly. "He is not dead then?"

"What would it matter even if he were?" Mary said nonchalantly. "Anne, he tried to kill our angel."

"I do not want to be hanged for murder," Anne replied, "that is all. I hate the exorcist as much as you!" There, now she sounded like a petulant child. She took a breath and tried to calm herself. "We need to hide him somehow."

"But Betty knows he's up here."

"We can tell her he has finished his work and gone." Anne frowned. "Though I doubt she'll believe it."

"She'll be too frightened not to believe it. Wait here. I shall go to my secret room and bring back something to hide him in." Mary disappeared out the window, leaving Lazodeus and Anne facing each other.

"Please," she said. "Do not interpret my anxiety as concern for the exorcist."

"I am sorry. For a moment I thought . . ."

The silence grew. Finally, she said, "You thought what, Lazodeus?"

He smiled sadly. "I thought you bore no more love for me."

"Love for you? Oh, Lazodeus if you only . . . I mean . . . my feelings for you remain unchanged. No, they have grown stronger, for seeing you so weak."

"Thank you, Anne," he said softly. Then leaned in and kissed her forehead with gentle lips. "I owe you my life."

"This should do." Mary was climbing in the window once more, and Lazodeus stepped away from Anne. She felt her heart beat frantically. Could it be that he loved her as she loved him? Loved her so much that the thought of losing her affection had frightened him? Loved her so much that he must hide his feelings from Mary? She barely noticed as Mary laid out a rich red velvet arras across the floorboards.

Anne tore her eyes away from Lazodeus. "What are you doing?"

"Hiding Father Bailey until we can get him out of the house. Will you help me?" She already had his feet held firmly in her hands.

Anne crouched near Father Bailey's head, and Lazodeus took his arms. They lifted him and placed him in the centre of the arras. Mary brought the edge up over his body, then rolled him over twice.

"Won't he suffocate?" Anne asked.

Mary parted the material near his head. "I'm sure he can breathe through there."

"But . . ."

"Stop worrying. Help me get him under the bed."

They pushed his body under the bed, letting the long covers drop so that he could not be seen. Anne sneezed from the dust. She stood back and brushed her hands on her skirt. "We won't leave him there for long, will we?" Anne said.

Lazodeus put a hand on her shoulder. "The very next time Betty leaves the house, I will help you take him to his home."

"And then he will be better?"

"No, he will always be like this."

"Should we not reverse the spell, then?"

"He may return," Mary said. "Don't be stupid."

Anne tried not to think about the strange, glazed look of the exorcist. Lazodeus was well again. That was all that mattered.

"You should set your sister free," Lazodeus said. "And I shall leave so that I may recover my strength in

Pandemonium. It may be some time before I can return."

Mary dangled the key in front of her. "I should very much like to keep this," she said.

"It belongs to Deborah," Lazodeus replied. "She knows how to use it. You do not."

"I know a couple of spells now — how to lock someone up, how to make them swoon."

"You were drawing on my power. It won't work for you without me near. Give it back to her. It is not worth you risking the love of your sister."

Mary sighed. "I suppose you are right."

"Let me have it a moment," he said. She handed it to him and he held it out and called upon the same demon who had locked the door. The five sweet notes rang out again. When their echoes had faded, Lazodeus returned the key to Anne. "I have unlocked it. She may come out." He offered Anne a smile. The white scar on his lip twitched.

"Farewell, Mary. Thank you." Then to Anne, "Farewell. I will return before he dies, do not concern yourself."

Anne watched as the glow around him gathered, shimmered, then disappeared with him. Her heart hammered, from excitement and love and fear.

"You can come out now, Deborah," Mary called.

Deborah emerged from her closet. Anne had never seen her look so enraged. Her face was flushed and her eyes glittering. She snatched the key and gave Anne a look of such abhorrence that she had to divert her eyes.

"How dare you?" she hissed.

"While we speak of daring, how dare you repeat the exorcism? Were you trying to get him killed?" Mary said.

"I care not if the angel dies," she said. "He is my enemy."

A long silence weighed heavily on Anne's ears, as the shock settled in.

"Be careful what you say, sister," Mary said, her eyes narrowed.

A new fear clutched at Anne's heart. They had fought before, they had squabbled with each other since their infancy, but the dark surge of anger between her two sisters now was unforgiving in its intensity.

"And you, Mary, be careful what you do."

"I shall protect the angel."

"And I shall protect the innocent."

"The angel is innocent."

"You know that is not true. Since the moment he first appeared, there has never been a trace of innocence about him."

Anne decided to intervene. "Please, do not fight. Are we not sisters? Do we not love one another?"

"I love her not," Mary said, her eyes never leaving Deborah's. "Not if she wants to hurt the angel."

"I do not want to hurt any creature," Deborah protested. "But I will be watching you. And if you dare to touch my belongings again," her hand went defensively to the key around her neck, "you may find that I am as formidable an enemy as Lucifer is to God."

The door to the bedroom suddenly swung inwards. Betty stood on the other side, clutching Liza's hand, peering in timidly.

"Hello, Mother," Mary said icily, her top lip curled.

"I —"

"If you are looking for your friend, he has left already. He did not have time to say goodbye."

Betty drew pale. "When did he . . . when did he leave?"

"Not long since. He passed on his best regards."

Deborah suddenly broke away from them and turned to Betty. "Betty, I shall join you in the kitchen anon. We should break our fast. Please go on ahead. Mary and Anne are still feeling unwell."

Betty, clutching the collar of her dress like a frightened child, backed out of the room.

Deborah turned to Mary and slowly extended her

forefinger so it nearly touched her sister's nose.

"You shall leave Betty alone," Deborah said.

"I shan't."

"You shall," Deborah returned, more forcefully.

"If she keeps interfering —"

"I will stop her interfering. I go now to stop her from ever meddling again in our affairs. Promise to leave her alone."

Mary shrugged, casting her eyes to the side in a feigning of nonchalance. "Perhaps. I shall think upon it."

"Ensure you do," Deborah said. A few moments later she was gone. Anne was terribly aware of a third presence in the room, of the exorcist breathing softly under the bed.

Mary strode to the door and slammed it with an exasperated sigh. "Does she think to make an alliance with Betty?"

"She said she would protect the innocent."

"I should kill her."

"She is your sister!" Anne cried, unable to stand the pressure of the animosity any further.

"Not Deborah, you fool. Betty. But no good would come of it. If she interferes again, though, I shall make her pay. I shall make her pay so dearly."

"Mary, you are frightening me." Her sister's cruel streak had always been unsettling, but this morning it was pure, undiluted by a jest or a flippant quip about Mad Mary.

Mary shook her head. "You do not understand my passion," she said. "I have an angel as my companion, and he shall not be taken from me."

"I care for the angel, too."

"Then you do not care enough, for to want to kill for love is its only true expression." She turned and stalked to the window, slipped out and left Anne alone.

Almost alone.

So Mary was in love with Lazodeus; she had all but admitted it. Anne sat heavily on the bed and put her head in her hands. Of all the rivals she could have for the angel's love, Mary was perhaps the most forbidding.

15
Seduce Them to Our Party

Betty — frantic, stomach fluttering and skull buzzing — paced the kitchen while blockheaded Liza prepared their tea.

Soon Father Bailey would be missed. Lettice would be at the door asking questions. Gossip would spread. Betty would be blamed.

The girls. What would they do to her?

A noise near the door made Betty look up. Deborah. She felt her whole body shrink away from her stepdaughter.

"What is it?" she asked.

"I need to speak to you, Betty."

"What do you have to say?"

Deborah glanced towards Liza. Of course Deborah wanted them to be alone. But if Liza were not there with her, who would protect her?

"I am . . ." Betty started.

"Afraid? Do not be."

Betty gazed at Deborah a long time, apprehensive. Then took a deep breath. "Let us walk into the garden. Liza," she said to the maidservant, "please do not disturb us."

She led Deborah out the back door and they sat on the stone bench against the wall. The sky was nearly fully light now, but the coming day did not fill Betty with hope as much as horror. How many hours would pass before someone came looking for Father Bailey?

Deborah turned to her and, to Betty's surprise, grasped her hand. "I fear for you, Betty."

Terror washed over her. "What do you mean?"

"You must not question what Mary does any more. You must not question any of us, but especially not Mary. Mary grows dangerous."

A small rage ignited in her stomach. "So I am being threatened by you? By my stepdaughter?"

"This is not a threat. This is a warning, a benevolent warning. Mary will leave you alone if you drop all your investigations into our conduct."

"Can you guarantee that? You are not Mary."

"I know far more than Mary."

"You are but a girl," Betty said. "How can I take my comfort from you?"

"What other comfort have you been offered?" Deborah shook her head. "Betty, this is not one of your childish superstitions. This is real, this is danger. I will protect you as much as I can, but if you delve into Mary's affairs again . . . I fear for you."

Anger and terror fought within her. "And what of Father Bailey?"

"I will take care of Father Bailey as best I can."

"Where is he? Sent to the infernal realm with the devils you worship?"

"I worship no devils. Father Bailey is in a swoon, wrapped in an arras, under Mary and Anne's bed."

A hot rush of dread moved up Betty's back. She groaned. "He will die," she said, "and I shall be blamed."

"I think I can save him. I think I can reverse the magic they performed, but you must promise me that you will leave us be, that you will turn a blind eye to our activities, and go on as if nothing has ever happened."

"And what of your father? Should he not know what kind of daughters he has raised?"

Deborah wove her fingers together as though trying to steady them. For the first time in this exchange she dropped her eyes and seemed at a loss for words. "Yes, what of

Father?" Slowly, she raised her head and looked at Betty with pleading eyes. "Betty, for the love you bear him and for the love I bear him, he is safer if he knows nothing."

Betty knew this to be true. As much as she wanted to be rid of the girls and recognised this as her best opportunity so far, there was too much danger in pursuing it.

"But are there devils in this house? Should I not fear them?"

Deborah lifted her eyes upwards, thinking. In that very serious, considerate way that she had, she said, "There is a force in this house that begins to run out of control, but all my endeavours are now bent towards solving that problem. And I do not believe it is necessarily evil, perhaps mischievous. I assure you, this force is not a devil. I believe you have nothing to fear if, as I have said, you stay away from our affairs, and especially from Mary's."

Betty shook her head. "I want to trust you, but . . . Father Bailey . . ."

"Let me think upon it. Today or tomorrow I will do something."

"I . . ."

"Betty, you have no other choice. You must trust me. I have little love for you, nor you for me, but at the moment we are united by a common enemy and a common love. I will undertake to manage Mary if you undertake to protect yourself and Father."

The girl was right. Betty had no choice but to trust her. And to be truthful, she had started to feel a sneaking hope that Deborah could protect her, that this nightmare of bad omens would soon be behind her.

"I agree, then," Betty said, and to say it was a relief. "I shall not tell your father."

Anne felt the covers slowly slipping from her upper body. He was coming for her. He was angry and he would repay her. Gently, gently, trying not to wake her, he was tugging the covers down. She was unable to stop him, tried to call out but couldn't. Could only make a grinding, guttural noise in her throat.

A long space where nothing happened. She almost relaxed, and then suddenly, with icy hands, he seized her feet.

She woke with a start. Looked down. Her covers were still in place, no cold hands touched her feet. The exorcist was still in his unnatural sleep in the arras, with the dust and shadows beneath the bed.

Anne took a deep breath. Her heart was thumping madly in her chest. *Merely a nightmare.* But it wasn't merely a nightmare — it was true. A man lay bewitched directly beneath her. She rolled over and watched Mary for a few moments, breathing deeply, sleeping the sleep of the innocent. How could she? Why was she not mad with anxiety as Anne was?

She wanted so desperately for the angel to return and remove their guilty secret from the room. Surely, when Father Bailey was returned to his home, she would sleep easily again. If the guilt did not trouble her too badly.

She flipped onto her back and stared into the dark. Over and over, she had berated herself for her guilt. The exorcist had tried to kill Lazodeus, and the revenge they took had saved her beloved from annihilation. No blame lay with her. She was simply saving the creature that she loved most dearly in the world.

But it felt all wrong.

Anne closed her eyes and tried to reclaim her lost sleep, but without success. She imagined she could hear the sound of the exorcist's breathing, or even a struggling, suffocating cough. Finally, she threw back the covers and got out of bed, went to stand by the window.

A light still burned in the window across the way. Happy people with less complicated lives. She watched the light for a while, trying not to let her thoughts return to the awful secret under the bed. What was taking Lazodeus so long? Did he not realise that if he didn't return soon, Father Bailey would die for want of food and water? Or would the enchantment protect him?

Protect him? He was dead in life in the state they had induced. Once again guilt rose, self-hatred on its heels. She put her head in her hands and pressed her fingers savagely into her face. *Why can't you be more like Mary? She loves him more than you do, and he will see it.*

If only he would come.

"Lazodeus," she whispered into the dark, but with no expectation. And, indeed, no luck. She watched the light in the opposite window until she was too tired to hold her eyes open any longer, then she went back to bed to dream of icy hands grasping desperately at her ankles.

When morning came, it was almost a surprise. Daylight once more. It took a few seconds to remember the horror under the bed, but then the memory returned swiftly and slyly. Mary was already out of bed and gone to breakfast. Anne lay there a few moments, then rolled over.

And found the note.

Gently positioned half under her pillow, a crisp piece of paper folded in half, then in half again. She did not recognise the writing at first, but soon spied his name at the bottom: Lazodeus.

> *Anne,*
> *I shall be with you soon. I am still recovering in my own world. Please do not call me again, because I find it so hard to resist your summons. I know you are afraid, but you must trust me. I will not fail you.*
> *Since my illness, I find my thoughts returning often to you. It seems so natural, and yet so wrong, for you are mortal and I am an angel.*
> *Perhaps it is just the gratitude of one whose life was*

*saved by a gentle spirit. Meet me next Thursday at
midnight in the park where last we danced. I should like
to dance again, and I think I know how to repay your
kindness.*

Yours, Lazodeus

She pressed the letter to her chest, realised she had held her
breath for too long. What a fool she was for mistrusting
him. Of course he would solve the problem with Father
Bailey. She had let her feelings of jealousy towards Mary
cloud her judgement. She would wager all she had that he
had never written such an intimate note for her sister.
She read it over and over, imbuing each word with new
significance. If she didn't know better, if this letter wasn't
addressed to lame Anne Milton, she may even read desire
into it. But that couldn't be so.

Or could it?

Thursday was nearly a week away. How she would ever
wait that long was a mystery.

Deborah crept as quietly as she could up the stairs.
Mary and Anne were in the kitchen with Liza and a wary
Betty. An opportunity which may not be repeated: her
sisters rarely left their victim alone, as though their guilt led
them to maintain watch.

She opened the door to the bedroom and went quickly to
the bed. Max lay curled up on the bed, sleeping soundly.
Kneeling, she lifted the covers. There, under the bed as she
had seen it in her scrying mirror, was a velvet-wrapped
shape. Father Bailey. She stood and hesitated. Too risky to
try to reverse the enchantment while her sisters were still in
the house. She chewed her lip as she considered.

Max. Still Mary's weak point.

Deborah picked up the little dog, and he whimpered
softly in his sleep. "Come with me, little friend," she said
softly, and took him to her closet. He settled on her bed

with a yawn, and went back to sleep. She closed the door and returned downstairs. Took a deep breath and burst into the kitchen.

"Mary, Max has run off!"

Mary looked up. Her sleeves were rolled up and her hands were covered in flour. "What do you mean?"

"I was in Father's study when I heard him whimpering at the front door. When I let him out, he saw a rat and went dashing after it."

"He can't have got far," said Mary, wiping her hands on a cloth and hurrying out of the kitchen.

"Anne, you'd better come help us find him," Deborah said, and Anne, as was her nature, complied.

"Which way did he go?" Mary was asking when they joined her near the front door.

"Down that alley."

They crossed the road.

"There's no sign of him. I hope he hasn't been strook by a carriage." Deborah almost hated herself for putting such an awful fear in Mary's imagination, but then reminded herself that Max was safe and well and Father Bailey was not.

"Don't say such a thing!" Mary cried. "Max! Max! Where are you?"

"You two go in that direction and I'll go back the way we came," Deborah said.

"He can't have got far," Anne said soothingly, laying a hand on Mary's shoulder.

"Stupid Deborah. You should never have let him out the front door. You should have let him into the garden." Mary stalked off towards the junction of the alley with the next street, Anne behind her. When they disappeared around the corner, Deborah dashed back to the house. Betty waited near the door.

"Deborah, are you —?"

"Just wait in the kitchen. I shall do what I can, and I shall do it better uninterrupted." She took the stairs quickly, threw open the bedroom door and dove under the bed. Dust irritated her nose and she sneezed once, loudly. The sound echoed in the room. With effort, she pulled Father Bailey out from under the bed. She tipped him on one side and rolled him over, rolled him out of the arras. By the time he lay exposed, face down on the ground, she was perspiring heavily. Her shaking fingers went to the demon key. Would it even work? She was such a novice. She suspected the reason Mary had been able to induce the swoon was that Lazodeus had been helping her. For all his protestations of illness and powerlessness, Deborah was almost certain that the angel had not been affected at all by the exorcist. The demons in her walls were still there. If they could withstand a Papist's prayers, then a creature like Lazodeus certainly could.

She held out the demon key. "Drachiarmus," she said, remembering the name from Lazodeus's instructions, "I call upon you with this key as your commander. Release Father Bailey from his unnatural sleep."

The notes rang out clearly, and as they did a profound thrill coursed through her, greater than she had ever felt it before. Momentarily, it seemed her body was formed of liquid gold. Then she was flesh and blood again, a laugh caught on her lips and a nervous excitement jittering through her.

And Father Bailey sat up. "Where am I?"

She knelt next to him. "Are you recovered?" she asked, astounded that the magic had worked so well. She had expected him only to wake enough to be helped home, not to speak and move so freely. "Completely recovered?"

Father Bailey shrank from her. "Are you one of the witches?"

"I have just saved your life, Father Bailey. You must leave now, and you must never return. I cannot vouchsafe you from my sisters' wrath."

"You are a witch," he breathed.

"If you must think me so, then at least consider me a good one. Come, rise. My sisters will return soon, and if they see you recovered they will not be satisfied until they have spilled your blood." She tried to help him to his feet, but he shied away from her.

"I do not wish to be touched by you."

"I cannot stress to you sufficiently, sir, how much danger you are in."

At once, he started reciting his exorcism and Deborah pressed her hands to her forehead in exasperation. Think, think. Which demon can be relied upon to induce forgetfulness? She reviewed the lists in her head, found the name and held up the demon key.

"Shayax, I call upon you with this key as your commander, make this man forget why he is here."

Five notes, each more delicious than the last. This time she fought down the thrill, knowing it would rob her of the composure she needed to solve this problem. Instantly, he forgot his exorcism.

"Who are you?" he said.

Once again, she was amazed that the key worked so effectively. Then the reason slipped into her consciousness. Lazodeus had used it and his power lingered on it, giving her the command that he boasted.

"Sir, you have wandered in a fit far from your home." She helped him up, and this time he took her aid. "I shall lead you to the street below."

"Which street am I upon?"

"Artillery Walk, sir."

"But I live on Leake Street."

"You have been a number of days away from home. You need to return to your sister and rest." She led him down the stairs, he with his hand pressed to his eyes in confusion.

"How did I come to be here?"

"You have been ill, Father Bailey." Deborah saw Betty out of the corner of her eye, watching them from the kitchen

312

door. She ushered Father Bailey out onto the street. "Do you know which way to go?"

He pointed up the hill and Deborah nodded. "Tell your sister you have been unwell, that the Miltons kindly took you in while the fit was upon you. You need to rest until Lord's Day."

His eyes were bewildered. "Yes, yes, I shall tell her that."

"And by Lord's Day, you will no longer recall an acquaintance with Betty Milton or with me. You will have only peace and happiness in your memory."

"Peace. Happiness."

"Go now. It is time you were away from here."

She watched him as he walked unevenly up the hill in the summer haze, and turned the corner. Betty stood behind her. "It is over then?"

"For Father Bailey it is," Deborah said. "You must not be seen to be my ally, Betty. Mary will not like that."

"You are not my ally," Betty said plainly. "Fear not."

"I must find my sisters, tell them that Max is retrieved." She ran up the street, her heart thumping wildly. Her fingers went to the key around her neck. Charged with Lazodeus's potency, what magical strength it now possessed! But she took little joy in it and that surprised her. All was fear and uncertainty, and nothing like the confidence and happiness one might expect from a girl who had the power of angels.

"Lazodeus!" Mary stood in the centre of her secret room. He had to come. He had to soothe the boiling rage in her heart. "Angel, come. Deborah has done an awful thing!"

He appeared in front of her, beautiful and serious in his black clothes, his head tilted to one side as he studied her. "You are angry."

"I shall strike her. I shall punch her black and blue."

"There is no need."

"She released the exorcist."

"She is a clever girl, Mary. She removed his memory of the events. She is more clever than I am, for I should have realised that that was the safest way to deal with him. I admire her."

Mary drew herself up tall, jealousy mixing with anger. "Oh? You admire her? Well, why do you not go to be with her instead of me if you admire her so much? I suppose that I am too stupid to keep your good company any longer."

Lazodeus laughed. "Mary, you are jealous."

Mary turned her shoulder to him. "I am not."

"You dear fool. Why do you think I come to you instead of her?"

"I know not, for your passion for her seems unstoppable."

"I fear the coldness of Deborah's embrace. She is all brain, no heart." His hand was on her shoulder. "Mary? Forgive me complimenting your sister?"

Mary sighed. She never worried about Anne. Naive, stumbling Anne with her idiot's gait and her pokey face. But Deborah was beautiful, statuesque, golden-haired and pink-skinned. "She is very beautiful," she said.

"Your beauty is greater." He slid around to stand in front of her. Picked at the laces of her bodice.

"I do not believe you."

"You need not believe my words. But you must believe my caresses." He pushed up her skirts, his fingers gliding up her inner thigh.

Her head fell back and jealousy and anger began to fade. "I believe I am addicted to your touch," she said.

"Then have your fill of me," he said, dropping to his knees and burying his face between her legs. The hot touch of his tongue on her core was a scalding silken pleasure. His fingers moved inside her and she was awash with bliss. She only lived in such moments.

"Do not prefer anyone to me," she whispered. "For I cannot bear the thought."

*

314

Deborah realised, as she walked up towards Amelia's house, that she now possessed a stronger ability with the demon key than Amelia herself: Deborah now knew two extra demons and their roles, and the angel magic left on the key made its use flawless. She had to admit, she was unsure how Amelia would deal with this news and so she decided not to hurry in mentioning it. Impulsively, she pulled the key from around her neck and tucked it into her placket. If Amelia asked for its return, she wanted a little more time to experiment.

The tall, dark house waited on the corner. Light summer rain fell, making her hair damp and the cobbles slippery. One of Amelia's cats — she thought it might be Tuesday — cowered on the doorstep from the rain.

"Hello, what are you doing out here?" she asked as she knocked. When Gisela opened the door, the cat dashed in.

"Are you wet?" the old crone asked.

"A little. 'Tis only a light rain," Deborah replied, as she came in, pulling off her gloves and hat.

"Amelia is expecting you," Gisela said. "Go through."

Just as Deborah was about to open the door to the sitting room, Gisela said, "And I'm expecting you later. I have a floor to be scrubbed." She smiled her toothless smile and Deborah felt her heart sink. One of the things she despised about Amelia's tutelage was performing household chores. Even at home she didn't have to scrub the floor — that was Liza's job. More and more, she felt such tasks beneath her.

"I shall be pleased to help," she muttered.

Amelia was waiting, sitting proudly like royalty, surrounded by her cats.

"Tuesday was outside," Deborah said.

"I wondered where she had got to. Where's your key?" Amelia gestured towards Deborah's throat.

"I left it at home. By accident."

"You must be more careful with it. What if one of your sisters took it?"

315

Deborah's memories of the awful night with Father Bailey returned. "I have so many questions to ask you, Amelia."

"Go on then."

Deborah sat down. Weary from the last few days, she slumped into a chair and put her head down on a cushion. "First, why can I not see Lazodeus in the scrying mirror?"

"He might have blocked you."

"Is that possible?"

"Of course. Why do you want to see him?"

"I don't trust him."

"Immerse the mirror in water. You will see and hear him, but the water will cloak your viewing. What other questions?"

"How can I stop Lazodeus from knowing things about me? He knew I had the demon key."

"He can only know about you by looking at you when you are physically in his presence. All you need do when you are with him is hold your hand over your forehead. Like this." Amelia demonstrated with one of her pale hands. "What else?"

"Can an exorcist hurt Lazodeus?"

Amelia laughed scoffingly. "Of course not. If it were that easy, I wouldn't have a business."

"You are certain?"

"Absolutely. Why?"

Deborah took a breath and told Amelia the story of Father Bailey.

"I don't understand," Amelia said when she was finished. "An exorcism should have no impact on him at all. Yet, what reason would he have for pretending it did?"

"I think he is trying to divide our loyalties," Deborah said.

"Surely not. I can see no purpose for it."

Deborah sighed and sat up. "Amelia, he has my sisters in thrall. They would do anything for him. They nearly killed for him."

"Angels are enchanting by nature."

"I doubt his motives."

Amelia waved a dismissive hand. "You doubt everything. That is why you cannot move forward. Less doubting and questioning, and you may find your magical practice expanding."

"'Tis not in my nature to be reckless," Deborah replied smoothly. This much she knew of herself and would not change.

Amelia caressed her pale hair imperiously. "Then perhaps you shall never be a great magician."

Deborah took a moment to think about this. Was Amelia right? She was so tired all of a sudden. Weary with worrying about the angel and the demons in her walls. She wished them all to be gone from her life, to be a girl again with two sisters who were friends and a father whom she adored. She said, "I have become a woman I suppose. That is why I am so unhappy."

"What are you unhappy about?" Amelia asked, leaning over to touch her hair.

"The demon key has changed. Since Lazodeus used it, it has more power."

"What do you mean?"

"Whatever I ask for comes to me immediately."

"It is not possible."

"Lazodeus, whether wittingly or not, has affected it."

Amelia withdrew her hand and sat back to stare at Deborah. "And is this why you didn't bring it? Did you think that I would try to take it from you?"

"No. I simply forgot it."

"Yet you have never forgotten it ere today."

"I assure you, it is coincident. Though I understand how you may suspect otherwise."

Amelia glanced around at her cats. Without meeting Deborah's eye she said, "Still, you should bring it back for me to examine."

"Yes, I shall. Next time."

"Come back tomorrow with it. You needn't scrub the floor today."

Deborah kept her voice even. "I shall not be able to get away from home until our usual meeting day next week. My father is returning and he will have dictation for me. Travelling stimulates his imagination."

Amelia narrowed her eyes slightly. "Are you certain you cannot?"

"There is more," Deborah said.

"Go on."

"Lazodeus called on demons I had never heard of."

"He did?"

"Did you not know there are others? Beyond the table that we have?"

Amelia frowned. "No, I did not know. Should we believe it?"

"We must believe it. He called on them and they complied."

"I am most perplexed."

Deborah felt such a sinking disappointment inside her. Amelia seemed to know very little indeed for one who was supposed to be so versed in magical knowledge. How was she to learn if every teacher she turned to failed her?

"I must go," Deborah said, getting quickly to her feet. "I have just remembered I am expected home."

"Come back tomorrow with the key," Amelia said. "I should very much like to see it and try it for myself."

Deborah smiled weakly. "I shall do my best."

She walked home by a long route, giving herself time to think things through. Once, knowledge had seemed such an admirable goal, but all she saw around her at the moment were problems. Mary and Anne barely speaking to her; Betty terrified; Amelia unable to answer her questions; Father no longer worthy of her veneration. Was this the lesson she was destined to learn? That people were horribly, horribly fallible and there was no security to be had at any port?

Perhaps it was time to be done with this magic. What could she do with it anyway, but command demons to do little things: open doors and find lost objects. Not healing, or protecting, or providing joy. Not changing the world enough for her to be allowed to travel alone on the continent, or study medicine. It all seemed so petty, somehow. For an activity that was supposedly of the highest spiritual importance, it reduced too easily to satisfying conceit or pecuniary interest.

With heavy feet she turned into Artillery Walk. Betty was home alone.

"Liza has taken your sisters to the markets. We are preparing a great feast for when your father returns. I have invited some of his friends."

Her sisters were not home. A good opportunity, she supposed, to turn her scrying mirror on Lazodeus.

"I shall look forward to his return," she said, and scooped some water from the bucket near the fire into a deep wooden trencher. Betty seemed about to ask what the water was for, but stopped herself. "I am going up to my room," Deborah said. "I shall be down for supper."

Safely in her closet, she closed the door. She lit a candle and it sputtered in the stuffy darkness. From her trunk, she pulled the scrying mirror out of hiding and laid it in the bowl. The water closed over it. Her own reflection, distorted through the water, looked back at her. Was she sure she wanted to do this?

Yes, absolutely. Her sisters were in too far with the fallen angel.

She positioned the bowl between her knees on the bed and passed her hand over it. "Show me Lazodeus," she said softly. Steam began to rise from the water, and she was puzzled. Amelia hadn't mentioned —

Suddenly, a blinding beam of light shot up from the mirror. She shrieked and put her hand in front of her face to protect her eyes. A burning sensation drilled into the palm of her hand, where the beam met her skin. What on earth was happening?

Of course. He was an angel, and he had only appeared to her in mortal form. The mirror was reflecting back his true appearance. She quickly said, "Show me Lazodeus in his mortal form."

The blinding light instantly disappeared. She checked her hand, and saw a red welt of scorched skin. She brought her palm to her mouth and sucked the wound to take the sting away. Through the water, in the mirror, she saw Lazodeus's familiar form.

He was not wearing his dark layers of beautiful clothes. Rather, he was clothed in a plain white robe, and appeared much more angelic, even vulnerable. He sat on an elaborately carved stone seat on a street she did not recognise. It seemed too dark, and a faint warm glow reflected on the dark stone walls and gleaming cobbles.

She drew a quick breath. Perhaps he wasn't in London. Perhaps he was in Pandemonium.

"Let me hear him," she said. But he was not speaking, merely sitting as though he were waiting for someone or something. She watched for half an hour while he sat unmoving, then grew bored and sat back on her bed. She idled with the demon key, flipping it over and over on its chain. Just as she was considering going downstairs to help Betty, she heard noise from the scrying mirror. She sat up and peered into the water. Lazodeus had stood, and a great elaborate iron door was opening in front of him. The door was carved with similar gargoyles and looping designs as the scrying mirror. A disembodied female voice said, "Come in, Lazodeus. His Majesty is ready to see you now."

His Majesty? That could only be one angel. One very fallen angel.

Lazodeus strode into a vast hall. It was dazzlingly lit with thousands and thousands of candles positioned against mirrors. A long fireplace ran to shoulder height along the wall. Her breath was tight in her chest; would she see Lucifer? He approached a black marble table which gleamed in the light of the flames.

"Greetings, your Majesty," he said as he approached. Deborah realised he was apprehensive. His gait was not so confident as when he was with mortals.

"Greetings, Lazodeus. You may approach."

His Majesty came into view. Lucifer was a perfect ruined beauty, with the same masculine dignified bearing as Lazodeus, in similar white robes. His face, however, was more exquisite, his hair black and his eyes green, an unimaginably perfect symmetry and proportion of features. A scar ran from one side of his face to the other, diagonally from forehead to chin. But it wasn't his physical characteristics which made him beautiful — though he was most certainly beautiful. It was something about his eyes, some addictive thrill cleaving to his brow, some dark promising kiss waiting in his glance. She held her breath. Lucifer sat behind the table in a carved chair and spoke.

"Why are you here?"

"It is about leaving guardianship behind and moving ahead."

"I understood that you were destined to remain a guardian because of your indolence."

"I am trying much harder, Majesty."

"You have not provided this realm with a single soul in hundreds of years. My Principalities and Thrones must be far more aggressive than that."

Deborah felt as though she had been kicked in the heart. Souls? After all this time, after convincing herself that this was not what Lazodeus wanted, was it really so simple? She composed herself, determined to remember every detail.

"I have found three girls . . . sisters . . ." Lazodeus began.

"Sisters? Decent girls? Pretty?"

"Yes, all three."

"Tell me."

"I was called as their guardian by an idiot witch who did not know what she was doing. I have been waiting their whole lives for them to call me. The eldest two trust me . . . love me. The youngest is wiser."

"Forget her. Tell me of the others."

"I want to seduce them to our party. If I can do it, will you elevate me to the position I rightfully deserve?"

Lucifer shook his head. "Too easy, if they are already in love with you —"

"Name me a sin, then. Any sin. I believe my sway is such that I can get them to do anything. In time."

"We have abundant time, Lazodeus."

"Name me a sin, and if I can get their souls that way —"

"You will become one of my Principalities. I suppose it is fair. I'd like to meet them." Lucifer took a deep breath and closed his eyes. "Are they pretty? Are they soft? Do they shed tears and tremble?"

"They are all that we adore about mortals."

Lucifer opened his eyes and smiled. "Go on, then. See what you can do for me. I shall be watching you closely."

Lazodeus stood, bowing obsequiously. "Thank you, Majesty. But you have yet to name their sin."

"Their sin?" Lucifer idled with the scar near his chin. Deborah held her breath, realised she was clutching the bed covers in anxious fingers. "Let me see . . . Ah, yes, I have it."

"Majesty?"

"Patricide," Lucifer said. "Their sin shall be patricide."

16
Sweet Reluctant Amorous Delay

Deborah's skull seemed suddenly made of granite. The shock froze her solid for a full minute. Then she pressed her fingers to her eyes and rallied her thoughts.

What to do? How to proceed? Her sisters would never believe her. She had declared Lazodeus her enemy just a few short days ago. To approach them with this story was to be destined to fail.

But she could not let Lazodeus have his way. Tempt them with . . .

Surely, he did not hold them so much in his spell that they would murder their own father. Her father.

Once more, she peered into the mirror, but Lazodeus had left the great hall and returned to the gleaming black streets of Pandemonium. She watched him as he began to wander silently through obsidian alleys indistinguishable from one another, twisting sickly into lonely places. Occasionally he would pass another white-robed, scarred creature and exchange greetings, then keep moving. Walking, as Father did, to contemplate a problem. The problem of patricide. For a long time she watched, and her heart would not still. Finally, she passed her hand over the mirror and it lay silent.

"Think, Deborah, think." Long since, she had heard Anne and Mary come home, take the rugs up for beating, call her angrily, then leave her alone when she claimed illness.

A terrible illness of the soul. *My sisters; my father*.

It would take time. Lazodeus had much hard work ahead

of him to convince Anne to kill Father. Mary . . . no, even Mary was not so completely without conscience.

"So I must not rush into warning them," Deborah said, falling back on her pillow and taking a deep breath of the stuffy closet air. "I must be prudent." Watch and wait a little while, and ask Amelia for help. Though Amelia was to blame for all this according to Lazodeus. Amelia and her reckless magic. So much for her exhortations to spontaneity. How was Deborah to know, now, whether or not the demon key was endangering her own soul? All Amelia's talk of amorality was now in question. Every instinct shrieked that she should destroy the key, but she needed it to protect Father. And herself.

She picked up the key and hung it round her neck again, tucking the bar of tarnished silver between her breasts. When all this was over — when her sisters were returned to their senses and Lazodeus was banished and Father was safe — then she would melt it and cast it into the Thames.

Until then, necessity dictated she consort with demons.

"How much do you love your father?"

Mary propped herself up on one elbow. "I love him not. You know that." She sipped her drink: spiced wine served in an ivory tusk, gold tipped. A special gift brought for her velvet room, from the exotic depths of the east.

Lazodeus smiled up at her from amongst the velvet cushions. His hand languidly caressed her bare thighs. "How much do you hate him?"

"He is an irritant rather than a blight. An itch rather than a pox. Why do you ask?"

"Some of those I affiliate with in Pandemonium are unhappy with his great poem."

"Unhappy with it? Why?"

"Will it be published?" he countered.

"I expect so. He publishes many things."

"The fear is of its influence, that its fame may live long

after him, that the true story of our nobility as a race will never be known."

"That tedious ordeal of a poem famous?" She sniffed. "I scarcely believe that to be possible."

"Still, these are our fears . . ."

Mary shrugged. "I should not mind if they wish to burn all the pages. But do not ask me to do it, for Deborah and I are at war, and I know the foul girl is watching me."

"It won't be necessary."

Mary smiled at him coquettishly. "I have brought something else for you to read, though. Something far more interesting."

"What is it?"

She pulled the letter out of her bodice. It had arrived yesterday, with "ERJENT" written across it in Grandmamma's hand. "Go on, read it aloud," she said, handing it to the angel.

Lazodeus unfolded the letter and read: "'Mary dearest, Lady Ruth Adworth has died of the gout, and now Sir Adworth asks me daily about you. I believe he purposes to marry you if you return. Do not delay, Mary. Write to him forthwith.'" He handed the letter back. "And why should I be interested in such a trifle?"

Mary felt her face fall; she had hoped Lazodeus would be jealous that some other man loved her and wanted her to be his bride. "I thought you might care that I was appreciated by so wealthy and powerful a man."

"Perhaps you should marry him, Mary, if he is so wealthy and powerful."

"No!" she cried. "How could I ever . . . I mean, now that I have known your caresses, how could I . . ."

"Did you hope to make me jealous by this?" he asked, and his voice was cool and puzzled.

"I . . ."

"Mary, trouble me not with the love letters of ageing suitors, when I have concerns about more important writings. I want you to watch your father for me: hear his

325

plans and aim to know what he intends. Can you do that?"

She nodded, chastened. "Of course, I shall do exactly as you say." She could do no differently.

Deborah watched her sisters and neither of them looked different. Neither of them looked like patricides. They sat in a circle in the sitting room, Betty and Liza behind them. All five of them were working on sewing up a new arras for the party on Thursday night. Father was expected home at dinner time and Betty was eager to have it done before his arrival.

So it was a surprise to all when the front door banged and Father's voice drifted up the stairs. "Where is everyone?"

Betty put aside her sewing and hurried to her feet. "Why is he home so early?"

"To torture us with his boring poem, I suppose," Mary said when Betty was out of earshot. She turned her eyes to Deborah. "Though I suppose you like the foul thing."

"Yes, I do," Deborah replied. "'Tis a great work of art."

"Please do not fight," Anne said, but it was a vague shadow of the adamant entreaties she had spoken in the past.

"Death, Anne," Mary said, "you sounded more convincing when you stuttered."

It was true; the lines between them were drawn deeply now, and Anne seemed not to care. Deborah held up her sewing to her face and examined it closely. Her stitching was uneven, compared to Mary's which was always excellent. She noticed her fingers shook a little; it was the anticipation of seeing Father. Once, she would have bounded down the stairs to greet him, excited at his return. But everything had changed. Somehow she had grown into a woman, disenchanted with her brilliant father, frightened of her sisters, overwhelmed with the responsibility of protecting them all, of healing this awful mess.

His voice carried up the stairs loudly. "Mary, Deborah, come down to my study at once. I am in need of your services."

"I shall keep sewing, shall I?" Anne said under her breath.

"Come down and say hello," Deborah said, touching her sister's hair.

Anne smiled up at her tightly. "I hardly think he's interested in my greeting."

With a deep breath, Deborah put aside her sewing and followed Mary down the stairs.

"Good morning, Father," Deborah said. "We were not expecting you so soon."

Betty stood outside the front door paying the driver and giving a coin to the boy who had been engaged as Father's eyes for the journey.

"I hurried the driver. My mind is on fire. I have so many new ideas for my poem, and I must dictate them immediately."

"Why do you require us both then?" Mary sniffed. "Surely Deborah will do."

"I require you, Mary Milton, to start making the fair copy of the poem. An old friend of mine named Samuel Simmons is a publisher at Aldersgate, next to the Golden Lion. We crossed each others' paths in Cambridge, and he has expressed a keen interest in publishing the work."

Betty, who had rejoined them, nodded her head smugly. "It shall be published then?"

"Of course," Father snapped. "There was never any question. He has promised me twenty pounds — the first five when I give him the fair copy, provided the work is to his liking."

"Twenty pounds!" Betty exclaimed. "Why we shall be able to afford some new rugs."

"'Tis hardly a King's ransom," Mary said quietly.

"Enough, Mary. I'm aware it is not a fortune. It is barely recompense for the many hours I have spent on it." No mention was made of the many hours that Deborah had spent on it, or any of the other scribes he had used over the years. But Father's arrogance was hardly a concern any

327

more. His safety was far more pressing.

"Well, I think twenty pounds is a solid sum, and we can use it," Betty said. "And 'tis a good reason for us to celebrate tomorrow night. John, I have organised a party in honour of your return."

"A party! Do I have time to make small talk with idiots?" Father shook his head in exasperation, but Deborah knew that by tomorrow night, when the guests started arriving, Father's excitement would match Betty's. "Now leave us be, Betty. We have work to do."

Mary set up on one side of Father and Deborah on the other. Soon, Mary was copying out lines in her strong, neat hand, while Deborah waited for Father's grand ideas to form into blank verse. He intended new and dynamic scenes, and in his dreams he had acquired ideas: grand ideas, heroic ideas, breathtaking ideas for speeches and descriptions.

And nearly all these ideas were about fallen angels.

Deborah tried to keep up as Father dictated. His words were almost frantic, and yet so beautifully chosen, so grandly joined together. At one point he stopped to ask her to read back a speech which Lucifer — Father called him Satan — made to his ranks of angels. Deborah straightened her glasses on her nose and read to him:

"Farewell happy fields where joy for ever dwells: hail horrors, hail infernal world, and thou profoundest hell receive thy new possessor —"

"Ha!" Father said, and he actually clapped his hands together with glee. "I *like* him, Deborah. I *like* my new Satan. Better than that vain, toadying weakling I had originally imagined. Now he has pride; now he has dignity."

Deborah looked across at Mary. Her sister's eyes were locked on Father's face, and a smug, knowing smile tugged at the corners of her lips. Deborah's gaze returned to Father, and he was smiling too, but it was a gentle smile, an innocent smile. In his moment of happiness, Deborah suddenly felt his awful vulnerability. An empty sick feeling opened up in her stomach, and she fought the keen urge to push aside the books and run to him, take him in her arms and tell Mary to get out. Tell her to leave them both and dally with her devils in some other part of the world and never to look at her Father again as though he were a fool, and she were his superior.

Father's fingers went to his throat. "I grow hoarse. I have been speaking too loudly in my excitement. Perhaps we should take a break until this afternoon."

Mary needed no encouragement. She put her writing tray aside immediately. "Good. I shall walk Max. 'Tis too hot to be inside." She was gone before Deborah had tidied her ink pot and rolled her pens. Deborah stood and walked to Father, knelt in front of him.

"What is it, Deborah?"

"You must be tired from your journey."

"I slept in the carriage."

"Father . . ."

He let the silence draw out between them. Finally, he said quietly, "What troubles you, Deborah?"

"Father, make no more mention of your poem to Mary."

"No more mention? But I must get a fair copy to Simmons by the beginning of September. How do you propose I shall do that without Mary's help?"

"I shall make the fair copy, Father. I shall take your dictation during the morning and make the fair copy in the evening. It stays light until quite late still, and I can work by candlelight just as well. Mary can do my chores — Lord knows she never really does work to the equal of the rest of us. But let me do it, Father. Mary should have no more involvement."

Father sightless eyes rested on her face, and it occurred to her for the first time she had been seen neither by her mother nor her father. Mother had died in childbirth; Father had been blind before she was born. Did that make her invisible? She reached out and touched Father's hand. He withdrew it awkwardly.

"And why should Mary not be involved?"

"You must trust me, Father. I cannot tell you."

"I know some of what Mary does," he said.

Deborah felt her blood cool in her veins. "You do?" Had Betty told him? And if so, would Deborah have been implicated? She suddenly couldn't bear for Father to know of the dark world she was now involved in.

"Yes, I've known for many years. A friend from Forest Hill told me. She flirts with men . . . she gives her favours . . ." He dropped his head as though ashamed. Relief; this was only about Mary's chastity. Father looked so embarrassed that Deborah produced a lie to reassure him.

"'Tis not true, Father. 'Tis an unfortunate rumour. Mary is chaste and brings no dishonour to you."

He nodded, but didn't seemed convinced. "Thank you, Deborah."

"Do you trust me, Father? Will you allow me to make a fair copy?"

"Deborah, I trust nobody. But I will allow you to do Mary's work. And I shan't mention it to Mary again. Perhaps one day, when you are a grown woman and you bring my many grandsons to visit, you shall explain to me what this is about. Until then, I have confidence in your judgement."

That old familiar sensation of pride rose up inside her, and she pushed it away with her reason. It would not do to rely on Father's praise. Father had little respect for women, Father expected her to marry and bear him grandsons, and Father would never understand her need to make her mark upon the world. She stood and moved to the door with a cool, "Good day."

"Deborah?" he said.

"Yes, Father?"

"Do not let me down. The fair copy must be complete by September the first. And I have many more scenes to draft. You must be reliable."

"You may rely upon me, Father," she said. She stood in the doorway and watched him a few moments, then turned to rejoin her sisters upstairs.

It had drizzled all day; a mournful misting summer rain which sent the party guests inside damp, with limp curls and sagging feathers. Enthusiasm was not dampened, though, and Father was in particularly high spirits, playing music and laughing with friends. Anne cared nothing for the party, and nothing for Father's good mood. She only cared that two hours stood between now and reunion with Lazodeus. From her hiding place near the window, Anne watched as Mary sang and flirted. Deborah, however, was nowhere to be seen. Anne had heard her upstairs in her closet, a pen scratching away at paper, and had asked if she would come downstairs for the party.

"No, I am far too busy," she had replied.

Deborah was becoming more and more a mystery to her. Once, not long ago, she had been her fresh-faced baby sister; precocious and delightful, kind-hearted and always trying to understand. But all that had changed. Lazodeus said she experimented with magic, and that seemed surprising as she had shunned the angel and his powers. No, more than that. Deborah had said that Lazodeus was her enemy. Anne pondered the statement. Was that the point at which her once innocent affection for Deborah had been soured, when Deborah had declared the creature Anne loved so much to be the enemy?

Anne sighed as she assessed the merry people enjoying the bright candlelight and the games and singing. Life had become so very complicated, but perhaps sisters could not play games and share secrets with each other forever. They must go their separate ways and, for the sake of the love she felt for Lazodeus, she was willing to let them go.

She heard a bell far away, ringing out the hour, and wondered at how time could crawl so slowly.

At a quarter to midnight, the party was still revolving around her. Deborah had been brought downstairs to read scenes from Father's great poem. Adam and Eve were being cast out of Paradise while an audience of enraptured faces oohed and aahed. Father sat proudly, back erect, listening to his dazzling phrases as if hearing them for the first time. Mary was nowhere in sight — perhaps gone to bed or to her secret room. For anyone else, perhaps, crossing the room and slipping out without being seen would not be so difficult. But she feared her ungainly walk would draw attention. She clung to the wall, shuffled slowly in the shadows. One or two glances darted in her direction but were soon diverted. She was the ugly sister; the lame, stupid one. Foolish to think anyone would care.

She made it to the stairs and began to hurry her step. To get out the front door before Betty or Liza called her back was her next goal. She did not have time to find a rain mantle or scarf. With a secretive glance behind her, she was out the door and on her way.

The drizzle had eased, thankfully. Lights from the window upstairs shone on the street, making the puddles glisten. She breathed the warm, wet air and savoured each second as it drew her closer to him. The bells rang out midnight as she crossed the street to the park.

He was there already, waiting. She approached from behind. He had not seen her yet, and she took a moment to admire the lines of his physique. His hand rested on a tree trunk.

"Lazodeus," she said. It felt so bold to say his name.

He turned around and smiled his slow smile. "Anne. You are late."

"Only by a matter of seconds."

"It seemed longer." He took her hand. "Come under the trees here towards the hedge. I have found a dry place."

"How can it be dry? It has rained all day."

"Angel magic," he said, tilting his head slightly. "What else?"

They moved into the hedges and the leaves were indeed dry. He helped her to sit and then joined her. She gazed at him in warm silence, the darkness faintly eased by the soft glow he radiated. She felt wild, womanly, even beautiful, because she knew the dark was kind to her pinched face and dull eyes.

With a slow breath, he spoke. "I have something to tell you, Anne, but it may not be as promising as it first sounds."

She shook her head, confused. "What do you mean?"

He pressed his lips together, thinking. Then he said, "You remember how I cured your stammer?"

"Yes. Of course. Not a day passes that I omit to give thanks."

"I have spoken to some of the potentates of my realm. I believe I may also eradicate your limp permanently."

For a few moments, she was desperately embarrassed. She squirmed. *Her limp*. Such direct reference to her physical shortcoming jolted her out of her romantic fantasy that she was somehow beautiful and womanly. He had never forgotten that she was grotesque.

"Anne?" he said. "You do not seem excited. I said I may be able to make you walk freely."

She looked up. Forced a smile. "Yes, it is exciting. But you warned that the promise of such news may be a burden."

He dipped his head in a nod. "That is true. I understand your caution."

"What is it, then? Will it turn me into a toad? Expose you to great hardship? Mean that my sister Mary will have her heart's wish and win your love?" She bit her tongue on this last, realising she had spoken too openly. Such a comment could only reveal her keen jealousy.

"Fear not, I am already aware of Mary's feelings," he said. "I return no such sentiment, though, and never shall, no matter what I make of my magic."

"Then what?"

Again he fell silent.

"Please just tell me so that I may feel the disappointment and grieve for lost opportunity."

"Anne, I do not mean to hurt you. My fears are for your dignity."

"My dignity?"

"You remember, do you not, how I cured your stammer?"

Anne felt suddenly light. "You kissed me."

"On your mouth. Because that was where the problem lay."

"Yes." A promise rolled in her stomach.

"Your limp is located in . . ."

"My leg. My left leg."

"No, Anne. In your hip. In the very joint of your hip." His hand reached out and touched her through her clothes. "Here."

"So . . ."

"I would need to press my lips to the joint. Through the skin, not through these layers of cloth."

Anne felt her breath jerked from her lungs on a fleet hook. "I . . ."

"I mean to offer you no indignity," he said, his hands held out in front of him. "I cannot believe I am even suggesting it."

"No, no. I am not . . . there is no offence taken. I . . ." She fell silent and he let her be quiet for long minutes. "Will you be punished again?"

"No."

"But last time . . ."

"Because I acted without permission. I have received permission from the highest source."

Lucifer, then. Lucifer could heal her hobbling gait. How far she had come from the frightened mouse who would not tell her sisters the angel's name. And yet, it mattered so little. For Lazodeus had locked his eyes upon her, and she was drowning in desire. Flutters of strange

334

sensation drew up inside her, made her feel vulnerable and hollow.

"I shall, then. I shall take your kind offer, and I shall walk and run and dance."

He let out a sigh. "Oh, I am so happy, Anne." He took her hand and pressed his lips to it. "I am so happy that you will let me do this for you. I have wanted to repay you for your kindness when I was ill . . ."

"I couldn't let you die," she said, her breathing shallow in her chest. Her fingers itched to touch his hair, but she held them back.

"Rise, then, Anne. I shall perform the magic."

Rise? She knew she could not stand. Her knees would buckle underneath her the instant he touched the hem of her skirts.

"I do not wish to stand," she said, trying to keep her voice even. "What if the cure upsets my balance and I fall?"

"I do not think you will —"

"I shall lie back," she said quickly. "I shall lie back and you shall perform the magic while I watch the stars."

He bowed his head. "As you wish it, Anne."

She lay back stiffly. The grass was cool beneath her, the cloudy sky dull white above, stars glimmered through clear patches. She could see drops of rain clinging to leaves.

"Forgive me," he said quietly as he lay next to her and his hands moved to her skirt. "Forgive me, Anne, for this indignity."

She tried to speak, to reassure him, but could not. Language had failed her. Instead she let her eyes drift heavenwards. She felt her skirt inching further and further up her leg, felt his warm fingers brush her skin accidentally. Her body was consumed by a twitching, pulling feeling, and she shivered deeply.

"Are you cold, my Anne?" Then before she could answer. "It won't take long."

But how long would it take? He seemed to be relishing the

335

slow advance of her dress up towards her thighs. Did he move so slowly so as not to startle her? It was unbearable. His hand pressed under her waist, lifting her gently so he could clear her skirts from beneath her. Although she kept her eyes fixed steadfastly on the clouds, she knew that she was now exposed below the waist, that her most private place was open to the summer breeze, to the drizzling clouds and the pale stars, to the angel's eyes.

"Please, do not feel embarrassed," he said. Embarrassment? No, this was the most liberating, thrilling sensation she had known. Again, he lingered. His fingers spread unhurriedly across her hip, pressing into the side of her buttock. She realised she had not breathed a few moments, and took a breath which shuddered down into her lungs like the foundations of a building quake when the earth trembles.

"I must administer the magic now," he said softly.

"Yes," she managed to say, but it came out sounding like a breath of desperation.

"Here, Anne." His hot mouth was on her skin, his fingers pressed firmly as if to hold her down should she startle and try to escape. For twelve feverish seconds his lips rested upon her hip, then he pulled away. Her centre had moved. Everything — pulse, thoughts, breath — emanated from between her legs. She waited for him to sit up and move away, waited for the awful cold tug of his relinquished touch. But he did not move. He lay next to her still, not touching her. Her lower body was still exposed to the elements. To her surprise, he groaned softly.

"Oh, Anne. Anne."

"What is it? Are you ill?"

"It is like a sickness, but I am in no danger of dying. I *feel* something, Anne. Something I should not feel."

"What do you feel?" Her heart hammered in her chest.

"I cannot."

"Please. Tell me. I shall die."

Once again his warm hand was cupping her hip. His

336

other pressed the grass on the right side of her body. His arm rested right over her quim. A warm looseness began to open up inside her. "Please," she said.

"I cannot love you for I am an angel."

He loved her? She could not speak.

"I cannot love you," he said again, more forcefully, raising his body up on his hands and covering her side with his, "because I am an angel."

Speak. Speak. Say something. He will think you do not care. The words, the words he had freed with his kiss so many months ago, came to the surface as though they had always been fated to be spoken. "I care not if you are angel or man. I would have you love me."

"Do not trifle with me, Anne." He sounded so stern, so harsh. She was almost afraid.

"I do not. It is true. For I have loved you as long as I have known you. And if you love me in return, then there is no impediment to our cause. We shall love each other."

"Anne, Anne." His lips descended and she was awash in kisses. She pressed her face to his fervently, felt his hands moving upon her body and did not care. For he loved her. He loved her! His fingers reached her core and passion exploded inside her. "May I, may I?" he said over and over, a little boy's voice, importunate, soft.

"You may do with me whatever you wish," she said, and she meant it so passionately that she repeated it. "Whatever you wish."

She heard the sounds of his clothes being removed, and she did not care. She wished for the whole world to see as she opened herself to him, as he entered her with his hard, ample prick. She wished for her Father and Betty and her sisters and all the guests at the party to gather around and witness her love, his love, their love.

Together as they were meant to be.

Eyes aching and hands cramped from writing in the

candlelight, Deborah finally put aside Father's manuscript and decided to sleep. The party still continued downstairs, though it was deep into the night. She had heard the toll for two o'clock a short while ago, and still Father played the harpsichord downstairs. His elevated spirits, she knew, proceeded from his delight with the newly rewritten parts of his poem. If only she could feel happy for him, and not fearful that he was being used by Lazodeus.

She massaged her fingers against each other. Footsteps approached from the staircase. Mary finally coming to bed. She got up and peered out of the closet. Anne was bent over her dresser, pulling a nightdress from the drawer.

"Anne?" she said, surprised. Where was her uneven gait? Coming up the stairs, her feet had sounded as regular as her sister's.

Anne turned around. She was flushed, her hair was loose and flowing around her shoulders. "Sister," she said, "you startled me. Good evening."

"Good morning, more like. Have you been enjoying the party?" Deborah felt her eyes drawn to Anne's feet, but she would not move them.

"I am tired and wish to sleep," Anne said, not meeting her eye.

"Go to bed, then."

"I shall. Why are you watching me?"

"Can I not watch my sister?"

"I feel you are suspicious of me."

Moments ticked by and neither of them moved. Finally, Deborah said, "I heard you, Anne. I heard you come up the stairs."

Anne threw her hands in the air. "Very well! Very well, look you." She strode, unimpeded, from one side of the room to the other. "You were right, are you satisfied?"

"Oh, Annie," Deborah said, leaving her closet and moving towards her sister. "What have you done?"

"What business is it of yours what I have done?" Anne

338

said, surprising Deborah with her vehemence. "Yes, I can walk now, see. I can run, I can skip, I can twirl . . ." She demonstrated to Deborah with a neat pirouette. "And I know you know how it came about, and I don't care that you know. I don't care for your opinion or anyone else's any more." She cast her eyes down. "Though I shall fain my limp around Father and Betty a while longer. They will ask difficult questions otherwise."

"You ask me why I care, why it is my business?" Deborah said. "I care because I fear that the angel may want to harm our family."

"Harm us!" Anne strode over and grabbed Deborah by the shoulders, her voice dropping to a vicious whisper. "You know nothing of him, Deborah. You know nothing."

Deborah felt her blood grow hot. "I know more of him than you do."

"You do not."

"I suppose you love him. I suppose, like Mary, you have lost your silly heart to him."

Anne released Deborah's shoulders and flung her hands in the air. "Do not speak about love, thus, as though it were a trifle. And do not compare me to Mary. She is fickle, I am constant, and I am the one the angel loves."

Deborah shook her head. "No, Annie, no. He has not said he loves you, surely?"

"Yes, he has, though I shall beat you if you mention it to Mary."

"He says it to manipulate you. He says it so that he may make you do things which are not in your nature to do."

"How dare you suggest it? Are you so jealous that finally somebody loves me? Loves me enough to help me walk and talk, when everyone else has only jeers and scorn for me?"

"But, Anne, already he persuaded you to harm the exorcist —"

"Who was trying to kill my angel!" Anne cried. "Do you not see?"

339

"Do *you* not see? For I have seen, I have seen something which terrifies me and . . ." She trailed off. Perhaps this was the wrong way to tell Anne about Lazodeus and the meeting with Lucifer she had witnessed. Not in anger. Not in a fight. Anne would hold it against her, refuse to believe her.

"What, what are you about to say?"

"Anne, do not trust him."

"It is you I no longer trust, Deborah."

"I have seen things . . ."

"Then tell me what things you have seen."

Deborah took a deep breath. She could not let this love between her sister and the angel develop any further. "Lazodeus gave me a scrying mirror, long ago. 'Twas his attempt to win my favour. I have lately learned how to turn it upon him. While watching him —"

"You have spied on Lazodeus?" Anne had drained of colour, and Deborah felt a fear grip her heart. What was her sister afraid Deborah had seen? How far had she taken the expression of her love with the angel?

"Why does it bother you so?"

"Because . . . because . . ."

"Are you in so deep, Anne, that you wish me not to see you with him?"

"It is private."

"I have not spied on you," Deborah said evenly.

"Then what have you seen which makes you so vexed?"

Deborah quickly explained the scene she had witnessed, all the while feeling her heart sink. For Anne shook her head rapidly throughout the whole story.

"No, Deborah, you lie."

"I do not lie."

"Then you are mistaken." Anne's expression clearly said that she still believed Deborah lied.

"Anne, what cause would I have to fabricate this story?"

"I know not. Jealousy, mischief, revenge."

"Revenge? For what?"

"I know not, Deborah. All I know is that I no longer trust you. You told neither Mary nor me about your demon key, you learn secret arts from somewhere and keep it all hidden from us. Your motives are a mystery."

"I shall show you, then!" Deborah cried. Her voice was shrill with weariness and frustration. "I shall get my mirror and show you." She knew it was madness. The possibility of Lazodeus meeting once again with Lucifer was surely nil. But if luck were on her side, she would overhear him speaking with another angel, or see him making a plan, or something which would incriminate him.

"Very well, I shall see this magic mirror," Anne said, "but I am confident you will not prove to me his untrustworthiness."

Deborah hesitated. Of course, if Anne saw something she didn't like she would simply say it was a magic trick. "Perhaps not . . ."

"Oh? You change your mind so quickly? Did you not think I would say yes?"

Deborah shook her head. "Wait here. I shall fetch the mirror." While Anne waited, Deborah returned to her closet. She found the mirror and the trencher she had used previously. On her return to the bedroom, she filled the trencher from a jug on the dresser and plunged the mirror into it.

"Come here, Anne," Deborah said, lying the trencher on the dresser.

Anne joined her. "Go on, then."

Deborah passed her hand over the mirror. "Show me Lazodeus in mortal form."

The picture formed and Deborah heard Anne gasp. Lazodeus sat with two other angels — neither as beautiful as him, but still far beyond the mortal notion of beauty — around a stone table. The pale, ghostly shape of a great building rose up behind, and the dark maze-like streets sprouted in all directions around them. The place where they sat was an open area, like a market place or agora.

"Can he see us?" Anne asked.

"No, I have the mirror in water to cloak my viewing." Deborah passed a hand over the water once more, this time her fingers were trembling. "Let me hear what he says." They were conversing. Deborah's breath caught in her throat; she willed him to mention his bargain to the other angels.

". . . for I do not believe it is possible," one of the angels was saying.

"I believe it is and I shall show you," Lazodeus replied.

"When?"

"When I am not so drunk on happiness."

Anne took a deep breath. "He is drunk on happiness, Deborah. You see? I was right."

Deborah turned to her sister. "What do you mean? How do you know of what he speaks?" The voices continued from the bowl of water, idle chatter and boasting.

Anne smiled shyly. "He has just been with me."

"You were at the party."

"Indeed I was not. I was in the park. We . . ." She trailed off.

Deborah was horrified. "Anne, what have you done?"

Anne shook her head. "Your experiment has failed, has it not?"

"We shall listen further." Deborah bent her head once more to the scrying mirror, but it soon became apparent that Lazodeus was merely indulging in the equivalent of mortal drunken revelry. His friends were speaking now, and he sat silent listening. They spoke of angels with names she had never heard, they spoke of places they had visited, and nobody mentioned a word about Lazodeus's arrangement with Lucifer.

"Deborah, I feel disloyal spying on him," Anne said after a few minutes.

"If we wait and listen —"

"What? Listen until he says something you may construe as harmful to us?"

"But Anne, I swear to you —"

"Be careful what you swear, sister, for you may find you poison old bonds of love." Anne looked away, arms folded in front of her chest.

"Anne, you don't mean it. Haven't we always been close? Haven't I always stood by you?"

"You try my patience. With your magic mirror and your false accusations."

"It is truth, Anne. This is an instrument of truth."

"It is an instrument of lies, of disloyalty, of your jealousy and your will to control me." Anne flung her hand out and upended the dish. The mirror clattered to the floor. "There, I hope your stupid mirror is broken into a million pieces."

"It cannot break for it is magic." Deborah picked the mirror up, realised too late that the water was no longer covering it. Lazodeus's head jerked up, and suddenly he was looking back at her from the glass with an expression of sneering rage. She made a quick move to pass her hand over it, but before she could it exploded in a flurry of silvery shards. She shielded her face from the flying glass, and felt the sharp slivers graze her fingers and wrists.

"Magic? Unbreakable? I think not."

"Anne, you must understand —"

"I shall call Liza to sweep up the mess. Take yourself to bed, sister, I am listening to you no more." Anne flounced out, slamming the door behind her.

Deborah sat a few bewildered moments amongst the debris of the mirror. A little blood trickled down her wrist and on to the floor. Lazodeus had seen her spying on him. Did he suspect how much she knew?

And if he did . . . There could no longer be any doubt that they were enemies.

17
Growing Up to Godhead

"Have you brought the demon key?" Amelia was eager to see her, standing at the front door with a cat cradled over her shoulder.

"Yes. But I need your help with a matter of urgency." Deborah followed her inside. The normally tidy house was messy and smelled of cats.

"Gisela is away until Wednesday," Amelia said in explanation.

"Oh." Deborah had always thought that the lovely smell and inviting surfaces were something inherent about Amelia. Not so. She brushed cat hair off a cushion and sat down.

"Let me see the key."

Deborah reluctantly pulled the chain over her head and handed it over to Amelia. If she wanted Amelia's help against Lazodeus, she had to share the demon key's new power.

Amelia's fingers closed over the bar of tarnished metal. "Oh, yes. I feel it already. Leave it in my keeping for a few weeks, Deborah. I shall experiment with it and then return it to you."

"But —"

"If not for me, you would not have it in the first place," she snapped, laying the chain and the key carefully on a dusty chest nearby. "And so, what help do you need?"

"I have seen the angel's real intent. He is in contract with Lucifer to tempt my sisters into patricide."

"Patricide! It is impossible, is it not? Your sisters are not capable of so great a crime."

"I know not to what lengths they will go to please him. They are both in love with him." Deborah was irritated. "And why are you not surprised to hear of his contract with Lucifer?"

"I have heard rumours of such things, but never had them confirmed. Advancement through the ranks of Principalities, Thrones and Dukes is sometimes possible if an angel can fulfil a task which Lucifer names."

"Why did you not warn us?"

"As I said, they were rumours. I have not had confirmation until now. And I certainly did not know that these tasks could involve a trade in souls."

"But you are not even surprised to find a fallen angel is wicked. Last time I was here you were still reassuring me about Lazodeus."

"Perhaps you witnessed part of a larger conversation, or misunderstood what you heard." Amelia frowned. "I cannot be expected to know everything."

"You are reckless with knowledge."

"And you are overly cautious."

"It seems to be that more caution would have been a good thing in this situation."

"Do not argue with me!" Amelia shouted, shocking Deborah into silence. "I am your mistress, you are my apprentice. Do not argue with me."

Deborah shrunk back in her seat. Her first impulse was to apologise, but she stopped herself. Amelia should apologise. "I simply want your help. I want to protect my sisters and my father. Can you show me a spell?"

"What kind of spell?" Amelia asked.

"A spell which will turn my sisters' minds against Lazodeus."

345

"I know no such spell."

Deborah threw her hands up in exasperation. "You know nothing!"

Amelia jumped out of her seat. "Leave immediately! I do not have to listen to your impertinence."

"Amelia, I —"

Amelia leaned over and grabbed her by the ear, pulled her to her feet. "Go on, get out. When you are ready to give me the respect I deserve, you may return for your key and further lessons."

"But —"

Amelia was marching her to the door, twisting her ear. "I do not want to hear an excuse, just go home and think about what you've done."

"Don't you see, this is more important than my disobedience?" Deborah pleaded. "My father's life is in danger."

"Oh, rubbish. Your sisters aren't killers."

"But he has them so in thrall —"

"I shan't hear another word about it. Amelia Lewis is not in the habit of putting young women in danger with evil angels."

The door swung shut behind her, and Deborah was left standing dazed on the doorstep. Her ear burned with pain. Amelia's pride was too great to admit her shortcomings, and shortcomings there were many.

"She has my key," Deborah said under her breath. That situation would have to be remedied very soon.

Deborah opened the door to her closet very quietly. That afternoon, she had spent two hours plotting her course down the stairs, finding which floorboards and stairs creaked, which were sound, where to place her feet to create the minimum noise. The last thing she wanted was to be caught by Father sneaking out of the house at one in the morning. At Amelia's place, things would be different. She would have to be quick, not quiet. But with Gisela away, she

346

trusted she could get in, take back her demon key and escape again without being noticed.

Amelia would notice it was gone, of course, and she would guess who took it. Deborah supposed this would be the end of their relationship, and it made her sad. Even though Amelia often did not know the answers to her questions, she had at least been an ally. Perhaps she was misguided, but she wasn't wicked. And there had been a time when Deborah had greatly admired Amelia: her vow of virginity, her steely-mindedness, her devotion to knowledge.

She watched her step as she crept to the front door. Father's study door was closed. He would be in there sleeping, perhaps receiving new dreams from Lazodeus. She could not bear how the angel had inveigled his way into her family. She wished him out, far away from her and her sisters and her father, back to Hell where he belonged. Cautiously she opened the door and in a few moments was out on the street.

Just as she allowed herself to breathe again, a hand caught her shoulder. "What are you doing?"

She whirled around. Mary in her housecoat and bare feet.

"Nothing of your concern."

"Yes, it is. You are my younger sister and I feel responsible for you." Mary smiled a snide smile. "I shall have to report to Father of course."

"Don't you dare."

"Then tell me where you are going."

"'Tis no business of yours where I am going."

"Then what shall I tell Father?"

Deborah drew herself up tall. "You shall not tell Father a thing."

"Oh, I should quake for fear seeing how tall you are," Mary said in a mock-frightened voice. "Oh, Deborah, do be kind to me."

"Mary, go home. I do not come to bother you when you

347

slip out to your secret room, though I am sure you behave outrageously when you are in there."

Mary mocked Deborah, made her sound righteous and pompous. "Outrageously. Mad mad Mary behaves absolutely out*rage*ously." She pulled open her housecoat, revealing her thin nightdress underneath. "How outrageous, I am." This time she turned and pulled up her nightdress, exposing her buttocks to the dark street. "Look, Deborah, even my arse is outrageous."

"Oh, for pity's sake," Deborah said, pushing Mary's nightdress down and rearranging her housecoat. "I do not want to be your adversary."

Mary turned back to her and flicked a curl off her shoulder. "A little late for that, is it not?"

"Is it?"

"You declared yourself the enemy to my angel."

"*Your* angel? You know, do you not, that Anne considers him *her* angel withal?"

"Anne is a pinch-faced dope. Lazodeus has no interest in her beyond a sense of charity."

Deborah pushed her lightly. "Leave me be, Mary. Go home to bed and try not to wake anybody."

"You will not tell me where you are going?"

"No. And don't think to follow me."

"Why, what will you do? Put a spell on me?"

"I should never do such a thing to one of my sisters," she said, wondering if it were true.

Mary shrugged. "I shall go back to bed, but I shall ask Lazodeus where you have been. He knows and sees everything. He knew you had the demon key."

Deborah shook the threat off. Mary obviously did not know how easy it was to block Lazodeus's prying eyes. "Go ahead and ask. I care not."

Mary turned around and began to walk away. Deborah waited until her sister had disappeared back into the house before she set off once more for Amelia's. Summer had grown ferocious this year. The usual sunny breezes and balmy warmth of July had turned to blasting winds and blazing days that clung on as though autumn had forgotten she was due. The hot streets were silent and deserted until she reached the wall. She went through Mooregate and headed down through the narrow crooked alleys towards Amelia's. Here people were still out, lanterns were hung in windows and loud voices swelled from pubs. The houses were built so close together in some places that the upper jetties almost touched.

No lights on at Amelia's. Deborah stood out the front for a few moments catching her breath. The clouds in the sky had parted revealing a half-moon. In the pale moonlight, the tall trees and the slender building seemed even more attenuated, throwing elongated shadows. The leaves rattled overhead.

"Go in, Deborah," she said. "Go in and take what's rightfully yours." Still, it took ten deep breaths to work up the nerve. She crept to the front door. The latch was on, but it was easy enough to tilt out the window next to the door, reach her hand in and drop the latch. She edged the door open quietly. One of the cats sat in a patch of moonlight nearby, looking up at her with curious unblinking eyes. Deborah stepped around it deftly and made her way into the house.

In Amelia's sitting room, the quiet lay very heavy over the velvets and silks. She waited a moment or two for her eyes to adjust. She didn't want to step on a cat and wake Amelia. The demon key was just where she had left it, on the chest under the window. She scooped it up and was nearly out of the room when she heard a groan from upstairs.

She stopped to listen. There it was again, but louder. Was Amelia sick? Deborah hesitated. She should leave; Amelia would be angry with her. But Amelia was alone. Gisela was away, and if she were sick or hurt, who would know? She could die up there, and Deborah would never forgive herself.

She hung the key around her neck and inched towards the stairs, stopping to listen. There it was again, a low groan. Deborah chewed her lip. What if Amelia were just having a nightmare? She couldn't go barging in there, letting on that she'd broken into her house. Suddenly, Amelia let out a loud yelp. And another. She must be in pain. Deborah firmed her resolve, and stole up the staircase.

Amelia's bedroom door stood in front of her. The groans were coming louder now. She pushed the door open a crack, Amelia's name poised on her lips. The sight within stopped her cold.

Amelia lay naked on her bed, legs and arms splayed in every direction. Three scaly red creatures, distant cousins to the creatures Deborah had seen squashed against each other in her walls, were arranged around her: two suckling at her breasts, the third shoving its unnaturally large member in and out of her quim. It took Deborah a moment to realise what was happening.

Pleasure, not pain. Her groans were sighs of sexual appreciation.

She backed out quickly. None of them had seen her, being so intent on their congress. Deborah felt a sick, heavy disappointment. So Amelia bragged of never having made love to a man? A mere elision of the truth. For she made love instead to demons. Not caring about the noise she made any more, Deborah ran down the stairs and out of the house into the moonlight.

She headed back home through cramped streets. Father had disappointed her. Anne and Mary had disappointed her. Amelia had disappointed her. They had let her down, all of them. She felt very young, very innocent, and very alone.

Her hand went idly to the demon key and she thought about its angelic charge. Did it matter that she knew nothing about love and sex and the congress of man and woman? For she knew about greater things well enough.

Loyalty, duty, family. The key was a tool for magic — petty magic. For trifles and baubles and the fulfilment of vanity. But she could use it differently surely. She could find a way to protect her sisters and her father.

She hurried home. Amelia's amoral recklessness was not for her. She had never been more certain of anything in her life.

Perspiration ran over her stomach and between her breasts, her hair flew in every direction, and her feet were starting to pinch in her shoes, but Anne kept running.

"Aren't you tired of it yet?" This was Lazodeus, leaning against a tree watching her, a smile playing on his lips.

"No, I shall never tire of it!" Anne cried, and took off once more for a loop around the field, her arms outstretched, laughing. It was mid-afternoon, summery and gusty. A couple cut across the field, but if they thought oddly of the girl running round in circles, or the handsome man who waited for her under the tree, they gave no indication.

Finally, he caught her in his arms. "Come now, Anne. Have you called me just to watch you run?"

Breathless, she laughed. "Yes, for I love it so much I had to share it with you."

He smoothed her hair down. "It is delightful. You delight me."

"I love you," she said, and pressed her lips against his, not caring if someone saw them.

"Sh, sh," Lazodeus said, pulling away. "We must be more careful than that."

"But I don't care who knows."

"We have to care, Anne. For our love is forbidden."

Chastened, she took a step back. "I'm sorry."

He took her wrist and pulled her to him. "Come, let's go further into the hedge where no one will see us. And I shall cloak us with invisibility so we may do as we please."

How beautiful, how reckless and delicious to make love in

the open, with dappled sunshine on her bare skin, as all those delectable feelings ran through her body. She had wondered on three or four occasions if their lovemaking was wrong. But how could it be wrong? It felt like the most natural thing in the world. And they were in love, Lazodeus would probably soon find a way to marry her so they could be together forever.

She frowned.

"What is it?" he asked.

"I was just thinking about how I'd like to be with you all the time."

"I'd like to be with you all the time too."

"Then why do you sometimes not come when I call?"

"Because I am busy."

Anne thought about the vision of Lazodeus with his peers, talking and joking. She couldn't bear that he had a whole life without her. "What will happen to us?" she said, not checking the mournful tone of her voice.

He smiled and cleared her hair off her face. "Annie, don't fret about the future. We have this wonderful moment together, let us enjoy it." He rolled off her and they lay naked amongst the hedges.

He was right of course. "I'm sorry. I'm simply so unused to being happy that I want to pin it down and make it promise to stay forever."

"You aren't to worry. You will be happy. I will always love you."

Every time he said it her chest seemed to grow wings. "I love you," she replied. "I love you, I love you, I love you." The words were already becoming worn out, could not express her feelings adequately.

"I know."

"Deborah said a terrible thing." She had been anxious to talk about it, to ask whether Lazodeus knew Anne had been watching in the scrying mirror when it broke. She did not want him to be angry with her.

"Deborah is full of terrible things, and so must excise

some of them by saying them aloud," he said evenly. Then he shook his head. "I'm sorry, I should not speak ill of your sister."

"No, I think you are right. I think that is why she said what she said, for what other reason could there be?"

"What did she say?"

"She said that she had watched you in a secret mirror and had seen you contract with Lucifer to tempt Mary and me into patricide."

"A secret mirror? No such mirror exists. At least, the figures one sees and hears in it are demons impersonating real persons or beings. One must be careful when using such a mirror, for it can be deceptive."

"She said you gave it to her."

"I gave her no such gift. Why would I give her a gift? You know that she and I are at odds." He sat up and looked down at her, growing agitated. "And why should I wish you to injure your father? I know him not. It is a silly accusation as well as a false one."

"It made little sense to me, too."

"Did you believe it though? In some small part of your heart did you wonder if it may be true?" His mouth turned down sadly at the corners, and Anne felt her heart contract.

"Oh no, no, of course not, my love. I merely mentioned it out of curiosity." She slapped her forehead. "I am such a fool. I should have anticipated such an accusation could hurt you."

"I am not hurt by the accusation. I am only hurt by the fear that you mistrusted me."

"No, my love. I trust you more than I trust myself. My life is yours to do with as you will." She reached a shy hand up to touch his face, and he leaned down to kiss her.

When he drew away, he said, "I think I know why Deborah said such a thing, Anne. But I am uncertain if you will relish hearing it."

"Tell me," Anne said. "I would like to know. For Deborah

and I were once close and . . ." She was suddenly sick at heart about how much distance now lay between her and her youngest sister.

"You must promise not to be too angry with her."

"Why?"

"Promise me."

"I promise," she said warily.

"Deborah made advances to me."

Anne was momentarily uncomprehending. "Advances?"

"Of an amorous nature."

"Deborah? My sister Deborah? The sworn virgin?"

"I do not think she desired any erotic outcome. In many ways she is still a child. But she had become infatuated with me."

"But the whole time she was protesting that we shouldn't call you. Was she . . . what was she doing?"

"She didn't want you or Mary to call me again. She wanted me wholly as her own angel." He raised a finger in warning. "Now you aren't to be angry with her."

Anne swallowed her indignation. "Yes, Lazodeus. I promised you."

"And it is best not to mention me to her ever again. Even in an argument, no matter what she says. You must promise not to talk of me to her."

"I promise."

He nodded. "When I turned her down, when I told her that such relationships could not form between angels and mortals, indeed that she was little more than a child and would love again elsewhere someone of her own kind, she grew enraged. She swore to be my enemy and so she has been ever since."

"When did all this happen?"

"Before you went away. If you think about it, you'll see it explains all her animosity towards me from very long ago. Practically right from the start."

Anne did think about it, and what he said made perfect

354

sense. She would never have guessed it though — Deborah had been so predictable with her urging of caution: wait until we know what he is, do not call him for he may be dangerous, and so on. All the time hoping to save his company only for herself. "I am amazed," she said.

"Deborah is not all that she seems. Like her father she is a veneer of reason and wisdom. But it is all conceit. It covers a great —"

"Vanity. A great vanity. For Father is so very vain and believes that he is wise and masterful. But he cannot even manage the most basic human dignity to me, and that is not the mark of a wise person. That is narrow and conceited."

"Yes, yes, you are right, Anne. And Deborah grows more like him every day."

"She has always been his favourite. She resembles him greatly."

"Again, where is the wisdom in such favouritism? To prefer a child because she resembles him in appearance?"

"Exactly! Exactly. He is the fool, not I."

"A fool? You? Why, you have depths which he cannot even aspire to."

She smiled up at her angel. "I am perfectly happy," she said.

"And so it shall remain," he replied quickly. "I shall ensure it. But beware Deborah and your father, for they shall try to undermine that happiness."

"I shan't let them. I know my heart and I know my mind, and for the first time in my life I shall trust to my heart and mind, and not assume that everyone else knows best." She sat up and shook grass out of her hair. "I shall not be a fool any longer."

A long time had passed since Deborah had been in Mary's secret room. She was astonished at how lavish it had become. Silk cushions piled high, deep crimson and royal blue velvet curtains sectioning off parts of the room, gold and crystal ornaments. And evidence too of her sister's carnal involvement with the angel: one whole wall decorated with explicit watercolours, pricks carved out of ivory and gold, and an assortment of silk bridles and velvet ropes whose uses she could barely guess.

Still, she couldn't spend all day looking around in here. Mary would be finishing the laundry with Liza soon enough, and might find her here. Deborah just needed a little uninterrupted time, a little uninterrupted space, and a nerve of steel.

She held the demon key out in front of her.

All the books had been no use in the end. No protection spell as far as the eye could see. Oh, she could change water into wine, worsted wool into silk, train a bird to be her familiar, create a storm or charm a man to fall in love with her, but nowhere could she find whom to call upon to ask for protection. She had even gone to her father's books. Nothing in Epicurus, Psellus or Dee. What were all these wise men doing if they hadn't considered how to cast a spell of protection or healing? Turning lead into gold was not about greed, they said, it was about self-purification, advancing to another level of being, harnessing the power of elemental spirits. It seemed so convenient, though, that there should be gold at the end of the process. Not peace, not an end to suffering and sickness, not insurance of the safety of loved ones.

But Lazodeus knew more demons than were listed in the mortal books. All she had to do was discover some of their names.

"Dantalion, I call upon you with this key as your commander, appear before me and answer my questions." The musical notes rang out and she felt the sweet shock of the magic run through her. She steadied her hand. She was not entirely sure if it were possible to call a demon to appear before her, and she did not relish having to look upon its hideous countenance. A few moments passed without incident. Then a low swooshing sound began to wash around her, and the velvet curtains rolled in a sudden gust of wind. "Dantalion?" she asked, keeping her voice even. She glanced behind her. When she turned back, it was there.

Deborah let out a little gasp. It was man-sized, not tiny like the ones mashed together in her walls, and not half-size like the demons who had pleasured Amelia. It wore a plain white robe over its scaly red skin. Its face was a confusion of animal features: cat, pig, bird. By far the worst was the sharp stench that arose from it. She had smelled rotten potatoes that were sweeter.

"Who are you, wench, that dare to command me personally?"

Deborah held out the demon key. "I have angel magic on this key."

"Angel? That has the mark of that cur Lazodeus upon it. He is no angel."

"He is a fallen angel."

"Is a fallen woman still a virgin? I think not. He is a devil as are they all in Pandemonium."

Deborah was curious, and her curiosity surpassed her fear of the creature. "You are at odds with the fallen angels?"

"We hate them. They control us. Would you not hate them?"

"And Lazodeus in particular? What is your argument with him?"

"He is frivolous in his use of us. He once called one of my apprentices to service your sister Mary to frighten her. Yes, it is true. You needn't looked so shocked. Your sister is well on her way to joining us all in Hell."

Deborah took a deep breath, concentrating on the matter at hand and not Mary's ruin. "What class of being are you then? Not an angel or a devil?"

"I am a chief among demons. We are elemental spirits, not meant to be applied to the purpose of good or evil solely.

Unfortunately, we are usually commanded by those who are evil. Like your friend, Lazodeus."

Deborah held her breath lightly against the stench. "Lazodeus is not my friend."

"Then why do you dare to command me?"

"He left his charge upon the key, and I need your help. I am desperate."

"Then call upon one of my apprentices."

"I don't want an apprentice, I want you. You teach arts and sciences. I want to ask you questions."

"Is it not enough to have the table of mortal desires?"

Deborah shook her head. "I don't understand. A table of . . .?"

"Mortal desires. Power, wealth, control over others." And when she still looked at it uncomprehending, it took on a sarcastic tone. "The list you have, my dear, of our names. The list you took my name from."

"It is incomplete. It offers no recourse for help in matters of healing and protection."

It snorted; perhaps laughed. "Healing and protection are out of the ordinary realm of mortal desires. Come, surely you'd like a little gold instead? A man to satisfy you?"

She felt herself grow angry; the demon characterised her species as so venal and corrupt. "I feel for a certainty that there are many mortals other than myself who are interested in less material things."

"Do not be righteous with me, wench. I have had contact with enough of you to know the narrow, dark alleys of your hearts."

There was no benefit in arguing with it, and Mary could not be far away. Deborah held up the key again. "I have the key. I shall command you."

"As you wish," it said, with not a trace of humility. Its oddly black eyes narrowed.

"I command you to tell me which demon I may call upon to protect my father from my sisters."

358

"There is no such demon."

"No demon of protection?"

"The devils — the fallen angels as you prefer to call them — destroyed all the elementals who could do good for mortals."

"That's appalling."

"They are *devils*, wench. Your stupid race has enough stories of them to suggest to you the truth of their nature, surely."

"I didn't think —"

"Then *think*. Think harder. What are you doing? What danger are you putting your soul in by dealing with Lazodeus? How much closer to Hell do you come every time you use the key for wealth and power?"

"I have used it neither for wealth nor power."

"No? Do you not feel a wonderful rush of power every time you command with the key?"

"I —"

"Stupid wench, stupid mortal. You know not what you're doing."

"I know I need to protect my father."

"The best I can offer is to let you know when your sisters are thinking ill of him."

Deborah almost laughed. "Sir, they think ill of him most days of the week. Most hours of the day. He is a difficult man."

"Then, I can warn you when they begin to think murderously of him."

"You can?"

It reached out a scaly hand. "Let me touch the key."

Deborah clutched the key tightly. "You will remove its magic."

"For pity's sake, you stupid girl. Who do you have left to trust if not me?"

Words failed her. She stood looking at the demon, assessing its hideous countenance and vile fetor, and knew it was right. It offered her clarity, unabashed truth. She held out the key; the demon brushed it with yellow-clawed fingers.

"There," it said. "It will ring — one note — when either of your sisters has designs upon your father's mortality."

"Designs, not just idle thoughts?"

"I assure you, wench, that I do not make mistakes."

"My name is Deborah," she said softly. "And I thank you."

"Well, *Deborah*," it said, its voice heavy with scorn, "have you decided yet what you will do should such an eventuality arise?"

"I . . . No, not yet. I believe I have time to work it out. My sisters are still very far from being patricides."

"Hmm, a blind father and two scheming sisters in love with a devil. I'd say you have a lot to worry about. Are you finished with me now?"

She met its eyes. "Yes. I thank you."

It smiled, and its mouth was little more than a ragged slit across its face. "Thank me for this," it said, then spat on her face and disappeared.

Deborah stood a moment unmoving. The sticky phlegm dripped down her left cheek. She reached for one of Mary's velvets and wiped it off, fighting down nausea and shaking herself to clear her head. As she slipped out the window and edged along the ledge, a strong gust of hot wind roared down the gap between houses, blowing dust into her eyes. The sky was very clear above and she took a moment to contemplate it before returning to the bedroom. Both of her feet were on the floor when Mary stepped in, the front of her dress soaked.

"Why do you look guilty?" Mary asked.

"Guilty? I believe you are imagining it," Deborah replied. "I'm just looking out the window."

"Well, I have been laundering since dawn and I am tired." She crossed the room towards the dresser.

This was an exaggeration. Mary had been laundering for less than two hours. "I am going to my closet to read."

"I care not what you do, you pious little twerp," Mary said as she pulled out a dry shift. "I'm going to change into something dry and go sit in my secret room."

Deborah considered her sister a moment, wondering where all the last traces of her patience and tenderness had gone. "Where is Max?" she asked.

"In the garden with Liza, making a mess of the washing. Why?" Mary's eyes narrowed.

"You spend so little time with him lately."

"He is frightened of going out on the ledge. I dare not take him with me next door."

"And it does not hurt you to spend so many hours without him? I remember a time when —"

"Oh, stop it. You cannot make me feel guilty. I care not for your opinion. Max is safe and well and . . ." She seemed at a loss for words and Deborah knew she had touched a tender space inside her.

"I shall be in my closet should you need me," Deborah said lightly over her shoulder. "Enjoy your velvet cushions."

Deborah settled on her bed with her writing tray and Father's manuscript all around her. She had begun to copy the book dealing with the war in Heaven, and it made her heart heavy to see Lazodeus's story so uncritically repeated. She dipped her pen and moved to write the first line, then stopped herself.

Father was blind. If she changed it a little, he may never know.

At least, she would be reading him the fair copy, she would be reading him the printer's proof. The first Father would know about her changes — little changes, subtle changes — would be years from now when she was gone and he had some other assistant to act as his eyes. And she would be far enough from him to avoid his wrath.

Her heart sped a little and she licked her lips. Strange that conjuring a demon and commanding it should not unnerve her so much as the prospect of changing Father's work. He was a great poet, she was just a girl.

But she had spent so much time with him while he dictated, so much time copying out this manuscript, that she practically thought in blank verse some evenings. And they would not be big alterations. Just a line here or there, pointing the readers' sympathies away from the fallen angels a little. Oh, Lucifer could keep his savage pride and noble bearing, but it was important that readers did not side with him wholly.

She took a deep breath and started copying, adding or deleting phrases here and there, keeping the rhythm consistent and, she hoped, the quality of the work congruous. Abdiel, once a cretinous traitor, now became the sole voice for God's loyalty. The archangels, once cruel and jealous brats, were now restored to their rightful noble cast. She found herself enjoying it, and though she made a few mistakes and had to put aside the pages, she soon slipped into the rhythm, deftly altering Father's manuscript in subtle, sophisticated ways to her own purpose.

Which would be his own purpose too, of course, if he knew that the stories were coming to him from a hellish angel rather than a heavenly muse.

18
To Lose Thee Were
to Lose Myself

Deborah passed many hours in each day working on Father's poem, as the summer heat sweltered on into late August. Mary still did not speak with her unless to ridicule her, Anne grew colder by the day, and she worked and worked on *Paradise Lost* until she was so immersed in the world of the angels and the first inhabitants of Eden, that she often lost track of which day of the week it was. Only when it became difficult to see the work in front of her did she realise she had missed dinner and evening was closing in.

She leaned back and stretched her arms over her head, then brought her hands down to massage her fingers against one another. Her stomach growled. Why hadn't Mary or Anne come to fetch her for dinner? But she supposed she knew why. Neither of them were affectionate towards her. They had probably made up a plausible reason for Father why she wasn't there, and been happy that she might go hungry.

Deborah leaned her head back on the wall and closed her eyes, yawning vastly.

Something changed in the room. The light was different beyond her closed eyelids. Subtly, but certainly. She opened her eyes. Lazodeus, waiting for her. She sat up with a start, and the door to her closet slammed shut. They were in almost total darkness, but for the faint luminescence from the angel's skin.

Deborah quickly lifted her hand to her forehead as Amelia had shown her. "I shall scream if you try to injure me," she said.

He strode towards the bed and stood over her. "I am not here to injure you."

"You know I shall never believe you about anything ever again."

He indicated her hand, pressed to her forehead. "Who showed you to do that?"

Deborah remained silent, looking up at him.

"How many times did you turn the scrying mirror upon me?" he said at last.

"I only watched you once. And that sole viewing provided all the evidence I need to hate you justifiably. When I tried to show you to Anne —"

"I know, the mirror broke. How do you dare to watch me?"

She tried to sit up tall, not to be cowed by him. "You have tried to read my thoughts. You have seduced my sisters. You intend harm to my father. How do you dare to ask me to justify myself?"

"You are a fool. You are so young and so ignorant."

"If I am such a fool why is it that my sisters have fallen under your spell and I have not?"

Lazodeus's shoulders drooped forward lightly, and suddenly all his enraged bearing evaporated. "Deborah," he said softly, almost pleadingly, "I could explain everything to you —"

"Go on, then."

"You would believe none of it."

He seemed so appealing in his softness, and Deborah hardened her heart against him. A trick, a ploy to weaken her. "Do you or do you not intend to seduce my sisters to commit patricide?"

"I cannot speak of it. I cannot speak of what oaths I have made in the Royal Court of Pandemonium."

"It seemed very clear to me from what I saw."

"But what you saw was but a brief moment in my life!" he protested. "Please, Deborah. I could be in great trouble for speaking of it."

"I heard what you promised."

His voice dropped to a whisper. "What I promised and what I do may be two different things," he said. "Now, I have said too much. You know that elementals live within these walls. I can speak of nothing more serious or specific."

Deborah narrowed her eyes against him. "I cannot trust you so easily as my sisters," she said.

"I have not injured you, have I?"

"You are under an oath not to harm anyone. 'Twas part of our original summoning."

"Deborah, I would not harm you, or your father, and especially not your sisters for the deep love I bear them both."

Deborah shook her head. "I am sorry, but my resolve will be firm on this. You have proven yourself unworthy of my trust at every turn. You and I, Lazodeus, are sworn enemies."

He stood up straight again, his mouth forming a rigid line. The scar above his eyebrow twitched. "As you wish it, Deborah Milton. I shall not endanger myself by speaking with you any longer. But you shall see, in time, that I am worth trusting. You shall see in time that I intend no injury to you or those you love."

Could he be sincere? The suggestion of relief that she felt could overwhelm her if she allowed it. He was right: she had only watched him for a few brief hours, after all. "I believe my mortal state allows me a limited amount of time, Lazodeus," she said, not meeting his eye. "Do not leave it too long to prove yourself."

The subtle luminosity of his skin flickered, and he disappeared. Deborah lay down upon her bed, kneading her tired hands. If only her tired mind was so easily soothed.

When Mary came down the stairs and into Father's study, she only intended to find a book she had left there many weeks ago. Father, who sat by the window listening to a bird's song, looked up when she came in and said, "Deborah, are you finished the fair copy of the tenth book yet?"

Mary frowned. "It is not Deborah, Father, it is Mary."

"Mary?" His eyebrows shot up. Did he look nervous? "I am surprised. It has been so long since you came to my study I assumed —"

"You no longer invite me to your study, Father." She looked at him closely. His mouth was very tight. "Is Deborah making your fair copy?"

"It is of no concern to you, Mary."

"I have a much better hand than Deborah. She writes like a spider who has dipped his feet in ink."

Father remained silent. Mary spotted the book she wanted and picked it up. Turning, she gazed once more at Father. Why had he given her task to Deborah? Deborah already took his dictation; making the fair copy as well was an enormous demand on her time. No wonder she was always yawning — she must be up half the night transcribing the poem. It would not be so unusual that Father should entrust all his tasks to his favourite if it weren't for the circumstances. For Mary knew, and was certain Deborah knew, that some of Father's great scenes were drawn directly from the nocturnal dictations of Lazodeus.

"Did Deborah dissuade you from using my writing skills, Father?"

"I shall not be drawn into petty rivalry between my daughters," he said, his blind eyes just a degree short of her own gaze. Amazing how he could do that. If she weren't examining his face so closely for signs of fear or mistrust, she would have believed him to be staring directly at her.

"I am not such a bad seed as she would have you think, you know," Mary said.

366

Once again, he fell silent. Typical. The old bore always refused to talk when he felt uncomfortable. She took her book and left.

So Deborah and Father were secretly working away on the manuscript together. She remembered what Lazodeus had said about spirits in Pandemonium being unhappy with what Father wrote. What was her sister up to?

"Deborah! Deborah, come downstairs please!"

Father's voice. He sounded agitated. It was unlike him to call to her up through the house, rather than sending Liza. But then, Liza was unusually busy this week. Betty had gone to visit her sister in Suffolk, and Deborah spent all her time finishing off Father's manuscript. All the housework fell on the poor maidservant and whichever of the hapless sisters were available. Needless to say, they made themselves unavailable as often as possible. The house was dusty and the kitchen was in chaos.

Deborah put aside her writing tray and bounded down the stairs. They were almost finished. Father had pronounced himself happy with the newly rewritten beginning, and she had made a fair copy of it for Simmons's approval. She was just finishing off the last few pages of book ten. Soon it would be all over. She would be able to sleep all night, instead of rising at three o'clock.

"What is it, Father?" she asked as she approached. His pale hand was pressed against the dark wainscoting as though he were holding himself up. "Are you ill?"

"No, not ill, Deborah. I have a letter just delivered. Could you read it for me? The messenger said it was from Simmons."

"Simmons?" Deborah snatched the letter from his hand. She was nervous, and knew he must be too. If Simmons did not like the poem the promised advance would not come, and Father would be forced to seek another publisher. And the damage to his confidence would be irreparable. Her fingers broke the seal and she unfolded it.

"Read it. Read it to me," Father urged.

Deborah grasped Father's hand. His skin was cool and smooth, and to her surprise, he returned her squeeze.

"'Dear John, I thank you for the opportunity to read the first two books of *Paradise Lost*. I am astonished, sir, by the scope of your work, your erudition and your unrivalled ability to write the most splendid verse. I am so very impressed with this superb work, and eagerly await reading the poem in its entirety. I believe that *Paradise Lost* may challenge the works of Virgil himself. Please deliver the complete manuscript post haste. I shall pay you the agreed sum upon its speedy delivery. I remain, your faithful servant, Samuel Simmons.'" Deborah looked up. Father was glowing.

"Challenge the works of Virgil . . ." she said.

"Let us walk, Deborah, for I cannot contain such an overmeasure of excitement in my heart by standing still."

"I'll fetch your hat."

Summer was refusing to give up her hold on the streets. September was only a few days away, but the heat and dryness of the season still clung to trees and houses. In fact, Deborah could not remember a hotter summer in the city. A warm breeze gusted up the Walk as they made their way to the Artillery grounds.

"Anywhere in particular, Father?" she asked.

"Let us head in the direction of the burial ground," he said. "Be my eyes, Deborah."

"The sky is dazzling blue and the clouds are moving fast, as though there is a great engine driving them, very high up. The sun . . ." They crossed the open road, emerging from the shadows of the crowded houses on the Walk. "Can you feel the sun, Father? It is still harsh today, as though it has no idea it must prepare for winter. I see a lark overhead, and two blackbirds in the field. Over the treetops the windmills are moving slowly." She glanced around. "A group of men approaches us. They are dressed like Quakers, four of them. Beyond them, across the road towards the city wall, a young man woos a young woman with a posy. Come, this way." She pulled his hand gently and led him across the road, down the hill and into the burial ground. She knew which game he wanted to play, but today it didn't feel like a game. The rows of graves laid out crookedly through the grounds only reminded her that Father could be at risk.

"Read me some dates, Deborah," he asked.

"Father, surely we could find a more cheerful place to be on one of the last mornings of summer?"

"Nonsense," he said, waving his hand as if to wave away her suggestion. "Go on."

Deborah moved forwards slowly, scanning the headstones. "Here, Father, Elizabeth Lincoln, born 1608, died 1636."

"Women aren't made of as strong stuff as men," he said knowingly. The comment should have angered her; it was, after all, his opinion about the capacities of her sex which had driven such a wedge between them. But seeing him standing among the headstones, an old blind man who did not know he was in danger from his own daughters, it was all she could do to stop from throwing her arms around him.

"And here, Father. Jonathan Harris. Born 1610, died 1660."

"In truth, there are not many of us that live as long as I, Deborah."

She smiled at him, his unseeing face in dappled sunshine, and squeezed his hand gently. "No, Father. And long may you live."

He shook her hand off and said gruffly, "No need for mournful sighs. The plague didn't finish me, nor did the return of the King. I'm meant to be here, Deborah. I was meant to write my great epic. I've always believed I have an angel on my side. I shall live a good long while yet." He wandered off by himself a few steps, stopping and putting his hand out to find a headstone to rest upon.

Deborah stooped to pick an errant wildflower from under a stone, wishing she could enjoy the morning. But such a heavy weight was upon her heart. How well she knew: the angel was not on his side at all.

Idly, idly, Mary slunk past Deborah's closet to see if she was in. No sign of her. The old man was gone, too. She supposed they were out walking. With Betty away, Deborah was on escort duty. She probably enjoyed it, toadying up to Father as she had always done. They were two of a kind, those two. Pompous, lily-livered, and impossibly dull. Mary checked around again, and entered the closet. She opened the lid of Deborah's trunk and quickly ploughed through. Nothing. She fell to her knees and peered under the bed. A flat wooden box lay there. She pulled it out, flipped up the brass fasteners and opened the lid.

Here it was. Father's manuscript. She riffled through the pages, sniffing derisively. Deborah's handwriting was appalling compared to her own. She could barely keep her lines straight. Father was mad to let her do the fair copy. Mary read a few lines. So very tedious. The parts she had heard by Lazodeus were far superior. At least they had a measure of intensity, of fire. She deliberately found such a scene; being close to Lazodeus's story was a sorry substitute for being with him in person, but he had not responded to her calls for three days.

When she read the lines, she was surprised. She had been sure it read differently. She read on.

"Why the little minx," Mary said. Deborah had changed it. This was why she had insisted upon doing all the copying, even though it was wearing her ragged. What lies had she told to Father? What would he say if he knew she had toyed with his words?

More importantly, what would Lazodeus think? All his hard work, finally trying to get the real story told, only to have Deborah make the archangels superior to Lucifer and the fallen angels. Superior to Lazodeus! Such a creature did not exist in the universe. Mary placed the pages back in the box and stood with it under her arm, not sure who she would read it to first: Lazodeus or Father. She turned to leave the closet and saw Deborah standing in the doorway.

"Hello, sister," Mary said evenly.

"Hand it over. It is not yours."

"It is not Father's either any more, is it? You've done quite a satisfactory job of ruining his poem."

"I have not ruined it."

"He wanted to tell it his way. You should not have changed it."

"It was not his way. It was Lazodeus's way and you know it."

"What would Father know about the war in Heaven? Lazodeus was there, Father was not."

Deborah put out her hands. "Give me my box."

"And if I don't? Shall you use your demon key? Shall you turn me into a frog, dear sister?"

Deborah took a step forward and snatched for the box. Mary lifted it over her head, remembering too late that Deborah had a good six inches on her. She whipped it out of Mary's hands and pressed it against her body, her arms crossed over it.

"Please get out of my closet."

"I shall tell Father you have changed his words."

"He won't believe you. He trusts me. He loves me."

Mary snorted. "He does not love you, Deborah, do not be a fool. He loves nobody but himself. If you could not take his dictation he would ignore you. Like he ignores Anne."

Deborah did not answer, she merely stepped aside to let Mary through the door. Mary slunk past. As Deborah slammed the closet door, Mary went to the window. She took a few breaths on the ledge, then slipped into her secret room.

"Lazodeus," she called. "You must come. It is important."

She didn't care either way about Father's poem, really. This was just a magnificent excuse for calling Lazodeus. Her body missed his touch, her eyes missed his seductive glow.

"I *must* come?"

She whirled around. He stood between two billowing curtains of blue velvet, in his familiar layers of black silk and lace. He bowed deeply.

"You have ignored me nearly a whole week."

"I apologise. I have been otherwise engaged."

"Are there other girls? Are you someone else's guardian?" She couldn't bear the thought. As it was, with only doddering Anne for a rival, she felt safe.

"No, I see no other mortal women except you."

"What about other angels?"

He smiled. "There is no attraction between angels."

She wasn't convinced. "Are there female angels?" If there were, they would be as beautiful as him. More so. How could she compete?

"We are ungendered," he said. "In our true form we have no distinguishing organs. We are pure light."

She shook her head. "I don't understand, and I don't care to understand. If you say I am the only one, I shall endeavour to believe you."

"You are the only one," he said gently, touching her cheek. "Now, what is the important matter?"

"Important? Oh, yes. Deborah has changed Father's poem."

"What do you mean?" His voice sounded urgent.

"She's making the fair copy — insisted upon it, warned Father to replace me with her — and she's changed it all about."

"What has she changed?" His eyebrows drew together, giving his face a dangerous aspect. Mary started to wonder if this matter were more important than she had originally perceived.

"Well, not all of it," she said slowly. "But she has changed significantly the scenes you told to Father."

For a moment, she saw his lip curl in rage, the scar drawing up into a puckered line. It was an expression almost animal in its intensity, but it was soon gone, replaced by a slow smile. "That wicked girl."

"Wicked? She's hardly wicked. That almost makes her sound interesting. She's rather too dull for wicked."

He shook his head. "Silly, silly Deborah."

"I've a good mind to tell Father about it."

"No, don't say anything to anyone. Let me think upon it. I need to speak to some of my peers."

Mary wrinkled her nose, pulling his hand to draw him closer. "Father's not really *that* important in Pandemonium, is he?" His body touched hers. Electric.

"Do you have no concept of his fame?"

"I suppose I know he's rather notorious. People sometimes walk past our house to see where he lives. But he is hardly as famous as a fine actor, or a courtier, or the King."

His hands closed around her waist. "Mary, there is no more powerful, persuasive, subtle and evocative force in this universe than that of words. Those who wield them mightily can change history, they can endure forever."

"Nonsense," Mary said, tired and a little repulsed about speaking of Father while in the angel's arms. "He's a doddery old blind man. His shirts are always musty and he eats his food like a nervous sparrow."

Lazodeus laughed. "Mary, Mary, one of the things I adore about you is your disrespect for knowledge."

She smiled. "You do?"

"Oh, yes, there is a certain charm in a woman who refuses to avail herself of the facts."

That didn't sound particularly complimentary, but he was gazing at her with such a pure expression of passionate desire that she could not find it in herself to question him.

"If you say so."

"Stay in the dark, Mary," he said kissing her. "I like you

there."

"Come, Deborah, are you ready?"

Deborah looked up. Father stood impatient by the door of his study, hat and coat on, ready for the walk to Simmons's printing house.

"Nearly, Father. Just a moment longer."

She bent her head once more to her task, checking that all the pages were in order. She had finally finished the copying, the censors had been consulted and duly ignored; Father was no lover of censorship. He had declared he would do no more revisions, the manuscript for *Paradise Lost* was complete and ready to take to the printers. Deborah's fingers trembled a little as she leafed through the pages. Here and there, she could see her alterations, alterations which would soon be in print forever. Although she wished every success upon her Father, she secretly hoped that *Paradise Lost* would vanish very rapidly after its publication. The thought of her deception being reprinted into a remote future was not one she relished.

"There," she said, squaring off the pages. "'Tis done."

"Then let us go, Simmons is expecting us."

"Mr Simmons will wait a few moments, Father. I must wrap it. We cannot have pages scattering far and wide between here and Aldersgate." As Father stood by, shifting his weight from one leg to the other, she placed the manuscript in the middle of a sheet of plain brown paper, wrapped it carefully and tied it with string. The result was a large, heavy package which required both hands to carry.

"Father, we may need help. I cannot hold your hand to guide you while I carry this package. Shall I call Liza?"

"Liza? No, I do not trust her. As Betty is not here, it will be just you and me, Deborah. I require no hand to hold. As long as you watch out for me, I shall walk just behind you, and I shall carry the package."

"Are you sure, Father?" she asked.

He reached out impatient hands, clicking his fingers. "Here, here. Give it to me then."

Outside, a fierce, hot wind blew. Deborah had been listening to it in her bed this morning as it rattled windows, lifted tiles and scattered the first dead leaves of autumn up the alley. The dry weather had made her eyes sore and her skin rough. The whole world appeared to be moving under the wind's impetus. She kept her head down as a particularly violent gust rushed up the street. When she turned to check on Father, his hat had vanished.

"Father, your hat . . ."

"Never mind the hat, I still have my manuscript and nothing matters more than that."

They made their way slowly down to Aldersgate. Deborah spotted the sign of the Golden Lion and found Simmons's printery next door. She took Father's elbow despite his grumbling that she would cause him to drop his package, and led him to the front door. The top half of the door was open, the bottom closed. Through it, she could see a small office where a pale, dark-haired man sat wearing tiny spectacles, reading closely. Beyond him, through a doorway, she could see men busy in the workshop, calling loudly to each other and clattering and banging. The man glanced up without a glimmer of recognition for Deborah, but as soon as he saw Father he leaped to his feet.

"John! How delightful to see you. I wasn't expecting you until later this afternoon." He spoke very rapidly as he rose and came to them, his hands emphasising every second word.

"Good morning, Simmons," Father said, and he tried a smile. But he was so nervous that it looked like a grimace. "I have brought my manuscript for you." He held out his manuscript with shaking hands, and Deborah looked away, unable to witness such vulnerability in him.

"I'm so pleased," Simmons said as he took the package

and carelessly dropped it onto his desk. "I'm very excited to be publishing this, John. There are many people who are waiting for it to appear."

"Is that so?" Father said, pleased with himself.

"Oh, yes, everyone I've mentioned it to is most eager for its publication." He suddenly broke off his address to Father and looked at Deborah. "Excuse my manners, my dear. You must be Mrs Milton. I'd heard that John had married a young beauty but —"

"She is my daughter," Father said, his face suddenly stony. "She is little more than a child."

Deborah had thought Simmons might respond with a barrage of prattling apology, but instead he fell silent for a moment, then withdrew into his office, calling behind him, "I shall find you the first part of your advance, John. Just you wait there."

The next few minutes as Deborah waited next to Father were deeply uncomfortable, but she didn't know if it was due to Father's anxiety as he waited for his payment, or his embarrassment that Simmons had presumed his daughter to be his wife. When she tried to touch his shoulder he flinched away, and she suddenly wished to have been his son; a young man with whom he could proudly walk down the street, free of speculation.

Simmons returned, held out some gold coins which Deborah took and pressed into Father's hand.

"Thank you," Father said, but Deborah wasn't sure if it was for her or for Simmons.

"'Tis my pleasure, John."

"And when will . . . when will it be . . .?"

Again, Deborah felt a twinge of compassion. Confronted with his dearest wish, Father became rather smaller and paler. He seemed not so frightening at all, and Deborah was unsure if she liked that. With the threat of Lazodeus over his head, she would prefer he seemed indestructible.

"As soon as we can. We have quite a few jobs waiting, and

this is a long work."

"Before Christmas?"

"Notwithstanding some unforeseen problem, I should say shortly after Christmas." Simmons smiled and reached out to grasp Father's hand. "Now go home and take a long rest, John. You must have worked on this for many years."

"In some ways, my entire life," Father said with a proud smile.

A life's work. Deborah was suddenly frightened. "Will you put the manuscript somewhere safe?" she asked, eyeing it perched precariously on the corner of his desk.

He winked at her. "Put your mind at ease, Miss Milton. 'Tis in my good care."

Anne was in mid-sentence, though she could not later remember what that sentence was, when she and Mary opened the door to their bedroom after an afternoon with the laundry.

Lazodeus paced the floor, his hands clasping and unclasping in front of him. His head jerked up as they came in. Before either of them could say a word, he said, "Where is your sister?"

Anne and Mary exchanged glances.

"Your other sister. Where is Deborah?"

"Out with Father," Anne said.

"What on earth is the matter?" Mary asked.

"Nothing on earth," he snapped. "The matter is in Pandemonium."

"You are angry," Anne said, afraid. Lately she had only experienced his love and sensuality. Anger was a shock to her.

"I have been waiting for you for hours. I would have appeared down in the kitchen, right in front of you and your stupid maidservant, if you hadn't returned soon." Anne had never seen him so agitated. His face was flushed, and his usual soft glow was dissipated. He would not stand still.

"What is the matter in Pandemonium?" Mary asked, growing impatient herself. "And what has it to do with Deborah?"

"How long has she been gone?"

"I know not. I didn't know she had left. Anne?"

Anne shrugged.

Lazodeus shook his head impatiently. "This is not a big house. How can you lose each other?"

"Lazodeus, tell us what the problem is," Mary said. "We cannot help you if you do not tell us."

He pressed a thumb and forefinger to his forehead and sighed. "Yes, yes. Sit down."

Anne and Mary sat on the bed. Lazodeus kneeled before them, leaned forward and began to speak. His words were deliberately slow. "I idly mentioned your father's poem to a colleague of mine. He is a seer angel, which means he has a partial ability to predict future events. Mostly in Pandemonium, but sometimes on earth. As hard as you may find this to believe, your father's *Paradise Lost* is fated to last through the ages, to be read many hundred years from now, to inspire generations."

"Death! Is the world destined to grow so much more dull? I should be glad to die if it is."

"Do not make light of it, Mary, for you have not heard the whole story," Lazodeus said.

Mary dropped her head, chastened.

"We went directly to Lucifer with the information, of course. Because of the poem's future wide influence, and because of Deborah's alterations, our story is destined to be mistold for generations. Our relationship with mortals, which I hoped to improve by dictating to your father, will be worsened." He took a deep breath as though trying to brace himself against an awful fear. "Lucifer was angry with me."

"Angry? But why? You were innocent of blame," Anne

378

said, feeling somehow guilty. She was related by blood to the two people who had brought him into mischief.

"I am not. For I did not tell him immediately of my involvement in its composition, I did not warn him of the . . ." He trailed off, and Anne thought she saw tears in his eyes, but they were soon blinked back. Her chest ached from trying to control her heart. She could not fling her arms about him and comfort him in front of Mary.

"I don't understand," Mary was saying, impatient with all this information. "'Tis just a *poem*. Why does anybody care? Why is it your fault?"

"Mary, I do not necessarily expect you to understand. Pandemonium is a different place with different rules. But in Lucifer's eyes, I am guilty for not stopping the progress of a work which will sully our name for centuries." He dropped his head. "He has named my punishment."

"You are to be punished?" Anne's heart beat a little faster.

"Yes, imprisoned."

"But you have been imprisoned ere now. It is not so bad, is it?" Anne realised she sounded desperate. "You will soon be free again."

He shook his head, met first her gaze then Mary's. "I am to be imprisoned for a century."

"A century?" Mary had grown pale. "But . . . I'll be dead when you are released."

"Yes. Such a punishment I could endure, were it not that it means . . . the end of . . ."

Anne's head suddenly felt light. Everything directly in front of her was sharply focussed, but around the periphery of her vision shadows collected. "I . . ." She stood, and a loud ringing started in her ears.

"Anne!" she heard Lazodeus cry, right before the floor rushed up and she swooned.

Consciousness seemed to grind back down on top of her, and she became aware of Mary roughly pinching her cheeks.

"Be gentle, Mary," Lazodeus said. "She has already hurt

379

herself by falling."

"Come, Anne, don't be a dolt. Wake up."

Anne's eyes tried to focus. What had happened? Then she remembered: her angel was leaving and she was no longer to see him. Her grief was too profound for ordinary tears and sobs.

"I can't breathe," she said.

Lazodeus gently scooped an arm beneath her shoulders and helped her sit. "Yes, you can. Come, in and out."

She took a few deep breaths.

"Anne, don't be a fool," Mary said. "He has been given until midnight on Tuesday to destroy the manuscript."

"Tuesday . . .?" Today was Friday; they had four days.

"Wait until she is better, Mary. Can you not see that she is still in a swoon?"

Relief crept into her fingers. "Is it true? Do you merely have to destroy the manuscript?"

"And any copies, but *you* have to do it. The two of you. Lucifer is afraid I will hide in the mortal world. I am expected back in Pandemonium in moments, to be taken to my cell. As soon as the poem is destroyed, you may call me and let me know." He pressed an object into Mary's hand. "Here. This should help."

Mary opened her palm and Anne peered over to see what was in it. A round, clay disk with a complicated symbol on it; all geometric lines contorted together. "What is it?" Mary asked.

"It is a fire charm," Lazodeus said. "For the manuscript when you find it. In case there is no fire nearby."

Anne was pained with jealousy. Why give the charm to Mary and not her? She was the eldest.

Mary, pleased with herself over this bestowal of favour, fixed Anne with a serious gaze. "Now, Anne, can you remember which publisher Father said was going to print the foul thing?"

Anne shook her head. "I was not present when he

imparted the news to you."

Mary chewed her lip. "If only I could . . . wait. Simmons, I think his name was."

"A common name in a city this size, Mary. We should ask Deborah."

Mary snorted. "Deborah will not tell us, you idiot."

"Think hard, Mary," Lazodeus said, grasping her hands in his.

Anne could not stop staring, assessing his grasp for any evidence of favour. Why did he hold Mary's hands so? Did he prefer her sister?

"Simmons at . . . Yes! Aldersgate! I remember, next to the Golden Lion."

"Well done," Lazodeus said. Mary turned her face up as though expecting a kiss, but Lazodeus ignored her and stood. Anne took great satisfaction in the downturn of Mary's disappointed mouth. "Now, you must destroy all the drafts of the poem."

"Yes. Anne, you search Deborah's closet, and I shall search Father's study. We must be quick, they could be home soon."

Anne nodded. "Lazodeus? Can you stay to help us search?"

He shook his head sadly. "I am afraid I must go to my incarceration. But I trust you, both of you. I know the love you bear me, and I trust you to help me." He touched Mary's hand again. "If nothing else, you have this charm to remember me by."

"Of course you can trust us," Anne said, her voice desperate.

"I shall not let you down," Mary said, with a competitive glance towards her sister.

"Nor shall I," Anne added.

Lazodeus placed a hand over his heart, the movement slow and mesmerising. "I thank you," he said. "For now, goodbye." The shimmering which signalled his disappearance began to emanate from his body. "Let us hope we meet again very soon."

Mary wished she could do this alone.

Most of all because then Lazodeus's favour would be hers only, and not stupid Anne's. She could not understand why the angel paid her pinch-faced sister so much attention. She was ugly, she was dull, and she always wore a slack-jawed expression of incomprehension which drove Mary wild with impatience. The other reason she would prefer to be alone was because she knew she would be more efficient. So far, Anne had baulked at scaling the back fence — "I have only just learned to walk properly, you mustn't expect me to climb" — so they'd had to sneak past Father's study where he sat snoring. Then Anne had been hesitant about walking down dark alleys at night. Did she not understand that if they walked through the glow of lanterns in windows they would be seen and perhaps recognised later? And now this, standing there wringing her hands together, biting her lip, pleading with Mary to be careful.

"One cannot break a latch with care, Anne. One must break it with force." She hefted the rock again and brought it cracking down on the edge of the door of Simmons's printery. She was rewarded with a loud snap. "There. Now we shall go in." Mary kicked the door gently, and the bottom half swung in. "You first."

"I . . ."

Mary rolled her eyes and groaned. "Lordy, you are no use to me at all." She ducked under the door and found herself standing in the office of the printery. Anne soon joined her.

"What if someone has heard us?"

"Do you want Lazodeus to spend the rest of our lives in prison?"

"I do not want to be imprisoned either."

"Stop worrying. There is nobody living here. The windows upstairs are boarded up." Mary edged around the side of the desk and towards the doorway to the printing workshop. "And the neighbours won't care. If they hear anything they'll think we are armed thieves and stay well away."

"You're right. I should be of more use to you," Anne muttered, for the third time so far that evening.

Mary stopped and fixed her sister with an exasperated gaze. "Honestly, Annie, how have you managed to get through life thus far? What is most important in this matter?"

"Lazodeus."

"And why did we burn the drafts from Father's study today?"

"For Lazodeus."

"And what if we don't find the manuscript?"

Anne hung her head. "Let us search for it then."

The printery was a large room with a profusion of benches and tables laid out at even spaces. The floorboards were bare and stained with spilled splotches of ink. Dark, iron boxes were stacked on the floor. A large black contraption stood next to the doorway, with a heavy handle and drawers on all sides. Fresh printed pages lay in tidy piles next to it. At another table were gridded boxes full of letters, rows and rows of them. Behind the table was a wall of shelving, and packed neatly into each shelf were manuscripts.

"There," Mary said, pointing.

Anne approached the shelf and started to leaf through the manuscripts carefully. Mary joined her and pulled a manuscript from the shelf. It wasn't Father's. She scattered it across the floor.

"Mary, what are you doing?" Anne asked, horrified.

"If a single manuscript is missing, Anne, they will know someone came for it deliberately. But if the whole printery is in chaos, they will suspect vandals rather than thieves." She violently pulled another manuscript from the shelf, checked it, then threw it behind her.

Anne followed her lead, but much more cautiously. "It seems a shame to upset everybody else's work."

Mary rounded on her. "You are simply not passionate enough, Anne. Do it for Lazodeus. Forget about everyone else."

Anne set her jaw and was soon creating as much chaos as Mary. After a few minutes, the two of them stood in a mess of paper, but Father's manuscript was nowhere to be seen. Mary, enraged by this, glanced around her. "Where else could it be?"

"I see no other . . . Mary!"

Mary had strode to the press and was pulling the freshly printed pages from the bench beside it. She glanced at them, tore them up, scattered them. She pushed a box of letters over, and they rattled to the floor. How dare Father write something which endangered her relationship to the angel? How dare this idiot Simmons think it a good idea to publish it? She turned more boxes of letters over. P's and M's crashed into piles of B's and K's; Roman letters mingled with italics; and numerals and foreign characters consorted. It would take the printers weeks to sort the mess out. Damn them. Damn them all.

She turned to see Anne watching her with her big, dull eyes.

"Yes, yes, I know," Mary said. "I'm behaving badly again."

"The manuscript is not here."

"He must have it at his house."

"Do you know where he lives?"

Mary shook her head. "No, I don't. But we shall find him. We shall return tomorrow and we shall follow him home after work."

"And then?"

"Simple," Mary said, blowing an untidy curl away from her cheek. "We shall burn his house down."

19
Thy Choice of Flaming Warriors

Deborah hated being in the kitchen in this hot weather. She could feel sweat in damp patches under her arms and across her stomach as she helped Liza prepare soup for the evening supper. This job should have been Anne's, but both her sisters had wandered off together just after dinner and hadn't been seen since.

Jealous. That's what she was. She wiped the back of her hand across her perspiring brow and tried to concentrate on cutting up the potatoes in front of her. Her sisters were friends with each other and she was excluded. She had never felt this way before. Anne and Mary had never been particularly close. Deborah had always seen herself as the connection between the two of them. But everything had changed, as Anne had warned them all it would, a long time ago when Deborah had still thought it a good idea to call an angel into their service.

Everything had changed.

"Miss Deborah, could you check the water?" Liza said. If Deborah was suffering in the heat, Liza was finding it worse. Most days she was confined to the kitchen with the fire, scouring the stone floor, or out in the blazing sun freshening rugs, linen and tapestries. There was no escape for her from the awful heat, which still refused to fade. The dry gusty winds still roared over the eaves, banging shutters and setting errant tiles free.

What Deborah wanted more than anything was to wade

fully clothed into the brook near Grandmamma's house, let the cool, deep water close over her, make her feel alive again. She savoured the fantasy as she turned to the fire to see if the water was boiling in the big hanging cauldron, but was distracted by something which caught her eye at the edge of the fire.

Her handwriting. On a piece of paper.

She gasped, leaned forward.

"Carefully, Miss Deborah, you'll burn yourself."

"Liza, were these pieces of paper here this morning?"

"I know not, Miss," Liza said, peering over her shoulder. "I didn't notice nothing. Is it important?"

Deborah grabbed the poker and coaxed the clump of burned fragments out onto the hearth. Leaned close to examine them. It was her handwriting, but her tired, messy scrawl; this was not the fair copy. Had Father burned the drafts? Surely not, he was not such a fool. To have only one copy of so many years of work was unthinkable.

"Liza, I have to go and see Father for a few minutes," she said, pulling off the cloth she had tied around her waist and dumping it on the big wooden table.

"But the soup —"

"The soup can wait. This can't."

She hurried to Father's study. He had moved his chair under the window in the hopes of a breeze. The window was open wide, but only hot air blew through it.

"Deborah?" he said, his head cocked to one side listening.

"Yes, Father, it is me. I'm looking for something."

"What is it?" he asked.

She walked directly to Father's desk. The drafts should all be collected in the lower drawer. "An old inkwell I used to use. I've been trying to remember what was carved on it. Mary and I have a wager."

"A wager!"

"Not money, just chores," Deborah said distractedly as she pulled open the drawer.

Empty. Completely empty. Her heart thudded hollowly

in her chest. She looked over her shoulder at Father, who gazed back at her oblivious. She could not tell him. How frantic would he be, knowing only one copy of his life's work existed? And that in someone else's care?

"Not here," she said, closing the drawer.

"You didn't look very hard."

"Father, can Simmons be trusted to take good care of your manuscript?"

Father smiled a tight smile. "I find your concern charming. Of course he can."

"But he doesn't live above the printery. What if . . ."

"He has it at home with him. He came by this morning to tell me how much he's enjoying reading it."

"It is not at the printery?"

"He sleeps with it under his pillow," Father chuckled. "At least, that's what he said."

Relief. Mary and Anne did not know where he lived. If they wanted to destroy it, they would go to the printery and be disappointed.

The window slammed shut in a strong gust of wind. "I wish we had made two copies," she said idly. She moved to Father's side, pushed the window open again and secured it with a rod.

"Deborah, child," Father said softly. "You must not worry. *Paradise Lost* is destined to be published. No impediment will arise. The manuscript is protected by divine intention. Trust me."

Hearing his gentle conviction was almost too much for her. There was so much he did not know, so many enemies he did not recognise. Tears were suddenly on her lashes.

"Yes, Father," she said, trying to keep her voice under control. "I shall be in the kitchen with Liza if you need me."

"Is it not thrilling to be alive, Annie?"

Anne watched her feet carefully as she trod upon the cobbles. It was so dark it seemed that each step she took was into oblivion. She thought being alive at this moment frightening. Mary danced ahead of her, full of energy and excitement. But setting fire to someone's house was not Anne's idea of an early morning's entertainment.

"Annie, think you not that it is thrilling to be alive?"

"I know not, Mary," she replied. Nearby church bells rang out the hour, startling her. Two in the morning. The tolling was snatched up and carried away on a gust of wind.

"That is because you are not really alive," Mary muttered.

"I am alive."

"You are so full of fear that you cannot even feel your heart beat."

"My heart is so far up my throat that I can barely breathe."

Mary doubled back and grabbed Anne, pressed her hand to her chest. "Ah yes, 'tis in there somewhere."

"Be not so cruel, Mary."

"I'm not being cruel."

"You are making a joke of me."

"Anne, we go to avenge our angel. We are saving him from a century of punishment. If you feel so uncomfortable about it, perhaps you should return home and leave the job to me."

Anne shook her head resolutely. "No, I shall not." She had an awful suspicion that Mary's plan to burn Simmons's house down was to discourage Anne from helping. Then Mary could take all the credit for saving Lazodeus. Anne wouldn't let that happen. "But must we burn down his house?"

"Yes. For the manuscript is in it, and it must be burned."

"Why can we not just steal it and burn it elsewhere?"

"Anne, you poopnoddy. It is one thing to break into an unmanned printery, another thing to creep about a person's house while he sleeps. We would be caught."

"But what if he burns to death?"

"Then it serves him right for printing the stupid poem."

"He may have a wife and children."

Mary made an exasperated groan. "Anne, once again you put the lives of others ahead of the life of our angel. I shall tell him, you know. When we have saved him, I shall tell him that the whole time you moaned about the needs of anonymous people." She stopped abruptly. "We've come too far. We should have turned right at the last corner."

Anne followed as she doubled back. The previous afternoon they had waited outside the printery for Simmons to finish work, and followed him to a house on Pudding Lane with a bakery beneath it. They sat across the street for two hours to make sure he did not come out again: to burn down the wrong house would be foolish, and they had no time to make foolish mistakes. The manuscript had to be destroyed by midnight Tuesday and the sun would soon rise on Lord's day.

Anne found herself breathing more rapidly as they came to a halt outside the building. The bakery window was shut, the windows of the three storeys above it were all dark. Anne almost imagined she could hear the slow breathing sounds of sleep, but when she strained her ears, all she could hear was the creaking of wind in the eaves.

"Here we are," Mary said, turning to face her in the dark. Anne could not quite make out her features.

"Do we have to go inside?"

Mary shook her head. "I have the fire charm."

"Do you know how to use it?"

"No. But I soon will." She fiddled around in her placket, then pulled the charm out. It glowed warmly, giving a little light to their scene. "Now, let me see." She clasped her hands together over the charm, then gasped.

"What is it?"

"'Tis so warm, 'tis almost . . ." She held out one of her hands. Her palm glowed orange. "It grows hotter. Ow. It is burning."

"Quick, let us run down to the river to extinguish it."

"No, you fool. We don't want to extinguish it, we want to use it." She flung out her empty hand in the direction of the bakery's window. A glimmer shook inside, then an amber glow began to reflect back at them.

"Ha!" Mary said, looking at her palm which had returned to normal. "I did it!"

"Are you sure?"

But Mary had pocketed the fire charm, and was already up against the window, pressing her face and trying to peer in. "Oh, yes, I'm sure. 'Tis spreading already."

"We should go."

"No, we should stay and make sure it keeps spreading."

"Then perhaps we should call out to wake up those in the upper storeys."

"Then what if Simmons wakes and saves the manuscript? Anne, you simply must let it go. Nothing is too much for the angel to ask us, you know that."

She did know it. She wished, though, that dealing with the angel was more to do with making love and speaking in hushed voices in the park, rather than running about in the dark breaking laws and endangering lives. But perhaps this was what being a woman meant: that pleasure only came at a price. And that price was surely not too much to pay, when the well of pleasure she drew from was so very deep.

"'Tis not moving very fast," Mary was saying.

"How fast should a fire move?" Anne asked.

"I —" A crash inside interrupted her. The flames suddenly burned much brighter. Mary scurried back to the opposite side of the road. "Something just gave."

Anne's heartbeat thudded in her ears. "We should leave."

"Just a moment longer."

Anne glanced at her sister, her face turned up to the building, clear in the fireglow. Mary was enjoying this. Glass suddenly shattered, and the fire curled out of the window and caught on the side of the building. They seized each other in shock.

"Now can we go?"

"Yes, yes," Mary said, backing down the street, but not tearing her eyes from the scene.

Anne found herself similarly transfixed. The fire was racing up the outside wall, and inside she could see the bright flames hanging ravenously from beams. A sudden blast of wind roared overhead, and for the first time Anne saw Mary show concern. Her brow furrowed as she watched the wind feed the flame, and a great arm of fire licked out and danced.

"Let us leave," she said breathlessly, turning on her heel and hurrying down the street. Anne followed her close behind. As she reached the bottom of Pudding Lane, she heard a cry.

"Was that someone screaming?"

"Anne, that's a good thing. It means they are awake, and will now save themselves. But the fire is so advanced, they will not be able to save the manuscript."

They rounded into Thames Street and ran straight down Cocks Key to the river. The strange sour, metallic smell of it was comforting after the close, hot lane. They stood on the sludgy bank, looking out over the water. Anne gulped big breaths of air, but could not seem to fill her lungs.

"Mary, what have we done?"

"We have saved Lazodeus from imprisonment. We have ensured that we will see him again."

A soft rushing grew behind them. Anne turned and looked back down the key. "Can you hear that?"

"'Tis just the wind."

"I believe it is the fire." She was rewarded by a long, low creak and then a crash. "We must go back. We must go back and help to put it out."

"Don't be ridiculous."

"But the houses are so close together. The whole street will burn."

Mary grasped Anne by the shoulders. "Calm down. The

city has engines which shoot water upon the flames. Within no time, the fire will be out. Besides, what could you do if you went back? Piss on it?"

Anne clutched her stomach. "I think I may throw up."

"No, Annie," Mary said, turning to the river. "Guilt and nausea may feel the same, but only one can escape your stomach. We should call Lazodeus and tell him what we have done."

For the first time this evening, the promise of comfort came to her. "Yes, you are right. For he will be free now, I expect."

"Lazodeus," Mary called, and the wind snatched her words and sent them echoing down the river. He did not respond.

"Perhaps it takes time for his release to be effected," Anne suggested.

"Perhaps . . . oh!"

Anne whirled around to see what sight had caused an expression of horror to appear on Mary's face. A squat, pig-faced creature stood behind them. She let out a short, sharp scream.

"Be not alarmed," the creature said. "I am a messenger from Lazodeus."

"Why does he not come?" Mary said, and Anne noticed she had slowly backed towards her. Her sister was terrified of the creature, and that terror suddenly became contagious. Usually Mary feared nothing.

"What are you?" Anne gasped.

"'Tis a demon, Anne," Mary said, reaching for her hand.

Anne could only stare as the creature spoke again.

"He does not come, my ladies, because he is in prison." The demon smiled as though it relished the thought. "He cannot go anywhere for a hundred years."

"But we burned the manuscript!"

Suddenly the smile disappeared and the creature shook his head. "You didn't burn a manuscript, you burned a bakery."

"No, Simmons lives above! We waited and watched for hours."

"He was visiting his sister's husband."

"Then the manuscript . . ."

"Was not there." The creature looked around, drawing Anne's attention for the first time to the orange smoke which slowly rose from Pudding Lane. "But haven't you made a nice fire?" it said, its voice thick with sarcasm.

"Go away, wretch," Mary said.

"No, wait. Where is the manuscript?" Anne asked urgently.

"I know not," it said. "Good morning." The demon vanished, leaving Anne and Mary clutching hands by the river.

"Oh, no," Mary said as a gust of wind roared overhead, and a cloud of sparks eddied up into it.

"What have we done, Mary?" Anne said softly. "What have we done?"

Anne could not bring herself to open her prayer book and read along with the congregation. In her addled state — she had only slept two restless hours after her early morning adventure with Mary — Anne imagined the angels listening to her praying would instead hear the false notes of her guilty soul, see her dark heart and judge her. She could not bring herself to utter the name of Christ, her mild and loving erstwhile hero, for she suspected that last night she may have become a murderer.

Master Allard began his sermon, and Anne glanced up and down the pew. Father's back was ramrod-straight, his hair combed neatly. Deborah sat next to him, her leg pressed against Anne's. On Anne's other side was Mary. She regarded her sister a moment. Anne suspected the black rings under Mary's eyes matched her own, but Mary bore no expression which indicated guilt or suffering. Anne dropped her gaze to her lap, pressed her fingers against each other.

Lord's day. She may have murdered on Lord's day.

If only there was a way of finding out if anyone had perished in the fire, but Mary had warned her not to open her mouth, not to mention the fire. They did not want suspicion brought upon them.

Perhaps she would feel comforted if they had at least been successful in their quest to release Lazodeus from his imprisonment. With Lazodeus's arms around her, she could be healed of any woe. He would no doubt be able to explain why it was more important to save a loved angel than to value human life . . .

But she must stop thinking like this. Mary had been quite clear: they didn't know that anyone had been hurt, and it was a good chance that all they had effected was a loss of property and not life. Besides, Mary had said, any consequence of the fire they started was accidental. They intended no harm to anyone.

And in some brief moments, Anne could even take comfort in knowing that it was Mary who lit the fire, not herself. Anne had pleaded with her not to. Why, she was hardly a murderer when seen in that light.

The sermon finished and Anne drew deep breaths as her family arose around her.

"Will you take me to Master Allard, Deborah?" Father asked.

"Certainly, Father."

Mary and Anne filed out into the bright morning air. Mary pressed her back against the wall and yawned. "Is it not foul how Father treats Deborah like his wife while Betty is away?"

"I do not believe he does. Father cannot see and so with Betty away —"

Mary waved a dismissive hand. "For goodness sake, don't defend them."

Anne looked back at her wordlessly. Too tired to speak.

"We have to find out where Simmons lives."

"We are not setting any more fires."

Mary rolled her eyes. "You can stay home this time. Lazodeus would probably prefer it if I saved him. He must be able to tell I care more."

"You do not care more!" This exchange was growing old between them. Anne shrugged. "I will do what I have to."

"Good, here comes Deborah. Ask her where Simmons lives."

"Me?"

"She doesn't trust me."

Deborah emerged from the church.

"Where is Father?" Anne asked.

"He is still speaking with Master Allard." Deborah adjusted her bonnet on her head. "You look tired, Anne. Did you not sleep well?"

Anne shook her head. "I have been troubled by terrible dreams."

Deborah glanced at Mary then back at Anne. "Some say that troubling dreams are the sign of a soul in torment."

"Deborah," Anne said, ignoring her comment, "does Father's friend Simmons live close by?"

"Why do you want to know?" Deborah narrowed her eyes.

"I am curious."

Deborah shook her head and laughed; a short cynical laugh. "Oh, Annie. It has come too far for this, do you not see? I know the two of you destroyed Father's drafts, I know Simmons's printery was vandalised, and I know it has something to do with the angel. Do you think I'm a fool? Do you think that you can once again be my dear, beloved sister, when all you have done of late is aimed at ruining Father's work?"

"Father only loves you because you are free labour," Mary hissed, leaning in between them. "You were better to take our side. At least we have always loved you for who you are."

Deborah turned wide hazel eyes on her, and was about to

open her mouth to rebut her comment when Father joined them, Master Allard guiding him by the elbow.

"Here are your girls, John."

"Thank you, Laurence," Father said. Deborah took his arm.

"What fine young women they have grown into," Master Allard said. "You must be mightily proud."

Father without a trace of irony said, "Daughters, Laurence, are nothing but trouble. Would that I had had sons."

Anne watched Deborah's face fall with disappointment. Mary gave a smile of triumph.

"Come," Deborah said, "let us return home."

"Where is Liza? I'm starving!" Mary paced the kitchen one more time while Father frowned.

"Mary, sit still. Liza will be here soon enough."

Mary leaned on the back of her chair. Liza had gone out for bread half an hour ago. Deborah had made soup for supper, but Father wouldn't let them eat until the bread arrived. The four of them waited around the kitchen table in uncomfortable silence.

Today had been a complete waste of time. After church, Mary had laid down for a second only to wake four hours later. Stupid Anne hadn't woken her, so nearly a whole day had been lost. Now she had to wait until after supper to take Anne aside and discuss a new plan. How hard could it be to find Simmons's address? Someone would know it. First thing tomorrow — Monday morning — they could go and ask questions at the printery, or perhaps she could press one of her friends of influence to help. Wallace certainly owed her a favour or two.

"I said sit down!" Father roared, and Mary dazedly realised that she had been pacing once again. Just as she dropped into her seat, Liza bustled in.

"What took so long?" Mary asked.

Liza turned agitatedly on Father. Her eyes were glowing and her face flushed.

"Sir, I have —"

"Where's the bread?" Mary asked, for Liza had laid nothing on the table.

"Is there no bread?" Father said. "You have been gone a long time to come back empty-handed."

"Sir, I have news," Liza managed to squeeze out. "There is a fire down by the river, burning out of control along Thames Street."

"A fire?"

"Yes, sir. There is talk of it everywhere. It started early in the morning, and has since burned down four hundred houses."

"Four hundred!" Anne gasped. "Has anyone been killed?"

Liza turned to her. "That I know not, Miss Anne. But my sister lives at the top of Fish Street Hill and I would like to go and check on her." She turned to Father. "Please, sir. I'm terribly worried."

"Of course, of course," Father said. "You must see if she needs you. How far beyond Fish Street is it burning, Liza? As far as Gracechurch Street?"

Mary saw Deborah glance at Father, her breath held tight on her lips, and knew instantly that this was the street that Simmons lived on. Perhaps their little fire was destined to destroy the manuscript after all. She waited calmly for Liza's answer.

"Not yet, sir, but folks are moving their goods out and taking to the river. The fire is so hot that the engines cannot get near it, and people are in such a panic that they've pulled the pipes out of the ground. There is no water to be had anywhere from Billingsgate to Cold Harbour."

"A terrible thing, a terrible thing indeed," Father said.

"What is the matter, Father?" Mary asked, hoping to draw him out. "We are so far from Fish Street, it surely won't burn our house down."

Father's eyelids shot up. "What? Is it only our losses that you feel concern for, Mary? Four hundred houses are burned, is that not a terrible thing?"

Mary cringed down in her seat. "Yes, Father," she murmured.

"Liza, go immediately, and stay safe. If your sister and her family need a place to stay they can sleep in Betty's bed until she returns." He turned to Deborah. "Deborah, we need to get a letter to Simmons immediately, to tell him to return *Paradise Lost*. To make another fair copy would take too long; we cannot lose it."

"We shall do it first thing in the morning, Father, for the post is finished for the evening," Deborah said, keeping a studied impassiveness to her expression.

"I shall take the letter to him myself, Father," Mary said. "If you tell me where on Gracechurch Street he lives. I shall take it tonight."

Father huffed. "It won't be necessary. The fire is still near the river. He lives at the top of Gracechurch Street near Bishopsgate. The manuscript will be safe for now."

Deborah hung her head with a barely audible groan. Mary smiled. A trip to Gracechurch Street at dawn would solve this problem easily. Lazodeus would be pleased with her.

Liza returned from her sister's around mid-morning the next day to pack some clothes, then left again. She was to accompany her sister to their father's house at Smithfield. Her sister had lost everything. Father told her to take two or three days, and Deborah chastised herself for being so surprised at his generosity.

"With Betty away and Liza away, the household shall fall apart," she joked as she sat with him to write the letter to Simmons.

"The household will manage, for I have three able-bodied daughters," Father replied gruffly. "Though only one is yet awake."

"I believe they were up very late. I heard much hushed talking until the small hours," Deborah responded, careful not to colour her voice. For the demon key was as much responsible for her sisters' long slumber. She wanted the letter to go to Simmons before they were lurking about to glean further details of his address, or worse, get there ahead of her.

"Only drunkards and babies sleep this late. If not for you, Deborah, I should despair of my children."

"Yesterday you told Master Allard you would have preferred sons."

"Of course I would have."

"You would have preferred a son to me?"

Father puffed up his shoulders and tapped his finger on the arm of his chair. "Enough nonsense. Let us get this letter written."

Deborah's hand shook as she dipped her pen. Why did her father's opinion still have such power to affect her? Why could she not just take his initial compliment without pushing to hear him disavow his sentiments to Master Allard? And why could she not trust that he would rather have her than a son?

A loud knock at the door startled her. She put her pen aside. "I shall see who it is, Father."

Simmons himself stood at the front door when she opened it.

"Mr Simmons?"

"Deborah, is your Father here?"

"Yes. If you wait sir, I shall fetch him."

She quickly brought Father, casting an anxious glance towards the stairs. She had only asked that her sisters sleep for a few hours longer, not deeper. The noise of visitors might wake them.

"Simmons, is everything well?" Father asked, extending a pale shaking hand.

"Yes, yes. You have heard, I suppose, of the fire?"

"I can barely take a breath without being reminded. The air is laced with smoke. And Deborah tells me the sky is the colour of dull bronze."

"'Tis unstoppable. The entire west side of the city is in uproar. You are lucky to live so far beyond the city walls. Fire posts have been established at all the gates, but already thirty churches have been burned, and as I left my home this morning the smoke was gusting up my street as though it intended to suffocate me."

"And my manuscript?"

"Safe, John. The stationers and printers have all stored their paper in St Faith's, below St Paul's. Only the very fires of hell could burn through Paul's stone. But I, alas, must take my leave from London. I do not expect to find a home when I return."

"Surely it is not so bad?"

"'Tis ravenous. The mayor has ordered a firebreak be made and buildings are now being pulled down south along Cornhill. My house stands between the fire and the break. A sacrifice." Simmons snorted a nervous laugh. "But your *Paradise Lost* is safe, John. A masterpiece. I wept when I finished."

"I am glad to hear it is safe, but I trust you did not trouble yourself too much. I have all my drafts still."

Deborah's stomach curdled.

"No, I dropped a number of important papers there. It is my business, not trouble."

He glanced behind him. "I must go. My wife waits for me at the bottom of the street. We have packed as much as possible on a cart, and we leave for her father's home immediately."

"Good luck, Simmons. Haply I shall hear from you soon."

They saw him off and Father turned to Deborah. "What do you think of this fire, then?"

"It has been extreme dry and windy, Father," she said as she led him back to the study. "But I think Mary was right when she said it would not reach us here."

"Yes. For the walls of the city will not burn."

"No, Father." She could hear the sounds of movement upstairs. "I think my sisters are awake."

Father nodded as he sat in his chair. Deborah took to the stairs, meeting Mary and Anne halfway. Mary was clearly annoyed, but Anne merely looked bewildered. Deborah knew she should have felt guilty: using the demon key on her sisters was a terrible betrayal. But instead she felt a great pride at saving Father's manuscript.

"You slept so long, sisters, you have missed all the excitement," she said, blocking the stairs.

"What excitement, you foul creature?" Mary asked. "Do you know how late it is? We have nearly lost half the day. Why did you not wake us?"

"Liza has left, and Simmons came by."

"Simmons?"

"Yes, his house is burned."

Mary smiled, but her smile soon faded. "Why do you look so happy?"

"Because the poem is safe, and you shall never find it."

"I *will* find it."

"No, 'tis no longer possible. Simmons has deposited it somewhere for safekeeping until the fire is out, and I shall never tell you where. So you may forget whatever wicked plans you had, for I have won this battle."

Mary stomped and let out a shriek. "I *hate* you."

"I care not," Deborah said.

"But the angel —"

"I care not a speck for Lazodeus," Deborah cut in. "So save your tantrums."

She swept past and went up to her closet, heard Mary and Anne arguing quietly on the stairs. The window was open and she went to it to take some deep breaths of air. All she could smell was smoke.

*

"It *is* up to you, Annie. I've not slept for thinking about it, and I've decided it is the only way we can find out where it is."

Anne grimaced against the suggestion. "But I am so very bad at deception. Father will see right through me, and then he'll be alert to us. Better if you do it."

"No, Anne. I cannot impersonate Deborah. My voice is too loud and clipped. You sound much more like her, if you just spoke confidently. He is not used to your voice, for you hardly ever speak. But our secret weapon is your walk, for Father does not know that your limp is vanished. If you walk into his study confidently and speak to him, he will never suspect it is you. I know he won't."

Anne regarded her sister. Mary sounded desperate, and certainly desperation was weighing upon them both heavily. Monday had passed by them with a solution still not apparent, and now scarce twelve hours remained for them to save Lazodeus from imprisonment. The city was in such chaos that all Mary's attempts to glean information about possible places the manuscript could be were foiled. Much time had been wasted in trying to contact Mary's rich suitors, who had all wisely vacated the city. "I want very much to believe that I can do this," Anne said.

"You can. You *can*. For Lazodeus."

For Lazodeus. For a chance to see him again. Anne nodded. "Yes, I will. Where is Deborah?"

"In the kitchen. We will be eating nothing but her mutton soup until Liza comes home." Mary grasped Anne's fingers. "Now, be careful not to touch him, not to take his hand."

Anne shuddered. "I wouldn't."

"And be careful how you word your questions. You are not to ask outright, for then he will suspect. For Deborah would not ask, as she already knows."

Anne felt her confidence waver. "I really don't —"

"You can do it, and I trust you. Lazodeus's hopes of being freed from prison rest upon it."

Anne smiled bitterly. Neither of them were desperate for

Lazodeus's sake. An eternal being such as the angel probably felt the passing of a century in an eyeblink. It was for their own sakes, for the possibility of continuing to see him. But neither of them discussed what may happen when he returned, their rivalry for his attention. "I shall do my best, sister."

"Remember the pretence I suggested."

"I will. You go to the kitchen and make sure Deborah is occupied."

They descended the staircase together, branching off at the bottom. Anne stood for a moment near the entry to Father's study, then took a deep breath and strode in. He looked up, and she could see the puzzled expression on his face. He could not tell which of his daughters stood before him, as Mary had suggested.

"It is Deborah, Father," she said, all the while hearing her voice and knowing she sounded nothing like Deborah.

"Deborah? You sound strange."

Anne's heart froze. What to do? What would Mary do? "Yes, Father, for I am most upset and it is hard for me to keep my voice steady."

"About what are you upset?"

"I dozed just now, and had a most upsetting dream."

"Ah. One should not doze in the day, for the dreams are too close to the surface and may cling to one for the rest of the afternoon." He nodded, and Anne was almost overwhelmed at the affectionate voice he used. Was this how Deborah perceived Father? A man who listened and offered advice? "Still, it was only a dream."

"But, Father, it was awful. The fire had wings and it burned your poem. All that work we did —"

"A dream, Deborah," he said more firmly.

Anne wanted to run out. She had no idea how to draw him further, to get him to mention the manuscript's hiding place. "You do believe, then, that it will be safe where it is stored?"

"Of course. For what can burn through stone?"

Stone. It was in a building made of stone. Her mind raced through the possibilities. A church? A public building? Too many options. "Are you sure that it is all made of stone, Father?" she ventured.

"You speak as though you never set eyes on St Paul's, Deborah. You know it is."

St Paul's. The warm relief was like thick liquid in her limbs. The manuscript was at St Paul's.

"Yes, Father," she said, almost forgetting to check her voice.

"So you are not to be concerned."

"Yes, of course. Forget that I came to speak with you, for now I am embarrassed for my feebleness." There, that sounded like something Deborah would say, and Father seemed to be convinced. "I shall see you at dinner," she said, backing out of the room.

Father did not reply. She raced to the kitchen. Mary had her back to the door, was trying to talk to a scowling Deborah as she chopped vegetables at the table. They both looked up as Anne came in, and she realised she was too excited. Deborah would deduce something was going on.

"Annie?" Mary asked.

"What's all this about?" Deborah said.

Anne smiled, and it was a smile of triumph. She could not remember ever having smiled like that before. "Nothing," she said. "Absolutely nothing."

20
At Our Heels All Hell Should Rise

Anne and Mary fought their way down towards Cripplegate, through a steady stream of people. Some had carts laden with expensive furniture, and some carried overstuffed trunks between them, clothes trailing out behind. Some, the poorest, carried what they could: a child under one arm and a cast-iron pot under the other, or a yowling cat in a box, or a bundle of rags which may have been a collection of favourite dresses. All of them were exhausted and harried. They were smudged with soot and running with perspiration, and three of them individually yelled out to the girls that they were going in the wrong direction.

"Idiots," Mary said, "what do they know about what we're doing?"

Anne still wasn't sure what they were doing. It was one thing to find out that the manuscript was in St Paul's, but another altogether to go running down there while a fire raged inside the city walls. The wind had picked up: mighty gusts snapped twigs from trees and threatened branches. Just before sunset they had heard word that the fire had spread along the river all the way to the Temple, that Fleet Street had been gutted and the fire had broken through the wall at Ludgate. But Paul's, the pedlar had told them, had held up.

"'Tis a miracle," he had said, much to Mary's irritation.

"But Mary," Anne had said when her sister had come to

405

drag her out just after twilight, "is it safe to go so close to the fire?"

"We have no choice. What if we wait until it is safe and midnight has passed?"

What if, indeed? Anne clutched Mary's hand now as they fought against the tide. It was an incredible thing to learn about herself, that she would risk her life for love. She tried to savour the pride, but the press of the crowd and the growing heat were of more immediate concern.

"There!" Mary called over the voices, the hooves, the rattling wheels and the ever-present background noise of the crashing, popping fire. "I can see the gate." She pulled Anne's hand and they dived through the crowd, only to be pulled up short by an armed foot soldier.

"Where are you going, ladies?"

Mary, always ready to lie, grabbed his wrist. "Our mother is in there, sir. We must get to her."

He shook his head firmly. "I'm sorry, I cannot let you enter. It is a furnace in there. Neither of you would survive."

"Is Paul's all burned?" Anne asked, wondering if she sounded hopeful.

"Not yet, though the scaffold on the front caught fire this afternoon. Provided the wind becomes no stronger, it should be safe."

Mary yanked Anne's hand and they were moving once again, but this time along the outside of the wall. Mary's hair was uncharacteristically loose, wild and long about her shoulders. She looked the part of Mad Mary this evening.

"Where are we going?"

"To Mooregate. There's no firepost there."

"But didn't you hear him? We'll be burned alive."

"We'll follow the fire, where it has already burned, where there is no more fuel to feed its flames. Paul's is out in the open, we can still get to it."

"Mary —"

"Stop whining and stay by me."

Anne put her head down and followed. Risking her life for love.

Father was anxious. He hadn't said so, of course, but his body betrayed his feelings. His fingers tapped. His jaw was tight. He was pale around the eyes. Deborah doubted he was concerned about Mary and Anne, who had disappeared around sunset. He assumed, like her, that they had gone up to the top of the hill to watch the fire. No, his concern was for the proximity of the flames.

The bells of alarm had grown nearer and nearer all day, and since the fire had burst through the wall at Ludgate, there was no guarantee that it would not also burn through Cripplegate and roar up Grub Street towards the Artillery grounds. Already, the park at the bottom of the Walk was filled with newly homeless people, their fancy furniture set up around them. Smoke gusted occasionally up the Walk outside, dark flakes of ash scattering ahead of it. Deborah had been to the top of the hill to look down over the city, and all she had seen was a pall of orange smoke. The heat was growing unbearable, and the crashing, banging clatter of the buildings succumbing to the fire, just a few miles south, had exposed her nerves. Still, she sat with Father, reading to him to keep him calm, and wondering how soon the bells at St Giles would ring, telling them it was time to pack up their possessions and flee.

"Enough!" Father said, as Deborah struggled to read on in the dim candlelight. "We shall wait for your sisters to return, then sup, and then sleep. By morning, we shall know if we are safe."

Deborah closed the book. "Can I get you anything, Father? Ale? Bread?"

"I shall be well enough until supper. I do not need to be watched like a child, Deborah. Have you no chores to do?"

Deborah stood. "Yes, Father, of course." She knew his

anxiety was making him irritable, that he was embarrassed for his neediness, for his cursed blindness which meant that he could not fend for himself when fire threatened his life, and she didn't take his gruffness personally. Instead, she went up to the withdrawing room to light a candle and find some sewing to occupy her until Mary and Anne returned.

She had just turned her back on the candle and reached for Betty's sewing box when she felt that she was no longer in the room alone. The light had changed subtly, and she was not surprised to find the angel there when she turned around.

"What do you want?" she asked, placing her palm gently across her forehead.

"To earn your trust."

She shook her head. "My trust? Are you in jest?"

"What you heard and saw in the mirror is not the whole story. You cannot know my motives."

"Your motives have always been clear: you intend to lead the three of us into sin and you have done well so far with two of us. You shall not win me over, Lazodeus."

"I shall, for I know how important your Father's poem is to you."

Her interest was aroused. What did he know about Father's poem?

"What about it?"

"He has worked on it for decades. It is his crowning achievement, and only a single copy remains."

She steeled herself. "What about it?" she said again.

"Your sisters want to destroy it because you made changes to my story."

"That's right, because you had no right to interfere with my father's imagination."

He shook his head. "That feud is behind us. This is far more important. They know that the manuscript is at St Paul's. They are at this moment on their way to burn it."

Deborah felt the overwhelming burden of responsibility drop once more upon her shoulders. "No, they cannot be. It is too dangerous to go to the city."

"They are determined. I tried to convince them not to, but . . ."

Deborah narrowed her eyes at him. "How can I trust you?"

"Because I am telling you this, and not keeping it from you. I have nothing to benefit from saving the manuscript."

"Perhaps your benefit is to see me burned to death in the city."

"Your sisters have been gone for an hour. Do you really believe they are still watching the fire from the hill?"

Deborah groaned. "This is all too much. Why have you come between us?"

"I have been allowed by the three of you to come between you. I have done nothing."

"You are not blameless, Lazodeus."

He raised his hands in the air. "I came to win your trust. If you do not listen to me and your sisters ensure the manuscript is burned, then perhaps you will realise how prejudiced you have become."

Deborah's mind ticked over the problem. "Give me something to trust you with."

"What do you mean?"

"I want a talisman to protect me from the fire."

He smiled. "Clever girl."

"Can you do it?"

He rubbed his hands together and then opened them. "Here, nothing may burn you while you wear this." He offered her a gold chain, with a fine gold circle on the end.

She took it from him with her free hand. "I shall test it ere I trust you."

He nodded. "As you wish."

She strode to the candle, gingerly reached out to the wick. She felt no bite of heat. With a quick movement, she passed her fingers through the flame. Nothing. She almost laughed.

"Are you satisfied?"

"I would be more satisfied if you had given these to every poor citizen of London who has so far perished in this blaze."

His smile faded. "Must you always be so pious, Deborah? Am I not serving you with a great favour?"

"That I still do not know," she replied. "But nevertheless, it appears I am to go to St Paul's this evening."

"And when you see, Deborah, that I mean you no harm, will you perhaps reconsider your feelings for me?"

She met his gaze evenly. He was so very beautiful that she found it difficult not to like him, merely for the magnetism of his face. "I shall consider that, angel, when I return whole and with Father's manuscript in my arms."

"If you see your sisters, do not mention that I sent you," he said urgently. "I am avoiding them at the moment, trying to wean them from their devotion to me."

"I doubt my sisters would believe a word I said on any topic related to you, Lazodeus. They know we are enemies."

He smiled. "Prejudice is unbecoming in one so young, but you shall learn to trust me. You shall." He vanished and Deborah stood for a moment in the sitting room, planning her lie to Father.

She was at the threshold of the front door before she said a word to him. With a light, "I'm going to find Mary and Anne," she stepped out into the street.

"Be careful," he called and she noticed his voice trembled a little. How could she leave him alone on such a night? She paused. He had to have some small comfort. She remembered Max cowering under the kitchen table and went to fetch him. "Come, little fellow," she said, grabbing him and delivering him to Father's lap. Father frowned.

"What is this?"

"Max is frightened, Father, and Mary is not home. Would you be kind to him?"

Father stroked the little dog's ears, and Max licked his fingers gratefully. "I suppose I can comfort him if he's frightened."

Deborah touched Max's head lightly then turned to go. "I won't be gone long, Father," she said. "I promise you."

It was all a great adventure. Anne, of course, looked like she would be sick from fright at any moment, but Mary was enjoying every second.

First they'd had to fight their way down to Mooregate. Moore Fields was packed with people and their possessions, and a steady stream of sooty faces emerged from the gate. Mary had dragged Anne down through the crowd and into the burning city.

They were hours behind the fire. Mary had never seen such a mess, never smelled such a burning, choking smell. They tied their kerchiefs around their faces, but Anne coughed like she might swoon from it. If the wind had not been driving the smoke so hard up into the sky, she may very well have choked to death. The heat of the smouldering buildings was enough to singe their hair, and even the soles of Mary's shoes began to grow tacky. Some buildings were still on fire, but most were blackened heaps of rubbish. Here and there, they saw a man or a woman squatting near one of the heaps, moaning or crying in distress. It was a scene from a nightmare. The wind gusted up periodically, swirling great funnels of ash and embers around them. One spark had caught on Anne's skirt and burned the hem, but it was soon put out. The wind drove it all in front of them, leading their way down to Cornhill, or what was left of it. They stuck to the middle of the cobbled street. Unidentifiable heaps of burning wood clustered around the sides of the road. The blackened shell of a church sheltered a crying child from the wind. Everywhere there were people, running in all directions, pressing their possessions to their bodies. There was no longer a cart or carriage to be had anywhere within the walls. Night had set in more than an hour ago, but all was lit up in a hellish light. The glow grew stronger the further they advanced down Cornhill, towards the epicentre of the fire.

"I shall choke to death," Anne said.

"Nonsense. The fire is blown all the way to the Temple by now."

"It seems we draw closer."

"Can you not see? This is where the fire has been. The wind drives strongly to the west and north. We are behind the fire front. The foot soldier at Cripplegate said the fire has already been to Paul's."

Anne blinked back at her in the firelight. Her dark eyes were round and glistening. "I am so frightened," she breathed.

Her sincerity bit through Mary's impatience. Mary pulled her sister to her and hugged her tight. "We are nearly there. We are almost on Cheapside."

"You are enjoying this," Anne said, bewildered.

Mary closed her eyes and listened. The crackling of the fire everywhere, the far away sounds of cracking timber and collapsing rooves, the endless cries of the people who ran past them. "'Tis an adventure, Annie. Do you not think it a thrilling adventure?" she said, opening her eyes.

"We started this fire. People have surely perished."

Mary tried to brush a piece of soot from Anne's cheek, but only succeeded in smudging it further. She noticed her own hands were black. "An accident, Anne."

"We started it on purpose."

"But its spread was accidental. We are not responsible for the wind, or the inefficiencies of the mayor who might have saved all if he had acted sooner down near Pudding Lane, or the stupidity of those who do not get out of the way of the fire ere it bears down upon them."

Anne shook her head. "When I see Lazodeus again —"

"Yes, yes, now stop whining and come on. Paul's still stands, and we must find this wretched manuscript." She was moving through the crowd again, dragging Anne behind her. "Oh, I shall relish feeding the damned thing to the flames."

Within minutes they had rounded on St Paul's. They stopped, gasping for breath, to consider it in the firelight.

The huge, grey gloomy building stood firm in the centre of an open area, across which the flames could not jump. Sparks had scorched the stone but not caught it. Fire had few places to cling on such a building, the scaffold on the north transept had burned incompletely, and blackened boards heaved precariously in the gusting wind.

"Death, that's an ugly church," Mary said.

"Is it safe to go in?"

"Perhaps."

"Then why are we not going in? We have but a few hours."

Mary could feel Anne's gaze on her face. A strong gust of wind blew up, sending flakes of burning ash rocketing across the sky. All around them, the city was turning to charcoal. It felt as though her very skin may be roasting. She felt in her placket for the little fire charm.

"Mary?"

Mary pulled the fire charm out and pressed it against her lips. With a mighty heave, she threw it hurtling through the smoke and ash, up towards Paul's. The wind seemed to slip under it, almost as though it knew her intent and wished to assist. It spun up and up.

"What are you doing?"

"Burning the manuscript."

"But —"

A loud pop cut her off. They both turned their faces towards the church. The roof had caught fire. Mary laughed. She felt a potent tide of excitement surge through her.

"Why did you do that?" Anne said, aghast.

"Because I could." She grabbed Anne's hand. "It shall make a pretty fire, Annie, you'll see."

They stood to watch. All around them, cries had started anew. "Paul's is alight!" A crowd began to gather on the edge of the square. The wind roared up, sending debris spinning across the churchyard. Mary could feel a smile broad on her face. As the minutes ticked by, the fire spread over the roof. The smoke was thick, but being blown away to the west. The city around Paul's was lit up like daylight. It was as though a grand festival was taking place, and all had gathered to enjoy the spectacular show. Half an hour passed, and the roof started to creak; lead was running in rivulets on to the stone. The east window of the choir exploded, sending shards of glass scattering across the open ground. Mary was about to suggest that they leave, when a strong feeling came over her that she should look towards the north entrance. A compulsion impossible to resist.

She saw a tall feminine figure hurrying towards the door. Deborah.

"That little —"

"My God, Mary, did you see? 'Tis Deborah, she's gone under the scaffold."

"She thinks to save the manuscript."

"She'll be burned alive! She'll be killed!"

Deborah. Killed. Mary felt as though she didn't know who she was suddenly. She shook her head and turned to Anne.

"We have to save her."

Deborah felt indestructible. She had passed through Cripplegate, where the fire post had disbanded due to the advance of the flames, between burning buildings only feet apart, and had not once felt the kiss of fire on her body or clothes. While the rest of the city fled in fear, she moved against the tide and down to Paul's, which was burning fiercely along its roof. She raced towards the north entrance, up the six stairs to the big iron door, lifted the latch and entered. The roar of the flames was immense above her, and she warily kept to the wall. The talisman protected her against flames, but burning beams may be another matter.

The transept was full of objects. Everyone in the near vicinity, it seemed, had attempted to store something in here, thinking to protect it from the fire: beds and chairs and cradles and desks, and piles of clothes and children's toys and books, all junked together in indiscriminate piles, blocking her access to the choir. A violent creaking groaned above as she picked her way along the transept. Behind the choir was the entrance to St Faith's, a subterranean church which she had visited with Father when she was a child. The wooden door was ajar, and she pulled it open and hurried down the stairs into the church.

In here, stacks of books and papers lay on every available surface, even along the pews and the altar. At the very top of the wall, a series of tiny windows revealed the street above. All she could see was the glow of the firelight. She glanced around her desperately. How would she find Father's manuscript here?

She stood at the first pile and scanned it for the printer's name. She didn't recognise it. She kept scanning, moving up the rows, looking for Simmons's name. A mighty crash from above in St Paul's stopped her heart. The fire burned louder now, and a thunderous crack rang out so sharp around her, that she thought she may be deafened forever. Her heart raced and she frantically began to plough through the piles of paper. They had been stored here for safety, but it was like a tinderbox in Paul's, and this paper would merely be fuel for the fire. The temperature had shot up, and smoke began to drift into the room. She coughed, held her kerchief over her face.

Here. Simmons.

She dived into the pile of papers, found a wrapped block

about the size of Father's manuscript. Anxious fingers tore the corner of the paper. No, not her handwriting. She tossed it aside, began to despair.

Then saw it. Brown paper and "*Paradise Lost — Milton*" written across the front in Simmons's hand. She snatched it up. Her lungs were aching. She ran back up the stairs and carefully peeked around the door.

Paul's was aflame. The piles of objects which she had passed only moments before were blazing. Her route back along the transept was on fire. She frantically looked around her. Parts of the roof had fallen into the choir and cracked the floor. Smouldering rubble lay everywhere and the roof was still creaking. The air was so thick she could barely see, and she realised now, too late, that her talisman did not protect her from the choking pall of smoke.

Through the flames, then.

She wrapped the manuscript under her cloak, pressed her arms around it as passionately as she might clasp a lover, and ran for the door. The fire from the burning pile of rubbish licked at her clothes, but did not catch, thanks to the angel's talisman. If she got out of this alive, perhaps she would have to assess her opinion of Lazodeus after all.

The door was in sight, the flames falling behind her. She coughed violently, head down. When she looked up, an unexpected sight greeted her.

Mary and Anne, standing on the top step beckoning her.

"Come, sister," Anne cried.

"What are you . . .?" She pulled up just short of the door, confused.

"The roof is about to give," Anne said.

Another mighty explosion sounded from the other side of the church. Deborah shrieked.

"The very stones in the walls are exploding from the heat," Mary said. "The south side of the church is ruined."

"What are you doing here?" she asked, her heart beating wildly. Her sisters were the very reason she was out here, they were her enemies. "You were the ones who wanted Father's manuscript destroyed."

Mary reached out a hand to Deborah. "Sister, save yourself. The manuscript is doomed; you may as well save yourself."

Without thinking, Deborah glanced down at the uneven shape poking from her cloak. In a fraction of a second, Mary's hand was iron on her wrist.

"Dump it," she hissed. "Burn it."

"No. No, I have come to save it."

"Deborah, please. Burn it," Anne said, her eyes frantic. "We haven't much time."

Another stone exploded on the south side of the church. Its sharp echoes cracked in Deborah's ears.

"I shall not burn it. It means all in the world to Father, and I shall not destroy it!" She had to shout to be heard over the flames.

Suddenly, Mary gave her a violent shove. "Then burn with it!" she shouted. Anne screamed. Deborah landed on her back, knocking over a burning chair which showered flames over her. When she looked up, the door was closed. She rose and tried to open it. Mary had dropped the latch. She kicked the latch on her side, but it wouldn't budge. Her sisters had wedged it, perhaps with a piece of the burnt scaffold.

They had locked her in.

She thought she heard Anne scream again, but it was hard to tell over the roar of the flames. The roof creaked ominously, and the smoke grew thicker now it had no portal from which to escape. She cowered against the door, her arms pressed over the manuscript, and gazed around her wildly. The heat was unbearable, the sound deafening, and her lungs were stinging from the effort of breathing.

But nothing hurt so much as the horrible realisation that her sisters intended to kill her.

*

Anne could not stop screaming. It seemed it was the only thing that would release the horror inside her. Mary tried to pull her down the stairs, but she would not move.

"Come, Anne, we have to get away. The roof will fall, we'll be burned alive."

"But our sister is in there!" she cried. Her voice was hoarse and sore. She felt herself to be a raw aching wound and nothing else.

"She had her chance!"

"She will die!"

"If she does not die, we will never see our angel again."

Anne stared in horror at Mary, the awful impossibility of the choice sitting ragged in her abdomen. Mary's face was streaked with tears. Another stone exploded, this time closer. It seemed to rock the very foundations of the staircase upon which they stood. Mary grabbed her and pulled her and she fell over, climbed to her feet, then started running.

This time she did not notice the route they took. Fires burned all around them, but these were in buildings which were already gutted, and had no more fuel to offer the ravenous flames. She felt her feet beneath her as if they were not her own, stumbling, running, burning on the embers which had long ago melted her shoes down to thin layers. Finally, she could see the river, reflecting the fire like an uneven mirror. Mary was taking her down to the docks. Hundreds of boats floated like black smudges upon the river, desperate folk with their possessions waiting it out on the water. Anne's feet skidded in the muddy banks. A man was loading a trunk on to a small skiff, and Mary grabbed his shoulder.

"Please, sir, help us. We flee the fire."

"I don't have room," he said gruffly.

"We have no possessions, just ourselves. Please."

"No, go away."

Mary took a deep breath. "Come, sir, it shall be all your pleasure."

Anne barely recognised her sister's voice.

The man paused. "My pleasure?"

"Provided you do not touch my sister, here," Mary said.

"But I may touch you?"

"All you want, sir. Until you bring us safely to shore."

The man grinned. "Climb in."

Anne was bewildered, but once again Mary dragged her along. They climbed into the boat, and the man left one of his trunks on the bank. They rowed out onto the river. An enormous crash drew their attention back to the bank. From here they could see St Paul's ablaze.

"The roof," Mary whispered.

"She is dead then," Anne replied, numb.

"Now where is my payment?" the boatman said.

"Yes, yes," Mary replied. "Anne, turn your back."

"I —"

"Turn your back, look to the south bank, and do not turn around until I say you can."

Anne was tired and in pain in her very soul. She did as her sister asked, watching the reflections of the fire on the water around her. She could barely hear the sounds of Mary debauching herself in the boat behind her, for the thumping and crashing of the fire. Her thoughts seemed too large, too unwieldy for her mind. Her attention was scattered everywhere, and every impression her mind lit upon hurt her, hurt her deep, deep inside, hurt her head as if it would burst it open. From far away she heard an animal, grunting sound. Her sister?

No. It was herself.

Mary was calling to her. "Annie? Annie, what is it?"

But the grey closed down around her and she didn't fight it. Better to turn it all off than to feel it any more. Better to descend into the dark.

Deborah lay herself out along the floor and tried to breathe under the crack in the door. It was no use. Her lungs would burst if she stayed in here any longer. She stood and tried the door again to no avail. Damn Lazodeus. He had set her up for this, she knew it. Why else send her down here? And damn herself, for not thinking of the smoke. For smoke killed as easily as flames. She kicked the door in frustration, sobbing and screaming.

"Help me!" she shouted. "Help me!"

Her throat was raw from shouting and from coughing. Was this what it had come to? Was she to die for her Father's poem? How unbearable, to die not for her own achievements but for somebody else's.

In a rage she dragged Lazodeus's talisman from around her neck, was about to cast it into the flames behind her when she saw that the chain she held was not the talisman, but the demon key. She raced through the tables Amelia had taught her. There wasn't a single door-opening demon among them.

And yet . . . Why did she have such a strong sense that there should be one?

She gazed at the key a moment, dangling on the end of its chain.

Of course! Lazodeus had named a demon to lock her in and let her free when the business with the exorcist had got out of hand. Now, if she could only remember its name.

She held the key out in front of her, shaking. Violent spasmodic coughs racked her body as she tried to centre her mind. Its name was . . .

"Paratax," she gasped. "I call upon you with this key as your commander. Open this door."

The five notes were barely audible above the crashing of the fire, but the sweet feeling still rocked through her, seeming to fill her lungs with air. She breathed, the door opened, and she ran. Father's manuscript pressed close against her body, she ran and ran. How she gathered her strength was a mystery, but she ran. Behind her, an immense crashing sound indicated that the roof had finally given. The exploding stones cracked and echoed around the city. She ran towards Cripplegate, through black smouldering ruins, then out of the city walls towards home. The fire had been controlled before it reached White Cross Street, and she knew that Father would be safe. But he didn't know it, and the frightful sounds of the fire, of Paul's going up, would have terrified him. She ran as though she would never need the energy to run again.

Gasping, up Artillery Walk.

Pushing the door open, calling, "Father!" breathlessly.

"Deborah?" A querulous voice. By the muted light of a sputtering candle, he cowered on the floor in the corner of his study, the little dog still clutched to his chest.

"I'm here, Father," she said, dropping the manuscript on his desk and going to him. She stroked his hair from his forehead, leaving a black smudge of soot.

"I heard such frightful sounds. As though the world were ending."

"Paul's is ablaze."

"My poem is gone then?"

"No, for I have just dropped it upon your desk."

He turned a blind bewildered gaze upon her. "Deborah . . .?"

"Never ask me," she said. "Never."

He shook his head. She helped him to his feet and back to the chair. Max ran away and hid in the same corner.

"I must go and wash myself. I am covered in soot."

"I do not understand."

"I will not tell you. Do not ask me to."

He nodded timidly. "You are safe?" he said, his voice quiet.

"Perfectly," she said, and began to cry. "Despite . . . despite everything, I am perfectly safe. We are both perfectly safe." For the moment.

Only for the moment.

Another Interlude

I waited as the old woman paused for a breath. And waited. The moment spun out, and the sick disappointment began to swell in my stomach.

"Keep going," I said. My own voice was barely recognisable to me; it sounded like a pleading child's voice. An unwieldy fear sat an inch outside my consciousness, the kind of fear that signifies that everything has changed forever in one's perception, because I started to understand that this was not normal, that me pleading like a child for the old woman to speak was not within the usual ambit of my experience, and that something bad had become uncontrollable in my life.

"I don't think I can, Sophie," she said with a huge sigh. "I grow so very tired."

"But I'll die if you don't finish."

"Do not misunderstand me. I want very much to finish. I am very close to the end now, but I am old and I am weary and I have been speaking for hours."

"But will I have to wait another week?" The thought was unbearable.

"No. For I wish this whole business to be over finally. No, come back whenever you wish."

"Tomorrow? No, tonight? I could wait here with you for a few hours."

"Tomorrow," she said decisively, "not before. Or the day after if you prefer. I'll wait for you. But now I need to rest. The next time I see you, as well as finishing the story, I have to explain to you the consequences."

"The consequences?" There was that fear again, lurking nearby, top-heavy and intrusive.

"Listening to my story comes at a price. I warned you."

"I didn't believe you. I still don't." Nobody would have been convinced by my words, but I felt very strongly that I had to say them aloud, and it did make me feel better.

"Scepticism is the supernatural's best friend. The supernatural can continue unchecked provided scepticism lags so far behind."

"But mundane explanations, while not as romantic, are always more common."

"Do you believe in nothing, Sophie? Have you never looked around you and seen the world? How can you remain a sceptic?" She sounded angry, though her face and demeanour remained impassive.

"I . . . I never thought about it."

"Go to my bookshelf."

I stood and did as she asked.

"Last week you were eager to look at the first edition of *Paradise Lost.*"

"Yes."

"Go on. You may take it and keep it."

I picked it up, with the insincere words, "I can't possibly accept such a valuable gift," poised on my lips; a first edition like this would be worth a fortune. But I sensed instantly something was wrong, the book was too light. I opened it. Scholars would weep; the inside of the book had been hollowed out, a square cut right through the centre of the pages. In the hollow was a dark piece of metal, about three inches long, strung on a piece of nylon cord.

"This book is ruined," I said.

"That is the demon key," she said.

Her words surprised me. I lifted out the metal bar and looked at it. "Deborah's demon key?" It was so impossible that I felt suddenly much better. The old woman was crazy after all. This was surely just a random piece of metal — an off-cut from a factory or a scrap from the side of the road or some such ordinary thing — and here she was telling me it was the magical key from a fictional story which took place over three centuries in the past.

"Yes."

"How did you get it?" I asked. I was being polite now, humouring her. The lurking fear receded.

"It comes with the story. You'll understand it all tomorrow."

Tomorrow; that sweet day when I could return. But that didn't make sense — how could such a paradox of feeling exist? This primal need to be in her company, to hear her tale, could not live side-by-side with my conviction in her quaint insanity.

"Take it with you, Sophie," the old woman was saying. "I have no use for it any more."

I tucked it into the front pocket of my jeans, leafed through the mutilated pages of the book. "This could have been worth a lot of money."

"I have no use for money."

"I sure do."

She shifted in her chair, turned to the window. "You'll have to leave, Sophie. I need to rest."

The moment I had been dreading. "Can't I just stay here? I won't disturb you." I shuddered at the idea of all those melancholy feelings descending upon me again, those feelings which were dispelled by her presence.

"No. Go. I shall see you upon your return."

I hesitated but knew she would not change her mind. I slid the mutilated book back onto the shelf and went to the door.

"Goodbye." What if she died before tomorrow? What if I felt like this forever?

"Goodbye," she said firmly.

I walked down the stairs — careful on the ankle I'd

twisted jumping from the bathroom window — and out onto the street. The wrench was terrible, like leaving a loved one to die. I was trying to rationalise it when I heard a noise directly behind me. Before I could turn around, a rough darkness made of cloth descended over my eyes, a hand closed over my mouth, and I was pulled to the ground. I could not scream. My hands flailed everywhere, but were soon caught. I guessed there were two people on top of me, lifting me, carrying me roughly. I couldn't make a noise for the hand over my mouth, and it was so firm I could not move my jaw to bite. I was dropped somewhere — it felt like old carpet under my skin through the gap between my shirt and my jeans. My hands were bound. The two attackers were completely silent — not a word passed between them. Then I heard a door slam and knew I'd been bundled into the back of a van. They hadn't bound my feet. I kicked at the wall, turned myself around and kicked where I thought the front seat would be. My shoes contacted a metal grid. I heard my assailants get into the van and start it. My ankle howled with pain, but I kicked out again.

"Help! Help!" I screamed. "Who the hell are you? Where are you taking me?"

They didn't respond, and ignored my continuing shouts. I was terrified, and only a massive effort of will prevented me from peeing in my jeans. But even through the primal terror, the thought that plagued me was that if I didn't escape, I wouldn't make my appointment with the old woman tomorrow.

We drove for an hour, maybe a little longer. I kicked and shouted the whole way but my assailants didn't respond. When the van stopped, so did my heart. I thought, *this is it, they're going to kill me and dump me*, and it seemed so unreal that I almost believed I must be dreaming, that I'd fallen asleep on the old woman's floor and all the psychological distress of the curse had generated this nightmare.

"Please don't hurt me," I said.

One of my assailants said, "Shh", very gently. This confused me. I had thought them to be thugs, rapists, burglars, not gentle people. I was puzzling this when the van door slid open. I bent my legs ready to kick, but they had the advantage of being able to see me and they grabbed my feet and hoisted me out of the van.

I screamed at the top of my lungs, but I could hear no traffic noises, just birds and the wind in the branches.

"Shh," the gentle voice said again, although his hands were not gentle on my ankles, and nor were his partner's around my shoulders. I wriggled and bucked to no advantage.

A door opened, and I sensed a third person there. No words were exchanged. I was brought inside and carried up a flight of stairs. The house smelled musty and old, but I gathered from the size of the staircase that it was large, an old manor home perhaps. I was dropped face down on a bed and pinned while my hands were untied. Before I could pull off my blindfold, my assailants had left and I'd been locked in.

"Hey!" I shouted, going to the door and pounding on it, wrenching the handle, kicking against it violently. "Hey, let me out!" Two minutes of shouting left me hoarse and frustrated. I turned to survey my surroundings.

I was in a bedroom. A mahogany four-poster bed took up most of the space, and between the windows there stood a large chest of drawers, a mirror and an armchair. On top of the chest was a towel, some toiletries, and some fresh clothes. I walked over to examine them. My clothes. So this wasn't a random abduction, they had targeted me specifically. I guess I knew then who was responsible.

I went to the window and looked down. A big drop. I wouldn't be jumping. The room was surrounded by tall ash trees, their huge round trunks bellied right up to a brick wall marking out the property. No branches stretched near enough to climb on to, and besides I expected . . . yes, the windows were locked.

On the other side of the bed was a door which led to a tiny windowless bathroom. I sank down on the closed toilet lid in the half-dark and put my head in my hands. How was I to get out of here by tomorrow? Already the sick compulsion was threading up through me like pins and needles, making me feel as though the entire network of my nerves was straining to break out of my body. I *had* to hear the rest, I *had* to be with her again.

I stripped off, leaving my clothes in a heap under the sink. I turned the shower on hard and hot and collapsed into the bottom of it, letting the water run over me. I cried for a little while. The threatening fear was back, and I didn't want to let it in, because to believe that the curse was for real was to undo my entire belief system. I was sick, I was tired, I was heartbroken, I was lonely; I was anything, *anything* but cursed. Anything but that.

The hot water ran out at the same time my tears did. I had left my towel in the bedroom, so I dried myself off with a handtowel which I dropped on the pile with my clothes. I dressed in the bedroom and then noticed that a tray of food had been left on my bed. I snatched up the folded card in the corner of the tray, lying on my stomach to read it: "Sophie, we're very sorry, but we feel this is for the best. Neal, Chloe, Marcus, Mandy, Art and Deirdre."

"Fuck you all," I shouted, hurling the card away from me. I lifted the lid on the plate, and found a chicken breast with vegetables and gravy. I thought about hurling it away, too, about making a big mess and tearing things up, but I was hungry and I was tired and the long shadows of the summer afternoon were growing deeper. I ate, I climbed into bed and, miraculously, I slept.

Nobody came to see me until the middle of the next morning, and by then I was mad with frustration. I had pulled up the armchair to one of the windows and was watching for any sign of movement, any walker on the other side of the brick wall whom I could call out to, tell them to phone the police. I had a bronze statuette in my right hand with which I intended to break the window if such an opportunity arose. But I had begun to suspect that on the other side of that wall were fields and trees and very little likelihood of pedestrians.

The door opened and Neal slunk in. Behind him, someone pulled the door closed and locked it. They were wary, they knew I'd run for it. He had another tray of food.

"Good morning," he said.

"Fuck off."

"Sophie, we're doing what's best for you."

"I said fuck off."

He placed the tray on the chest of drawers, and stood beside it nervously as though he waited for inspection. A marvellous smell filled the room — fresh coffee in a pot. I found myself approaching the tray, pouring a coffee, gulping it down.

"Can we talk about this? Without you abusing me?" he asked.

"Listen," I said, drilling my index finger into his chest. "You let me out of here, now. This is illegal. The police won't go for your stupid story about a curse; this is abduction, this is holding me against my will, and you're kidding yourself if you think I won't report it when I'm free."

Neal dipped his head in a nod of acknowledgment. "We happen to believe that by the time you're free you'll be thanking us."

"Thanking you?"

"You're not yourself, Sophie. You know that."

"You know nothing about me. I'm like this all the time." Nobody was going to be convinced by that lie, and hearing it out loud keenly reminded me how unlike myself I felt. I was strung out and depressed and a little crazed, and it was all new to me. "Where the hell am I, anyway?"

"This house belongs to Chloe's uncle. He's in America on business."

"Yes, but where is it? North of London? South?"

"I'm not going to tell you. We have one purpose in bringing you here, and that's to give you the time and the distance to sort out this mess you're in. What we really want to do is to perform the Ritual of Calith over you."

"The Ritual of what?"

"Calith. I learned it on the thirtieth path of Resh."

I felt myself squint in disbelief and disdain. "This sounds like a bad fantasy novel. The thirtieth path of Resh? Are you a complete moron? None of that is *real*, Neal. It's all in your silly head."

"Then if it isn't real, you won't mind if we do it for you. It's a deep psychic cleansing ritual for those in extreme psychic danger. As you are."

Extreme psychic danger. My stomach turned to water. I took two steps back and sat on the edge of the bed. "I refuse," I said.

"The curse is making you refuse. You have to fight it."

"No, I have to get out of here. I have an appointment which I don't want to miss."

Neal sighed and ran his hand through his hair. "Sophie, if the appointment is what I think it is, you must miss it. When you've heard the whole story, no amount of psychic cleansing will save you. You will be cursed."

"Cursed? What does that even mean?"

He came to kneel in front of me. "An unending curse of misery. That's what I've heard."

"That's what you've heard? You mean you don't know for sure?"

"I've never met anyone who —"

"Ha! You don't even know for sure!" My moods were spinning rapidly after my thoughts — from believing in extreme psychic danger to taking refuge once again in the gullibility of Neal and his friends — and my emotions could barely keep up. Crying suddenly seemed appropriate so I began to sob.

"Sophie, Sophie," he said, trying to put an arm around my shoulder.

"Leave me alone!" I pushed him away and he fell on his arse.

He looked embarrassed as he struggled to his feet. "You should allow us to do this ritual as soon as possible, Sophie. You know you're only going to feel worse tomorrow. All that suffering can be prevented."

"I said leave me alone."

He moved to the door. I watched him anxiously. He knocked on it twice and it unlocked and opened. I sprang to my feet and ran for it. Neal caught me, Marcus on the other side of the door pushed me. Neal slipped out and I was locked in again. This time I only kicked and shouted for thirty seconds. I was growing bored with my own desperation. I went to the chest of drawers and poured more coffee.

For the first time since I had left the old woman's house, I caught my breath. I lay on the bed and tipped out the contents of my bag, put aside my tape recorder, notebook and pen, then scooped the rest — lighter, two bent cigarettes, keys, purse, old tissues, the adaptor for my tape recorder, a half eaten packet of mints — onto the floor. I stretched out with my arms over my head and closed my eyes. The itching, impossible feeling of deprivation seized me. She was expecting me and I wasn't there. How long would she wait for me? Would she give up on me, refuse to see me another time? My burning anger with Neal and the others was fused with unbearable longing for the old woman's voice and company, for the end of this journey she was taking me on, which I knew deep down had very little to do with the daughters of a famous poet and everything to do with who I was and what I stood for in the universe.

I opened my eyes, sat up and found the adaptor for my

tape recorder, plugged it in and rewound the tape. The only thing for it was to write it all down.

It was oddly soothing to transcribe the tape, though a shadow of the relief felt when in her presence. The hours passed quickly and I didn't notice that nobody had brought my dinner. I turned on the lamp next to the bed and treated the grumblings of my stomach with the mints from my handbag and a cigarette. Still no food.

I went to the door and called out: "Hey! I'm hungry. The least you bastards can do is feed me!"

A silence of carpeted hallways and stairs was my response. I listened closely, could hear nobody moving around, no clatter of pans in a far away kitchen.

"Neal?" I called. "Chloe?"

It seemed they had decided to starve me into submission.

I couldn't sleep for hunger and for my psychological distress, which were equally acute. I turned the light off and sat by the window, watching and watching. I was so tired that my mind started doing flips and arabesques around groups of words. I would find "extreme psychic danger" beating a rhythm in my brain, over and over like a mindless song one cannot excise. Then it would be replaced with "Ritual of Calith" or "path of Resh" — collections of vowels and consonants which meant nothing to the Sophie I was at the start of the summer, yet which now led me on an obsessive, head-aching path away from something lost, something which I could not even name. I gazed out at the huge ash trees, and I said, "I am experiencing a crisis of the soul." And so I took up the echo of those words in my head, "crisis of the soul", and they repeated until they made as little sense as a children's nonsensical rhyme. I remembered being told once, recently, that words could cause pain but I could not remember where I'd heard it. The memory caused a vague stirring of fear and I leaned my head on the cool glass of the window and bumped it once, twice, three times before I caught myself and stopped.

And this is what it was really like; this was the reality of confronting the supernatural in a life where it had previously held no sway. A thousand thousand so-called ordinary people in a thousand thousand stories had seen ghosts or vampires or monsters and taken a few pages, a few breaths to accept it. But in reality, the confrontation was an impossible grinding pressure on my brain and it was making me deranged and dizzy.

I smoked the last cigarette when grey dawn bled into the room, and fell into an uneasy doze in my chair.

I was, of course, beset by nightmares. Most were unpleasant, but ridiculous and fragmented, shards of scenes from the old woman's story interwoven with the awful cravings of my immediate situation. So I would be sitting with Deborah at the kitchen table while she ate and I starved; or I would be fighting my way through fire to a great church where all the coffee and cigarettes in London were stored. But the worst dreams were not even formed into narratives. I would find myself in a grey darkness, surrounded by small, sharp objects which I knew were words but *live* words, and they would rise up through my body and lacerate my skin, work their way into my veins and pulverise my joints. I could not speak, all meaning was lost. Over and over I returned to this dream as I slept, and my eventual wakefulness was such a relief that I had to leap out of my chair and run to the bathroom to throw up.

Everything hurt. My gullet and throat stung, my neck and shoulders ached from sleeping crooked, and my very spirit was twisted in a knot. I simply could not spend another moment in this place.

I strode to the window, picked up the bronze statuette and hurled it at the glass. With a loud smash it splintered. The statuette thudded to the ground below. I picked up my towel and wrapped it round my hand, used it to poke out the remaining glass. A gust of fresh morning air rushed in and

432

my lungs sucked at it gratefully. I leaned out the window and with all the energy I could muster, screamed, "Help! Help!"

My screams were deafening to me, and yet they reverberated off nothing outside. They seemed, instead, to be soaked up by the trunk of the nearest ash. I screamed again, no louder because I was already hoarse and years of smoking had seriously reduced my lung capacity. Silence answered me. A moment later a bird called, almost as though it had heard my cries and was curious for a translation.

Grey clouds scudded over and threatened rain, and I realised how foolish it had been to smash the window. Somehow the flesh of my right palm had been cut shallowly. Disastrous. Absolutely disastrous.

No food. No coffee, no cigarettes, no old woman. I was ready to bite my own fingers off in frustration. I went to the door and called out to the empty staircase over and over again. The day ticked on. My stomach was grumbling and I was light-headed, achey and anxious. I returned to the tapes, proceeding with the transcription, going over parts again and again just to hear the inflections of her voice, the rhythm of her words.

Finally, around five o'clock in the afternoon, I heard sounds from downstairs. By this stage I was whimpering at the door like a family pet. "Hey!" I shouted. "I'm starving up here."

They didn't respond immediately, but after half an hour I heard footsteps coming up the stairs. If they thought they had made me too weak to run, they were mistaken. I waited at the door, ready to make a dash.

"Sophie, it's Chloe," she said from the other side of the door. "Neal and Art are with me. I'll only bring your food in if you promise not to run."

"I promise." Like hell.

"If you try to run we'll put you right back where you are and you'll get no food." This was Art, clearly more

433

comfortable with playing tough guy than Chloe.

"Okay, okay, I promise." Really promised the second time because I was starving and now they'd returned I was confident I could find another way to escape. Cutting my wrist on the broken glass in the window, for example, so they had to call an ambulance. I stood back from the door. "Okay, bring it in."

The door opened a foot, the tray was shoved in, the lock fell back into place. I didn't even bother to pick up the tray. I sat on the floor, right there next to the door, and I had half a cup of coffee in me before I even lifted the lid on the plate. Ravioli, huge fat pillows of it swimming in chunky tomato sauce. I gulped it down. After more coffee I demolished the apple pie and ice-cream and sat back to contemplate.

But couldn't quite contemplate. I felt very fuzzy suddenly, which was odd because I had hoped food would nullify the dizziness.

I tried to stand up but found myself grabbing the bedpost to stop myself falling.

Damn them, they'd poisoned me. They were lunatics after all, and they thought I was cursed so they'd poisoned me after starving me for two days to make sure I took the whole dose. I tried to call out but my tongue was a stone. I collapsed on the bed, blinking rapidly against what I had convinced myself was my death. A low buzzing sounded in my ears and I tried to prop myself up on my elbows with no success. My fingers were clutching at the bed covers as the world turned grey.

When I became aware of voices, I realised I wasn't dead. I tried to open my eyes, but my eyelids were very heavy so I squinted at the scene in dazed fear. Black figures surrounded me: two on either side of me and two at my feet. It seemed as though I had been suspended by a long cord threaded down my spine, and my neck felt like it had hardened into porcelain. But when my fingers moved over the bed covers beneath me, I knew that I was still exactly where I had collapsed. The black figures were speaking, but I couldn't make any sense of what they were saying, and it put me in mind of my terrible dream about the words which rose up through my body and injured me. I panicked, but I had been drugged and all the anxiety was contained within a couple of wheezy grunts and an unsuccessful struggle to raise my head. I felt my eyes roll as I surveyed each black figure in turn. A light came from somewhere nearby and as I looked at it my eyes hurt so I closed them.

"Magister, the candidate is prepared for the ritual."

"She must pass through the fire of Calith for cleansing."

The word fire jumped out at me and became confused with the fire in the old woman's story. I struggled, believing I would be trapped in St Paul's as it burned, and then some word of relief came to me but I couldn't place it. *Paratax*. A nonsense word.

"This is one who has suffered extreme psychic damage. I commit her to your care and command that you lead her through into the pure light of knowledge." This voice came from my right, and I was trying to look in that direction when my arm was grasped from the left. "Come, hear the voice of light on your path of darkness."

My other arm was grasped and one of the figures at the foot of the bed began to sprinkle water on me. One of the drops landed on my lower lip and trickled into my mouth. In my addled state I believed it to be more poison. A strong smell of incense was clogging my lungs, and smoke floated over me.

The figures continued speaking to each other, like dark ghosts muttering incantations. Nothing made any sense and I was anxious and bewildered. But then I felt something move inside me; deep inside me, not within my skin or within my organs, but somewhere else, and the anxiety turned to terror. For suddenly, I felt something about myself begin to change, something crucial to my identity. It had been found and was being pulled out of me on a hook.

"No!" I managed.

"We must be getting close," one of them said, a woman.

The squirming feeling plagued me, and I knew that I would lose something I cherished any second. The old woman's face came to me, and it was deathly sad. Would I never see her again? The thought was too painful to contemplate. A sick feeling of inevitability overwhelmed me and I began to surrender myself to it, almost relieved.

Suddenly, though, there was a loud crack and the room was plunged into darkness. Three or four of the voices called out in pain, their hands jumping off my body. I tried to look around me but couldn't make out anything clearly in the dark.

"What happened?" a woman asked.

"Psychic shock. The electricity's gone out, my watch has stopped."

"It *hurt*."

"What does it mean?"

"She has an object from the Wanderer. The Wanderer has protected her with something."

I closed my eyes and the sheet of unconsciousness was slowly pulled back up. I felt my body relax as their panicked voices swelled and fell around me. Somehow I knew that I was safe, that they wouldn't be able to steal that crucial part of me. The relief had me drifting off again, into an unnaturally deep sleep.

Bright daylight woke me, or maybe it was the presence of Neal sitting on the end of the bed. I noticed in one glance that the broken window had been covered in plastic and that Neal held a packet of cigarettes. I could smell coffee. I sat up and rubbed my head.

"Why the hell did you do that?" I asked.

"We thought it was the best thing for you."

"The list of grievances I'm taking to the police is going to be long. I'm glad you and Chloe are loaded because I'm going to sue you until you bleed."

He offered me a cigarette and I took it. While I lit it he poured me coffee. I eyed the clock. "It feels later than that."

"The clock stopped. Every clock in the house stopped, and the electricity's gone off. The ritual didn't work," he said.

"I figured that bit out for myself. I'm one giant craving. Why don't you just let me go to my fate, whatever it is?" Because it couldn't be something too bad, because all of this was nonsense, right? I felt like a climber who had just put her foot on an empty space instead of a rock.

"Do you have some object, some gift from the Wanderer?"

I shook my head, but at that precise moment remembered the piece of metal. The demon key. A crack was opening up in my mind.

"Are you sure?" he asked, peering at me closely.

"Please just let me go."

"I have to talk to the others."

"It's none of your business."

"It is. It's our fault you're in this mess."

I had woken up sufficiently by now to feel the weight of longing on my heart, and I shook my head. "I just want to go home."

"You want to go to the Wanderer."

"The Wanderer! She's just an old woman."

"You know she's not. Sophie, you know she's not."

I sagged forward, dropping my cigarette in the ashtray. My hands went to my forehead and my hair spilled through my fingers, and I felt utterly terrible. Neal's fingers brushed my own and I grasped them desperately.

"Please," I said lifting my head. "Please help me."

"We're trying to help you."

I sank into his arms and found that I had no tears left, just a soggy numbness. His comforting pats on my back became loving caresses and I responded to them as any strung-out, melancholy, half-crazed, unsatisfied woman under a curse would. I pressed my body against him and I longed for him to continue. I longed for some kind of bodily distraction

437

from the turmoil in my mind. Despite the fact that I hadn't brushed my teeth for days, I turned my face up to kiss him. He took the opportunity hungrily, and I let the warm swoon of desire take over my body. His hand was under my shirt, his fingers cool on my breast when the door opened and Chloe walked in.

"Neal?" she said querulously.

Neal leaped from the bed, leaving my arms empty. He was out the door and it was locked before I could rearrange my shirt. Damn Chloe.

I lit another cigarette, forgetting the one in the ashtray, and went to the bathroom. In the corner I found my dirty jeans and I felt in the pocket for the piece of metal on the nylon string. I was still resisting calling it the demon key, but I think at this point the crack in my mind had opened wide enough for some belief to trickle in. I think at this point I could no longer cling to my scepticism.

I lay on the bed and studied the key for hours. The word that had been plaguing me during the ritual last night came back to me: Paratax. It was the demon Deborah had called on to escape the burning church. I eyed the door and thought about whether or not I would use the demon key, and what it would signify if I did. If I burst out of my room now, Neal or Chloe or the others would be bound to catch me, and then they might confiscate the key. But if I waited until dark, until everyone was gone or sleeping, I could slip out unnoticed.

But I didn't really expect it to work, did I?

I groaned and put my hands over my eyes. It was all too complex and the worst was yet to come. Because if I listened to the rest of the story I would receive some kind of psychic punishment, which was okay by me as long as I was a sceptic. But if I was going to bust out of here with a demon key . . .

I decided to stop thinking. Thinking was hurting. I focussed instead on the primal drives within me. *Get out.*

Return to the old woman. They were in there right along with *eat, sleep, smoke.* My mind was made up.

In the end, I waited until the very early morning. This was not by design, but because I dozed through the middle of the night which was when I had originally planned to escape. I had only candlelight. The electricity had not been restored and Marcus (not Neal, not Chloe) had brought me some candles with my dinner that evening. I wished for a nice, safe electric light because candlelight reminded me of all those teenage seances back in boarding school, where creepy stories and sleep deprivation made shadows alive in the walls.

I woke with a start, as one does when one didn't expect to be asleep, and sat up. The candle had burned down to a waxy well. The clock on the wall was still stopped, but I estimated it was around two or three o'clock. The house was completely silent. I pulled the demon key out of my pocket and eyed it warily.

"You're going to change everything," I whispered to it, but it didn't respond. I stood and walked to the door, held the key out in front of me and repeated the words which Deborah had said. "Paratax, I call upon you with this key as your commander. Open this door."

Three distinct and undeniable things happened at once, though I'm not sure in which order. Reflecting upon it now, they are still all muddled up together, one big breath of shock pushed into my lungs simultaneously. But I think it must have gone like this:

First, music; a collection of notes which I've since pinned down as rising from F#, A#, C#, down to C and up to G. But it's no use trying to play them to get the same feeling, because it was more than the melody; it was the sweetness of the sounds, the aching clarity with which they echoed down through my synapses and seemed to touch my spirit, both beautiful and yet somehow sinister.

439

Second, the door opened; the lock clunked and the door swung in an inch, letting in a quick breeze of cool air.

Third, I lost my mind. Momentarily, that is. All the strange events which I had been holding at arm's length rushed into the crack, and suddenly I *knew* I was under a curse; I *knew* the old woman was a Wanderer who had a magic power over words; I *knew* that Deirdre could read minds and that the Lodge of the Seven Stars had a limited power to affect the world; I *knew* that John Milton had a fallen angel in his attic and that his youngest daughter had a key to command elemental spirits. At that moment I would have believed in the Bermuda Triangle, alien abductions, the second coming and little green men.

And consequently, I finally realised that I was in grave danger if I returned to the old woman to hear the rest of her story. But still I was determined to see her. I cannot explain why any more than I can explain why I still smoke even though I cough like a steam train every morning and two of my grandparents died of lung cancer. I was compelled. I was being pulled along on a chain which had enmeshed me so inexorably that there was no hope of escape.

I took a deep breath and attempted to pull myself together. *Think about it later, think about it later.* I picked up my bag and walked out the door, found my way down the staircase to the front entrance and, without hesitating, left.

Of course I had no idea where I was, but I followed the curving driveway in the weak moonlight out onto a narrow road. I looked from right to left, wondering in which direction I would find London. All I could see was the road winding into the darkness, past more country homes no doubt, leading me no closer to the city. I stopped and listened in the dark. Very faintly, a long way off, I could hear cars. The motorway. I crossed the road and headed into a brambly field, following my ears towards the traffic. The world felt emptied and soft.

Mist lay low over the field, filling the ditches I stumbled

in and out of on my way. I peered ahead into the darkness and could see the shadows of trees in front of me. Ordinarily I might have found the scene eerie or forbidding, but I had far greater pressures acting upon me and I pressed forward, one foot in front of the other, until I reached the wood.

I saw myself, almost as if I were outside myself, picking over uneven ground, over fallen logs, around glistening spider webs, listening through the intense morning silence for traffic on the motorway, and I had a profound sense of how this may be the last silent peaceful moment in my life so I tried to relish it. I took deep breaths of clear dewy air, felt myself soothed by the damp leaves which caressed my face as I passed, and revelled in the almost perfect tranquillity of the wood.

But I drew closer and closer to the motorway, and the roar of a lorry shook a spider web in front of me, sending drops of dew plummeting towards the ground. I broke out from between the trees and found myself standing on the edge of the road. Once again, I had no way to tell in which direction London lay, but while I was deliberating a car sped past then pulled up two hundred yards in front of me, its indicator flashing. It was a beat-up white utility, with crates tied in the back. I hurried down and leaned in the window. A skinny, greasy-haired man who could have been twenty or fifty peered back at me.

"Are you going to London?" I asked.

"Yes. Want a lift?"

"That's the idea."

He shrugged. "Get in."

I got in and soon we were pulling out. "Do you have a cigarette?" I asked.

He handed me a mashed packet from his dash and pressed the lighter in. "So what are you doing out here in the middle of the night?"

I indicated the dawn creeping across the horizon.

"Morning," I corrected him, lighting my cigarette. I took a drag and released the smoke, coughed once and tried not to count how many cigarettes I had smoked in the last two days. "I'm under a curse."

"A curse?" He smiled.

"I didn't believe it either. But now I'm fairly certain."

"Whatever you say, love. Where do you want me to drop you?"

"As close to City Road as you can."

"I'm delivering to Shoreditch."

"That'll do nicely."

I didn't even stop to think whether or not it was too early for me to arrive on the old woman's doorstep. It hardly seemed important given the momentous change in perspective which had just overtaken my life. The house was dark — indeed, it was barely light outside — as I thundered up the stairs calling for her.

"Hey, there. It's Sophie. Are you awake?"

Her voice, those addictive inflections. "I'm ready, Sophie, if you're sure you are."

I arrived at the doorway. She sat where she always sat. I had assumed that she went into one of the adjoining rooms to sleep, but now I started to suspect that she didn't move from her place under the window. And that made perfect sense, for a Wanderer, a woman under a curse, probably had little use for mundane things such as beds and toilets.

"I'm afraid," I said to her.

"It's probably too late."

"You're right, of course."

"I'm sorry it had to be you. I quite like you. But I'm selfish, you see. It's been a very long time."

"Can you explain what will happen to me?"

"The story will lead us there."

I sat on the floor in front of her. "Go on."

She began to speak and I listened. God help me, I listened.

21
The Hollow Deep of Hell

Betty returned to a city razed nearly to the ground and a household in chaos.

She had raced home at first news of the fire. By Thursday morning, when she had taken John in her arms in surprised realisation of how deeply she had grown to care for him, the fire had been brought under control. But the stories of the extent of devastation were almost impossible to be credited. Most of the old city was gone, the wall had failed to contain the fire which burned west past Newgate, Ludgate and Bridewell, jumped the canal at Fleet Ditch and burned all the way down Fleet Street, nearly to Temple Bar. The field at the bottom of the Walk was filled with people and whichever possessions they had managed to gather. They turned their eyes anxiously heavenwards as the gusty winds of summer gave way at last to grey skies.

But John's first words at her anxious inquiries into his well-being were, "It appears my eldest daughter has lost her mind."

Betty took a step back and looked at John's face. "Lost her mind?"

"She sleeps in your bed. Liza returned yesterday morning, after Anne had paced the kitchen and raved half the night while Mary tried to calm her. They tried to move her upstairs, but Anne grew violent, shouting that she could not look upon that room again. She refuses to eat, though Liza has made her drink."

"What is the nature of her raving?"

"It has to do with Deborah. Anne has said a number of times that she killed Deborah, yet Deborah is alive and well."

"And Deborah has visited Anne?"

John lifted his shoulders. "It is not a Father's role to negotiate such disputes." As if on cue, a mad groan echoed down the stairs from the first floor. "I believe a woman's intervention is more appropriate, and you are their stepmother."

Betty anxiously glanced over her shoulder. John did not know what the girls were capable of. The tightness around John's jaw told her how uncomfortable a raving daughter had made him. "I shall go to her forthwith," Betty said.

"She will not go to Bedlam, Betty. Not a child of mine."

Not fatherly love, she knew. Simple pride. "No, John. It may be that the raving passes, that she has a fever of the brain. Perhaps we should call a physician."

He shook his head. "We cannot afford it. We have lost Bread Street."

Betty did not comprehend for a moment, then realisation seized her. John's house on Bread Street; the rent had supported them. "Burned?"

"Yes, to the ground. We are near destitute, Betty. Anne and Mary will have to find employment or return to their grandmother, we will have to sell what we can of books and possessions, perhaps let Liza go, and then live more frugally on the tiny pension I have remaining from my father."

Betty felt her stomach sink with self-pity. She could have married better. There had been that civil servant at Shoreditch; a drunken fool though wealthy ... But John stood before her, proud in his ruin, and she took his hand and squeezed it. "We shall manage, John."

"Let us deal with one problem at a time. Look in on Anne."

She dropped his hand and he felt his way back to his chair and lowered himself into it, his head cocked to one side in his characteristic way, as though listening for some far off music. She went through to the hallway where her trunk still sat by the door, and up the stairs. Liza sat in a chair in the withdrawing room, dozing into her chest.

"Liza," Betty said sternly, jarring her awake.

"Ma'am," Liza said, shaking her head to rouse herself. "I'm glad you are returned."

A long, mournful groan from the other side of the curtains drew her attention. "What has happened?" She removed her gloves and unfastened her bonnet.

"Mistress Anne is mad, ma'am. She says over and over that she has killed her sister, and will not listen to a word of reassurance. Mary tries to sit with her but Anne spits at her and says it was she started the fire, it was she burned Deborah to death."

"And Deborah? Does Anne respond to her presence?"

Liza dropped her gaze. "Deborah won't come, ma'am."

"What? 'Tis no wonder Anne believes her dead if we all say she is alive and she does not appear. You should have forced her to come."

"I . . ." Liza hesitated, then seemed to form her resolve and proceeded. "I'm frightened of Mistress Deborah, ma'am. I went to tell her she should look in on her sister and she glared at me as though . . . as though she would turn my soul to stone, ma'am."

The old rolling, tumbling fear returned. Maybe this malady of Anne's was a product of witchcraft, and here was the girl sleeping in Betty's own bed! An extremely bad omen. One that would take more than salt water and a name said backwards to overcome. She braced herself and pulled back the curtain.

Anne saw her, sat up and howled. Betty put her hands to her ears, as the howl stretched out for long moments. Her eldest stepdaughter was a raving mess of wild hair and bruise-black eyes, her thin face pale and drawn, her bottom lip red and scabrous from having been bitten to pieces.

"Hush now, child, hush," Betty said, trying to sound soothing despite her wariness. To call Anne a child did not seem ridiculous even though she was a scant half-dozen years younger than Betty, for the girl had only the capacity of a babe in this state. Betty pushed her gently down onto the bed and adjusted the covers.

An icy hand shot out and grasped Betty by the wrist. Despite herself, she jumped.

"I killed my sister, Betty," Anne said, in a voice so matter-of-fact she could have been reciting the alphabet.

"Hush, child, no you didn't. Deborah is alive and well."

"No, I burned her. Mary and I burned her to death. We burned everyone to death."

"'Tis not true, Annie. Deborah is well. I heard that only six people had been killed by the fire, and Deborah is not one of them."

"Six?" Anne said mournfully. "Six?" Then she released Betty's wrist and held up her hand to count them off. "One, two, three, four, five . . ." She made a fist with her fingers then raised her pinky again. ". . . six. Dear little Deborah. She was such a pretty child."

"Deborah is well."

"I do not believe you, for I burned her myself. I saw her on fire and calling to me to save her, but Mary had bound my hands and I could not save her." She began to thrash her head back and forth, a violent shaking. "No, no, no. I could not save her." She descended once more into the howling, and Betty reached forward and clamped a hand over her mouth.

"If you saw Deborah, if she stood right here in front of you, would you believe me?"

Anne bit her hand and Betty released her.

"She is dead, Betty," Anne said, her voice becoming shrill and loud. "Dead, you hear? Dead. I killed her!" She flipped herself over and exploded into sobs, guttural grunting sobs, and Betty found herself wondering about demon

446

possession and how it might show itself. She could not risk Father Bailey's return, however.

"Ma'am, what are we to do?" Liza asked.

Betty turned on her angrily. "I'm going to fetch Deborah."

"She will not come, ma'am. We've all asked her, even her father, but she refuses. Mr Milton shouted at her like he'd bring down the house, and she said no, she would not go to Anne."

Betty was surprised. "John admonished her?"

"Yes, ma'am."

"And she wouldn't come?"

"No, ma'am."

Then what hope did Betty have? Still, Deborah had proved her ally once before, and if nothing else, Betty needed to know whether this madness had anything to do with witchcraft. "I shall speak with her," Betty muttered.

"Best of luck, ma'am," Liza said sarcastically, then when Betty turned on her, she added, "Pardon me for saying."

"'Tis well for you that I am too busy to box your ears."

"Yes, ma'am."

"Watch her closely. I shall return anon."

With trepidation, Betty advanced up the stairs. They seemed to lead up into the dark, and she knew why Liza found Deborah frightening. All of the girls scared her if she were honest, for they seemed to belong to part of a shadowy, sinister world which Betty had spent her whole life avoiding. Steeling herself, she knocked on the door and pushed it open. Mary was nowhere in sight. The door to Deborah's closet was ajar.

"Deborah?"

"I'm in here."

Betty approached, leaned around the threshold. Deborah sat on the bed with her writing tray in front of her, surrounded on all sides by papers. She didn't look up.

"What are you doing?"

"Making a second copy of Father's poem."

"To what purpose?"

"'Tis not for you to know."

Betty felt a surge of irritation. This girl — not long out of her childhood — spoke as though Betty were her inferior. "I am your stepmother."

Deborah placed her pen aside and released a weary breath. She fixed Betty with a gaze through her glasses. "You, of all people, know that common customs do not apply in this household."

"Why do you not go to Anne?"

"Because I do not care a speck for her and I wish her to suffer."

Betty was so surprised that she actually had to steady herself on the doorframe. "I cannot believe I hear correctly what you are saying! Your sister raves —"

"She says she killed me, does she not?"

"Yes."

"Perhaps I wish her to believe that she did."

"Why would you wish that?"

Deborah shrugged. "Caprice? Does that answer satisfy you?"

"No, it could not. You know it could not."

"There is little purpose in your coming here, Betty. I assure you, if Father cannot make me visit my sister, then nobody can."

Betty hesitated, then advanced into the room and sat on the end of the bed. "Then, for the sake of my peace of mind, Deborah, tell me if she is bewitched."

Deborah smiled, then snickered, then laughed out loud.

"Do not laugh at me!" Betty exclaimed, indignant.

Deborah's laugh faded. "I merely laugh because I am tired of crying," she said, her voice thick with venom. "Anne is not bewitched. Anne suffers under the burden of a terrible guilt and deservedly so."

Betty shook her head slowly, the pieces falling into place

in her mind. "You are not saying . . . Anne surely did not attempt to . . ."

"'Tis better for you to know nothing, Betty. You and Father both. All I can say for a certainty is that it appears my sisters and I are now enemies, and should I have the chance to go back in time and change one thing, it would be my reluctance to see them off to Surrey as apprentices. For a great deal of affliction may have been avoided by such a circumstance."

Betty watched her for a few moments, as she dropped her head once more to her work. "You will not be moved, then?"

"I will not be moved," Deborah replied, eyes on the page in front of her.

"What am I to do for your sister's madness?"

"Her cure will come. I have no doubt it is lurking nearby, waiting for an appropriate moment to push its advantage."

Betty's bones grew cold. "You sound as though you speak of a person."

"Not a person."

"Then of whom . . . of what do you speak?"

Deborah answered dismissively, a schoolmaster's inflection to a pupil. "Stay ignorant, Betty. 'Tis the safest route."

Betty rose and left, wishing she had stayed in Suffolk.

Mary kicked a stone along the path disconsolately. Where was the benefit in taking a walk to clear her head when all around smelled like stale firewood, when smoke still rose in choking whirlwinds from beyond the city walls, when all of it had been to no purpose?

Her angel was gone. A hundred years' imprisonment, and she had not been able to save him. She blamed Anne, she blamed Deborah, and eventually she blamed herself. Long fantasies plagued her, where a century passed and somehow she was miraculously still alive, where he came to her and confessed his love, his undying love. For now the pleasures of the flesh seemed far less significant than the longings of the heart.

She idled up the hill and pushed the front door open. The house was quiet. Anne must be sleeping. Mary found her ravings impossible to bear; the sign of a weak spirit, not a weak mind. Mary had done what needed to be done, and would not have done otherwise. Lazodeus was the centre of the firmament for her; any sacrifice was a small one. Betty's trunk blocked the hallway. When had she arrived home? She glanced in and saw Father sitting in his chair, his eyes closed. Was he dozing? Impossible to tell. She watched him a few moments and felt a violent rage brewing inside her. It had all started with him, hadn't it? Father and his grand epic. Why could he not write plays or limericks? Why did he feel it so necessary to inquire into the affairs of angels?

He roused and opened his unseeing eyes, appeared to fix them directly upon her. "Who is there?"

"'Tis Mary, Father," she said.

"Why do you stand there?"

"I'm looking at you, Father."

"To what purpose?"

"To memorise the face of the author of my miseries."

Father frowned. "Have you caught your sister's madness? Are you raving withal?"

"Oh no, Father," she said, approaching him and standing over his chair. "I am perfectly sane."

"Then why do you speak to me so? Where is the respect due to me?"

"What is due to you is affront, what is due to you is denunciation."

He straightened his back in his chair, eyelids pulled up menacingly. "Well then, daughter. Denounce me."

A moment passed, her breath was caught in her throat. Then, with a gasp, she unleashed some of her rage. "I wish your *Paradise Lost* to be a spectacular failure. Your words are a blight on humanity, a testament to your unbridled

450

vanity and arrogance. You are so swollen with pride it has strook you blind, and you think it nothing to justify the ways of God to man. Who are you? Who are you really but a sad little blind man whose best days are behind him, whose ugly wife married him for want of a better offer, whose daughters despise him and laugh about him when he cannot hear?" Mary's heart fluttered wildly in her chest. The room seemed terribly warm. She had said it, but she felt no better.

Father's face was carved in stone. "I gave you life," he said quietly.

"Would that you hadn't. For it is all misery." She turned to leave, but at that moment Max ran in, glad to see her return, and she tripped over him. To break her fall, she threw her arm out but overbalanced with a painful pull in her ankle. Father caught her.

"Let me go," she said, although he had already pushed her gently to her feet and released her. "Max, bad boy!" In angry humiliation she kicked him. He yelped and ran, and the guilt sucked all the air from her lungs.

"Max? Max, I'm sorry." She ran after him, hobbling slightly on the ankle she had pulled. She couldn't see him in the hallway or on the stairs, so moved as quickly as she could through the kitchen and out into the garden. "Max? Max, I —"

She stopped short when she saw Deborah sitting on the stone bench under the wall, cradling a grateful Max in her arms. She and her sister had avoided speaking with each other, avoided even meeting eyes, since Tuesday night, when Mary and a crazed Anne had returned home after midnight, sooty and soiled. After Mary bathed Anne and put her in Betty's bed, Deborah had been waiting for her in the bedroom.

"Sister, you are home exceeding late," she had said.

The first shock was seeing Deborah alive and well; the second, bitter shock was knowing she had failed. Midnight had passed, the manuscript had been saved, and Lazodeus was gone.

Now, here in the garden, Deborah met her gaze evenly. Max licked her face and hands.

"And why are you not locked away in your coop like the foul creature you are?" Mary said.

"I sought fresh air. But now you fill it with your fetid words."

Mary approached, and Max shrank against Deborah's chest.

"Give him to me," Mary said.

"He is quite happy in my arms for the present," Deborah said. "Look you, he is frightened of you."

"I accidentally kicked him."

"In the same way you accidentally locked me in Paul's while it burned?"

"I thought I was doing the right thing!"

"You'll forgive me for not sharing such a view."

"You could not understand, for you have never loved."

"Never loved!" Deborah put Max aside and rose. "How dare you say such a thing? I loved you, I loved Anne. And do you see where it has brought me?"

"It is different when one loves a man, an angel. He is gone, Deborah, because I failed to destroy the manuscript."

"What do you mean?" Deborah narrowed her eyes.

"He was under threat of a century's incarceration if Anne and I did not destroy the manuscript."

"So I was to be sacrificed along with it?"

"You would not listen to reason."

"There was no reason to be had! It pleases me, Mary, that you will never see him again. I feel that you have been punished sufficiently."

Mary wanted to stamp her feet, to cry out, to pull Deborah's hair. But she had never been so keenly aware that they were both grown women, not children fighting over a toy. "I am in pain!" she wailed. "I die for the loss of him."

"I care not, Mary. As long as nobody else has to die, I care not." She brushed past, and Mary couldn't help herself shoving Deborah with her shoulder.

Deborah stopped and turned her head. "My relief at his disappearance is immeasurable."

Mary saw the glint of silver at her throat and remembered the demon key. Suddenly the idea came to her that she may be able to get a message to Lazodeus somehow, if she had the nerve to steal the key and call upon a demon.

"I do not expect you to understand," Mary said.

"Sister, if I understood your motives, I would not like myself." She moved away. Mary knelt down to beckon Max, and he approached her warily.

"I'm sorry, little man," she said, rubbing his head. A tentative lick told her all was forgiven. Would that Deborah was so pliable. Would that the whole universe would bend so easily to her will.

Anne woke but reality was no relief from the dreams; dreams where she left her sister to burn to death. She was lost again, though she remembered something about the curtains which surrounded her. What was it, though? What was it about the curtains? A panic seized her and she heard an awful moan, like someone in terrible pain. *Who is that poor soul? She sounds very close.*

The curtains were Betty's, that was it. Betty had been here and said the words that everyone was saying, "Deborah is alive." But it made as little sense to Anne as a sentence in Greek, because it didn't fit the world at all. Deborah was in the church and the church was on fire, but Mary closed the door. Mary propped it shut with a piece of wood. Mary dragged her to the river.

And then the curtains fell down and there they were still, pale and amorphous in the sunlight. She was missing something . . . where had she put it?

453

"Lazodeus," she said, and Liza thought the call was for her and approached.

"Mistress Mary."

"Not you."

"You called my name."

"Not you. It could never be you!" She picked up a burning ember and flung it at Liza, but Liza didn't even flinch. When she looked at her hand it was white and clean. Where had that ember gone?

"Calm yourself."

"Where is my angel?"

But Liza didn't answer and Anne was falling back inside her head now, where the grey was not as confusing as the many bright colours and sharp shapes which made up the world. *Who is that poor soul?*

The least he could do was to come to her. She had killed her sister for him. Where was he? Had something gone wrong? She groaned, thinking about how slowly the hundred years would pass. She would be hungry again long before that, and how could she eat when he was locked in a cold dungeon with nothing?

"Where is my angel?" a woman said. Perhaps it was her. Everything remained grey and all the voices in her head were sobbing as though to shake the earth.

"Father? Liza said you wished to speak with me?"

"Yes, Deborah. Come in and sit down."

This had to be about Anne. He was going to command her again to talk to her sister, convince her she was alive and well. Deborah didn't know if she was capable of refusing him a second time. Wednesday night's disagreement still haunted her, his exasperated annoyance, his glowering disapproval of her.

"Of what did you wish to speak?"

He steepled his fingers together in front of him and tapped his chin. "What do I spend most of my time doing, Deborah?"

"I know not, Father." An odd question. It threw her.

"Come, make a guess."

"You like to be read to, and you like to compose letters, and to walk . . ."

"But when I have no one to assist me in those things — for well you know I have no eyes — what do you think I do with my time?"

She ventured an answer. "I expect you sit here and think, Father."

"Indeed, I do. I think and I think. Not much escapes my notice or my scrutiny."

This line of conversation was headed in a direction which made Deborah uncomfortable. "I should imagine not."

He released his hands as if banishing the thought. "Enough of that. I merely meant to show you that I may sometimes understand more about a situation than you are aware."

"I see. Is that all, Father?" She moved to leave.

"No, sit, sit. I am not finished."

She settled again, watching him. He smiled and she smiled back, a small invisible smile.

His face became serious again. "Deborah, the fire destroyed my house on Bread Street."

"I guessed it might have. Are you sad, Father? Was it not the house of your childhood?"

"My childhood I'd soon enough be rid of. No, the problem is that the rent from that house was supporting us all."

"Indeed? I knew not."

"And why should you? You are a girl . . . a young woman. What need you know of your Father's fortunes?"

Deborah found herself confused by Father's meandering logic. The feeling of discomfort returned. "Then why did you tell me?"

"No reason, no reason. Or, perhaps there may be a reason, but only you would know."

She shifted in her seat, as though being an inch closer

might bring her closer to his meaning.

"Deborah? You have not answered."

"Sir, I can make no sense of your words."

"I shall be more plain. We are all but penniless. If there should be a way to regain what finances we have lost — I have no wish to be a rich man, you understand — but if there should be a way . . . I leave it to you. My best and brightest daughter."

And suddenly she understood. *Not much escapes my notice or my scrutiny.* Had he some suspicion of her dealings in the unseen world? Indeed, why should he not? She had returned miraculously unharmed from a burning church with his manuscript just days before, and perhaps over the passing months he had gleaned some hushed mentions of magic or angels. Now he seemed to suggest that she, through some occult intervention, reinstate his lost fortune.

"I . . . I know not how to respond," she said, for the silence required filling and she knew it was her duty.

"Respond as you see fit, Deborah. Do not mistake me, I advise no greater loss for such a gain. I trust to your judgement. I trust you." He said this last grudgingly, and leaned back in his chair. "You may go."

She stood though her knees felt oddly jointed, and made her way back up the stairs. Certainly, she could pretend that she knew no magic, and perhaps that would be a relief to him. But how would they live without money? How would they eat and keep warm? She could endure hardship for herself, but Father was an old man.

Yet to use the demon key for such venal ends was sure to send her soul spinning down to Pandemonium.

22
This Horror Will Grow Mild, this Darkness Light

Mary did not sleep. How could she? Her mind was full of the possibilities in Deborah's demon key. It commanded spirits, and spirits lived in Pandemonium. She could find one to pass on a message to Lazodeus, to tell him she loved him and she was sorry. Or even gather information from him about some other method to effect his release.

But Deborah was her enemy and would be guarding against her.

"I have done it once ere this," she whispered to her pillow in the dark. The dolt wore it on the same chain about her neck as she always had worn it.

Mary flipped over again, stared at the moon above the neighbouring house. What had Betty once said? Bad luck to look at the new moon through glass? Long ago, when such innocent superstition had been all she knew of the mystical, she had been a different person. She had been a girl playing at womanhood with red satin and strings of pearls in her hair. She could barely contemplate how far she had travelled since then.

She threw back the covers and rose. Since the fire the weather had begun to cool, and her feet sought out the rug. She crept, one foot quietly in front of the other, to Deborah's closet.

Opened the door.

Approached the bed.

Deborah sat up. "What is it, Mary?"

"I . . . are you awake?"

"I woke the instant I heard your foot hit the floor. You'll understand that I no longer trust you."

"I thought I heard you crying out, having a bad dream."

"Perhaps it was Anne downstairs."

Mary assessed her sister, her long pale hair and even features. She knew it was wrong to feel such a tug of anger that Deborah was more beautiful than her, but she was so tired of applying civilised laws to her more primal feelings. She pounced on her and began wrestling the chain off her neck.

"Ow. What are you doing?"

"Give me your demon key," Mary said. "Don't make me hurt you for it."

"Indeed, it is you who shall be hurt." Deborah grabbed Mary's hair and wrenched it, then got her elbow between them and used it to pry Mary off.

Mary fell to the floor with a thump. Deborah was much stronger than her and Mary felt keenly aggravated by this fact. Deborah was her baby sister.

"I hate you!" she cried.

"I care not how you feel for me, Mary." So reasonable, so irritatingly reasonable.

"Keep your damned key."

"So I shall."

Mary stood and stormed out, slamming the door behind her. What now? She was far too agitated to contemplate sleeping. Max was curled in a ball on the corner of the bed, and she sat next to him and stroked him gently. How was she to trick Deborah out of her key? Violence? Poison? Pleading? Blackmail?

Then her perspective widened out and she considered for the first time that perhaps she needed no key to command a demon. She remembered that awful day when a demon had come disguised as the King, and Lazodeus had said that some elementals could hear one's wishes and respond to them. Perhaps she had something to offer such a creature in return for contact with Lazodeus.

She scrambled out her window, still in her shift, edged along the ledge and dropped into her secret room. It was much warmer in here, with all the floor coverings and thick curtains. Mary had avoided coming to the room since the fire; all these reminders of her time spent with Lazodeus were painful to her. She lay down on a pile of cushions in the centre of the room and looked up. It seemed impossible that his warm body, his faint luminescence, his clear eyes should now be denied her. He had become the most significant element of her life; without him, it was almost impossible to imagine herself.

She sat up and brushed her hair off her face. Courage now. The demons were awful, disgusting things, but if making a deal with one was her key to seeing Lazodeus again, then she would do it.

"I call upon whichever demon is nearby . . ." Was that the right thing to say? She couldn't imagine how else to call them. She cleared her throat and started again. "I call upon whichever demon can hear my plea. I wish to trade whatever I can of value to make contact with Lazodeus."

The air seemed suddenly full of a hushed chattering. One voice grew louder and louder, and she realised it was saying her name: *Marymarymarymary . . .*

"Who is there?" she said, looking around.

The chattering suddenly stopped and a demon appeared before her. Although the confusion of features was the same as the other demons she had seen, it was recognisably a different individual. She hoped it had a kinder nature than others she had met.

"What is your name?" she asked.

"You could not pronounce it."

Mary shook her head. "You appeared so quickly."

"There are many of us living up here now. Your sister Deborah attracts us."

"Deborah?"

"Yes, but she has yet to make an offer the like of the one you extended. Whatever you have of value. Oh, I am most excited to have arrived first."

She scanned the room anxiously. "Will others come?"

"No, I am here so you are mine."

Although its voice and its nature seemed more gentle than the others, she was still made uncomfortable by its words.

"You are frightened of something?" it asked.

"Of you."

"But I can bring you in contact with Lazodeus."

"Is he well?"

"He is well enough."

"Does he mourn? Is he very sad?"

"I have heard no reports of his sadness."

Mary took this small comfort. Of course Lazodeus would be brave in his punishment. It was she who could not bear it; for her it was a lifetime of anguish. "I wish to see him again. Can you deliver messages between us?"

"Yes, that is within my capabilities."

"I need you to ask him what I can do to bring us together again. I will do whatever he says, so he is not to feel any request is too great. Can you reassure him? Can you tell him that I love him and I will do *anything* to see him again?"

"I can. But what about my payment?"

"I would give anything. I would give my soul."

The creature snorted and took a step towards her, towering above her menacingly. "Your soul is not worth much, Mary Milton. Nor is your body for so many have enjoyed it."

A meagre relief that he would not want to mix flesh with her. "Then what?"

"How badly do you wish to see him again?"

"My heart is bleeding. I will do anything, provided I am

alive and well when he takes me in his arms again."

"Your sight?"

"No, I have to see his face."

"Your hearing?"

She shook her head impatiently. "I have to hear his voice. Do you not understand? It is his absence which pains me. Suggest nothing else which will compromise my experience of his presence." Her heart was beating very rapidly, but she was determined to go through with whatever it asked of her. At the back of her mind a tiny voice was pleading, pleading, *don't mention Max.*

"Ha!" the creature said, picking the thought from her mind. It knelt next to her and leaned close. "And what could I do with your ugly dog?"

Mary held her breath against the awful smell of the creature. "He is what I love most. After Lazodeus."

"A wiser love, Mary Milton. One for which you need not suffer so much." It shook its head. "No, I have decided upon my payment. I want your youth and beauty."

Her breath seemed pulled from her lungs. "My . . ."

"'Tis the only thing of value you possess."

"And how is such a transaction to be effected?"

"You merely have to agree to it."

"Then you will go direct to Lazodeus?"

"Direct."

Mary licked her lips. Her youth and beauty. She would lose them eventually anyway. And if it meant she may once more hold Lazodeus in her arms . . . should he still want her to hold him . . ?

"What is your answer, Mary?"

"I consider it yet."

"Make haste."

"Perhaps I shall call upon another demon."

"Another demon will want the same thing. 'Tis all you have, my dear."

Moments ticked past and Mary could not decide. Part of

her ached to say yes, to be done with this agony of separation from Lazodeus. But no guarantees existed that her bargain would bring them together again. Was being in contact with him via a messenger enough?

She nodded. It would be enough, for once contact had been established, he would tell her how to proceed to release him.

"May I interpret that nod as a yes?"

"I —"

He sat back with an exasperated sigh. "You cannot call out to us that you will make such a bargain and then hesitate."

"I am almost persuaded."

"What can I do to persuade you further?"

"Let me see how I might look."

"Very well, go to the mirror." He indicated the large looking glass hung on the far wall. She advanced to it with trepidation, gazed at herself. The round cheeks and bright eyes would fade anyway. Was it really so great a loss for such an enormous gain?

"Show me then, demon."

In a blink the reflection had changed. A hag stared back at her, with white hair still ridiculously looped into a fashionable hairstyle, with sunken cheeks and not a tooth in her head. Long crevices of age scarred her cheeks and her neck fell in haggard folds. Mary looked down at her own hands, still soft and white, then held them up to the mirror where they were gnarled and spotted with age. In the mirror, her breasts sagged nearly to her waist, and Mary had to put her hands on her own body to reassure herself that they were still where they had always sat. Thick nausea rolled into her stomach.

"Your answer, Mary?"

"I . . ."

"I shall give you ten seconds, and then you shall be transformed."

Mary stared and stared. *This will be what you see every time you pass your reflection.*

"One . . . two . . . three . . ."

"I need longer to decide."

"I have no more time to wait. Four . . . five . . . six —"

"No!"

"No?"

Mary turned from the reflection and looked at the demon. "No, I cannot do it."

"You shall be separated eternally from Lazodeus."

"I may live another hundred years."

"And you will be that hag upon his return."

She shook her head, and although her guilt was acute, she felt such relief. "No, I cannot . . . I cannot look like that. There must be another way."

"Do not waste my time. You are an idiot. You do not love him."

"I do love him!" But the demon was gone. "Come back!" she shrieked. "I may change my mind, come back." She wouldn't change her mind, though, and she suspected the demon had realised that. She turned back to the mirror, to her restored prettiness, and she spat upon it. "You vain wench, I despise you."

Betty had to stand on a short stool, and still couldn't quite reach the top of the bed. She stretched up on her toes, felt the stool rock slightly beneath her, but steadied herself and persisted. Carefully, she arranged in a row on the tester three wax figures, a clove of garlic and a string with a knot in it. She had no idea what kind of bad emanations a lunatic might leave in her bed, but she wanted to alleviate them as much as possible.

A noise on the stair outside nearly sent her crashing to the floor. She hurried down and sat upon the stool, looked around to see Mary come in.

"Now, Mary, you know it upsets her to see you."

"'Tis no business of yours, Betty." Mary sank down on the edge of the bed where Anne slept peacefully. "Leave us be a few minutes."

"But you . . ." Betty thought better of finishing her sentence. Of all of them, Mary was the most frightening. "I shall return anon. Do not work her into a state."

Mary was not listening; she had leaned over Anne and was whispering, "Annie, Annie wake up. 'Tis Mary; I need to talk to you."

Betty went through the split in the curtains to the withdrawing room, but hesitated nearby so she could listen. If Mary made Anne begin to howl again, she would have to go in and put a stop to it. Betty couldn't stand the sounds of her madness. They made her feel as though she were being driven mad herself.

"Sister, wake."

A soft grunt.

"Annie?"

"Leave me alone, Mary. You are a murderer." Anne sounded distressed, but not in her usual state of screaming panic.

"No, I am not."

"We killed Deborah." The same refrain.

"No, we did not. Deborah is alive."

"If she were alive she would come."

"She is angry with us."

"I do not believe you." Anne's voice started to grow louder. "I killed my sister and it is because of you, because you started the fire, because you pushed her inside . . ."

Betty listened carefully. The ravings of a mad person, surely. But Deborah had suggested that perhaps her sisters had intended her harm.

"Will you be quiet!" Mary hissed. "Be quiet and listen, for I come to speak to you of the angel."

Then Anne said a word which Betty did not recognise. Lass-something. What was this talk of an angel? She suddenly felt edgy, as though she should not be listening. Mary would be angry if she knew.

"When will he come?" Anne said. "Has he been to see you?"

"Annie, listen. Deborah escaped with the manuscript. The angel is not returning."

"No, no!" A wail of such anguish that Betty was surprised. The guilt over the imagined killing of her sister was expressed at only half the intensity.

"Shh! Do you want Betty to come racing back in here?"

"It cannot be, Mary. I shall die, I shall die." Her voice was little more than a whimper.

"Would that we were both dead."

"What can we do?"

"Nothing, for he was all our magic. And Deborah, with her foul magical key, will not help us."

Betty's knees nearly buckled underneath her for relief. Mary's magic was gone. Only Deborah had some remaining, and Deborah had vowed to protect her. Was it all over then? Was her only remaining concern with her stepdaughters to be Anne's lunatic fit?

"I don't believe you, I don't believe you. He must come, he must." Anne choked on a sob. "I don't believe you, I don't, I don't. He's coming, he's coming back, he must come back."

"Hush, hush, your tongue runs on wheels. Be quiet now."

But Mary's entreaties for quiet only seemed to anger Anne, and soon she was shouting again about how she hated Mary, how poor Deborah was all burned, and how she would die with the pain in her heart.

"Anne, listen, you must recover so we can steal Deborah's key."

"Deborah is dead! Deborah is dead!"

Betty heard Mary rise in a rage and a slap of flesh on flesh indicated she had struck Anne. Then Mary came storming out. At first, Betty tried to hide the fact that she had listened in, but then she remembered Mary's words. All her magic was gone.

"Why do you stare?" Mary demanded.

"Because I cannot believe such an ugly soul is allowed to walk God's good earth."

Mary stepped up to her. "How do you dare to say such a thing?"

"'Tis nothing daring. I invite no danger."

"Why, I should —"

"Should what? Lash me to death with your tongue? I quake."

Mary puffed up with rage, but could not manage a single word. She stamped out, her face as red as her dress. Betty smiled to herself. Months of tyranny concluded. A little revenge would satisfy her greatly.

Deborah watched for the next few days as Mary did everything within her power to convince her dog that she still loved him. From a distance, she was the Mary of old who loved a small creature immodestly and bent all her care towards him. But up close she was a snarling opponent, with a permanent groove in her forehead from frowning. Sometimes Deborah almost felt pity for her sister, that she was so inexorably removed from her love. But Mary had placed herself outside the circle of pity with her actions, and so they continued adversaries and, Deborah expected, would do so until she could convince Father to send her older sisters away. She was merely waiting for Anne to recover her wits.

From the window of the withdrawing room, Deborah saw Mary walk down the hill with Max. Now was the time to act. Betty was occupied in tending to Anne, Liza was cooking, Mary was gone. She crept up to her closet and had the demon key held out in her right hand when Liza entered the bedroom.

"Mistress Deborah?"

She stepped out of the closet. "What is it?"

466

"I need help with the mats from Mr Milton's study. I'm not tall enough to hang them."

Deborah hesitated, and almost went with her. Housekeeping was preferable to calling upon demons. "Not now, Liza, I'm busy."

"But Mr Milton wants his mats beaten."

"My Father can wait an hour."

"But he said —"

"I care not! Go away. I shall be down as soon as I can."

Liza made a grudging curtsy and left. Deborah picked up the demon key again. Who was to say the stupid servant wouldn't come back in the middle of her incantation? What she wouldn't give for more privacy, her own house like Amelia's where she could do what she wished.

Mary's secret room, then. She climbed out on the ledge and crept along. The stone was beginning to crumble at the far end, and she inched around it carefully. Once inside, she found herself looking around impatiently. All these rich things. Mary had commanded an angel and asked for this. What was wrong with her? Why had she not asked for protection for Max, for the continued love of her sisters? She was as base and corrupt as the demon Dantalion had suggested.

And yet, here was Deborah, about to invoke the demon of treasure.

"For the greater good," she muttered, pulling out the demon key. Then in a clear voice, "Asmodeus, I call upon you with this key as your commander, provide me with treasure."

Five notes, but this time they pained her. No sweet after-shock, only an abrasion of her most delicate organs, only a dark corrosion of her soul. The tiny sound of coins clinking together drew her attention. Under the window, a red velvet bag. With a deep breath, she approached it. She could not have been more loathe to touch it had it been a snake. Her hands shook as she opened the bag, and saw it was full of guineas.

A small fortune. She dropped it. What had this cost her? What had happened to her soul while those notes had rung out? A rage boiled up inside her and she picked up a pillow and flung it towards the fireplace. It felt good, so she picked up a candlestick and made to hurl it at the wall.

Then a voice of reason inside told her, *Control your temper, these belongings are Mary's*.

Mary who had left her for dead in a burning church. The crack of the candlestick as it hit the wall was infinitely gratifying. She found another, which she aimed at a looking-glass on the opposite wall. It split in the middle, then fell from the wall. She took a velvet tapestry in her hands and wrenched at it, pulled away its hem and tore the stitching. Before she had even realised what a rage had taken her over, she was tearing through the room, pulling things apart, pushing statues over and breaking every candle she could find. It felt good, it felt so good. Tears ran down her cheeks and she became aware of an animalistic grunting and gasping; her own.

Deborah had a brass statuette in her left hand, about to smash it into a painting hanging above the fireplace, when a voice from behind her startled her back to herself.

"I believe you are enjoying yourself."

She whirled around. Lazodeus, dressed as black as his black heart.

"You!"

"You seem surprised."

She dropped the statuette and pushed her hair off her face. Her cheeks felt flushed and her heart was racing. "I am surprised on two counts. One, that you should dare to appear before me after sending me to my death in St Paul's. Two, that you are not imprisoned for one hundred years as my sister believes."

He frowned, looked puzzled. "I am amazed on both counts."

"Amazed? Are you stupid and evil both?"

"Deborah, I did not send you to your death."

"My sisters locked me in!"

"I had no inkling of what they intended. If they, in fact, intended it. Was not the act opportunistic? They did not know you would come to find them."

"I . . ." She was surprised by logic.

"Did you not save your father's manuscript?"

"Yes."

"And instead of being thanked for —"

"I do not wish to listen to this!"

"Should you not thank me for warning you though, Deborah?"

"I will not thank you, for I do not trust you."

"Still? What more can I do? You are determined to consider me your enemy."

Deborah sighed and wished that he was not so beautiful to look upon. If he at least appeared evil she knew she would not be moved. "I cannot trust you, Lazodeus. It is not within my ability to trust you."

"And as for the second charge, that I am imprisoned. Why, as you see, it is not so."

"Then why would my sister say such a thing?"

"She lied to excuse her actions. Which is like Mary. You know it is like Mary."

Deborah looked around at the destruction she had caused, then her eyes drew back to Lazodeus. She only remembered at that moment that she hadn't protected herself from him. She put her hand to her forehead. "Why are you here?"

"I was once your guardian."

"You never did anything of benefit for me."

"And so now I wish to. You used the demon key for the acquisition of wealth. It has injured you."

"I feel no injury." But she was lying. She remembered the awful feeling of erosion that the music had caused.

"It has injured you in your subtle body, not your mortal body."

"My soul?"

"If you like to call it so. And every time you need more money, for that will last you but a year or two, you must do it again, causing further and further damage."

A cool gust of air washed into the room. The torn tapestries danced and Deborah shivered. "My father is destitute."

"I can remedy that."

"I want nothing from you."

"I can remedy it, Deborah, as was my original mission in being your guardian, and it will cause no further harm to you." He nodded towards the bag of coins. "That is someone else's money, you understand. Demons cannot make it out of nothing."

She looked at him warily. Father's words returned to her; *I advise no greater loss for such a gain*. He would not want her to endanger her soul.

"Is this the sin that Lucifer has named for my soul?" she said suddenly.

"Deborah, if you do not believe me, you must at least believe the signs that you experience. Did not the demon key hurt you when you used it then?"

"Yes, it did."

"And has it ever hurt you when I have used my magic."

"You have never used it to my benefit."

He shook his head with a smile. "I should cry for your ingratitude. Did I not ensure that you were not separated from your sisters when they were under threat of apprenticeship?"

She regarded this information carefully. It was right. She had thought nothing of using his magic then, and she had felt no unnatural pain as she felt when she used the demon key. And it was true that this bag of money would eventually need to be replenished. Father may live another thirty years — was she willing to do it more than once? What harm would be caused if she did?

"Very well, Lazodeus. You have another chance to prove

your trustworthiness. With no ill effects caused to anyone, you may attempt to reinstate my father's fortune."

He approached her, and she felt her skin prickling lightly. No man had ever looked at her in such a way, as though she were the sole focus of his life, as though he wished to express it in unimaginably sweet ways. He placed a hand on each of her shoulders. "I shall prove myself to you yet, Deborah. It is my dearest wish that you should come to consider me with the deep regard I feel for you."

She pushed his hands away, but felt her fingers linger involuntarily on his warm skin. "We shall talk anon. Go to. I have mats to beat."

He disappeared, and Deborah picked up the bag of money. Perhaps she should hide it away and never look at it again. But she pressed it against her as she climbed out the window, and it sat cold next to her heart as she stood on the crumbling edge, drawing air deep into her lungs.

"Anne, Anne."

A soft voice close to her ear. But no, she didn't want to wake up. Lazodeus had burned to death in the church and Deborah was in prison for the crime, and somehow it was all Anne's fault and she wouldn't wake up, she wouldn't come up through those grey layers to look at a world without her angel.

"Anne, my love. Awake."

Mary had said such awful things, and to stay under here was better than to consider them, because if they were true, she found herself wishing Deborah had remained in the church. A hundred years was a long time, a long, long time. "Leave me be," she said, burrowing further under the covers.

"Anne, look at me."

"I killed my sister and I wish she had stayed dead," she whispered.

"Look at me."

The voice was familiar, achingly familiar. The grey began to swirl around her and she couldn't make sense of the shapes. "I want to stay under here," she said.

A firm hand took her chin and turned her towards him. She opened her eyes. Through the gloom she could see a face.

"I do not believe it is you," she said to the angel.

"I assure you I am here."

"I have dreamed so many times and been disappointed."

"You know I am real; you can feel I am real." He took her hand and led it to his face. Her fingers clutched at his skin. The grey was tumbling backwards.

"Lazodeus?" She struggled to sit up. "Can it be that you have come at last?"

"Anne, my Anne." He enclosed her in his arms, and it was real, thrillingly real.

"Oh, my angel." The relief was overwhelming. In his arms clarity began to return. "Oh, thank God you are safe. Thank God you are returned to me."

"Yes, I am returned to you," he said, his warm voice rumbling in his chest. "But, Annie, we have a problem."

She sat back and gazed at his beloved face. "A problem?"

"My love, how far will you go to keep me?"

23
Devising Death to Them
Who Lived

"'T is a miracle, Mary. Your sister is well again."

Mary eyed Liza warily. "What do you mean?"

"Come down and see her. She sits up and speaks perfect sanely, she eats and she has asked for you."

Mary threw back the bed covers and approached Liza in puzzlement. "What, overnight?"

"Yes, she has woke recovered."

Mary saw Deborah idling near the entrance to her closet, watching the proceedings with curiosity.

"I shall come and see her anon," Mary said. "Tell her I shall be with her as soon as I have dressed."

Liza backed out and Mary pulled open her chest of drawers to find clothes.

"Miraculously recovered?" Deborah said.

"Yes, no thanks to you."

"I should have wished upon her another year of suffering, and two years for you."

Mary did not answer. She dressed hurriedly and went downstairs. Anne sat up in bed, eating leftover soup. She smiled when Mary came in.

"Sister, I am eager to speak with you. Go, Liza. Mary and I need privacy."

Liza took Anne's empty bowl and left them alone. When Mary was sure she was gone, she said, "You are completely recovered then?"

"My madness has passed. I now find only clarity in my mind."

"So you know that Deborah is alive and well."

"Yes, for I have it from a trustworthy source." She smiled coyly, and Mary found herself intrigued.

"What do you mean?"

"Lazodeus came last night."

With disappointment, Mary realised that Anne's madness had simply transformed itself into another obsession. "Sister, Lazodeus is gone."

Anne shook her head. Her limp hair hung in greasy strands around her face. "Indeed he is not. He has been given a short reprieve."

The hope in her heart could not be allowed to soar. "Anne, you are not thinking clearly. Lazodeus has been imprisoned for —"

"For pity's sake, Mary, are you listening to me?" Anne said crossly. "He came to me last night, he cured my madness, and he has asked that we both meet him this evening in the garden so he may tell us how we can help him."

Mary's breath caught in her throat. "He is really returned?"

"Briefly. He has been given another chance to prevent his imprisonment. We are instrumental."

"What is it? What does he want us to do?"

"What does it matter? We shall do it. We are capable of all manner of terrible things, are we not?"

Mary shook her head slowly. "Anne, I know that I am willing, but are you? Your conviction that you murdered Deborah sent you mad."

"I no longer feel any misgiving, for I have suffered his absence and it is worse than any pain." Anne leaned close, her dark eyes gleaming. "Sister, I will not suffer it again."

Deborah arrived home from the bakery to find Father pacing his study.

"Father?" she said, untying her bonnet.

He whirled around at the sound of her voice. "Deborah?"

"Yes. Whatever's the matter? You are agitated."

"Indeed, I am. Come in, I wish to speak with you."

She stood just inside the entrance of the study, her hands folded before her. Father continued to pace around the furniture as though he could see it. Finally, he came to stand in front of her.

"I had a letter this morning."

"Would you like me to read it for you?"

He shook his head. "The messenger read it for me. For he was a messenger of the King."

Deborah was surprised into momentary silence. Eventually she asked, "What did the King want of you, Father?"

"He has offered me a position. The same position I held under Cromwell, as Latin secretary."

A deep ache of regret moved inside her. This was Lazodeus's doing, with no doubt at all. She almost admired him for how subtle the return of Father's fortune was to be. But to work for the King was no honour for Father, who was a sworn opponent of the monarchy.

"I am glad for you, Father. It appears your concerns about money are resolved."

Once again he shook his head. "No, Deborah."

"No?"

"No. For I did not accept the position."

Deborah felt a smile break out upon her face. She hesitated before saying it, then decided she would. "I am glad."

"You are?"

"Yes, for to take that position were against your principles, and no price can be named for principles."

He reached out a blind hand to her. She grasped it firmly. "I know not how much you had to do with such an offer, Deborah," he said quietly.

"Why, nothing at all, of course. What could I do to influence the King?"

He opened his mouth as if to say something, then closed it again. He dropped her hand and nodded curtly. "I expect we shall manage without royal appointments. I expect we shall make what little we have last."

She loved him so much in that moment that it baffled her that she ever grew impatient with him. Clever, principled, compassionate Father.

"Mary and Anne will have to go," she said in a small voice which betrayed her attempted confidence.

"It surprises me to hear you say that."

"Much has passed between us."

"Betty is already making enquiries into apprenticeships for them. Or they can go to your grandmother."

Another pang of regret. So paradoxical that their attempts to stay together would at last separate them. "I care not where they go, Father," she said. "I just wish order and harmony restored."

Betty was walking past the kitchen when she spotted Mary sitting at the table, feeding her dog. Her first impulse was to keep walking and not say a word, but now she remembered that she was no longer in danger from Mary and she paused in the doorway.

"That mongrel animal should not eat our food."

Mary looked up and scowled. "Be quiet, you foul creature."

"It is he who is the foul creature." She strode forward and pushed him off the table. He yelped and ran. "Go to, get out of my sight."

Mary shot up from the table and grabbed Betty's wrist. "Leave him alone," she hissed. "Next time it will be scorpions in your pot."

Betty shook her off. "You frighten me no longer, Mary. I know your source of power is gone."

Mary took a step back, a startled look upon her face.

"So," Betty continued, "I have sent letters to lacemakers in Kent and in Dartford and expect to hear a result at any time. We can no longer afford to keep you or your dog." Betty derived such satisfaction from Mary's smouldering indignation that she persisted. "You are a drain on our resources and I long for your departure."

"You should be quiet," Mary said, in a voice so evenly poisonous that it gave Betty pause. She had expected — wanted — rages and tears and empty threats.

But no, she would not be terrorised any longer. "And why should I so?" Betty asked boldly. "Your apprenticeship will soon knock all the arrogance out of you, Mary Milton. You shall trade your fine red dresses for a blue apron and grey shirt, and you shall regret your disrespect and cruelty to me. And as for your dog, I doubt that your new master will allow you to keep him and so —"

The slap across Betty's face was unexpected and left her stinging. Mary shook with rage, and Betty began to laugh.

"Be quiet," Mary said. "You shall regret this."

Betty doubled over and laughed harder, all the aching anxiety of the past few months rocking out of her body. When she looked up, Mary was gone.

When Anne came down to the kitchen shortly before midnight, Mary was pacing the room.

"I wondered where you were," Anne said.

"I could not sleep. I can barely believe he will be here."

Anne yawned. "He will be here. He promised me, and I know he would do nothing to cause me injury." She was rewarded by a jealous glance from Mary.

"Why did he come to you and not me?"

"Perhaps my need was greater," Anne said, all the while thinking, *because he loves me, and not you*.

"Come, let us wait in the garden."

They sat on the long stone bench under the wall and

waited. When the church bells in the distance rang out midnight and still he hadn't come, Anne could sense Mary's restlessness.

"Anne, are you sure you didn't imagine this in your state of delusion."

"I am certain."

"But it is after midnight and —"

"Mary, Anne."

They looked up to see Lazodeus sitting on top of the garden wall, between the broken jugs and urns which decorated it. Anne heard Mary catch her breath.

"It is true, then," Mary said.

"Come over the wall and out into the street behind. I must talk to you in the utmost privacy."

Mary deftly scrambled over the wall, but Anne lagged behind. She was not yet particularly co-ordinated when challenged to climb. She stood on the stone bench and tried to heave herself up on her arms, but fell back. Lazodeus caught her with a strong hand.

"Here, Anne, let me help you." For a few sweet moments she was pressed against him as he helped her over the wall. Then he released her. She knew it was important to hide their love from Mary, but she could feel herself glow from his touch.

Mary eyed her suspiciously. It had always been clear that Mary considered the angel her own. There was a special satisfaction in knowing she had enjoyed Lazodeus in a way that Mary had failed to. Her sister had always been so sure of her desirability; had never considered Anne anything but a bony-faced oddity. Anne smiled to herself as Lazodeus beckoned them to follow him out onto the road.

"Where are we going?" Anne asked.

"We need to find somewhere where Deborah won't hear us. Or your father, or Betty."

"Are you returned completely safely, Lazodeus?" Mary

asked in a whining voice. "Will you attend upon us again? May we call you?"

"I shall explain all presently. First let us find a place where we can speak in confidence." He pointed to a tavern on the corner of the hill. "There."

"But it is closed," Anne said.

Lazodeus smiled at her, his eyes tender in the dark. "Angel magic, Annie. Have you forgotten so soon?"

Mary glanced from one of them to the other, clearly growing suspicious. "Forgotten what?"

Lazodeus came to a halt in front of the closed tavern. "Your sister has forgotten that I have special powers." He moved his hand delicately in front of the tavern door. "Go on, open it."

Mary moved forward and pushed the door. It swung inward. "It is unlocked," she said with pleasure.

"Go in, Mary. You too, Anne. We do not want to be seen."

They went in ahead of him; he closed the door and indicated that they should sit at a round table near the fireplace. Anne looked around. There was a curiously desolate feeling about the place. The rushes were soaked with the smell of stale beer and the dying embers of the fire provided a little gloomy light in the dark. She sat and Mary sat across from her, Lazodeus between them.

"Now, explain everything," Mary said, leaning towards him so her skin touched his.

Lazodeus didn't seem to notice. He slumped forward with his head in his hands. "I shall only tell you if you make me a promise."

"Anything," Anne said, beating Mary by half a second.

"Anything," her sister echoed.

The angel looked up and in the firelight Anne saw for the first time how careworn he was. His usually clear blue-green eyes were clouded, his smooth brow furrowed with concern. "I need you to promise me that you will say no if you have the slightest misgiving about what I am to ask you."

"I will have no misgivings," Mary said.

"Nor I."

"Promise me," he said, fixing Anne in his gaze.

She nodded solemnly. "Yes, I promise."

"I promise, too," Mary said. "Come, tell us what is so grave. You make me uneasy."

He took a deep breath. "I am free only temporarily."

"Why so?" Anne asked, her heart caught on a wire.

"I have been given a reprieve as long as I can perform a certain duty. I am, indeed, considered the best candidate for it. Because I am in your confidence."

"Go on," Mary said.

"Your father's poem will be published. We can no longer change that. But we want to ensure he writes no more."

"What do you want us to do? Destroy his study? All his books and papers? Lordy, we'd burn the whole house down if you asked us."

He shook his head sadly. "Unfortunately, it is not that easy."

Anne looked from Lazodeus to Mary in the dim firelight. Her chest was tight with horrified realisation. "I think I understand," she said. "You want us to kill him."

Lazodeus nodded. "I am afraid that is it."

Anne's breath seemed stolen from her lungs, and yet part of her stood outside herself and said, *That is not so very bad; you do not love your father, it is not the greatest sacrifice you could make.*

"I am willing," Mary said forcefully. "If it is what keeps me from losing you."

"And it must be Mary and I who perform this deed?" Anne asked.

"Death, Anne, just say yes!" Mary said indignantly. "Lazodeus shall think you bear no love for him." It was a challenge.

"No, Mary, Anne is right to ask. Your original summoning of me, the reason I am here and in your confidence, bore a condition that I injure nobody. I cannot injure your father. It would violate that condition."

"You see?" Mary said to her. "'Tis your fault the deed falls to us. You had better agree to it."

"I do not want her to agree to it if she has misgivings." Lazodeus touched Anne's hand lightly, and all the love he felt for her was concentrated into his fingers. "I shall accept my punishment and take comfort in knowing that I caused you no distress."

"I have no misgivings," Anne said easily. "All is well. We shall do it."

Deborah sat up with a start. Had she dreamed it?

No, no dream, for the sound still rang in her ears and was as unmistakable as the sound of cannon fire, though infinitely quieter. One note, sweet and splendid, from her demon key.

Her sisters had resolved to patricide.

Her thoughts had kept her awake for two hours after Lazodeus's proposal, and now Mary had decided there was no point in trying to sleep through such excitement. She found her way to her secret room only to find it torn to pieces.

"Deborah," she hissed. Then put all thoughts of her sister aside. It was her stepmother she wanted to hurt. She called Lazodeus.

"Mary?" he said. "I thought I told you we must limit our contact over the next crucial days."

"Anne sleeps a troubled sleep. She tosses and turns as one possessed. I know not if she is capable of such a great service to you." She launched herself into his arms. "She does not love you as much as I love you."

He held her close and stroked her hair. "Do not compete with Anne. It is not fair on her. She has none of your charms and she is ugly and thin."

Instant gratification. "I want to scare Betty," she said.

His mouth tightened momentarily as with impatience, but then he found his smile. "As you wish."

"I know you can't harm anyone, but can I make her ill? A little ill?"

He inclined his head and thought about it. "I can furnish you with a charm, like the fire charm. If you put it under her pillow it will be dissolved by morning and she will be gripped for a day by a vomiting malady."

Mary clapped her hands together. "It sounds perfect."

"Only be careful not to name an illness while she suffers. The magical illness you give her will instantly transform into the one you name."

She wondered if he told her this to tempt her into the very thing he warned against. "I see," she said, mock-seriously, "so I should be careful not to say 'measles' or 'whooping cough.'"

He nodded. "Precisely." He extended his hand and a black charm lay in his palm.

She picked it up and popped it in her placket. "How about 'small pox.'"

He held out a stern finger. "Now, don't you go too far. I trust you."

She closed her lips around his finger and rolled her tongue around its tip.

He pushed her away gently. "Mary, I am too anxious to consider love."

"I am not anxious, and I am the one who must kill him."

Lazodeus touched her hair gently, and his gentleness caused a swooning desire to race up through her body. "Please?" she asked.

"No, I must go. I will see you again, soon."

"Very soon?"

He smiled. "When your Father is dead, we will be together all the time."

"I yearn for the day."

A moment later he was gone. Mary climbed out onto

the ledge and took a moment to breathe. As she looked down she saw a white shape huddled outside the house across from theirs. It took her a moment to realise what it was.

"Max?" she said under her breath. Suddenly she couldn't get into the house quick enough. She had thought the dog asleep in Father's study, where he had taken to sleeping since the fire. She raced down the stairs and out into the street, not caring who she woke. He had seemed so very still.

"Max!" she cried, running across the street and scooping him up. He was still warm. She felt his side. He still breathed. But he whimpered softly. "Oh, oh, where does it hurt? What has happened to you?"

"What is going on?" This was Father, calling out from the front door.

"My dog is hurt," Mary cried, whirling around. Betty stood at his shoulder smiling. "You!" she said in sudden realisation. "What have you done to him?"

"He was underfoot so I gave him a beating and turned him out," Betty said defiantly.

Father frowned. "Betty, such extremes are not necessary."

Mary advanced, Max in her arms. She should have taken better care of him; she should never have let him sleep in Father's study; she should not have been so involved with the angel that the poor creature whimpered on the street in pain while she enjoyed herself. But all her rage directed itself towards Betty. "You are evil," she said, her voice shaking with her attempt to control her anger.

"Nonsense. It is just a dog."

"I return to my slumber," Father said. "And so should both of you. Mary, your dog will likely recover. Calm yourself."

Mary suddenly remembered the charm in her pocket, and she produced a perfect smile for Betty. "Yes, let us return to our beds, Betty. I shall keep Max upstairs away from you, as we agreed."

483

Betty looked at her with suspicion in her eyes, but no fear. How she would regret that.

Dawn was a half hour off the horizon when Mary crept down to Betty's bedroom. Silently, silently as a ghost she slipped the charm under her stepmother's pillow. Betty frowned in her sleep and whimpered, but didn't wake. Mary leaned close and whispered, no louder than the sound of a drawn breath, "A plague on you, Mother." And once again for good measure. "A plague."

24
The River of Oblivion

Deborah had no idea whether Amelia's house on Leadenhall Street had survived the fire. As she walked down through Cripplegate, past the ruined Guildhall and along still smouldering Cornhill, she prepared herself for the eventuality that Amelia may have gone. If that were so, she didn't know who she would turn to.

The stench of a million burned substances curled around her. In places, despite the recent rain and the passage of a week, embers glowed in hollows of wrack. Black smoke still surged in columns from the ruins of larger buildings, where wood had turned to black dust, and stone had calcified to purest white. To look around was not to recognise that this place had ever been a city. The close, dark buildings had been transformed into a flattened landscape of wreckage and smoke.

She cursed herself for a fool for giving Lazodeus a chance to prove his trustworthiness. Perhaps she had just wanted so badly to believe that the exchange she had witnessed between him and Lucifer was only part of some other scheme which she did not understand. Perhaps some of the spellbinding ways which had snared her sisters had worked on her. Perhaps the idea of Father's fortune being restored seemed worth the risk. But now, there could be no doubt. Her sisters were contemplating the murder of her Father, and Lazodeus was clearly the instigator.

As Deborah picked her way over blackened remnants of

buildings, up Cornhill, she was rewarded by the sight of intact buildings ahead on Leadenhall Street. Although everything to the west of Gracechurch Street was ruined, St Peter's on the other side was still standing — scarred with shadows of flames and the trees all around burned — but still standing. She advanced up the road, finding Amelia's house and pausing a few moments out front to consider.

Amelia would not be happy to see her. She had stolen the demon key and not returned. But Amelia was responsible for calling Lazodeus to them in the first place, so only she could tell Deborah how to banish him back to where he came from.

"Miss Deborah?"

Deborah turned to see Gisela approaching, a basket on her back.

"Gisela."

"We haven't seen you for an age."

"Is Amelia here?"

"She was in the garden when I left. Go through."

Deborah hesitated. "Will she want to see me?"

Gisela stroked her wrinkled chin. "I reckon so."

Deborah followed Gisela inside. She had already decided that if Amelia wanted the demon key in exchange for information, she would give it to her. They went through the citrus-scented lounge room and the echoing kitchen out into the garden. Amelia bent her head to tending a bush of tiny, coloured berries.

"Amelia, Miss Deborah is here."

Amelia straightened her back but did not turn around. "And why should I wish to see Deborah Milton?"

"I have come to return the demon key."

She turned her head and glanced at Deborah over her shoulder. "How mightily decent of you," she said sarcastically. "Am I to believe that is the only reason you are here?"

"No, I —"

"Gisela, you are dismissed. Deborah approach. We shall discuss it further."

Deborah had never seen Amelia's garden before. It was laid out perfectly, with flagstones running a path through four distinct beds and towards a carved bench under the wall. The beds were marked out by neat rows of sheep bones, their bleached knuckles stark white against the deep green of the plants.

"I recognise none of these shrubs and flowers," Deborah said, fingering a shiny leaf.

Amelia pointed around. "Rue, angelica, wormwood, mandrake, burdock and henbane. I use them in my practice."

Deborah tilted her head sceptically. "Not in healing?"

"Yes, in healing."

"But the Royal College of Physicians has said —"

"Why have you come to me?"

She took the demon key from around her neck and held it out. "Here. I am sorry that I stole it."

"Thank you." Amelia picked it up gently and hung it around her own neck. "You are in some kind of desperate straits are you not? I do not believe you would have returned to me otherwise."

"Indeed I am. I need to banish Lazodeus."

"Why?"

"My sisters plan to kill my father. I suspect that if Lazodeus were gone they would not go through with it. They are under his spell, and his absence will return them to their true selves."

Amelia eyed her carefully. "Are you certain?"

"I hope so."

"And if you banish Lazodeus and your sisters still kill your father?"

"I will stop them by any means possible. But first I will rid our household of the angel, of their supernatural assistance."

Amelia returned her attention to her plants. "I cannot tell you how to do that."

A rage stormed up inside her. "What? But you must! 'Tis your doing that he was given to us, and now —"

"Do not lose your temper. I would tell you how to banish Lazodeus if I knew how, but I do not. Ordinarily, a prudent commander would be able to banish her angel merely by telling him to go. But your sister broke the bond of command very early on. It is irreversible."

"You jest with me. You are angry with me and you mock me with this."

"No jest, no mocking. I am sorry, Deborah."

Amelia moved about her garden, from plant to plant, trimming leaves and flicking bugs away. Deborah watched her with a barren longing in her chest. How was she to protect Father? She remembered something Amelia had told her long ago, and now she began to turn it over in her head.

"Amelia, what if I set about acquiring an angel key?"

Amelia sniffed. "Don't be ridiculous."

"But tell me, if I had an angel key, could I banish Lazodeus?"

"I will not encourage such a foolish notion."

"Tell me. You owe it to me to tell me."

Amelia whirled around. "I owe you nothing."

"My father may die."

"We all die."

"I love him. I would do anything to preserve him."

Amelia sighed and sank down on the bench. She put down her basket and touched the seat next to her. "Come here."

Deborah obediently sat next to her. In the sunlight, Amelia looked much older, with tired lines under her eyes and along the sides of her mouth.

"With an angel key," Amelia said, "you could annihilate Lazodeus. Do you know what I mean by that?"

"Yes, destroy him completely. The only way to kill an immortal creature." Deborah felt excitement build in her chest. Not just banish him back to his own realm, but to erase him forever.

"But an angel key is an extremely dangerous prospect. You may die in trying to obtain it."

"I care not." She did care, but hoped that feigning bravery would help her to feel it.

"And how would you help your father if you were dead?"

"'Tis not just my father who is at stake. 'Tis also my sisters. I must break the spell he holds over them. They tried to kill me, Amelia. They are not themselves."

"Perhaps they are themselves. Perhaps this is merely a side of them you have never seen ere now."

Deborah shook her head. "Not Anne. I hate to despise her. I hate to be her enemy. And Mary . . . we were friends once. I loved my sisters, Amelia. I would like them returned to me."

Amelia patted Deborah's knee. "I may do you a great favour by not telling you."

"You already told me once. Vaguely."

"But you were not so keen on the idea then. I told you to discourage you, for one needs to be —"

"On the point of death, I remember."

"There is no guarantee you will remain alive long enough to command angels. And even if you do, they are said to extract the highest price."

"I wish to risk it," Deborah said decisively, and knew it to be true.

"I cannot let you risk it."

Deborah jumped up and turned on Amelia. "How dare you be so prudent when you are usually so reckless! 'Tis mightily unfair."

"Lower your voice," Amelia said imperiously.

"No, I shall not. You carelessly command spirits, you have demons to love you, you recommend the learning of necromancy and never stop to think it may be dangerous to your soul's health. And yet you now draw a line in front of learning and say, no, she may not cross this line. How do you dare, Amelia Lewis?"

"Because I do not wish you harmed."

"Harmed? Has not my family already been irrevocably harmed? My sisters are enchanted into evil, my father is under threat, I nearly burned to death in Paul's! I would put a stop to all this and return things to the way they were."

"You may die. And things will never be the way they were. All things change, and they change forever."

"I shall not listen to you," Deborah said, leaning forward to press her index finger into Amelia's chest. "You know so little but pretend to know so much."

"You are an arrogant brat who has only one way of looking at the world."

Deborah pulled herself up to her full height. "I have enough information on the angel key, and I shall go to the river and dive in, and you will not stop me."

"I will not be party to a young woman's death," Amelia said calmly as Deborah turned to leave.

"A large part of this suffering is attributable to you," Deborah called over her shoulder. "Perhaps you should not have been party to a young woman's ruin."

"How are you feeling, Betty?"

Betty woke up suddenly. "What? Who's there?"

Mary crept out of the shadows. "'Tis only me. I merely asked how you were feeling."

Betty shifted uncomfortably in her bed. "I am ill. Do not vex me so, Mary."

"You are ill?" Mary said, enjoying her stepmother's discomfort.

"Yes. Where is Liza? Tell her I am awake."

"Liza has fled the house."

"What nonsense are you speaking?" Betty was trying to

sound forceful but managing only to sound weak and sick. As yet, she did not know how sick she was.

"Yes, for she no longer wishes to share your bed."

Betty shook her head. "Leave me alone, Mary, and do not torment me with your prattle. There will be time enough for us to quarrel again when I am feeling better."

"*If* you should recover."

Betty turned her back to Mary as if she intended to sleep again.

"For when Liza changed your clothes this morning she was most shocked to find something," Mary continued.

Betty was silent, but her breaths were not the slow breaths of sleep. They were shallow and anxious.

"Do you not want to know what she found?"

"Leave me be, Mary."

"Is your throat not raw? Are you not uncomfortable in all your joints?" Mary eased herself onto the bed next to Betty, stretched out beside her and stroked the back of her hair. "Check beneath the pits of your arms, Mother. You may find them all swollen with buboes."

Betty turned violently and shoved Mary away. "I said leave me be!"

"There can be no doubt that it is the plague you suffer."

"It cannot be. The sores beneath my arms are some other malady, for it takes many days for such sores to develop."

"Unless, of course, the illness is attributable to magic."

Betty was suddenly racked by a fit of coughing.

"Oh, oh," Mary said, in a small, mock-sympathetic voice. "Poor Betty, your illness advances apace. Never mind, 'twill all be over soon." Mary sprang off the bed and stood at the foot a few moments. "Max is feeling better, by the way. At least one of you will live and prosper."

Betty shook her head from side to side, racked with coughs, then sank back on the pillows, her eyes closed. Her breathing was laboured and wheezy. Mary leaned forward to pat her hand, then returned to her room.

Lazodeus was waiting for her.

"What do you think you are doing?" he demanded, and her delight at seeing him was suddenly replaced with an awful anxiety.

"I was visiting my stepmother."

"Yes, but what have you done to her?" His blue-green eyes were glittering with anger.

"I gave her an illness."

"Did I not warn you not to take it too far?"

"She beat Max! The poor thing can barely move he is so sore."

Lazodeus moved forward and grabbed her by the shoulders. "This looks very bad for me, because it was my angel magic which was used. I am under oath to injure nobody."

"That was a silly oath. Surely you should not be concerned for it now."

"I am, because the laws of the cosmos are inexorable on such things. Mary, I told you not to take it too far." He shook her lightly and she suddenly became aware of the massive physical strength which resided in his hands, the hands that had touched her so tenderly and so expertly.

"I am sorry," she wailed, heart-sick.

"When will you carry out our other plan?" he said urgently, his voice dropping to a whisper.

"Anne has just this morning gone to the markets to obtain what we need," Mary offered, eager to please him. "We shall decide this afternoon, depending on the availability of the substance, which day shall be his last."

He released her suddenly and she staggered back a few paces, rubbing her arms where he had held her. "All your attention should now be bent to that purpose, Mary. Do not disappoint me. Do not make me doubt your love."

She opened her mouth, wanting to blurt out the story of how she had almost traded her youth and beauty for contact with him, then realised that the word "almost" made the story all but ineffectual. "I shall endeavour to be more focussed."

"Leave your stepmother be. I care not what her fate is. It is her husband who must be routed."

She nodded, keen to be back in his favour. "You shall have no more reason to doubt me."

"See that I do not." He disappeared without any return to his usual tender self. It left her bereft.

When Anne returned to the house she found Mary pacing the bedroom floor.

"Sister?" Anne said, shrugging off her cloak.

"Annie, you are returned. What have you found? When can we act?"

Anne held a finger to her lips and indicated Deborah's closet.

Mary shook her head. "She is downstairs with Father."

"I went to a market near Duke's Place. They will have the poison mixed for me on Friday."

"Then we shall feed it to him on Lord's Day, for I always make supper on Lord's Day and he will suspect nothing out of the ordinary."

Anne fought down the rising tide of paralysing guilt which threatened to engulf her whenever she thought about their plan. Lazodeus's arms would make it all well again, and he had promised her they would be together always and eternally as soon as Father was dead.

"And what of Mary?" she had asked. "Will she not expect such reward as well?"

"We shall solve that problem in due course. For now, concentrate on the task at hand," he had replied.

And so she would, but with an eye on the future. "Yes, Lord's Day will be perfect," she said. And a perfect time, perhaps, for Anne to keep a little of the poison aside for Mary. How else could she ensure her sister's foolish love for Lazodeus would not stand in the way of their eternal bliss?

Betty became aware of voices through the haze of her sleep — for sleep was the only relief from the aching in her joints and the burning of her throat. Mary's words from that morning still haunted her. *There can be no doubt that it is the plague you suffer.* What an unbearable terror her words brought, for she had all the symptoms. A magic plague, pushed upon her by Mary and her witchcraft. It had been foolish to assume her stepdaughter was no longer a threat.

"Father, there is no doubt in my mind." It was Deborah's voice. She could see the shadows of her and John on the other side of the curtains.

"It cannot be, Deborah. Yesterday she was completely well. One does not contract such an advanced case of the disease overnight."

"I know it is unusual, Father, but we must not ignore it. We must send for a physician."

"We can no longer afford a physician, Deborah. You must nurse her. Liza is fled, I cannot see, and your sisters bear Betty no love."

A short silence, and Betty felt herself dropping back out of awareness. Then Deborah's voice again. "Father, will you allow me to bring someone who may help?"

"Deborah, I am wretched. I wish not to lose another wife."

"Very well. You sit with her. I shall be back as soon as I can. If Mary or Anne try to enter, prevent it by all means."

"I shall."

Betty fell into an uneasy slumber. She doubted this time whether Deborah's good magic could help.

Deborah paced anxiously in the withdrawing room.

"Sit down, Deborah. You make me nervous," Father said from his chair.

Deborah sat, winding the material of her skirt through her fingers.

"You must have little faith in this physician you have brought," Father said.

"She is not a physician."

"Then what is she?"

"She is a healer. She healed her maidservant of this very illness, many years ago." Deborah glanced towards the curtain, wishing that she could watch, but Amelia had insisted that Betty needed quiet, not a legion of people hanging apprehensively around her bed.

Father had fallen silent, his hands pressed between his knees. Deborah could not bear to see him so distressed, and to contemplate her sisters' plan froze her very soul.

"Please do not worry, Father," she said quietly, but he did not answer.

At length, Amelia emerged from the bedroom. Deborah looked up at her with guilty eyes. After their argument that morning she had been surprised that Amelia even responded to her request. Perhaps Deborah had underestimated her.

"She is resting," Amelia said.

Father jerked to his feet, straightened his shirt. "Will she live?"

"Oh yes. The illness may have strook her quickly, but it has not had time to cleave to her very strong. I have dealt with the sores, and checked that her lungs are clear. She will be well in a matter of days, given rest."

"Is it . . . safe to go near her?" Father asked.

"Yes, she is past the stage of infection. But should you suffer a sore throat or a fever, you are to tell Deborah to call me immediately."

"Thank you, Mrs Lewis," Father said, extending a hand.

Amelia shook it with a smile. "It is Miss Lewis. I knew your wife, Mr Milton."

"Katherine?"

"No, Mary. Your first wife."

Father frowned. "I see. Well, you have done a great service to our family. If Mary lived yet, she would be grateful."

Amelia suppressed a laugh and Deborah bit her lip. If

495

Father's first wife were still alive, he wouldn't have a third to tend to. But Father was finding his way through the gap in the curtains to sit with Betty, oblivious to his unintentionally comical remark.

Deborah took Amelia's hand. "I apologise for my behaviour this morning." They had spoken only of Betty's symptoms on the way from Leadenhall Street; Deborah had avoided any reference to their earlier conversation.

"You are forgiven," Amelia said in her imperious tone.

"I remembered you saying you had healed Gisela of the plague. But I never questioned you about it later because I thought . . ."

"You thought that if I hadn't studied on the continent and didn't belong to the Royal College, I could not be a proper healer?"

Deborah dropped her head. "Precisely."

"Doctors of physic study many years in stuffy libraries, Deborah, and still know less than the least village witch. Knowledge takes divers forms."

"I know. I am sorry. I was disappointed in you."

"I could not have disappointed you so greatly if you had not expected so much of me." She indicated towards the curtained room where Father sat. "You may look to others all your life as paragons and never learn about yourself. Look inside for your own strength, and stop expecting others to bestow it upon you without struggle."

Deborah pressed her lips together, chastened. "I shall think upon it," she said.

Amelia glanced around. "Walk me into the street. There is something we must discuss."

Deborah called out to Father that she would be back shortly and accompanied Amelia out onto the Walk. Slowly, strangely, London was staggering to its feet around her. The night soil man was back on the job, the endless procession of carts had come to life along the main street and the Walk was once again clogged with traffic. Amelia picked her way around a muddy hole and hitched her bag of medicines further up her shoulder. She seemed reticent, so Deborah prompted her.

"What do you wish to discuss?"

Amelia took her time in answering. They were on the main street and heading towards Cripplegate. Amelia stopped. Across the road in the Artillery grounds, the makeshift village was already growing smaller as the unfortunates within found alternative accommodation. They watched two children playing with a kite, running around in a large circle, their laughter being snatched away on the autumn breeze. Finally, Amelia turned to her.

"Your stepmother's illness was probably advanced by magic."

Deborah considered a moment. "Mary."

"With Lazodeus's help."

"Yes."

"It will recede as quickly as it came upon her, but still watch her carefully." Amelia held out the demon key on the chain about her neck. "Your demon key made an unexpected sound."

Deborah shook her head. "I'm sorry?"

"It rang out, once."

"Oh," Deborah said. "That is the alarm."

"I know it now, for I was curious and set about scrying for the answer. It rings when your sisters are together and planning your father's demise."

"I did not know it would ring more than once, more than the first time."

Amelia put a hand on Deborah's shoulder. "In the scrying water I saw your sisters planning. They intend to murder your father on Lord's Day."

Deborah took a breath against the dread. "I have little time, then."

"You could prevent them by persuading your Father to leave the house on Sunday," Amelia said.

"Then they will murder him upon his return. No, I must remove Lazodeus. He assists and inspires them."

Amelia cast her glance away again. When she returned it to Deborah, her countenance was softer than Deborah had ever seen it. "I am not angry with you for this morning's argument, because I am culpable. I know now that I am culpable."

Deborah merely nodded. It seemed inappropriate to say anything. A couple with two spaniels walked past and eyed them suspiciously.

Amelia pulled Deborah into the shade of a tree, close to a wall on which a vine crept and spilled. A handful of the leaves were turning yellow. "I did not believe that Lazodeus had tempted your sisters into patricide, because I could not believe that I had been so wrong. To call a guardian angel from among the fallen is . . . well, it is the work of an amateur, which I suppose I was then. I did not know fully what I was doing, and did not believe that it would lead you into danger." She touched her hair nervously. "I was wrong and too proud to admit it. I accept that. And I'd like to help repair the damage."

Deborah felt such a gust of relief billow into her lungs that it nearly knocked her over. "You will help me?"

"All that I can. I will tell you about the angel key, and whatever your punishment is, I will share it with you. It is the least I can do."

"I feel not so alone now."

Amelia nodded slowly. "You must understand that ridding your family of Lazodeus may not change everything back to the way it was."

"But it will release my sisters from Lazodeus's spell."

"Not if they love him. Or at least, I'm not sure. You may still have to protect your father from them. You may have to protect yourself. I cannot say for sure what will happen if you succeed."

"I will still try, Amelia. It is everything to me. My father is everything to me."

Amelia grasped Deborah's hand in her own. "Listen carefully. Take yourself to the river when you are least likely to be disturbed. Go to an empty place; it should not be difficult with so many of the docks destroyed by fire. If someone pulls you up out of the water ere you have the key, all will be foiled. Angels cannot be tricked twice."

"I see."

Amelia took a deep breath. "When you are on the very point between life and death, an angel will come to identify you, to assess your fitness for Heaven. He will lean over you, and then you must take both his hands in yours, as quickly as possible. But be not surprised if it feels curious, for you must use your subtle body, not your mortal body."

"Will I be dead then?" Deborah felt a chill creep across her skin despite the warm sunshine on the street.

"Momentarily. All that happens next will take place in the space of moments, although it may feel like much longer. You must say to the angel, 'I demand an angel key.' He will then take you away to present your case before a delegation." Amelia stroked Deborah's fingers with her own. "Be careful, Deborah."

"What will they ask me at the delegation?"

"I know not. I have never met a person who survived an attempt to command angels."

Deborah swallowed. Her throat felt dry. "Do I have any hope?"

Amelia considered. "I believe you do, for you are young and strong, and drowning is a gentle, slow death. If I do not hear from you, I will come to find your body and ensure you are properly buried."

Deborah drew her hands out of Amelia's. "I am so very frightened," she whispered.

"Are you certain you want to do it?"

Deborah looked back up the Walk towards home. "My life for Father's? Yes, I am certain."

*

The world seemed very quiet at four o'clock in the morning, and that was the clearest sign to Deborah that the city still had much to recover from. Ordinarily, a cacophony of carts and merchants would be parading the streets within the walls, but the blackened ruins lay still and silent in the half-light. The sky was not yet aglow, but Deborah could see no stars, only clouds. A light drizzle misted down as she made her way to the river.

Queenhythe was the very centre of the devastated riverfront, and Deborah headed there. A stone wall was built here, rather than the ordinary muddy banks, and Deborah climbed over and sat upon it. She shivered in the cool morning air, and flinched against the idea of how cold the water would be. Reluctance now weighed upon her. Need it be so serious? Need it be so dangerous? The answer was yes, but her body felt as though it were saying no, over and over, in every twitch of her frightened muscles.

She sat upon the wall a few minutes, then a few minutes longer. The rain came down harder now, and beat its mournful cadence on the sour ashes behind her. She turned her face up to it, let the water run into her mouth, and wondered if she would ever feel the rain on her face again.

You are young and strong. Amelia was certain that counted for something. Deborah slid into the water. It came up above her calves. She put out an unsteady hand and sunk to her knees, took a breath and plunged herself backwards. Cold. She stretched out full on her back, her arms over her head, her pale silky hair floating in strands about her.

And waited for an angel to arrive.

25

This Continent
of Spacious Heaven

Her lungs began to panic almost immediately, as if they disagreed violently with the resolution in her mind. *Breathe, breathe.* Spasms lurched through her body. A black stain crept across her field of vision. *Breathe, breathe.* Her lungs seemed poised to explode, her fingers tingled and her stomach clenched. *Breathe, breathe.* But she would not breathe. She said it over and over in her head, I will not breathe I will not breathe I will not breathe. Her ribs felt bruised by the effort, it was becoming impossible to clench them any longer. Under the river, she cried out, "Father!", and the water gushed inside her, poured through her nose and mouth, seemed to fill every crevice of her body, sour and acidic. Her head was weighed down with it, she screwed her eyes closed and felt herself fading from the world, slipping, slipping away . . .

A light above her, a circle at the end of a dark tunnel. *All is confusion, I know not where I am.* Her body was suddenly weightless and felt as though it was being pulled gently in all directions. A moment of wonder, then a blazing light flashed before her and she knew this was the angel. But how to catch him? She had assumed he would appear in mortal form. There was no time for deliberation, she propelled herself up and lunged at him. Her own hands looked ghostly and pale, yet they seized something solid. She pulled gently, and found herself looking at a pair of perfect hands. The angel had suddenly transformed into mortal form. In that moment she was nearly undone, because the great beauty of the angel fleetingly eradicated her ability to think. Here was a creature hand-carved by God, neither recognisably male nor female, a slender seraph with blazing eyes and marble skin. Lazodeus, by comparison, seemed base and dark.

"I demand an angel key," she managed, though not forcefully.

The angel fixed her with large, sad eyes. "Are you certain?" he asked. In this place between life and death, his voice seemed to emanate from all around her.

"I am certain. I must save my father."

"All will be well if you leave things as they are."

"My sisters are about to kill him."

"It is not such a loathsome thing to die."

Deborah remembered what Amelia had said about angels, that they could be cruel and despised to give mortals power over them. Despite his comforting words, she hung on. "I demand an angel key," she said again, this time with more certainty.

He blinked slowly then smiled. "Very well, hold on to my feet." He suddenly slipped from her grasp and began to move away from her. She desperately grasped his ankles and felt herself pulled upwards and upwards. From his back two mighty wings had sprouted, snowy white and beating rhythmically above her. The dark earth below moved slowly away and she felt a rolling, spinning fear of falling. A million miles seemed to fill the space between her feet and the ground. They moved towards the light above them, through the dark tunnel between the worlds.

"Can you hear it?" the angel called behind him.

"Hear what?"

"Listen."

She listened. As they drew closer to the circle of light, she could detect a sweet shimmering music: viols and pipes and harpsichord. The music seemed to sink inside her and fill her with a calm joy. "'Tis beautiful," she said.

"It is Heaven," he replied.

They swept up and up, the music grew louder and louder, vibrating through her with mellow resonance. Suddenly the circle of light opened up like a great eye, and they broke through it. Deborah closed her eyes with fear. A mighty swooshing sound shuddered over her, jolting her like a tiny boat on a stormy ocean. The music reached a desperate crescendo, breaking like colossal waves. She clung to the angel, her teeth clenched hard, her eyes screwed shut. Then a soft quiet descended upon her, the music pulsed gently as though moving on a summer breeze, and she realised she was lying on the ground.

"Open your eyes, Deborah," the sweet angel voice said.

Deborah opened her eyes and suddenly, miraculously, all anxiety and urgency evaporated. She sat up and gazed around her. A twilit landscape stretched out as far as the eye could see around her; soft grass and a balmy breeze which shifted in the treetops like a gentle caress. The trees were dark against the velvet blue sky, the stars a magnificent landscape of shimmering points. In the distance, almost hidden behind a copse of trees, was a great hall which gleamed softly in the darkness. As she was trying to make out its lineaments, a tiny pulse of light darted from behind one of the trees and raced across the sky, a cross between a shooting star and a firefly. Her eyes followed it into the darkness where it disappeared. Another light detached itself from a tree and zoomed towards her, over her head and into the twilight behind her. As it passed her, a soft feeling of well-being descended over her, and the music grew suddenly louder. She remembered in a brief instant a moment of her childhood, sitting with her first stepmother in a sunbeam in the kitchen, as a fly grazed itself against the window. Her stepmother's hands in her hair, gently stroking the silky strands. It flashed over her and then washed away; the music faded off. More of the lights darted around her, and she could feel glimmers and edges of old memories, of soft peaceful moments in ordinary corners of ordinary places, where a first breeze of autumn, or a touch of a bird's wing, or a glint of sunlight through leaves had made a fleeting impression of happiness on her then been forgotten. The memories spun out around her like a glimmering net, one suggesting another, enveloping her in a sense of flawless peace. She sank down to the ground again, felt the dewy grass beneath her fingers and gazed at the sky, temporarily dumbfounded. The firefly thoughts whizzed around her and the music swelled and sank.

"That is my favourite music," she said at last. "I am so glad to know it is also the favourite music of Heaven."

"Everyone hears different music," the angel said, "just as everyone draws different memories from the lightspinners."

"'Tis so very wonderful here," she said, knowing how profoundly understated such a sentence was.

"You cannot stay, Deborah. You are to return with your angel key if it is granted."

She sat up again. The angel sat across from her. "I do not know your name," she said.

"Natiel. I am a seraph."

"And you know who I am?"

"We know all the children of earth."

"I feel I should be frightened, but —"

"Heaven is a place of peace."

"What must I do now?"

"You must meet with a committee of angels." He indicated the gleaming hall in the distance. "You may wait here while I arrange it. I shall call you. Enjoy Heaven, for I fear a separation for you."

"What do you mean?" Deborah asked, but he had turned to leave, and nothing seemed urgent or frightening here, so the comment slipped off her. She lay down again and watched the lightspinners dart about in the soft twilight. Memories glimmered and faded, over and over, and she felt herself sinking further and further into a mood of deep serenity. Hearing her name roused her.

"Deborah!" Natiel called again. She sat up and saw the angel beckoning her from the hall in the distance. She rose and began to walk towards him, feeling weightless and tranquil. The trees were cool and dark around her and she slipped between them, a soft breeze lifting her hair. She drew closer to the hall, and a sweet smell of cinnamon and flowers enveloped her. Natiel opened the door of the hall, and somewhere in the very back of her mind, a nagging doubt occurred to her. He had said something to her earlier which she should be concerned about.

"Let everything be as it is," Natiel said, and his words instantly neutralised that fleeting doubt.

Let everything be as it is.

She ascended the gleaming stairs and entered the hall. Muted white light rose from every marbled surface, a chandelier of lightspinners hung above her, and as she looked up she momentarily forgot where she was, submerged suddenly in memories. Father touching her little head and calling her a good girl; running after Mary with a kite; the way the long grass moved one afternoon in spring; the snow that had clung to her shoe and glittered like diamonds before it melted in front of the fire; crying in Anne's arms while listening to the warm beat of her sister's heart; one of Amelia's cats purring gently in her lap; hot potato soup on her tongue; the feel of her favourite nightdress; the delicate touch of her own eyelash on her skin — oh, the miracle of an eyelash ... infinitely, infinitely perfect moments stretched out in an immense shimmering web around her.

"Deborah, welcome to the Hall of Morning."

She blinked and fixed her eyes on a trio of angels who sat before her at a long carved table. "I did not realise my life had been so filled with joys."

505

Natiel shook his head. "Hardly anyone does. Deborah, this is Huzia, warden of this celestial hall, and Poiel, a Principality."

She greeted each in turn, trying to tell between them. Magnetic perfection and symmetry characterised each face, leaving no distinguishing feature for her focus to light on.

"Do you like our kingdom of peace?" Huzia asked.

"'Tis heavenly," she said, then realised what a absurd thing it was to say and started laughing. The angels laughed with her, but she saw them exchange conspiratorial glances, and again the doubt flickered in the back of her mind.

"Let everything be as it is, Deborah," Natiel said again. "It is of no concern, for one way or another eternity will come and every man, woman and child will eventually find the pathway to this place."

It soothed her. *Let everything be as it is.*

"I need an angel key. My sisters plan to kill my father, and it is due to a fallen angel."

"We know," Poiel said. "We know the entire story."

"Then you will grant me an angel key? I wish to destroy Lazodeus."

"Are you willing to pay the price?" Natiel asked. His face seemed to darken suddenly with seriousness.

"What is the price?" she asked, that niggling doubt recurring to her.

"The price we name."

"Yes, but what is it?"

"We will tell you after the angel key is returned to us. We will confer upon it until that time."

She considered for only a moment. "I agree."

"You are certain? For as well you know, we do not like to be commanded by mortals, and expect a high repayment from them," Natiel said.

She nodded.

"Very well," Huzia said, "approach the table."

Deborah did as Huzia asked and he held out a silver rod

on a chain. She took it from him reverently and examined it closer. The silver was shot through with rainbow colours. If she focussed on it very keenly, she thought she could hear a faint ring of music emanating from it. She carefully hung it around her neck.

"Listen carefully," Poiel said. "The angel key bears mighty and dangerous powers. You are protected by angel magic now and are not susceptible to its dangers, but you must not use it near any other mortals for they may be injured or die. You must deal with Lazodeus alone. The key protects you from his subtle senses, so he will not know you are nearby unless he sees or hears you, and nor can he read your intentions. As soon as the key has appeared in his presence, he will be earthbound and must remain so until the end of the matter. When the time is right, you must say, 'I command Lazodeus's annihilation.' Seven Seraphim are contained within that key, and they will carry out your command. Then they will go, the angel key will disappear, and you may expect Natiel to call upon you soon after with your price."

Deborah nodded, trying to commit it all to memory.

"We wish you luck, Deborah," Natiel said. He glanced towards the door of the hall. "Morning fades. The sun will soon be upon us."

"Have you ever seen the sun rise in Heaven, Deborah?" Poiel asked with a slightly mocking smile.

"You know I have not."

"Go and watch it, for Father Infinite passes over at sunrise to tell his love to all angels," Huzia said.

"It is a moment you will never forget," Natiel said.

"Even if an eternity might separate you from our kingdom of peace," Poiel said.

She turned towards the door and saw that light had begun to grow outside.

"Go, Deborah. Go and witness what you may never see again."

A coldness began to grow in her stomach. "What do you mean?"

"Let everything be as it is," Natiel repeated. "Go quickly."

The sense of peace returned and she hurried her steps to the world outside. She ran through the trees and out into the open field to watch the sun's rising. The lightspinners shot past, bringing their happy ordinary memories and she stood with her back to the night, watching as the orange blaze broke over the horizon. Golden light bathed her, drawing a long shadow behind her. Birdsong rose and the sweet taste of morning kissed her lips. A swelling of promise; something wonderful was about to happen, and she could feel it at the very core of her being. Something magnificent and brilliant was about to erupt from the horizon and wash over her and it was . . .

She collapsed, fell backwards. Light moved and scudded above her, a giant tide of indescribable splendour and golden shadows, and she was suddenly awash in joy, in love, in ecstasy. *He loves me, he loves me, he loves me, he loves me, he . . .*

Cold, spluttering, choking.

"Miss, Miss, you must try to breathe."

Gasping, coughing, suffocating.

"Turn her over."

"Her lungs are full of water."

Flipped violently on her stomach. Cold, hard water splashing from her nose and retching out of her. She opened her eyes. The docks, the Thames, three men in simple clothes. She fought for air, her lungs felt bruised and twisted. Her fingers grasped at her neck, ensuring the angel key was still there.

"I saw her move."

"She is alive."

Their rough hands pressing her back, pushing the gagging water out of her. She spat and she coughed and at last she breathed. She breathed. She breathed.

"What happened, Miss?" one of the men were asking.

"He loves me," she said, and her voice broke over a sob and tears began to mix with the river water. "He loves me."

Betty clung to a corner of her bed and kept one eye open at all times. The slightest noise on the stair would send her curling up into a defensive ball, John's name on her lips. If she saw Mary again, she knew her tired heart would stop beating and she would no doubt die of fright. But what was she to do about the girl? Run away? This was her home. Any attempts to banish the girl, however, would draw more repercussions. She wished she were not too weak and tired to think about it properly.

Someone approaching. She cringed under the covers, pulling them up over her face. Not John, with his careful feel-step, feel-step on the staircase. Not Liza, who had chosen not to return. One of the girls.

"Betty?"

It was Deborah. She steeled herself. Just because the youngest girl hadn't yet turned her witchcraft on Betty, it didn't mean she never would. "What is it?"

Deborah found her way through the part in the curtains and Betty saw that she was drenched. She had an expression of such serious intent upon her face, that Betty felt herself flinch.

"What is it?" she said again. "What has happened? Why are you wet?"

"Betty, listen to me," Deborah said, sinking on the bed next to her.

Betty scrambled away.

"You are so serious. You frighten me."

"I know you are still ill," Deborah said. "But you and Father must get out of the house."

"Why?"

"Be not so frightened. You will be safe. I am on the verge of putting an end on this whole wretched affair."

"Get off the bed. You are wet. I shall catch a chill and die if you soak the covers."

Deborah did not respond. "This afternoon, you and Father must purpose to go for a walk —"

"I am suffering from a terrible illness!"

"You are recovering rapidly. The illness was advanced by magic, it did not take hold of your body completely. Trust me. To stay here a moment longer is far worse. You must walk with Father, and at the bottom of the hill I shall have a hackney coach waiting for you to take you to Dartford for the night, where the driver shall drop you at a good inn and return to collect you the next morning."

"We cannot afford a hackney coach. We cannot afford an inn."

"Betty," Deborah said, raising her voice, "you must listen to me and you must do as I say. If you do not wish to preserve yourself I would allow it, but you must preserve Father."

Her stern tone jolted Betty into silence.

"I will pay the driver of the coach in advance for the whole expedition. He will arrive at five of the clock. You are to take Father for a walk, saying you are much recovered and you wish to take some fresh air. You are to lead him to the coach, put him in it and say it is Deborah's command, and Deborah says he must trust her. He *must* trust me."

"If he does not? If he purposes to turn and come home?"

"You must not let him." Deborah reached over for her hand, but Betty withdrew it. "Betty, it is of extreme importance that you take care of this matter."

Betty felt a terrible frightened sadness well up within her. "I despise you," she said. "I despise all of you."

"When you return tomorrow it will be over. None of us, not me, not Anne and certainly not Mary, will have anything beyond the ordinary powers to control the world around us. My older sisters may be sent away as apprentices and they will have no means to stop you." Deborah sighed.

"All will be well for you."

Betty knew she had little choice. What Deborah promised was her dearest wish. As much as she didn't want to give Deborah the gratification of seeing her bend so easily to her will, she nodded once. "I shall do it then."

Deborah sank forward, and Betty noticed for the first time the dark shadows beneath her eyes. "What happened to you, child?" she said, more softly than she intended.

"I believe I may have done something foolhardy." She pressed her face into her hands then looked up to meet Betty's gaze. "What is your fondest memory, Betty?"

"Why, I don't know."

"You must have at least one fond memory. You must know a moment in which all was happy."

Betty shook her head, wondering why Deborah was asking her. "My life has been very ordinary up until recently, when it has become frightening and precarious. There have been no great moments of joy."

"What about small moments of joy?" Deborah said.

Betty waved her away. "Go and dress in dry clothes. You will catch a chill and then be no use to anyone."

Deborah rose and left, heavy footed. Betty watched her leave and then pressed her fingers against her lips. All so complicated. She hoped Deborah was right. She hoped it would soon be over.

Father was grumbling and Betty was coughing and Deborah was sure her plan was doomed to fail as, that afternoon shortly before the bells had rung five, she realised just how stubborn Father could be.

"Betty, you are ridiculous. Just yesterday morning you were on death's door, and now you want to walk! Go back to bed and rest. A dead wife is of no use to me."

"But I am well!" Another cough. Deborah winced.

"You sound unwell."

"I believe it was a short illness which has now passed. My

heart beats strongly and I wish more than any remedy for fresh air. Please, John, we needn't walk far."

"Father, I can vouch for Betty's colour," Deborah said. "Her cheeks are rosy and her eyes bright." This was very far from the truth, and Betty's look of exasperation acknowledged it.

"And what if she should fall ill while we walk? What if she collapses and I cannot revive her?"

"'Twill not happen, John," Betty said.

"I shall walk with you, then," Deborah said suddenly. "I will be the guardian of you both."

Father relented. "Very well, if she is determined to walk."

"Yes, I am," Betty said.

Deborah heard footsteps on the stairs and her skin itched with anxiety. How was she to get her sisters out of the house next?

Still, one problem at a time.

"Very well, let us go, for evening will soon be upon us," Deborah said, leading Father to the door and fixing his hat upon his head. "Come, Father, here are your gloves."

Betty looked very pale and Deborah hoped she was not sending her stepmother into the arms of a greater infection. She steeled herself against such thoughts. It must be over. It must be over soon. She ushered them out in front of her and began the descent down the hill. She could see the hackney coach waiting at the bottom of the Walk — she had paid for the whole venture from the bag of conjured guineas — and felt her pulse rise. It was up to Betty to get Father into the coach. They approached it slowly. A few yards away, Deborah said, "I have a hole in my shoe."

Betty turned to her and gave her a determined nod. "Return home then. We shall wait here at the corner."

Father stood staring into blind nothing, unaware of the plan.

Deborah pressed two guineas into Betty's hand. "I shall return presently."

Betty eyed the money in shock. "Good luck," she managed, as Deborah ran up the hill.

Deborah paused at the door of their house, could see Betty and Father arguing. Long moments passed. She watched, her breath held in the hollow of her throat. Then, miraculously, Father was climbing into the coach and the driver was assisting Betty.

Thank you, Betty, thank you.

She turned to the house and was suddenly hit by a wave of sensation. He was here. Lazodeus was already here. Upstairs, in the bedroom.

Would she leave him be? Or would it be imprudent? After all, she had no guarantee that he would come when she called, other than a faith in his cunning and his desire to ensnare her as firmly as her sisters. Perhaps he was alone.

She felt around her neck for the angel key. Its cool weight rolled between her fingers.

"It is time, Lazodeus," she said under her breath. "You shall let my sisters go."

26
Our Circuit Meets Full West

Anne had laid down for only a moment — a brief rest from the immense load of holding her head up under such unbearable pressure — and the dream was upon her as soon as her eyes fluttered closed. *A funeral, her dead father in state, she comes to kiss his brow, his skin is smooth and cool, voices in the distance chatter and laugh but she is very cold and alone, he opens his eyes, his hand reaches up to seize her face, he hisses, "I see you, Anne, at last I see you."*

She woke with a start, her hand pressed to her breast. Was this what the rest of her life would be, suffering this awful burden of guilt? She rolled onto her side and her dark hair fell over her face. She had been fighting back sobs of terror and exertion since the night Lazodeus had proposed his plan. Her fear was that if she began to cry, if she let the thoughts that plagued her overwhelm her, she may lose her resolve. That resolve was growing weaker and weaker by the day, and she both longed for and dreaded Lord's day. She knew that to keep Lazodeus — to have him by her forever, her dearest wish granted — she had to do as he said. But every time she slipped into that dream, she wondered if she would be capable of it at the end. Would her softer nature, her damnable timidity, undo her at the very moment she was to prove herself to him?

A soft touch on the back of her neck made her catch her breath. Anne turned over to see Lazodeus crouching by the side of the bed.

"Hello, my love," he said, and for an instant — just an instant — she wondered if he had read her thoughts and made this visit to sway her more keenly to her purpose. But then he smiled at her, and any suspicion of manipulation evaporated. He loved her.

"Why are you here?" she asked. "I thought your visits were limited until the deed is done."

"They are, but I missed you so badly." His fingers grazed her cheek. "And here I find you looking so sad. What is the matter?"

"I am afraid."

"We all know fear."

She opened her mouth to speak again, but he trailed his finger over her lips and moved onto the bed next to her.

"Lazodeus, my sisters may be nearby."

"No, Mary is in the garden and Deborah is not here. We are quite alone."

The sheer curtain on the window moved in the breeze, sunlight diffused through it. Anne found herself beginning to relax. "I have missed you, too, angel."

"Soon we shall be together always," he said, his lips touching hers in tiny, butterfly kisses. "Do you not look forward to that?"

"'Tis all my pleasure to think upon it," she said. His deft fingers were unlacing her house dress and loosening the buttons on the top of her shift. "Shall we make love every day?"

"Perhaps," he said, his hand enclosing one of her small breasts.

"What else shall we do, tell me?"

His lips moved down her neck and across her collarbone. "We shall do whatever you wish, Annie."

"Will you be happy?"

He looked up at her and fixed her in his green-blue gaze. She was astonished again by the clarity of his eyes. "I will be happy, I promise I will be happy. Will you? Will you be happy that you have saved me from imprisonment, that you will bring me praise and honour in Pandemonium?"

"Of course, of course I will be." His lips descended and her dream was forgotten.

Deborah took the stairs with painful slowness and care. To give herself away now would be foolish and irreversible. Her presence would bind Lazodeus to the earth so that she could finish this business finally. If he fled before she got there . . .

Strange how she could sense him in her mind; like a warm itch in the field of her perceptions. She saw her own hand stretched out before her, reaching for the door. It swung in. She stopped and caught her breath.

A naked woman lay upon the bed in Lazodeus's arms, her dark hair covering her face. Deborah's first thought was that it must be Mary, but the arms and wrists were too thin, the hair too straight and long. Anne sat up and shrieked.

"Get out!"

Lazodeus staggered back, fixing her with a desperate look of fearful wonder.

"How did you —?"

"Get out!" Anne screamed again, throwing a pillow and pulling her shift against her naked body.

"No, Anne," Deborah said, taking two steps into the room and standing firm. "'Tis you must get out. Leave me with the angel."

"I shall not."

A look of horror began to grow across Lazodeus's face, and his mouth moved once, twice, without him saying anything.

"What?" Anne said, looking to Lazodeus. "What is it? Why do you look so horrified? You are frightening me, my love."

"Oh, Deborah," Lazodeus said, his voice quiet yet heavy with portent. "Deborah, what have you done?" His fear seemed to be as much for her as it was for him, and a frosty finger touched her heart.

"I have done what I had to do. Now tell Anne to get out, for you know she will be harmed."

"What is going on?" Anne said, turning a frightened and confused face to Deborah. Tears had begun to stream down her cheeks and her attempts to dress herself had stalled. "Why do you both look so pale? What is happening?"

All at once Lazodeus seized Anne by the shoulders and pressed her in front of him like a shield. "You will not harm your sister," he said boldly, and he was right.

"Lazodeus, what is happening?" Anne sobbed.

"Her purpose is to annihilate me," Lazodeus said, his eyes never leaving Deborah's. "She has an angel key . . . she may command angels against me."

Anne looked in gape-mouthed horror at first one, then the other of them, and began to scream. "NO! No, Deborah you shall not! No! I won't allow it. I love him, I love him!"

"Be quiet," Deborah said. "Lazodeus, let her go. Be not so timid that you cower behind a mortal woman."

"As long as you are with me, she will not do it," Lazodeus said to Anne, "for to use the angel key in the presence of a mortal is to cause them terrible injury."

Anne dropped her shift and spread her arms in front of Lazodeus in a protective gesture. "Ha! Hear that, sister? I can protect him."

"I can finish him anyway, and choose to let you be harmed," Deborah said, but there was little conviction in her words and she knew it. She had acquired the angel key to protect her family, not to destroy them.

A noise on the stairs. Mary. Deborah felt her heart sink.

"What's all that noise? Why are you shrieking so, Anne?"

Lazodeus let go of Anne. "Cover yourself," he said. But it was too late. Mary already stood in the doorway, gaping at naked Anne in Lazodeus's arms.

"Lazodeus?" she said, in a little girl voice.

Anne was pulling on her shift, buttoning it unevenly.

"Anne?" Mary said.

Deborah wondered if this revelation could work for her. "I came in here to find them making love, Mary. Your sister has betrayed you. Your angel has betrayed you."

Mary turned a contemptuous gaze on Deborah, but Deborah could see her chin working against the effort of holding back a sob.

"Mary," Lazodeus said, "Deborah purposes to destroy me, but she will not as long as you and Anne are with me."

Mary seemed hesitant to react, and Deborah found herself feeling as though time had slowed, and that they would play out forever this one scene. The angel key, faithless Lazodeus, her sisters regarding each other as enemies. But then Mary took four quick steps towards the candlestand by the bed and seized the heavy brass candlestick with purpose. Deborah quickly went to stay her hand, for she thought Mary intended to strike Anne with it. But Mary turned, and with a mighty heft, brought the candlestick down on Deborah's head.

Deborah staggered back, her palm flying to her forehead. Blood. A loud ringing in her ears, darkness on the periphery of her vision. Mary pushed her, she crashed to the floor.

"You shall not harm him," Mary said to her. Then to the others. "Come, I know where we can go."

All three of them fled, Anne fiddling with the buttons on her housedress. Deborah tried to sit up, but her head was a millstone. Her hand clutched at the mat, but then the ringing in her ears became too loud to bear, and she slipped into a swoon.

Mary led Lazodeus and Anne down the Walk and along Bun Hill, then through the gate into the city.

"Come, Anne, keep up," Mary called cruelly, for Anne was without her shoes and the streets of the city were still strewn with blackened rubbish.

"Go slower," Anne cried. "I will hurt my feet."

Mary hoped she would hurt her feet. Mary hoped she would cut them to ribbons. Lazodeus belonged to Mary, and if Anne had to learn that through pain and suffering, then so be it.

"I cannot go slower, for I must save Lazodeus's life," Mary called behind her.

Lazodeus urged her forward. "Where are we going?" he asked.

"Sir Wallace's house is part burned. He removed his possessions and went to the country, but the house still stands and Deborah will not thinking of looking for us there."

"Wait!" Anne cried out, as they pulled ahead of her.

Lazodeus was a few steps in front now, and Mary quickly doubled back and grabbed Anne's elbow.

"Thank you, sister," Anne said.

Mary smiled, then kicked both Anne's feet from under her, tripping her roughly to the ground.

Anne cried out in pain. "Oh! My ankle!"

"I am sorry, Anne, we have no time to wait. Lazodeus's safety is at stake." She didn't look behind her, but hurried her step, urging Lazodeus on. "Come," she said, "we proceed faster without her."

"I may need both of you."

"She can't keep up. She slows us down and Deborah might catch us."

He glanced over his shoulder. "You are not to think that I encouraged her to expose herself to me. The poor girl has been in love with me for some time."

Mary felt a little satisfaction settle her troubled heart. "I know not what to think. But I assure you we need her not. I will cleave to you closely. Deborah cannot win this."

Anne sobbed wretchedly as she picked herself up. Her feet were bleeding and her ankle felt as though the very bone had been twisted, but she could not let Mary and Lazodeus out of her sight. She saw them disappear up an alley ahead and hobbled in that direction, every step an arrow of pain, leaving bloody footprints behind her on the filthy, ash-stained cobbles. This part of the city had been touched by the fire but not levelled, so it would be easy for Mary to lead Lazodeus via a convoluted route in order to lose her.

She struggled to the corner and saw Mary's red dress disappear to the left. Hobbling as fast as she could, she gave chase. The sun was sinking, and it had stained the sky blood orange. Amongst the approaching shadows of evening it was hard to distinguish the shape of her sister darting through alleys. A moment later, she emerged on the remains of Cradle Alley and saw Mary and Lazodeus running. The city had cleared a path through the wreckage here, and Anne gritted her teeth and ran after them. They disappeared into a house at the end of the alley. One side of it had been burned, the other was still intact.

Mary met her at the door. "Stay out, sister, we can manage this ourselves."

"Please, Mary," Lazodeus called from within. "Stay by me. Let Anne in."

"What did you think you were doing with him?" Mary asked in a hiss. "As if he would ever love you."

"He does love me," Anne replied, her face straining to hold itself together. "Let me in."

Lazodeus appeared at the door beside Anne and pulled her in, then dropped the latch. "Both of you, stop arguing and stay here by me."

"Lazodeus, tell her it is me you love!" Anne cried.

Lazodeus roughly seized first Anne's shoulder then Mary's, held them in front of him and leaned forward with a dark face. "I may die!" he shouted. When both of them cringed away, he dropped his voice. "Do you understand that? Your sister has acquired the power to annihilate me. I do not know how many Seraphim she has with her, I do not know what she intends or when. All I know is that she will not destroy me while other mortals are nearby, for she knows it may destroy them as well. So you must stay with me and you must stop fighting with each other. I have to think about a way to save myself." He released them and stalked to the window to watch the street.

"We'll do anything," Mary said quickly.

"Why do you not return to Pandemonium?" Anne suggested.

"Do you think I have not thought of that?" Lazodeus said impatiently. She could not bear his anger, it hurt her heart more than the cruel ground had hurt her feet. "The key has me earthbound. I am already falling under its power."

"Haply I strook her hard enough to kill her," Mary said.

"No, she is alive, or the key would not still be exerting its influence. I cannot escape."

"Maybe we can —"

"Quiet!" Lazodeus roared, turning from the window. "Both of you be quiet and let me think. Anne, wash your wounds, you bleed upon the floor."

Anne looked around properly for the first time. They were in a rich man's house — she could tell by the coloured paint and the oriental carpet tacked to the floor — but none of the rich furnishings were present. The house was a hollow shell. Stairs led up to other rooms, which she presumed would also be empty. The carpet was faded in patterns around where furniture had stood. She could pick out the shape of a grand couch, a large table. Her own bloody footprints stained the carpet.

"The kitchen is through there," Mary said, indicating. Anne hobbled in that direction. Water had not yet been restored to the pump, but a bucket stood by the fire and she plunged her feet into it, feeling the sweet pain of relief. She took a few moments to dress her wounds with an old apron which she tore into strips, then returned to the large room where Mary and Lazodeus were pulling up the carpet.

"What is happening?" she asked, hurt that she had been left out of this plan.

"We have decided to call one of Lazodeus's colleagues through," Mary said. "In the same way you and I and Deborah did when we first summoned Lazodeus."

"He may be able to take me back with him, as he has not yet been in the presence of the angel key," Lazodeus explained. "Can you find something to draw a triangle with?"

Anne nodded, eager to be involved. "Yes, certainly." She went back onto the street to find a lump of charcoal good for drawing. She glanced around. The street was deserted. Deborah was nowhere in sight.

"Hurry, Anne," Lazodeus called.

"I am here," she replied, latching the door behind her again. She handed Lazodeus the charcoal and he bent to the floor to draw a triangle on the boards. She watched him lovingly, becoming slowly aware of her sister's gaze. She looked up. Mary met her eyes and there was nothing but venom and hatred within them. Anne realised then that each of them wished death upon the other, and her heart waxed sad and sick.

When she could raise her head, Deborah took a moment to assess how far across the sky the sun had moved since Mary had struck her. Late afternoon, an amber-gold glimmer still upon the clouds. It had been perhaps half an hour then. She put a hand to her aching head and felt the congealed blood, the swelling lump. Then her fingers went to her throat and found the chain for the angel key. She pulled it out and considered it, its rainbow colours moving and shifting as she rolled it between her fingertips.

Where was Lazodeus? Again, the feverish prickling began. He was in the city somewhere. She tried to stand, but it took a few moments as a fit of dizziness seized her. She hoped that she was well enough to go through with this.

And then what?

She refused to contemplate it, though the question raised itself at every gap between her thoughts. The decision had been made; she had acquired the angel key, and now matters were irreversible.

An eternity might separate you from our kingdom of peace. Poiel's words, returning to her as on a random breeze.

"I will not contemplate it," she said aloud, holding her head between her hands. She breathed; she attempted to restore her reason, to pull the threads of her judgement together. It was important to be fixed to her purpose. She stood. The dizziness came, then passed. A tentative step towards the door. Steady. She drew a poker from the fireplace — protection from her sisters. Another step towards the door. She paused, leaning on the doorjamb. Then kept moving, down the stairs and out onto the street, down the Walk and through the ruined gate into the city.

It was growing dark. The stench of sour smoke and ashes surrounded her. Here and there, embers still glowed within the wreckage. She used the fire poker as a walking stick to support her. A wave of dizziness descended. How far away were Betty and Father now? Would he expect an explanation on his return? The thought discomfited her momentarily, but then perhaps she had more to be frightened of than Father's disapproval.

She paused and closed her eyes, located Lazodeus once more in her senses. To the east. She reoriented herself and hurried down between the collapsed houses and half-burned churches, through smouldering alleys and across wreckage still hot enough to be felt through the soles of her shoes. A last finger of daylight faded out behind her, and she turned to watch it slip over the ruined horizon. The unwilling comparison to the sunrise she had witnessed that morning was a shock to her perception: this hellish landscape of devastated, smouldering London and her knowledge that she was despised by her sisters and feared by Lazodeus, compared to the soft heavenly twilight where she had felt an infinite love beyond imagining, an absolute annulment of every lumbering woe and weary longing. She stumbled and almost fell, used the poker for support as she caught her breath and headed down Cradle Alley. The house suggested itself to her almost immediately. Mary had pointed it out once, long ago, as Sir Wallace's home. The side closest the street was crumbling and hollowed by fire, but the side off the street was unharmed. She slunk into shadows and paused to assess it. Oh, he was in there, for certain. She could feel it like the hot tingle of a flea bite, and she actually had to reach up and scratch her scalp to alleviate the irritation.

"I shall finish this business with you, angel," she said, under her breath. They would have latched the door, with no doubt. But through the ruined side of the building she could see the remains of a small room, a broom closet with a sagging door exposed to the elements. It would lead under the stairs, and it would not be barred for only a fool would fit a latch to a broom closet.

Deborah edged up the alley, cleaving to the shadows of the half-ruined houses, sinking into crevices to hide and peer, then moving slowly, slowly up the alley. At last she dashed across and into the side of the house, among the blackened wood and fallen beams. The remains of the closet still retained their shape. She picked her way carefully towards it, misjudging the height of the lintel and striking her head on it. The wound reopened, and blood once again began to trickle from it. Deborah bit her tongue to control her cry of pain, and paused to still her dizzy mind. She pressed her hand to her head, and when she brought it back to check for blood, she saw her fingers were black with soot. She was filthy from head to toe. The door was less than two feet away and she paused to catch her breath.

Show him no fear. Show him no mercy. Make him believe you would sooner see your sisters dead than in his thrall.

She stilled her trembling hand and opened the door.

"You must repeat exactly what I say." Lazodeus positioned Anne by grasping her shoulders and moving her to the first point of the triangle. She nodded, then watched as Lazodeus positioned Mary similarly.

"Very well," Lazodeus said. "Listen carefully and repeat." He grabbed their hands and indicated they should do the same. "Rimmoneus, angel of the order of virtues, come to us and stand within this triangle so that your brother may be saved."

"Rimmoneus," the girls intoned with him, "angel of the order of virtues . . ."

Anne felt a warmth growing in her bound feet. As they reached the end of the first chant, it had grown to a sharp heat.

"Rimmoneus," they began again, and this time the heat flared to such an unbearable intensity that she had to jump from her place.

"What are you doing?" shouted Lazodeus.

"I am sorry," Anne cried wretchedly. "Something burned my feet and they are already so sore."

"Get back in your place," Mary said imperiously, and Anne did as she was told.

"Rimmoneus, angel of the order of virtues . . ." She saw Mary shift from foot to foot, and anxiety gripped her. Nothing like this had happened when they called Lazodeus, but then there hadn't been an angel in the triangle. Anne endured the heat as long as she could, and this time Mary jumped.

"Ow!"

"What is wrong?" Lazodeus snapped.

Anne moved from her place and saw that the floorboards were beginning to smoulder. "Something is wrong,

Lazodeus," she said. "A terrible heat radiates from the points of the triangle."

"And you will allow that to stop you saving me?" Lazodeus cried. Anne had never heard him sound so desperate and it terrified her.

"I —"

"What matter is it if you should both be burned to ashes? Will you not save me? Will you not save the angel you love so greatly?"

Mary stood across from her, agape. Anne shook her head. "I . . . of course I will save you. I would die for you."

"Then stand in your spot."

"Must we die for you?" Mary asked, and Lazodeus turned on her.

"Why do you plague me with these questions? Can you not simply do as I ask?"

"We shall do as you ask, my love," Anne said. "Here, I stand again upon the point. I shall suffer the very flesh to be burned from my feet if only you will —"

"Quiet, Anne!" Mary called. Then to Lazodeus, "Must we die for you?"

The question remained unanswered when a sudden thump from under the stairs drew their attention. Deborah emerged, smeared with soot and blood, brandishing a fire iron.

Lazodeus shrank from her, pulled Mary and Anne in front of him. "Your chances of success are not improved," he said. "You see, your sisters have decided to stand by me."

"I care not for my sisters," Deborah spat.

Lazodeus cowered behind them. "You will not see them harmed. I know what you are, Deborah Milton, and you know what you are, and you will not see your sisters harmed."

"See you not this wound?" Deborah said, pointing two fingers at the gash in her forehead. "My *sisters* did this. See me covered in soot? 'Tis not the first time my *sisters* have seen me like this, but last time they were locking me in a burning church."

Anne had never heard Deborah sound so furious. All her usual cool reason appeared to have burned away.

"So you'll forgive me if I now believe that my *sisters* should have their lives forfeit for my father's life, and for the pleasure of destroying you."

Lazodeus shook his head, and Anne felt his fingers drill harder into her shoulder. "I do not believe you."

Deborah merely pulled out the chain around her neck and dangled a silver rod in front of her. "Do you not? It will hurt you no more or no less to be annihilated should you not believe me."

Anne felt his fingers tremble and could bear his fear no longer. She sprang forward and made to snatch at the angel key, but Deborah raised the fire iron and grazed it across Anne's shoulder. Anne braced herself for the pain, but when she looked down, her dress had been torn and the wound was very shallow. She understood immediately that Deborah was bluffing. If she were serious, she could have run Anne through completely.

"She is lying," Anne said, turning to Lazodeus. "She will not harm us."

Lazodeus and Deborah locked stares across the room.

"Look you, she has barely grazed me," Anne said.

"I am dizzy from the blow to my head," Deborah said stonily. "I had aimed for your heart. But fear not, Lazodeus, I have not forgotten a word of the command for your annihilation."

Lazodeus shook his head. "Anne is right. I do not believe you would do it in the presence of your sisters."

Deborah raised the key. "I command —"

Lazodeus fled, nearly knocking Anne and Mary over. He dashed to the stairs and Deborah was fast on his heels. Anne heard a door slam above; she and Mary were on the stairs in moments, running up, arriving at the door and pushing it.

Deborah had latched it.

"Don't hurt him!" Anne screamed. "Don't hurt him!"

Mary pelted the door with her fists. "I hate you!" she shouted. "I hate all of you!"

"We must break the door down," Anne said, grabbing Mary by the shoulders. "Calm yourself, we must find something with which to break the latch. A stone, or a piece of hard wood."

Mary shook her head. "It is over."

"I will not see him destroyed," Anne said, racing down the stairs. "I *shall* save him."

27
Eternity, Whose End No
Eye Can Reach

Deborah dropped the latch behind her and turned to see Lazodeus cowering in a corner. He had run into a windowless bedroom, and now she had him trapped. The only light in the room came from under the door, and from the angel himself, and Deborah waited a moment for her eyes to adjust.

"You are not so magnificent now," Deborah said to him.

"Please, Deborah, show me mercy."

She held out the key. "I intend as much mercy to you as you intended my father."

"Then listen to reason!" he begged, dropping to his knees. "Please, put the key away a moment and listen to reason. You are rational, you are clever, you must be swayed by reason."

Deborah did not drop the key, but she was curious. "What reason will you offer me?"

"You have been to Heaven. I know you have for you possess an angel key."

"That is correct."

"You know, then, that your father will proceed to that place upon his death."

"Yes."

"But I have no hope beyond my destruction if you choose to proceed with it. Once I am annihilated, I cease to be. I am no more." He began to sob. "Do you not understand what a terror that is to me? Where will I be? What will happen to the spark that I am now? I cannot contemplate such a profound darkness. Will everything I *am* be gone? My memories, my aspirations, my desires? I cannot bear it, can you not see? Can you not imagine such a terror?"

His fear was a cold spark in the room. She felt it keenly for she had known such questions in her life: *What if nothing awaits me after my demise?* But now she knew for certain that something did await her, and Lazodeus knew equally for certain that nothing awaited him.

Her hesitation encouraged him. He stretched out his great length full on the floor. "Deborah, you are wise and you are reasonable. Please do not assign to me such a fate."

"You lied to me, you betrayed me. You've poisoned my sisters against me and sought to kill my father."

"I am that which God made, just as you are that which your Father made. I have been banished for countless millennia from my homeland, from that perfect world which you call Heaven." He looked up at her, his blue-green eyes gleaming. "Deborah, you have seen it. You have felt his love. Is it not punishment enough that I am so irrevocably separated from him?" Tears coursed down his face and she felt herself moved. "I beg you, I beg you."

"Yet if I exercised my mercy, how could I ensure you stayed away from my sisters?"

"Use the angel key to banish me back to Pandemonium under condition. It is easy and it is binding. The Seraphim within that key must do as you say to the last letter." He drew himself up to his knees. "Please, Deborah. I do not want to be nothing."

Moments ticked past, and Deborah felt herself to be very young to make such a decision. Yet if he was forbidden from interfering with her sisters and Father, who was she to take the last essence of such a creature? She flinched from killing spiders; she hated the sound of a pig being slaughtered or the mad flapping of a fish in the markets. And yet, these creatures may very well also proceed to that kingdom of peace, of which Lazodeus would have no hope.

"Lazodeus, I will grant you the mercy you ask," she said quietly. "But you must go with the Seraphim, and not look upon me more."

His head bowed forward and she could no longer see his face. "Very well, Deborah. I await my fate."

Mary waited at the top of the stairs, her ear pressed against the door. She could hear nothing. The wood was heavy and thick.

"Out of the way, Mary."

She turned. Anne trudged up the stairs with her bandaged feet, a large rock held in both hands.

"Tell me, sister," Mary said, "why were you naked with Lazodeus?"

"There isn't time for such a conversation," Anne said, averting her eyes.

"Do you know that I have laid with him?" Mary said.

"I believe you not."

"Why do you not? I have laid with many."

"Out of the way, Mary. I shall break the latch."

"He says he loves me, Anne."

Anne paused, her fingers white as they gripped the rock. "You lie."

Mary cocked her head and gave Anne an inquisitive look. "Are you certain?"

"Yes I am certain," Anne said softly. "For he says he loves me."

"And after we killed Father, you and he would be together eternal?"

"Yes."

"And has he laid with you? Has he touched your body and made you sigh?"

"Yes," Anne said more forcefully. "Now, out of my way."

Mary rose, descended two steps towards Anne, put her hands on her sister's shoulders. "You have all betrayed me." She felt the fury twist up through her like a storm. The only way to stop it bursting out of her body was to push with all her might. "Let him die!" she called, as she watched Anne tumble down the stairs, the rock flying from her hands. "You may all die for I care not!"

She ran down the stairs after Anne, stepped over her motionless body at the bottom, and fled into the dark.

Deborah held the key up and took a deep breath. She wanted to be sure she got it right.

"I command Lazodeus's banishment to Pandemonium, that he may never interfere with my sisters, my father nor my stepmother for the rest of their lives and into eternity."

Faintly, faintly . . .

Approaching . . .

Looming out of the very walls . . .

Music! The joyous ring of music washed through her and surrounded her, and she was once again as content and at peace as she had been in Heaven. Lights began to gather in the room. One, two, three . . . all the way to seven. They grew in intensity enough to blind her, but she stood and watched awestruck, protected somehow by the key, able to see all the way into the burning light to its perfect core.

The lights became larger, and Deborah glimpsed the flash of a wing, the curve of a shoulder. Yet they did not take mortal form. Their growth began to shake the walls of the room, and a loud creak sounded from somewhere below. The house, already half destroyed, began to shift precariously. Even so, Deborah did not flinch.

Lazodeus shuddered on the floor before her, began to cry out in fear.

"Let everything be as it is," she said.

The Seraphim crowded around him now, picking him up

532

under the arms and lifting him into the air, so that he appeared to hang suspended upon a wall of light. The music grew louder and louder, shuddering through her body and through the walls. Lazodeus looked up at her, his blue-green eyes met hers and she felt a shock to her heart for his beauty in this moment of his ruin.

"Deborah," he said. "I shall be with you upon the day you die."

"What do you mean?"

"I shall compete for your soul. I shall battle whichever angel is sent for you and I shall have you with me in Pandemonium."

"What do you mean?" she shouted, but the music had grown to a deafening roar and the lights had intensified to a blinding sheet and the house began to shake.

Whiter and whiter. Louder and louder. Lazodeus's dark figure being sucked into the perfect brilliance until he was no more than a grey speck at its centre.

In an instant, it stopped. The key dissolved from between her fingers.

The sudden absence of the music was nearly as deafening as the music itself. Her eyes saw everything blue, but she could tell that the room was empty except for her. Lazodeus was gone. The house shuddered and then stilled, but nothing could still the violent quaking of her body, the riotous course of her blood through her veins, the jumping of her heart.

"What do you mean?" she asked again in the silence. A chunk of plaster fell from the ceiling and bounced on the carpet.

No answer came.

The house on Artillery Walk was dark and silent. Mary closed the front door behind her and sagged against it. She took a moment to catch her breath, then straightened herself and strode in.

"Max? Max, little friend? Where are you?" She went to the kitchen and lit a candle. Under a cloth she found a round of cheese. Max limped in. He was recovering well from his beating, but still required delicate handling. She picked him up gently and lowered him onto the table. He licked her hand and his tail wagged.

"Dear little friend," she said, cutting him some cheese and feeding it to him. She cut another chunk for herself. "We're going away, Max. We're leaving horrible Betty and horrible Father behind and we're going back to Forest Hill. You like it there, don't you little man? You like the big fields, I know." She continued cutting bites of cheese, one for Max, one for herself. Max devoured them eagerly. "Mary's going to marry a rich man, Max. Do you remember Sir Adworth? I think he shall die before you, but he has pots of money. You shall have a diamond collar and a velvet cushion to sleep upon."

She sank into a chair and Max licked her fingers, finding every last smear of cheese. "Grandmamma will have us until Adworth invites me, but you must be good in the coach and don't watch Mary. She has to pay the fare somehow."

The dog squirmed into her lap and she held him for a long time, felt his warm heart beating. Just as he was settling down to sleep, she rose. "Come, Max. I shan't pack, for Adworth will no doubt buy me many fine dresses. I shall live a life of finery and I shall not love again, except for you."

Max barked happily at her heels as she led him out into the street, down the Walk to the main road. She hailed down a coach and did not look back.

"Could it be true?" Deborah asked Amelia as they sat amongst the cats in her withdrawing room. "Could he have a claim on my soul?"

It was morning, but Amelia, as always, had drawn the

curtains against the sun. Deborah had come early to tell the whole tale. She hoped violently that Lazodeus's last words to her were an empty threat.

Amelia cupped her chin in her hand. "Let us go over it again. You ordered that he stay away from your sisters and your father?"

"Yes. Even Betty!" She cursed herself for the millionth time for her short-sightedness. Perhaps it had been the earlier blow to her head, or perhaps he had worked some of his magnetic magic on her. Either way, she had made a crucial error. "But I forgot to order him to stay away from me."

"Then he can return. But I should think he will not."

"Why?"

"Because he is afraid of you now. You have commanded an angel key. He may think you too great a risk to antagonise."

"And yet he said he would return on the day of my death."

"Because you will be weak and old or sick. You will pose no threat."

Deborah leaned forward. "And he may compete for my soul?"

"'Tis possible. Few angels would bother certainly, for God appoints every soul an angel."

"For revenge he would?"

"Yes, perhaps. I think. I am not as sure as I would like to be."

"And can he? Can he take me to Pandemonium?"

"I do not believe so. You have led a virtuous life and intend to continue."

"The demon key?"

"You used it only a handful of times. And demons are not evil, you know that."

"The scrying mirror?"

Amelia frowned. "Oh, I had forgotten that."

"Why do you frown? You frighten me."

535

Amelia took a deep breath before continuing. "It was an instrument of Lazodeus's, and he, we have discovered, was evil —"

"Therefore it was an instrument of evil."

"Precisely."

Deborah sagged back in her chair and rubbed her aching eyes.

"But one small spark of evil in a life of good . . . I think he has little claim."

"He has a claim though?"

"A small one. He would have to fight ferociously."

Deborah remembered the look in his eyes as he had been taken away by the Seraphim. She believed him to be equal to the fight. She rose wearily. "I must look in on my sister. She was injured last night."

"Mary or Anne?"

"Mary has disappeared. 'Tis Anne who is injured. I will have to call a surgeon. I believe her leg is broke. She is still in a swoon, but I think it is only from the pain, and she breathes as easy as a baby." Deborah sighed. "It is hateful. I cannot help but despise both of them. For all that I tried to save them . . ."

Amelia stood and squeezed her hand. "It may pass. Time may heal the rift."

"Part of me hopes you are right, and part of me wishes to hold on to the hatred."

Amelia led her to the door. "If you need anything, please ask. Here is a powder to help ease her pain."

Deborah took the small pouch. "Thank you, Amelia."

"And when the angels come to name your price . . ."

"I shall let you know," Deborah vowed. "Immediately."

Through the haze of pain, Anne perceived someone was in the room with her. She opened her eyes. Deborah bent over her, stony-faced, with a damp cloth.

"Deborah?" she said, "I am in such terrible pain."

"I know." Deborah handed her a cup. "Here, drink this. It will help."

Anne sipped it and looked around. "How did I get home?"

"A gentleman assisted me after the awful trouble. Two days have passed and the surgeon has been. Your leg is broke."

Anne let her eyes roll back, focussed on the black beams which ran across the ceiling. "Then I shall be doomed to hobble after all."

"Is she awake, then?" This was Betty, hovering near the door.

"Yes, Betty."

Anne tried to brace her whole body against the excruciating ache in her leg. It barred almost all thoughts from her mind; all thoughts, except Lazodeus.

"Where is Mary?" Anne asked.

"In Forest Hill," Deborah replied, mopping Anne's hair away from her brow. "We had a letter from her this morning. She is the especial guest of Sir Danderfield Adworth. I do not expect her to return any time soon."

"Betty, leave me alone with Deborah a moment," she managed.

Betty sighed in exasperation and closed the door behind her. She grasped Deborah's hand.

"Is he dead?"

"Lazodeus? No. He is banished forever from seeing you, under threat of annihilation." Deborah spoke coldly, as though she expected Anne to scream at her.

"I had dreams of him, when I was in a swoon."

"Well, you may dream of him no longer —"

"No, you misunderstand. I saw him for his true self. It is so clear now: I once begged you and Mary not to call him for fear he would injure somebody. And yet he came and made us all injure each other and I did not see it. I did not see it." She despised the awful blindness that had descended upon her, and barely knew the person she had been these last months.

537

"Do you not love him still?" Deborah asked.

"I . . ." Something still moved inside her, but she could not name it. "I feel as though I have loved once, long ago, in another lifetime, and lost it. I feel it shall never come again, and it makes me sad. But I cannot see how such a feeling ever attached itself to a creature like Lazodeus."

Deborah fixed her with a cool gaze. "And so am I to be your friend again?"

"I would like that."

Deborah turned and wrung the cloth out in a bucket. "I would not. I cannot forget how energetically you and Mary sought to kill me." She picked up the bucket and made for the door. "Betty's found an apprenticeship for you in Dartford. You will leave as soon as you can walk."

"But Deborah . . ." Anne started. To no purpose. Her sister was gone.

The confrontation with Father could not reasonably be put off any longer. She had excused herself from attending him by saying that Anne needed her, but his anger was growing apace. She descended the stairs with trepidation and found him sitting straight-backed in his chair, his face carved of stone.

"Father?" she said meekly.

"So you have finally decided to attend me?"

"I am sorry. Anne is in most excruciating pain and —"

"Explain yourself."

She took a moment to catch her breath. "What would you have me explain?"

He laughed bitterly. "Why I was dragged off to Dartford by my sick wife? Why I return to find Anne's leg broken, Mary betrothed to a Royalist and my youngest daughter gashed in the head — yes, Betty has told me — and treating me as though I am a fool!" His voice grew louder as the list went on.

"I cannot explain," Deborah said, bracing herself for the response.

"You can and will explain!" he roared.

"Do you not trust me, Father?"

"Do you think me a fool, daughter?"

Deborah watched him for a few moments and stilled her hands. She was grown now, she was not a child, and Father's temper need not rule her any longer. He had no inkling that she had saved his life. How blindly ungrateful he seemed in light of that thought.

"Well?" he asked.

"Father, Mary and Anne were in love with a devil and so I had to call a legion of angels to destroy him."

The silence beat out for one minute, two minutes. His face was impossible to read, a mask. Then his expression shifted, just a fraction, and Deborah thought she sensed in that shift some kind of surrender. She remembered the day he had hinted that he knew she was involved in magic, and wondered if this had any bearing on his abandonment of the matter.

"Deborah, if you are going to answer me with nonsense, then perhaps it is best if you do not answer me at all. Now, take a letter to Adworth. He shall have as his bride price the money that your grandmother owes me."

Deborah was momentarily frozen by Father's response, but then forced herself to action. She found paper and a quill, her writing tray and inkpot. Then she turned and saw him sitting there, his head tilted slightly, and she abandoned these items and sank at his feet.

"What's this?" he said.

"Father, please," she said, reaching for his hand.

"Please, what? What is this about?"

"Father, do you love me?"

He pulled his hand away. "What is this nonsense? Why do you ask such a thing?"

"Father, I love you so dearly and I have . . ." Her voice caught on a sob, and she knew she could not relate to him the awful sacrifice she had made for him. "I only wish to know if the feeling is returned."

"Why do you vex me so with this prattle? Do you not have a place to live and food to eat? Do I not trust you with my dictation?"

"Yes, yes, Father. Only I would like to hear you acknowledge me in some fond way."

"This is most irritating, Deborah."

"Please. Are you not a great poet? Could you not spare a few of those grand words for me?"

He pressed his lips together and fell into the irritated silence she knew so well.

"Please, Father."

He would not speak. She stood and kicked over her writing stool. "You are the cruellest man on earth!" she cried as she stalked out.

"Deborah, you have a letter to write," he called in a stern voice.

"Write it yourself!" She ran through the kitchen and into the garden. What a fool she had been to ask him. Where had her reason gone? She sat heavily on the bench and put her head in her hands, breathing deep to still herself a few minutes. Then she raised her head. There was much to be done. Liza still had not returned and with Mary gone and Anne sick, much of the work fell to her. Deborah took herself into the kitchen and began to chop and wrap vegetables for supper. About an hour later, Betty leaned in the kitchen doorway.

"Your father and I are going for a walk."

"You are feeling better?"

"Much, now that Mary is gone."

Deborah tried a smile. "Take good care of him, Betty."

Betty sniffed and was gone. As the front door opened, Father called out to her, "Deborah, tidy my desk while I am out."

Then she was alone in the house, but for Anne upstairs who rested. She dumped the net of vegetables in boiling water and wiped her hands on her apron. Slinging the apron on the back of a chair, she left for Father's study.

She saw it almost immediately. A white sheet of paper with a mess of inky letters upon it. A careful scrawl, and yet still awkward and almost childish. It could be no neater nor more precise, she knew, for its author was blind. She picked up the slip of paper and read it.

Deborah, you are my eyes.

Seized by the heart. Her breath contracted as she clutched the note to her chest and, for the first time since this last catastrophe had entered her life, sobbed like a tiny girl.

A week passed, and then another, and still Natiel did not return to name his price. Deborah was not foolish enough to believe he wouldn't come, that she would be able to continue her life as normal, but as the days changed one to the other and life picked up a routine, she began to think that perhaps it would not be so bad after all, or that she would not hear from him for many years. Mornings would be spent with Father, and some days with Anne who was frustrated and bored from being in bed so long. Often Amelia would drop by and bring one of her herbal remedies for Anne, though Deborah still wasn't convinced they worked as well as a surgeon's might. Father even grew to like Amelia in a guarded way, for her Italian was perfectly fluent and she thought nothing of conversing with him for hours while a possessive Betty looked on in wariness.

The leaves had turned on the oak above their garden when, after dinner on a Friday, while Father dozed inside and Amelia read to Anne in the bedroom, Natiel finally came. Deborah sat on the stone bench cleaning candlesticks, a barrel of sand for scrubbing between her knees, when she looked up and saw him standing there. She let out an involuntary shriek.

"What is the matter, Deborah?" he asked.

"It has been so long. I thought you had forgotten me."

"We do not forget."

Amelia, who must have sensed his arrival, appeared a moment later, closing the kitchen door behind her. Natiel turned to her and asked, "Why are you here?"

"It is my fault this girl found herself in so much trouble," Amelia said, standing erect and proud in her black mourning dress in front of the angel. "I intend to share equally in whatever expense she finds herself responsible for."

The angel smiled gently, and held out two pale glowing hands. "This creates something of a mathematical problem, for how does one halve eternity?"

Deborah saw Amelia draw pale, and a chill finger tapped her heart. "Please," she said to Natiel, "I am terrified. Tell me quickly."

"You have seen Heaven, Deborah Milton, and you have felt God's love. We only ask that you describe your experience to others so that they may be drawn back into God's truth. He loves every mortal because they were created for him to love. His love is infinite and alleviates all suffering. You know this to be true?"

"Yes," she said, nodding. This did not seem too difficult, and the weight upon her heart began to lift.

"This is your burden."

"It hardly seems a burden."

Natiel smiled again, and this time it was not so gentle. "However, you sought to command angels which is well beyond the station of mortals, and for your arrogance and for the distress you caused us, you must wander the world alone until your story is told, and nor will you die and return to the kingdom of Heaven until you have."

Deborah heard Amelia gasp and she glanced up nervously. "'Tis not so very bad is it, Amelia? We can certainly find one who will listen to such a story?"

Amelia shook her head slowly and Natiel kneeled in front of Deborah. "This is a punishment, foolish girl. For you are now cursed. People will shun you, no man will marry you, no stranger will listen to you." He touched her hand. "In other words, you may *never* find a listener for your tale."

She felt the safe mundanity of ordinary life rolling away from her as if on giant wheels. To wander alone? To be separated eternally from that mellow twilight world of Heaven?

"Wait." This was Amelia. "I said I would share in this payment and so I will. Deborah is a young woman, I am old. I prefer the company of my cats to the company of people. I am not afraid of living indefinitely. Let me take the first half of eternity."

Natiel stood and turned to her. "You never touched the angel key."

"I am responsible for this young woman."

The angel bowed his head in acknowledgment. "A foolish sacrifice. I shall relate it to the committee. Take this burden, Amelia Lewis. Take it and make of it what you will."

An Resolution

The old woman paused, looking down at her gnarled hands. "Deborah was too young to deal with such an immense burden of guilt and responsibility. Soon she began to freeze Amelia out of her life, sent her away if she tried to visit, returned letters unopened. Eventually, in desperation I suppose, she eloped to Ireland. Away from London, away from her beloved father, away from the woman who had taken her curse." A huge sigh, a sound of finality.

"You're Amelia Lewis," I said.

The old woman looked up. "No, my dear. I'm not. I'm Deborah Milton."

"But the demon key . . . Amelia had it last."

"I inherited it with the rest of her effects when she passed on at seventy-eight. When I'd heard she had died I was at first excited, presuming she had found someone to whom the burden could pass, but soon after Natiel returned to explain to me that the angels would not let Amelia keep paying a price which was wholly mine."

I sat back on the floorboards and looked at her astonished. "You have lived for centuries."

"It's not really living."

"You mean you're dead? Like a ghost?"

She shook her head. "I have been suspended at the moment of death for many long years now, with all its pains and discomforts. I'm not a ghost, for as you see I'm made of flesh, but yet I needn't sleep or eat. I have waited, waited, for so long and now I'm happy to slip away. Now you've taken my burden."

I fell silent for a long time. My burden now, my curse. The awful craving had evaporated, but there was no denying any more that I was in some serious supernatural trouble.

"I am sorry, Sophie," the old woman said. "It's a terrible thing to pass on to an innocent listener, but I am so very tired."

Still I couldn't find words in my mouth for her.

"Would you like me to explain some of the things I have learned about the curse?"

I nodded dumbly.

"There are two phases," she said, stretching out both her hands. "Your life, and death-in-life. During your ordinary life span, things may seem almost normal at first. But as soon as you start asking people to hear your story, they will be repulsed by you. Gradually, all with whom you come into contact will start to shun you. But death-in-life is worse."

"Why do you call it death-in-life?" I managed.

"Because you are at the point of death and you remain there. You don't slip over to the other side, your suffering is unrelieved, but you are no longer a part of this world. You are no longer repulsive — a small mercy — you are now merely invisible. Only the psychically sensitive will sense your presence, but they'll also sense the danger and keep your existence hidden from the more vulnerable. The sceptics, like yourself."

I swallowed dryly. Long moments drew out. "Any . . . ah . . . any advice you can offer me?"

"Yes. Be ruthless."

"In what way?"

"You need only get someone to *ask* you for your story. Once they have asked they are in the snare. So use trickery, or subterfuge, or exploit the ones you love. If your mother says that you seem depressed, tell her it's due to a sad tale you heard. The shudder of revulsion she feels at your implied suggestion will be overridden by her natural love for you, and she may ask you to relate this sad tale. Your warning — and you must give a warning — will mean nothing to her because she trusts you. And then . . . then you can snap shut the trap." She smacked her hands together and the noise echoed loudly throughout the empty building.

"Give someone I love the curse?"

"Better her than you. Eternity's a long time, Sophie."

"Why didn't you do it then?"

Her head drooped. "I nearly did. When my daughter was ten she asked me what troubled me, and I nearly told her." She lifted her head and met my eyes. "But I loved her unwisely; I always loved unwisely. Soon after, she turned against me too. I should have passed the curse on to her."

"Your own daughter?"

She shrugged. "It's much easier while you live. Though a consolation I can offer is that your ability to generate the compulsion grows stronger and stronger. I have been close many times in the last few years. Even psychics who should know better have been tempted to listen, though they escaped early enough. In a few hundred years, you will find that you too have the ability to weave such a spell of magnetism around your words that people will start to be tempted. Then someone, like you, will ask you to tell the story. That's all you need, one person to ask. Once they've asked, once they've accepted the warning, it will all be over."

A few hundred years. Ridiculous visions of the Jetsons came to mind.

"I simply can't believe it," I said at last.

"You do believe it. You didn't when you first came, but you do now." She shook her head sadly. "I am sorry, I truly am. But would you leave me by myself now? I wish to spend my last moments in contemplation of my life; of what it has amounted to and how I treated those around me."

I stood — difficult under the circumstances. I moved unsteadily to the door.

"Goodbye, Sophie," she said.

I didn't reply. I walked down the stairs on legs of rubber, hit the street and headed towards the cemetery. A devastatingly good-looking man dressed in black barrelled past me, nearly knocking me over, but I didn't give him a second thought until I was waiting to cross the road.

Something niggled me about his appearance. And then I realised: he had a scar through his left eyebrow and across the top of his lip. Lazodeus, returning to compete for her soul.

I turned and ran back towards the old woman's house. She had been waiting so long for Heaven that I couldn't bear the thought of her being wrenched into Pandemonium, separated from the relief which she craved so much. I raced up the stairs and to the old woman's room, but it was empty except for the chair and the few books on the shelf. No body, no withered skeleton, no empty black dress: none of those spooky-story tropes to heighten the atmosphere. Nothing.

I hope she made it.

My newly cursed life didn't feel particularly different at first. I had no real friends at the time anyway, and my guess was that Neal and the other Lodge members would not be rushing to invite me for drinks any time soon. Mrs Henderson didn't seem to notice I had changed forever, and a libidinous weirdo smiled unsteadily at me on the Tube that weekend. Clearly, I wasn't revolting to him. The first time I tried to tell the story, however, I realised the full extent of the problem. I saw a junkie sitting in Russell Square. She had long, greasy hair and she stank like a goat, and she was wearing a Motorhead singlet top and a red kilt. I thought she was an easy target, so I sat down and said, "Hi."

She fixed bleary eyes on me.

"Do you want to hear a story?" I asked.

"Leave me alone, you freak," she muttered, and got up and walked away.

I tried it on a couple of other people, and they all had the same reaction, as though I had offered to sell them child pornography. Quite simply, *nobody* would listen to me, and I started to feel that I was the very freak the junkie had accused me of being. Worse, in small ways the generalised shunning began soon after. Gradually, shop assistants stopped meeting my eye, beggars stopped bothering me, nobody asked to sit with me in the pub any more, even when it was full, and I found myself playing a lot of squash by myself, bouncing that ball up and back on the wall alone.

I barely slept for thinking about it. I fantasised about Terry Butler that day in the cafe with Chloe, and how he'd asked me what was wrong. If he did it again, would he be out the door before I said, "It all started in the 1660s"? In really guilty moments, I imagined him passing on news of my misery to Martin, and Martin phoning to check on me.

What's the matter, Sophie?

Funny you should ask, Martin . . .

But I couldn't do it, not to someone I loved. I simply could not see my way out of this problem and it frustrated me terribly because I like solutions, I like to overcome adversity, I like to *win*.

Was I frightened? Oh, yes. I often woke in the early hours of the morning, my heart racing and my palms sweating, as I contemplated an eternity of growing loneliness. I imagined seeing the world change all around me, but not being part of it, being a lonely old woman sitting in a room marked for demolition somewhere, waiting and hoping for someone to come by and listen to my story. It was not a pleasant notion. My thoughts were bent all the time towards solving the problem. The question which repeated itself over and over in my mind was, "How can I get somebody to ask me for the story?" What trickery could I use, what extortion, what coercion?

In the end, none was necessary.

I received a letter one morning from Imelda Frost, a literary agent on the Strand. I had sent her a query letter early on in my research with the Lodge, when I had yet to meet the old woman and still thought an exposé on urban magicians would make a good project. Every other agent I had written to had rejected the idea long since. Imelda's letter read like this:

> *Dear Sophie*
> *Thank you for your query. I would be very interested to read the manuscript arising from your experiences with the magical Lodge. I have a long-standing interest in matters both anthropological and supernatural, and know of a number of publishers who may be interested in such a work. Please send it or drop it in.*

Poor Imelda. Still, it was easy enough for her to pass it on, too, what with publishers distressed by their slush piles and always asking for hot properties from reputable agents. And then, with enough intriguing advertising and a stylish jacket, a publisher can always make a buyer think she wants it. One buyer is all it takes, really.

So, as you see, I'm off the hook. Martin and I are back together and I expect I've a good sixty years left in me yet, and that's enough, that's just fine. But what about you? This is a serious business, and you don't want to take it lightly. I suppose you could pass this book on to a friend. If you can find one.

I warned you, you know. It's right there on the first page. You can't say I didn't warn you.

Author's Note

Anne, Mary and Deborah Milton were real people. When I found out that John Milton dictated his epic to his daughters, I immediately started to speculate on whether they could have changed his work without his knowledge, because of his blindness. The thought amused me enough to look up some biographical information about them. To my absolute joy I found out they didn't get along with their father, that Mary actually said the words spoken in Chapter One ("that was no news to hear of his wedding, but if she could hear of his death that was something"), and that in his will he left the girls a family debt and called them his "unkind children". Various accounts list Anne as subnormal, retarded, and in one biographer's words "dippy," though not much evidence exists beyond the fact that she had a limp and some difficulty speaking. In fact, the biographers seem to have it in for all the girls, one implying that they must have really tried poor Milton's patience, and another suggesting that they were very irritating to live with; but I'm sure living with an egotistical genius who has a sharp tongue and a cruel sense of humour would be no picnic. Milton's earliest biographer, Edward Phillips, summed up the situation in this way: "It had been happy indeed if the Daughters of such a Person had been made in some measure Inheritrixes of their Father's Learning; but since Fate otherwise decreed, the greatest Honour that can be ascribed ... is to be Daughter to a man of his extraordinary Character." Hmm. So consider this book a kind of redress, a speculative account which, I hope, requires no previous knowledge of Milton or his great poem. I had long wanted to write about the loyalties of sisters to sisters, of daughters to fathers, and this provided me the perfect opportunity.

One important caveat: even though this book has its inception in fact, it is a work of fiction, and the astute will no doubt spot the bent truths. As far as possible, however, I have adhered to recorded dates and facts. But no, there are no records which suggest that a fallen angel lived in the attic of Milton's house on Artillery Walk. Which I think is a very great pity.

My heartfelt thanks are due to a number of people. Philip Birger at the Milton's Cottage Trust in Chalfont St Giles was kind enough to open the cottage for me in the dead of the winter tourist slump. Without his support this book would have been impossible for me to imagine. Thank you, too, to the Eleanor Dark Foundation and Peter Bishop at Varuna Writers' Retreat, a magical place in the Blue Mountains where I finished the story on a misty morning while the maple leaves quivered in the breeze outside my window. My support team at HarperCollins are due the greatest thanks for their passion and commitment, especially Stephanie Smith who humours my hysteria with good grace. A little dog named Max, who was murdered in winter last year, has kindly provided his name for my purposes. I know he is still sorely missed. For some small but crucial details I owe debts to Ian Mond and Julia Morton. A close circle of truly great friends always exercises its patience and understanding with me when I am in "the zone," and I count among that number Drew Whitehead, who once loaned me a book on Milton even though it meant he had nothing to read on the train that day; Lynnie and Vinnie — everybody needs good neighbours; and my beloved Mirko, who provides live music while I write and somehow lives through my mood swings. Thanks also to my family, especially Frank Wilkins. I am eternally sorry that I do not write cowboy books, Grandad. Finally, and most crucially, thanks to super-agent Selwa Anthony. She is an unstoppable force, and her faith in the power of the word can move mountains.